MW01615043

DESTINY'S SLAVE

a novel

By T. K. Laverents

Copyright © 2021 Todd Kelly Laverents

All rights reserved. No part of the text, except for public domain
material by other authors and poets, may be reproduced in any form
without the express written permission of the author.

This book is a work of fiction. Names, characters, businesses, orga-
nizations, places, and events (other than those clearly in the public
domain) are either the product of the author's imagination or are
used fictitiously. Any resemblance to actual persons (living or dead),
events, or locales is purely coincidental.

ISBN-13: 978-0-578-88050-1 (Tickle Books)

Cover art by Martin Fuks

Formatting by pen2publishing.com

(For Maria and Martin.)

By T. K. Laverents:

(available on Kindle and Amazon paperback)

Blood Sacrament: a crime thriller

The 4ᵗʰ Manifestation: a crime thriller

Still Waters: a noir mystery

The McConnell Crime Saga (the three books above)

Visitation Rites: a comedy

Before the Winds of Spring: a novel of the pre-apocalypse

Destiny's Slave: a historical and religious satire

If you managed to read this or any of the others to the end, drop by my website, and let's get acquainted.

Table of Contents

Part I

TO THE END OF THE WORLD

CHAPTER ONE

OF LOST HEADS AND LOST FREEDOM

1

The Tenchteri tribe into which I was born holds the belief that one's life begins not at birth, but at the moment which defines a man's destiny. In my long travels through this life, I have learned that different cultures hold different opinions regarding this matter. If I keep to my tribe's view, however, my life began when a platoon of Roman soldiers, accompanied by a band of Chauci warriors, entered our village, and a chieftain swung his sword blade through my father's neck, then raped my mother before beheading her ... after the rest of his platoon and the Germanic warriors followed his leading deed upon her. These events occurred when I was but a little boy, and they are the collective moment that forged my destiny.

My name is Bern—or that is the name I was given by my captors. I was a short and stout tree-trunk creature who plodded behind the cart to which my neck was tethered. I was one of eleven survivors of my people's first and only encounter with emissaries of the Roman Empire.

"Why do we take the wee one? He slows us down!" barked a warrior.

"We sell him and the others south of here. Then we are rid of them and have that much more silver in the bargain," answered the chieftain who ordered my parents killed.

"But who will buy him? Who needs a dwarf bear?" The warrior yanked on the cord, causing my feet to leave the ground and my neck to nearly break. "Dance, bear!" All the soldiers and warriors shared a nice laugh.

"Little bear," mused the chieftain. "*Kleiner Bern* ... You can never tell ... He could prove amusing for the right customer." With my shaggy mane of blond, I suppose I resembled some sort of baby golden bear.

"I wonder," said the warrior who released the cord, "who the lucky owners of those two will be." He leered at the cart where my cousins Frida and Linza, the youngest girls of the six taken along with five boys, lay bound and hidden from view. He licked his lips.

"Put it out of your mind," the chieftain said. "Virgins bring a higher price, and those two remain virgins." He smirked. "Besides, you should be satisfied after this morning."

"And I'm sure I speak for the lot of us when I thank you for removing her head. She was screaming so much I could barely concentrate on my business!" They all roared at that.

Only hours earlier, though, they were not such jovial fellows.

The sun had risen to mid-morning height, and I was playing a game of chase with one of the village dogs—the one named Kamik—when I heard a woman's screech beyond the village fence. Both Kamik and I stopped and looked that direction. The weaver's wife had been working in the fields, and was running into the opening at the fence shouting, "They're coming! They're coming! Romans and others!" She had begun to turn and point when a spear pierced her. She ceased her shrieking and gawked with moon-eyes at the spear tip protruding from her chest. It is odd to me now I knew upon seeing the blood-soaked spearhead that it was of our people, Germanic work. The weaver's wife pulled her hands away from the spear and raised the red-streaked hands to the sky. "We die today!" she cried. Then she fell to the earth.

Through the fence opening poured a few dozen men. Half were Romans, decked in their red cloth and metal plating, and half were warriors from a neighboring tribe, the Chauci. They all stood, legs wide, swords and spears at the ready, in a half-circle around the courtyard.

Suddenly the weaver burst from his hut and ran to his dead wife. He cradled her head in his lap and placed his hands in her blood. He rose to his feet and scanned the soldiers and warriors with his accusing eyes. "Who did this thing?" He held out his red palms. "Whoever did this thing, come to me, and we shall settle now!"

A Chauci warrior stepped out of the semi-circle. He held out his empty hands. "I seem to have misplaced my spear." He smirked down at the dead woman. "Ah ... There it is! Now how could that have happened?"

The weaver ran at this warrior screaming in a rage. Three steps short of his target, he fell as an arrow pierced his neck from a side.

While this occurred, the Chauci warriors ferreted all the villagers from huts, stalls, and surrounding gardens, and had us stand huddled together at the center of the fenced compound.

A Roman optio—there were no officers present—strode before us. He waved the Chauci warrior back. The warrior stepped over to the weaver's wife. He placed a foot on her back and yanked out his bloodied spear before returning to his place. The optio motioned to another Chauci warrior. This man, a Chieftain, stepped out and stood beside the optio. The Roman optio nodded to him.

The chieftain took a step forward and regarded the small throng of frightened people that composed our village. "My Roman friend here cannot speak our tongue, so he bids me to deliver the message." He spat the direction of the dead weaver and his dead wife. "What a pitiful lot you are ... Not a single warrior among you!" He sneered down at the bodies. "But perhaps you can at least tell us where we can find a warrior. We march in the service of General Germanicus, and we seek the butcher called Arminius, the one who led his men to slaughter innocent women and children at Teutoburg Forest!" This was most likely a lie, as we all had heard Arminius led several warriors from various tribes to wipe out three legions of Roman soldiers led by General Varus. The chieftain signaled to a fellow Chauci warrior. This one stepped to the throng, which had now become a gathering of sheep huddled against imminent slaughter. He reached out and snatched an old woman by her hair. Borgia was her name, grandmother of an occasional playmate of mine. He dragged the screaming old female before his leader, spun her to face the throng, and shoved her to her knees.

"Now," the chieftain called out, "you will die, one by one, until you allow us to leave with your gold and silver ... and the name of the place where we can find the butcher of Teutoburg!"

The warrior who had a handful of the old woman's gray hair in his left fist checked with his leader as he moved the blade of his short sword before her face, the handle gripped in his right. With a nod from the chieftain, the Chauci warrior lowered the blade to her throat and pulled hard on the handle. Her scream was brief, more like a bleat from a baby lamb. Blood spurted from the wide slit. He released his hold on her hair, and she crumpled into a useless, awkward heap of wrinkled flesh attached to brittle bones.

Still no one stepped forward to offer that which did not exist. "Choose another!" the chieftain ordered.

"No!" a voice from the throng screamed.

All Chauci warriors craned their necks to find the owner of such a bold voice.

My father was our metal worker, our smith. Not a warrior, nor a leader of men. He chose that moment to lose his mind and become a hero. For insanity is what defines heroism. A man who charges outnumbered into battle will either be defeated or emerge victorious, the former among the decided majority. If defeated, he merely dies forgotten, his name sinking into oblivion, especially if his cause loses. If victorious, whether he lives to a ripe old age or dies before his hairs turn gray, he becomes hero, legend. My father always lost in the games when he gambled, and he chose that moment to gamble with his life.

The man who sired me pushed his way out of the throng of frightened villagers. "No, please do not continue this! We have no gold, no silver! And this Arminius, to us he is only a name. Only a rumor! We know nothing of the man you seek!"

The chieftain smiled widely, displaying a set of missing and rotting teeth. "So, one among you wants to show his balls after all ... Step forward, you," he said to my father. My father obeyed and walked toward the chieftain until the Chauci leader held out a palm to halt him. The chieftain regarded my father for half a minute. "So do you speak for this village? Are you their chief?"

"I speak for no one. I only ask you in the names of the gods— "

"It's in the names of the gods that we come! Ours and theirs," the chieftain said with a cock of his head back to the Roman soldiers. "Their Emperor Tiberius orders revenge, as do their gods. Our gods demand that this abomination—this slaughter of women and children—does not go unpunished."

8

"I agree abominations must be dealt with," my father said. "But we know nothing of the slaughter of women and children. And if it occurred, we cannot help you to carry out the punishment. We know nothing, I swear!"

"You say you speak for no one, that you are no leader. What is your trade, then?"

"I am a smith ... I work with metals."

"With metals ... So do you work with the shiny metals? With gold and silver?"

"My lord, we have no— "

"I have already heard this from you." The chieftain stepped around his warrior and the old woman's body, and stood directly before my father, staring into his eyes. "But have you ever worked with such metals?"

My father bowed his head. "When I have been commissioned. When the metals have been provided for the service."

"But of course, the gold or silver would need be provided from elsewhere since, as you say, you have no such metals here." The chieftain pulled his sword from its sheath. I feared my father would die by the sword at that moment, but my fears were a few moments premature. The chieftain held out the weapon as if it were on display, the handle resting on one open palm and the side of the blade tip on the other. "Do you make arms?"

"Again, my lord, when I have— "

"—been commissioned," the chieftain finished. "And when the metals have been provided for the service."

My father nodded to the dirt, at the corpse, like a little boy caught in a misdeed.

"Have you ever made a blade such as this one? Come, my good smithy, you must look at the blade in order to answer the simple question."

My father raised his face. He trembled visibly, which could not work in his favor. For like wolves, Chauci warriors feed on fright. "I may have," he said.

"That is unfortunate, for this very blade—from the Cherusci of Arminius—was found in the chest of a Roman skeleton, in the Teutoburg Forest." The chieftain resheathed the sword and resumed his place behind the executioner. "You do not need to choose the next to die," he said to the warrior. "This one has volunteered."

He spoke in a tongue I had never heard, probably translating his previous words. He looked at the Roman optio, who merely said, "*Ita sit!*"

"On your knees, scum!" the warrior ordered my father, who instantly obeyed with whispered prayers to the gods.

"Please, no!" Now it was my mother who decided to play lunatic. She broke from the group and ran toward my father.

"Hold this woman!" the chieftain bellowed. Two warriors raced forward, grabbed her arms, and lowered her to her knees. The chieftain strode over and knelt before her. He studied her, then reached forward and placed a hand inside her dress from underneath. She struggled and squirmed against his explorations. He rose and faced his men. "Choose one of these vermin to live and tell of our visit! Take a few boys and only the fair young females as prisoners. We'll march south and sell them."

He repeated his orders in that strange tongue, the Roman optio's tongue, obviously, for this emissary of Tiberius and his imperial legions suddenly paid full attention to the chieftain. As the chieftain rolled out these words in the tongue of the Empire, I realized something odd. I not only enjoyed the sounds of this foreign tongue, but I also felt I understood some of the text. And I knew what he had said by the tone, by the sense of finality the words conveyed.

The chieftain turned to my father. "This woman is yours, I know. Do you wish to watch us enjoy her before we kill you both?"

"No! No! No, please!" my father screamed. I always hoped since that day I would be able to muster something wiser and braver—something more worthy of memory—than my father's as my own last words.

The chieftain said, "As our friend from the Empire said, *Ita sit* ... So be it!" He stepped behind my father and faced us, the chosen children. He smiled at us with his mouth closed and his eyes nearly twinkling, like a favorite uncle. Then he unsheathed his sword, spun, and gripping the handle in both fists, swung with all his might.

My father's head rolled and landed at my mother's knees. He had spent his adult life at his wife's feet, so it was only fitting he did so as well in death. She bowed her head and wailed and wailed.

"She is mine first until I am finished!" the chieftain said. "Then anyone who wishes, may have a go. How you determine the order is up to you: draw lots, fight for it ... your choice."

"The order shall be determined by the number of kills!" offered a warrior.

"Then by the number of kills it shall be!" the Chauci chieftain shouted. "*Ita sit*!"

The slaughter began. The throng was surrounded, and there would be no escape. I stood in the middle silently praying for survival to all the gods whose names I could remember. And I believed I owed my survival on that bloody day to them. After nearly everyone had fallen with their torsos pierced or their throats cut, eleven of us—five boys and six girls—were led out of the pile of corpses by one long length of leather thong tied around each of our necks, binding us together as a squad of pitiful offal.

Though they had my mother, nothing prevented the warriors from satisfying themselves on what other females they found in the throng before killing them. And *after* killing them in a few cases.

We future slaves stood to a side in full view of the display, my mother taken by warrior after warrior. She had ceased struggling and screaming, and merely allowed each man to position her as per his preference. Once, she was tossed to the dirt on her back, and as a warrior lay himself atop her and thrust his hips, her head lolled to a side, and our eyes locked. Mud caked onto her hair, and her face was now one massive bruise. She mouthed *I love you, my son. Stay strong*! I stood observing like a statue. I merely prayed to live the next day, though I knew not how or why.

I stared in curious awe at the ground. The blood from the pile of bodies in the center of the village was so thick, it had spread several paces from the edge of the slaughter to our feet. I was amazed by the sudden redness of the very dirt. There had always been much blood after the slaughter of a single pig or cow, but never before had it created a red pond such as this. I somehow knew when we were long gone from here and decades from now not so much as a weak memory, this ground would be unlikely to support any life, not even a blade of grass or a weed.

I eventually came to the understanding that these Chauci never believed they would find any gold or silver here, nor that anyone among us would know anything about the where-abouts of this Arminius. Tiberius in Rome wanted Germanic blood in repayment for the Roman blood lost a few years ago in a nearby forest. And these Chauci warriors were quite willing to spill the blood of their fellow Germans in exchange for Roman silver. If not them, warriors of another tribe would have just as willingly obliged.

Only when I felt the sharp tug of leather on my throat did I know I was in the lead of this train of worthless living flesh. Pulled along by a warrior with the most massive back and shoulders I had ever seen on a human, we were led away from the village. "Burn it!" shouted the chieftain's voice. "Burn it all to ashes!" Though I did not see the flames, I could feel the heat of them on the back of my head. Somewhere behind me, I knew, my mother was losing hers.

We had been marching south at a steady pace for what I had counted as five days. My fifth day as an orphan, as a slave.

"When do we get rid of this shit?" one of our captors complained. "I'm itching to go back and make another surprise visit!"

"You're still holding to hopes of gold and silver?" another answered him. "In those peasant villages? Would you also like me to tell you a babe-story of magical faeries tonight before you go to sleep?" Several of his comrades guffawed.

"My feet are sore from this march! Also," the complainer said drawing his short sword and raising it to the sky, "my blade has been the wrong color for five suns now ... *That* is what I hope. After all, are we not warriors?" He was answered with a guttural agreement from the two dozen.

"We sell them at *Castellum apud Confluentes*, then we return north to fulfill our purpose."

"*Castellum* what? What in the gods' names is that?"

"A Roman settlement and fort south of here. At the meeting of the two rivers."

"How far south?"

The chieftain kept his eyes forward as he guided his horse around tree roots in the path. "At this pace, another five, maybe six days."

"We'll starve to death before then!"

The chieftain twisted on his mount and pointed ahead. "If ever you are a leader, you will also ride on a steed where you'll also note from this height the village only an hour ahead ... unless those home-smokes are lying."

"Keep your pace, men!" the complainer called out. "Food and rest—and maybe even luck—await us!" A cheer rose from those guttural throats.

Since the events in the Teutoburg Forest some five years prior, German villages and settlements had become less accepting of strangers than before. Everyone for hundreds of leagues around knew of that massacre in a vague sort of way, of course. But to residents of tribal villages, this occurrence was like a violent argument between a man and wife elsewhere in the village. You would hear rumors about it, but you minded your own business and your life went on separately.

I am certain this Arminius, whom I came later to believe was merely a man and not a god or demon, had hoped he would stir all Germanic tribes to action, and he would grow to lead a nation of Germanic peoples. It did not quite work that way. Arminius faded into historic oblivion, and the Germanic people lived on edge, especially after Roman soldiers representing Tiberius arrived in the north on their own mission of stirring the Germanic tribes toward complacency mixed with fear.

On our way south, the village in a forest clearing a short run off the path made no foolish attempts to bar the entry of a platoon of Roman soldiers and a couple dozen Chauci warriors and their captives. But neither did they so much as acknowledge our presence. The chieftain dismounted and bellowed, "Food, drink, and shelter! And we pay nothing or you pay the consequences!"

The village suddenly awakened with attention for our every need. Rather, for every need of the Romans and Chauci. We eleven captives were left bound in or to the cart. While our captors ate and drank and made noises of cavorting within a hall made of timber, mud, and grass, we dropped in exhaustion and attempted to rest.

The afternoon sun had sunk to the trees by the time the chieftain emerged from the hall. He staggered drunkenly toward us escorting an old woman, a hag-thing who bored her eyes our direction. "You brew a great ale in your village!" the chieftain slurred, having difficulty with the *g* sound, and the *l* sound seemed not to wish to leave his mouth. "They're over there. L-l-l-le'sss go to the cart."

"If you can make it so far," the old woman said. We had all sat up as she stopped before us. She ran her eyes over us focusing on the girls and said, "I count four, not six. Where are the other two?"

"Innna cart," he answered, motioning to the covered cart.

She stepped to the cart and peered within. "All right," she said. "My hut is behind the ale hall. Bring them to me, and I'll tell you by nightfall how many of these six are virgins."

Because of the knowledge possessed by the old woman—the village seer and healer, two older girls, each of thirteen winters as our next brief master guessed, rode the rest of the journey to *Castellum apud Confluentes* in the cart with Frida and Linza. It must have been crowded in there and a strain on the horse, with four girls and two big, burly Chauci warriors. Since I was first in line tethered to the cart, I could hear how loud it was as well, with the incessant screaming and crying, the occasionally-coherent protests of the two new female riders. From the warriors, who were in constant substitution, came the intermittent grunt and bellow of release.

These two girls had already lost their virginities, according to the old woman, whom the chieftain paid four silver coins for her troubles. To appease the warriors, the chieftain gave these girls over to them for the remainder of the trek south. Since he wanted neither virgin in the cart defiled, he heated his knife blade and pressed the side of it against the forehead of each of the non-virgins. This way, the desirous men would recognize their targets. And now, if they survived the journey, the two non-virgins would fetch only a pitiful price at a slave auction.

Although their names escape me, I do remember a whore-master bought them both for a total sum of ten silver coins.

2

Castellum apud Confluentes was a confusion I could liken to nothing I had known before in my young life. I had often studied ant piles in my summer hikes with Kamik in the forests surrounding the village. Those tiny creatures at least seemed guided by purpose, whereas the humans in this fortress settlement scurried hither and thither, stopping here, moving there, without apparent discernible reason.

I understood much of the conversations I heard, albeit with some difficulty. The words of many here were our words, meaning of the German tongue, but so rearranged and mispronounced they may as well have been a foreign language. However, there was also the Latin I had heard briefly on my village's last day, in much more abundance. Another tongue broke through now and again, which I later came to learn originated from far across the river separating our people from the conquered Celtic tribes.

To the chieftain's chagrin, the next open slave auction would not be held for another week, and he kept us quartered outside the fortress walls beside the smaller of the two conjoining rivers. He and his band of warriors slept in tents made of leather hide while the rain pelted cold and unrelenting upon us. We made ourselves as comfortable as we could in our bed of mud. The warriors also erected a tent for the two branded girls—and the unsated Chauci males of the moment.

A Roman officer stepped out the gates accompanied by what appeared a German dressed in strange garb. Some kind of white cloth wrapped around his torso and draped over his shoulders. Beneath that was a skirt around his waist. And on his feet he wore no leather bootlets; rather, some sort of open-toe affair. This man served as the Roman's translator. Both men approached our makeshift camp. "We seek your leader!" the translator shouted. The Chauci chieftain emerged from his tent and raised his hand. The two squished through the muck to him.

The translator leaned into the officer's words, then looked into the chieftain's eyes. "This is General Pontilius of the Fourteenth Legion." The chieftain and Roman officer bowed slightly to one another. "He was told about you by fellow

Roman soldiers returning for replacements from the Emperor's campaign against the northern tribes. You performed well, and the Emperor is grateful. You will be aptly compensated."

The chieftain replied in the General's tongue of Latin. "I have no need for this German's services," he said in reference to the translator. The General laughed. I observed while attempting to appear as dumb as possible, yet I understood each tongue, all of my first tongue and much of this new language of the Empire.

The General reached forward and grasped the chieftain's forearm in the Roman style of greeting. "It is a pleasure to meet such a warrior as you," the General said. "As Loka, our translator friend here, said, for your services we will give you food and shelter within the walls, and silver to help you on your way, to use as you wish on your journey north with a new full company of our best soldiers."

"We will be happy to continue our service to the Empire," the chieftain replied. "And the silver you give us will add nicely to what we'll receive for the slaves we brought."

The General glanced our direction. "Yes ... which brings me to my next point." He took a few steps toward us, and the translator and chieftain followed, both halting when he did. Without facing the two men—as though he were addressing us—he said, "Only Roman citizens are allowed to sell slaves or profit from the selling of slaves." He turned to the chieftain. "And though you may soon be awarded such an honor, such an honor has yet to be bestowed upon you."

The chieftain's eyes flashed, and the way he flexed, it was as though he had doubled his size. "Perhaps I should find Arminius and have him sell these slaves."

The General narrowed his eyes. "What do you mean by that?"

"Is Arminius not a Roman citizen?"

"Yes ... A Roman citizen who is guilty of treason. Once he is taken back to Rome, I am certain he will be stripped of his citizenship ... then his flesh." The General pointed a finger at the chieftain. "But as you are new to Roman law, I will forget the treason I heard just now ... And I vow that if I hear any more such words out of you, you may be the first non-citizen in Roman history to be flayed for heresy to the Empire." He winked at the translator. "Normally we simply behead our enemies if the gods smile upon them. If not, we crucify them on the road outside the city gates ... Is this not true, my German friend Loka?" Giving the chieftain a furtive glance, the translator nodded at his muddy feet.

"Once we are within the walls, Loka will pay you whatever price he deems correct. Then after a day of rest it is back north for you, under the escort of your new Roman leaders." General Pontilius watched with disgust as we scooped muddy rainwater with our hands and drank greedily. "If we do not get your new property proper food and water, Loka, you may have no living slaves to sell by auction day."

A Chauci warrior band is a fierce collection of men who strike fear into the hearts of simple German villagers, especially the very old and very young. But such ferocity as theirs is no match against the machine of Roman law and order, not to mention Roman bureaucracy. After a stay of merely a day within the walls of *Castellum apud Confluentes*, the Chauci chieftain and his band of more than twenty warriors rode north with a company of over one hundred experienced Roman legionnaires. I don't know how much silver the warriors received from Loka for the eleven of us, but from their expressions, it didn't nearly match their previous aspirations.

Before their convoy exited the gates, the chieftain shouted with a scowl to his fellow warriors, "We will never again make this journey, I promise you!" This met with grunts of agreement.

I knew then I must pray to all the gods for the souls of any unfortunate villagers these belligerent Chauci would encounter in the future. There would be none spared for a life of slavery.

3

Loka housed us in an empty livestock stall, our neighbors a family of pigs who squealed the full day and night through. We ate well enough, far better than the warriors fed us during the two-week march from home. Right after we were given our bowls, we would hear the pigs squeal loudly, followed by slopping. At least we received the first portions.

As the days passed, we entertained many visitors. Though they were not proper visitors, they were nonetheless strangers we had never before known, and they came alone, in pairs, and in small groups to gawk at us. The fortress of *Castellum apud Confluentes* had not hosted Germans from so far north, not in the lifetimes of these gawkers.

Children the world over are naturally curious and just as naturally brave. Young Germans, young Romans from so many conquered territories, and the strange young Celts—all came to view us. And they chattered to one another and hurled insults at us in their various tongues. I learned some of my first non-Germanic words there in that stall. "They smell like shit!" does not sound pretty in any language, I decided. I often felt myself the direct target of these words. "Shouldn't the fat little one be with his family?" a Celtic boy laughed as he pointed from me to the pig stye.

The morning of the slave auction finally arrived. Now we were visited by adults for a preview before the display and sale. "Maybe the offerings will be better this afternoon," one man said in Latin as he wrinkled his nose.

Loka came, a couple of Roman soldiers at his sides. "Take them out," he told them, "and bring them with me."

"Where are we going?" a soldier said. "It's not time for the auction."

"To the baths."

"The baths? Barbarians do not bathe!"

"I know," Loka said. "I also know these particular barbarians smell awful, and no one will want to buy them. I may fetch a profit if I rid them of their stink!"

I had never seen so much water for human use. I thought it such a waste when out of this building it was a hot day and there were panting horses, cows, and goats hugging walls for bits of shade. What good are clean people without meat or milk for their survival? The dead of all species tend to smell alike, and no bath can wash the stink from their rot. One thing is certain: when I emerged from the bath house in fresh Roman-style clothing and my wrists bound by shiny new metallic manacles, I smelled like a blossom. For once, I was glad not to be back home in the northern forests where my aroma would attract bees.

Loka then took us to a house where ladies painted the girls' faces and brushed our hair. I later learned Romans prefer to appear to the world outside their homes as someone other than who they are inside their homes, with their faces painted in unnatural hues, with their hair clipped and brushed. Before my encounter with those ladies, the natural elements like the wind determined my hairstyle, and my mother had cut my bangs only when they fell into my eyes, and clipped the sides when the hair dipped into my broth. And in such circumstances, a Tenchteri hunting knife proved apt for the purpose.

Now we were marched to the center of the settlement, the market square at the foot of what I learned was a temple in honor of a Roman god. I came to love the imagination of this Empire. Our gods, the gods of my Germanic youth, were merely names and ideas. But the gods of the Romans were encased in physical form, and resembled their human worshippers, but to perfection. The Roman artisans were paid well to create stone likenesses of these deities. This Mercury, whose likeness loomed in stone above me, became one of my favorite Roman gods, perhaps because he was the first I beheld. And what a handsome figure! His face was chiseled—literally of course, but any young female would dote over such a visage in real life—and his body was that of a lean and muscular athlete. What caught my attention more than anything, though, were the wings on his heels. As though he could lift himself right off the pedestal if he so desired and fly far away.

A crowd had gathered before a raised platform in the middle of the square, and I asked Loka if it were erected for the auction. "When there is entertainment, it happens there," he replied.

"Is a slave auction entertainment?"

He nodded at the gathered people. "Nearly no one here has the money to buy a slave, nor the need of a slave. Most come here out of curiosity ... to see people captured from distant lands. The poorest among them come to feel fortunate, seeing others worse off than they. The platform remains for other entertainment that may come our way. The occasional traveling players, the odd execution." He tugged at my curly blond locks. "And do not ask a question of me again unless you ask for proper permission!"

He led us eleven into a gated pen to the right of the platform where I could gaze up in admiration of the god Mercury. There would be entertainment today in plenty. The pen was crammed standing room only with the captured from distant lands. I heard many Germanic dialects and some of the lilting sing-song of the Celtic tongues.

I raised my eyes to Loka, who stared ahead firm. "Master Loka, may I ask a question?"

His head quivered as though he were awakened from a dream. He looked down and found my eyes. "What is it, little Bern?" he said, an exasperated sigh.

"What happens to a slave who is not sold at this auction?"

"Then said slave remains property of current owner and master."

"So if nobody buys me here, I go home with you ... to serve you?"

Loka averted his eyes from me. "I live in a small apartment in the house of General Pontilius. There is room for no other in that apartment, and the General has all the slaves he needs."

"Then what would happen to me?"

"I would be forced to release you ... to total freedom," he said, the last two words sounding like a gasp.

My heart fluttered. "Then if no one wants me, you will free me?"

He returned a steel gaze to me. "To give *you* freedom requires a payment that can last you through a season of days ... after the Empire receives its twenty percent tax fee." He knelt and grasped my shoulders, tight. "Little Bern, I have no such money. When the General is recalled to Rome, he wouldn't take me with him because in Rome no one needs a German translator. And if his replacement doesn't take me on as translator, I am homeless and no better off than a slave. If, as your owner and master, I release you to total freedom, you will be branded with a mark here," he said, pointing at his cheek, "for all to see ... And all who come across you are totally free to do with you as they wish."

I realized then it would probably have been far better for a Chauci blade to have taken my head back home.

Loka, my master for only a short while longer, rose, and focusing over the crowd away from me, he said, "You will speak with me no more on this matter ... or any other."

With a bang on a gong, the auctioneer began the sales. As the last into the pen, my group would be the last up the steps to the platform. Each slave on display—half Germans and half Celts—was sold to a member of the raucous crowd, to one of the few true customers. Receiving the loudest roars were the fairest females. With each sale, the size of the crowd shrank, one-by-one. I kept glancing from the platform to the winged feet of the god, to whom I began praying instead of my Germanic gods. It made sense to me that the gods I grew up with had their hands full protecting unsuspecting villagers from Roman soldiers and warriors of the Chauci and other tribes. Mercury was here now, standing above me here and now. He was my god of the moment. If I hoped to be sold to a Roman citizen here in Roman territory, I would need to beg the help of a Roman god.

By the time Loka's slaves were summoned to the platform, the crowd had thinned perceptibly, and I wondered if there were any real buyers remaining. The two non-virgins were the first to go, both to a *pleasure house* where they would soon earn back the silver paid out by the new sex slave master, and especially when a Roman infantry company returned from a triumphant campaign, when their pleasure would be paid on the General's tab. My cousins Frida and Linza were sold to a bronze-skinned man who carried a staff bearing a Roman eagle over some markings, which I learned later to be Latin writing. The bidding for my beautiful cousins rose rapidly, and this man must have been very wealthy indeed, for he won them both for the sum of seventy-five silver coins. The six remaining on the platform with me sold as well, but not for such a high price as did Frida and Linza.

I stood last, alone with the auctioneer. "And what bid you for our final offering on this beautiful afternoon?" he sang. "Just behold! A lovely little boy, a veritable cherub with his fair skin and golden curls!" Nobody in the audience moved a muscle. No one was in the market for veritable cherubs with fair skin and golden curls on that beautiful afternoon. "Come now!" he pleaded. "This fine creature will be an ideal play-mate for your young child at home." He clapped his hands, and his eyes grew moon-wide as a new idea popped into his brain. "That's it! You will have a real doll, a living puppet for your and your children's amusement!"

They were not amused.

I looked to the side. Loka stood on the steps scowling at me, as if it were my fault I was neither a big slave who could work in the forest and field, nor a fair budding virgin girl. I gazed over the crowd, most of whom felt the festivities were over, for they turned to leave the square. I begged into the chiseled face of my new god Mercury. *What do I do now, my Lord and Master? I cannot survive a day of total freedom!*

Then as my mother and father had done two weeks previous, I lost my mind. And I found my voice. "Stop!" I shouted in what at that time in my life must have been a tiny shrill voice. "I will be bought today or Mercury will pay a dire visit upon your houses!"

About one-third of those who were leaving stopped and spun to see what puppy dared throw a curse upon them. I then realized the trilingual nature of my intended targets. I repeated the same words in Latin based on what I had heard from soldiers. Another percentage stopped and turned toward me, many darting their eyes in trepidation from the screaming golden-haired dwarf on the platform to the stone god before the temple. Finally, I mustered the best Gaulish Celtic I could from my memory, given my one-week immersion beside the porcine family.

After that final attempt, someone shouted, "But what about Rosmerta?" in the Celtic tongue.

I had not prepared to speak, so I certainly was in no form to answer a question without any prior research. I gazed down at my pesky new shoes with the open toes. "Ros ... um ..."

"Our goddess!" the man shouted. "She is the one we pray to, the one we fear!"

"*Fruchtbarkeit*," came a voice from the steps. I glanced over and saw Loka pretending to cough into a fist. He brought down the fist and pantomimed the motion of rocking a baby in his hands.

"Oh, yes," I said. "Of course, and then there is the problem of Ros ... merta." I stood to my full height of a young briar bush. I decided to toss all caution aside, for I had nothing to lose, and only my life to gain. "If I do not leave here a bought slave, Rosmerta will shit upon your crops, and your next child will ... um ... will look exactly like me! Only shorter!" A mild gasp emitted from the crowd, who now gave me their full attention. In fact, some of those who had previously vacated the square were now streaming back in.

"He is enchanted!" a woman cried in the local Germanic.

"Do not buy this one!" came a male voice in Latin.

"Right!" a Gaulish Celt shouted. "Burn him!"

The man holding the staff in his right hand and the chain to which Frida and Linza were shackled in his left stepped forward grinning. He winked at me, then waved the auctioneer to the front of the platform. He placed coins in the auctioneer's open palm.

"So, can anyone beat the price of five silver coins for our dwarf of the many tongues?" No one said a word. "Then sold to the House of Tavarius for the sum of five silver coins!"

As I climbed down the steps, Loka bent and whispered into my ear, "I know not where you come about this gift, from our stone friend above us here or from the pits of the underworld, but may it serve you well, my little Bern." He grasped my manacled hands in his, turned, and left the pen. My eyes followed until he became swallowed into the crowd.

The man I believed was my new master stepped into the pen. He had a leather strap tied to his left wrist, and he encircled my neck with the dangling end and secured a tight knot. "I am called Vebru," he said in Latin. "Come, we have a long journey south."

4

We received permission to attach ourselves to the rear of a Roman regiment patrolling the west bank of the great river the Roman soldiers called the Rhenus. My master told me it was called the Rīnaz in the Gaulish Celtic language of his birth. The Roman soldiers were always eager to have someone besides themselves at the rear, which is where they normally received the first attacks. By the evening, the horse and foot traffic traveling north toward border settlements had decreased, and the regimental commander called his soldiers to halt for the night. They set up a semicircular perimeter of guards against our boundary of the river, erected canvas shelter, and built fires for cooking and warmth.

As the sun sank beyond the running water, Vebru pulled dried rabbit meat from a pouch and heated a pot of stew for the four of us. I bowed as he handed forth a steaming bowl. Then I cupped it in my palms and brought it to my lips. I sucked in the broth and chewed the strips of meat like a wolf after tearing muscle off a bone. The man whom I still regarded as my master chuckled. "Slow down, little one!" he said in his Celtic tongue. "Little ... Bern, is it?" I pulled my face from the bowl and looked at his twinkling eyes, then brought the rim back to my lips. With a final slurp, I emptied the bowl. I chewed on the last piece of meat and listened to the swelling river currents carrying the water south.

I was not certain what I should—or was allowed to—do, so I sat staring into the fire. To my right, Frida and Linza lay curled against one another. And on the other side of the fire Vebru sat staring to the west, beyond the river's opposite bank. "I wish to know," he said, and I nearly jumped with a start, "how do you come to know my tongue? You are from the north, is that right?"

At first I wondered if he were speaking to me, but with my cousins asleep, who else? I nodded.

"So up there, the barbarians speak many languages?"

"What are the barbarians, Master?"

"Barbarians ... your people, the uncivilized. And I am not your master."

I could feel the skin tighten on my forehead with the furrowing. He asked a question, which I was obliged to answer. But then I, too, had a question of him. "No, Mast— ... um, no. My people have spoken only one tongue in my memory."

"That Germanic growling." He rubbed his chin. "So again, my question. How do you come to speak their tongue?" he said, darting his eyes to some Roman soldiers. "And mine as well?"

I searched into the flames for an answer. I recalled the legend of our origin—the origin of all humans—told around the village fire. The gods, having no physical form, could not create the things they desired. Crops, spears and arrows for hunting, strong drink. So they created the first people from the fires deep in the mother earth. It was all very good for the gods, but they had not counted on the fact that what they created had the gift of procreation. Soon the people far outnumbered the gods who created them. And soon the people became stronger than the first gods, and created their own gods far superior to the original. These new gods replaced the old, and served the people. And since then, people had always deferred to the power of fire when they needed anything, such as inspiration and answers to difficult questions.

It had never worked for me in the past, and it was not working for me now. I raised my eyes over the flames to Vebru, who continued to rub his shaven chin as he studied me. "I don't know," I said. "My people have a belief what a man will become—the gift he is given by the gods—will be revealed in time. Maybe mine is the gift of language ... All I can tell you is I listened and learned. I listened to the Roman soldiers after I was taken and brought to the fortress. I listened to these other people— "

"Celts," Vebru said. "My people."

"I listened to these Celts in the fortress until I understood them."

He tilted his face. "Little Bern, how old are you?"

Now I tilted my face back at him. "Old? I don't understand. I know I am older than new-born babies because I remember when they were born, but not as old as the big trees because they were always present in all my memory."

"How many years since you were born?" My blank thoughts must have shown on my face. "All right, then how many winters do you remember?" I blinked at the flames. "Oh, that's right, you're from the north. Where I am from, they say if you travel far enough north, all the way to the top of the world, it is just one forever winter."

"They say that where I am from also. But I remember five winters. There were more before my memory, though."

Vebru chuckled. "I will say to our master that you are eight."

I thought that would do. Eight is still safely on the fingers of both hands. "I want to ask you a question, but I do not know how to address you."

"I have told you many times. I am Vebru."

"Then ... Vebru, you have told me you are not my master, yet you bought me with silver coins from your own pouch."

"I bought you on behalf of my master—now your master as well—with his money, on his behalf. In his name."

A slave bought me? A slave bought a slave? "But ... how is that possible?" I said. "I thought only a Roman citizen could sell or buy a— "

He held out a palm for my silence, then rose and grasped the staff. He brought it back to his place and sat. He reached inside his tunic and pulled out a rolled parchment. He unrolled it and showed me markings that meant nothing to me. "I carry this from my master to show I am a slave who acts on his behalf." He rolled the parchment and stuffed it back into his tunic. "Also, Roman citizens understand that the man who bears this staff represents a Roman citizen." I leaned forward to view it better. Vebru beckoned me forward. "Come, Bern, and behold the seal of a family of Roman nobility."

"The eagle?"

"That is Rome."

With the fingers of both manacled hands, I probed the bronze bird's head, his outstretched wings. Then I rubbed the tips of those fingers over the figures below. "These ... markings, and those on that paper. Are they some symbols of the gods?"

He smiled. "Perhaps they are. Perhaps the gods created these, and gave them as a gift to humans so that humans could honor them better." He looked at my perplexed expression. "Do your people not read?"

"What does that mean?"

"I suppose not, then. Here, let me show you something of the Roman writing." He pointed at each marking. "The first two are the same. A *C* and another *C*. The first letter in the first and second names of our master. Caius Cinna. This next letter is *T*, for the family name Tavarius. Caius Cinna Tavarius, the *praefectus* of the colonia. Our master."

"So you, a slave, were sent here by our master to buy slaves?"

"As steward of his house, I was sent on behalf of Master Caius Cinna to buy *two* slaves." He nodded at my cousins. "I will find a proper explanation for the third. At least I hope I will."

"Vebru, can you understand the Roman writings?"

"Enough to understand most of what I read. Why do you ask?"

"Could Master Caius Cinna use the services of an interpreter who can write the words he speaks and speak the words he writes to the Germans and Celts?"

"Our master is first of all a shrewd businessman." Vebru tapped the dirt with the end of the staff. "If we were to find such an interpreter, I am certain he would be pleased."

I patted Vebru's shoulder. "How wise and thoughtful of you to find such an interpreter as a gift to show your gratitude for all Master Caius Cinna has given you." I bowed. "And for only five coins silver!"

Vebru's eyes widened. "You? But you have only begun to learn. And you had no idea what these markings on the staff meant!"

I returned to my place on the other side of the fire. "How many days until we reach Master's house?"

"The villa he owns where we are going, *Augusta Raurica*, ten or more days' march."

I smiled across at him. "Then you have ten or more days to teach me what our master will need to see and hear from me." We laughed together, nearly awakening my cousins. I cocked my head and studied him. I was dying to know something. "Vebru, you traveled alone north carrying that staff. What would have stopped you from running and declaring yourself a free man?"

"I like my head wedged firmly between my shoulders, Bern. Besides, I do not possess the skills to survive as a free man." He shook his head at the flickering flames. "So I would be caught and brought back where I would be freed of my head ... or I would lose it out here as a runaway slave. Not much of a choice there." He continued his rumination staring across the water.

I turned my face to the opposite shore hidden now in black shadow. "What lies on the other side of the water?" I asked.

"They used to be my people when I was your age," he said. "Now they are only another danger to our master's house and to me."

He unrolled a blanket for himself, then for me. I thanked him and lay down. I stared up at the stars and felt that he was looking at me. He stepped over and knelt beside me as he pulled a thin piece of metal from a pouch. He inserted the metal into a hole of each manacle, and with a twist, my wrists were freed. He slipped the piece of metal and the manacles into the pouch and returned to his blanket. He lay upon it and said, "If while I'm asleep you wish to run to your freedom, you know the direction north, back to the German people."

I searched the stars for shapes and thought about the last German people I met. I closed my eyes knowing I would remain with Vebru and try my luck as a slave in the House of Tavarius.

⤳

From a Roman soldier, Vebru had borrowed parchments bearing Roman writings. "What writings do you require?" the soldier asked.

"Oh, it matters little. I simply need to practice my script." Vebru handed the man a pouch that jingled from the few pieces of precious metal it contained.

The soldier regarded the strange Celt, then shrugged. "I don't understand, but I'll find what I can for you."

Upon our solemn promise of secrecy and with our guarantee of the safe return of the parchments, we were soon walking along reading letters from home in the Empire, written to men in the regiment we did not know, by people we would never meet.

"Am I reading this correctly?" I said. "One of the platoon leaders is having secret—what is this?— "

Vebru leaned toward me and read the word phonetically. "Trysts ... Meetings of a private nature." He glanced to the soldiers marching ahead of us in a column two-by-two, and satisfied we were not heard, he added, "The Romans are known not to be able to get to the direct point when speaking of certain matters."

"Well," I said, "this man is having these ... meetings with the Regimental Commander's daughter."

"Oh my!" he put his hands to his heart. He bent and whispered into my ear. "We must speak of this to no one once we give the letters back. But do read on, please."

"So if she misses having sex with him, why does she not simply say so?"

"Well ... it is a rather delicate matter."

I looked at him as if he had suddenly become a dotard. "I would not call what I have witnessed *delicate*. In fact, it often appeared to me rather athletic and sometimes even painful."

"Um ... well, yes ... But you must understand that for the Romans, when a man and his wife— "

"A man and his wife? What does that have to do with sex?"

"For the Romans, it means a great deal. The joys of the flesh are the rewards of marriage."

"Without at least a good fight between the rival men?" I wondered how the Romans were able to populate their military with such numbers amid such restrictions. "The language and markings— "

"Writing," he corrected me.

"Yes, the spoken and written words will not be the most challenging part for me of learning the Roman ways."

"I dare say," Vebru said. "Now back to our practice ..."

We marched along thus, travelling south while news and images of life back in distant Roman homes kept us occupied.

The occasional so-called private matters kept up our spirits when they arrived between the long stretches of descriptions of lost cows or old acquaintances who had died of boring ailments. But I believed I was getting the hang of the Roman scribblings. I had begun practicing the art of making the markings after Vebru had found some blank parchment and a charcoal pen.

Two days after receiving the parchments, the attack came.

From the other shore across the river, a chorus of shouting in the Gaulish tongue preceded a hail of arrows falling into the water about two-thirds across. "Come over here," a male voice shouted, "so we can carve the skin from your bodies! But not your females! We have other plans for your females!"

The Regimental Commander rode back our direction on a well-groomed speckled stallion. Vebru hastily folded the parchments and stuffed them into a shoulder pouch. "You!" the commander said to Vebru. "You're one of them!" He pointed toward the opposite shore. "What does he say?" Vebru translated the Gaul's words of threat. "Do they have boats?" Vebru let him know in all probability, the Celtic warriors would remain hidden safely within the wood line on the opposite shore. "Julius wrote over a century ago that he subdued these people," the commander said. "It would appear he missed a few." He galloped his stallion back to the front of the ranks.

The arrows continued to fall well short of our shore. I asked Vebru for a piece of parchment and charcoal. It took several minutes, but I managed to write a sentence. I handed my work to Vebru. *Pedit fortior mihi sagittas*, I had written. He laughed and nearly fell to the path clutching the parchment in his fist. "Yes," he said, "you can probably fart stronger than they can shoot arrows." To the opposite shore he shouted in Gaulish, "My German friend's gas can outshoot your arrows! You should go back home and eat bean stew! Then come back and try again!"

We laughed, our arms around each other's shoulders as we continued on the journey south.

CHAPTER TWO

IN THE SERVICE OF A NOBLE HOUSE

1

Around half a century before Vebru brought my virgin cousins and me to Augusta Raurica—also called Colonia Augusta Rauricorum, depending on which person (Celt or Roman) is speaking—Lucius Munatius Plancus, then a senator, came through this region and that of the southern Germanic tribes, founding settlements here and there. My new home was among them.

Gaius Julius Caesar had subdued—or so he had boasted in his writings—the Gaulic Celts only just over a decade prior to the arrival of Senator Plancus, so he and his escort of Roman soldiers could concentrate more on recruiting local Celts to work on building projects, and less on fighting and killing them. Once he had completed enough structures for occupancy, he sent word back to Rome, where Augustus offered positions to freemen nobles and an alternative to death—removal to these new settlements—to convicts, debtors, and others who had fallen into disfavor.

Through the back gates, Plancus left the new settlement with his military escort on the day the train of nobles and others entered the front gates. He did not bother to meet, greet, or brief his replacement leader. The founder was more than happy to vacate his property, and according to reports, was heard having said he was leaving a bad cesspool to make a better one elsewhere. Among the lessor nobles through the gates was my new master, widower Caius Cinna Tavarius.

What followed was typical Roman urban planning. The structures for every purpose were ready for use and occupancy. The granaries were full, and cellars were stored with casks of wine aplenty. All that preparatory labor had been performed by Plancus and his soldiers. The only problem lay with the most unreliable of resources, the new humans pouring in from Rome. The convicts and debtors knew all too well what to do with the stores of wine. The minor noblemen immediately fell into argument over which of them would best serve as leader of this settlement.

After a few days of this nonsense, Caius Cinna Tavarius had had enough. He knew the basics of Roman politics, namely that threat of physical harm worked hand-in-hand with bribery and corruption to bring about a desired outcome. Caius Cinna approached General Spanto and offered him the position of Chief Consul to the future *Praefectus* for the mere cost of five crucified convicts, debtors, and what-have-you—it mattered not a whit whom the future Consul chose—and the heads of three minor noblemen on spikes, also of the General's choosing.

Caius Cinna Tavarius, now *P*raefectus *U*rbi Caius Cinna Tavarius of his newly-created Roman colonia, assumed his office in a peaceful transition. After that initial display of business, there was no further need of blood spillage, at least not of fellow Roman citizens. In not too many years after Caius Cinna's ascent, Colonia Augusta Rauricorum had become a strongly-fortified center of culture and trade along the routes from Rome to Gaul. Caius Cinna Tavarius had had no real experience in politics, but his business instincts and decisions were unparalleled. He simply applied what he had learned from his father and grandfather in the business of the grape and the olive to the operation of a town. Soon the town would grow into a veritable city, and the city into the capital of a province. Someone would need to govern the province, and who better than the master of the grape and the olive whose business life had been stuck in the mire of politics back in suburban Rome?

Though from his marriage, he had a grown son back in Rome to keep an eye on the vineyards and olive orchards, he knew all good political leaders must have a woman beside him to keep the house in order. Shortly after he secured the position of *P*raefectus *U*rbi, the widower sent a letter to Rome and in absentia married the daughter of a wealthy senator, owner of a rock quarry, through an arrangement meant to mutually benefit both families. Upon the aging senator's death, Caius Cinna Tavarius was to inherit twenty-five percent interest in the quarry. As to the senator's benefit? Ridding his house of the youngest of three daughters freed up the elder two for arrangements more financially beneficial to the family name. The girl, Dalina, was quite beautiful and quite young. Only fourteen years old, eleven years younger than her husband's son.

Master Caius Cinna was out negotiating peace with a Celtic encampment in the northwest corner of the province when Vebru brought my cousins and me to the villa in Colonia Augusta Rauricorum. Young Lady Dalina, who had been in the region for barely a year, was home, and she had an adult female slave escort Frida and Linza to their quarters. That left me to stand alone with Vebru before her. She gazed upon me with a knowing smile, her hazel eyes reflecting all she took in. I noticed how smooth and unblemished her white, white skin. Her golden blonde locks rested before her, framing her inticing curves.

At her age, any female I had ever known before was nearly as muscular as the men I had known. In fact, after a woman had had a baby or two, she soon became not pretty but handsome, barely distinguishable from males.

"My Lady, I can explain," Vebru said in Latin.

She held out a slender, soft palm. "We asked for two virgin German females," she said. I am certain my mouth dropped open. Her feminine voice resembled the Roman musical instruments I would later come to know, and not the raspy noise I was accustomed to hearing pour through female lips. And she did not feel the need to clear her throat and spit, like the women in my village did after every few sentences. She gazed upon me with those captivating eyes, and I felt myself dissolving under their hazel spell. "So what do you have to say for yourself, golden boy, or can you even understand me?"

I balled up my right fist and pounded my chest twice, as was my tribe's custom among males when introducing oneself. The Lady Dalina tittered at this. Vebru cleared his throat. He bent and whispered in my ear, "Here among the Romans, you bow, like so." He demonstrated the motion. I mimicked the bowed trunk and head. "Remain so when you answer," he said.

"In which language would you prefer me to say something for myself, my lady?" I said in Latin to the tiled floor.

"How interesting!" she replied. She switched to the Gaulish of the Celts, but with very bad grammar. "Which languages do you speak?" she attempted.

Since her mother tongue was obviously her strength, I answered in Latin. "I am fluent in my home tongue of the Germans," I said. "I am nearing that in the tongue of Rome ... and I am learning to converse in the tongue of Vebru's people."

"Former people," he corrected.

"Yes," I said, "his former people. The Celts."

Again flowed the birdlike chirping laughter from the lady. "What a gifted little one!" she said. She had been leaning back in the well-padded chair. But now she tilted forward, a hand resting on one armrest and her elbow propped on the other. She rested her tiny chin on the backs of her slender fingers and, with a half grin stared at me with those reflecting hazel eyes. Simply stared at me. I felt they were like the rare whirlpools you may come across in the swamps back in the north. And I was being pulled into them, to be sucked in, to drown, and to be lost forever. "And how pretty ... Tell me, do all your people have such golden hair, such fair skin, and sparkling blue eyes?"

I merely stood gawking like some garden satyr sculpture, several of which we had walked past outdoors before entering the villa.

"The Lady Dalina has asked you a question, Bern," Vebru said, his voice suddenly becoming uncharacteristically gruff.

I awakened from my spell. "Um ... no, my Lady, not all of us. It depends on family and tribe, like all people everywhere, I imagine."

She raised an eyebrow, a seductive motion that made me shudder. "All people everywhere? Listen, young—Bern, did he call you?—I stem from a long line of noble blood. I am from no barbaric tribe."

I bowed my head in shame of my faux pas. "No, my Lady."

She settled back with both palms on the armrests. "Bern, raise your face to me." I did as she bade. "Your master, Caius Cinna, is strictly a businessman, and knowing him as one, I can predict how he will react when he returns. He will order you to be sold to another highest bidder." She eyed me up and down, measuring my physical worth. "In his eyes, you will be a short and stout Germanic boy who could not produce in the wheat fields or vineyards." Again she leaned forward. "Step up to my chair, Bern." I stepped forward, bowing my head, stopping when I could see her painted toenails poking from the open-wrapped shoe I later learned was called a sandal. "Raise your face, Bern, and look me in the eyes with those beautiful sparkling jewels." I did so, believing it would not be long before I would be sent away, never again to gaze into the Lady Dalina's pools of hazel. "Yes, we know how Master Caius Cinna would deal with you. But I am his wife, and unless he gives you to me as my pretty pet, his bed will not be so warm."

I grinned at her machinations. She reached forward and stroked my hair. "You find it amusing that we women wield such power over our men?"

"No, my Lady," I said. "It is so familiar. When my mother wanted something from my father, it took only a night of sleeping with the oxen or sheep to change his thinking."

She burst into a round of laughter, and it felt wonderful to be the cause of this mirth. When it subsided to giggles, she reached out both hands. "Come, little Bern," she said, patting a place beside her on the chair, "come sit beside me." I climbed onto the chair and she pulled me close against her. She hugged me and kissed the top of my head. "You are mine, all mine ... And together we shall share the secrets about those of us of the fairer sex who truly rule the Roman Empire ... and indeed the known world." She pulled herself away, and we looked into each other's eyes. "And I will correct and improve that horrid Latin given to you so briefly and incorrectly by our Vebru." He bowed low. "I will teach you to read and write properly."

Again she pulled me into her. This felt so lovely. I could not recall such show of affection even from my mother. "Oh," she said, "and may I interest you in another tongue, my little prodigy? It's called Greek ... You may leave us, Vebru. Bern and I shall busy ourselves straightaway with our lessons."

Vebru remained bowed but raised his face to us and winked at me as he stepped backwards out of my Lady's parlor.

2

I became accustomed to the Roman calendar and the Empire's concept of the week, the month, the year. After two Roman calendar years I had become fully fluent in three new languages—Latin, Gaulish Celtic, and Greek—gods be thanked for the aid of my Lady Dalina and my Celtic friend and fellow slave Vebru. With speed I was able to read and write anything I wished in Greek or Latin, which pleased my Lady, yet she still had given me no official task as translator. I spoke often to Vebru about my desire to serve a useful purpose for the House of Tavarius.

"Patience, Bern!" he told me in final exasperation. "You are yet young, and our masters will avail themselves of your talents in due time."

In due time ... Perhaps that was a Celtic measurement of time. It could not be Roman. They were always so precise and punctual.

"Besides," Vebru added, "are you not satisfied to pour wine for our Lady? To stand beside her as she pets you?"

"There must be more," I sighed. "What about my destiny? What am I meant to be? To do?"

"Enough of this Germanic nonsense!" he bellowed. "You are a slave in the House of Tavarius!" I was still short enough so that his eyes were aimed slightly downward as he looked in mine. He bent slightly and placed his hands on my shoulders. "My young friend Bern, your destiny unfolds and changes with each moment. What you are meant to be at this moment is the cup bearer and the pourer of wine for our Lady. That and her preferred object of distraction ... But what you are ultimately meant to be will be revealed— "

"—in due time," I said, making a duet of his worn phrase.

I had scarce little direct contact with Master Caius Cinna, a stoic man who was apparently living a life as a model for one of those popular marble busts of Roman greats. On occasion I would exit my Lady's parlor and nearly bump into him as I turned a corner to fetch whatever she wished. One time he said, "Is it you again, little Mister Underfoot?" and he continued sauntering out of the villa to inspect the vineyards or fruit orchards. Often, though, I would find him simply sitting just outside the parlor after a session of reading the Greek of Homer or the Latin of Virgil, Cicero, and Gaius Julius Caesar. I would bow to him and exit the outer room backwards bent at the waist, but never did he acknowledge me after the initial eye contact.

In those sessions with the Lady Dalina, I learned much of the written arts. Cicero, writing in his native Latin, borrowed or perhaps stole from the poetic style of the Greek epics from Homer, while Virgil simply stole whole stories from the old Greek master, and made the Greek heroes Roman with Roman names and settings.

"Is it not wrong, my Lady, to take another's work as your own?" I asked.

"Bern, let us pretend you are suddenly rich and free. You wish to build a house. What do you build?"

I had limited experience with any kind of dwelling, so I decided on the best I had known. "I would like a villa like this one," I said. "Or perhaps something like Master's hunting lodge near Arialbinnum."

"Both excellent choices," she said. "There are abodes back in the countryside outside Rome I would choose, but then I have seen more in my time than you have in yours ... Back to the point. You chose two that already exist. So your house would not be original, not your design."

"Ahhhh," I said, "I think I understand. If the original story was a masterwork, then why should it not serve and be used as a blueprint?"

"Precisely! The characters and setting are altered, and the style is that of the new author, so it is only fitting." She shrugged and said, "Besides, so many stories have already been written; therefore, it will continue to become more increasingly difficult for new authors to compose completely original works."

"Yes, I understand." Then I stared out toward the vineyards and orchards with another thought.

"If your brow becomes any more furrowed," she said, "Master will mistake your forehead for a new plot to plant fruit seeds." She chuckled and ran the backs of her fingers across my cheek. "Come, little Bern, what else is troubling you?"

"We read *The Gallic Wars* by Gaius Julius Caesar ..."

"Yes, Bern, and what of it?"

"Well, I trust Vebru, who is from Gaul."

"As do I, Bern. So what is the problem with Vebru?"

"Nothing about Vebru, but about Caesar." She raised those beautiful eyebrows as she awaited an explanation. "Well, my Lady, in those wars, Caesar emerged triumphant, but according to Vebru, much of what Caesar writes did not occur that way."

She was grinning, like a guarded secret had been exposed. "First, Caesar did in fact win that war. Otherwise, we could not be here now. To the victor goes the spoils, and part of that is the story. For example, what stories would we have now if Troy had won that war? Something quite different, I dare say. So Caesar had the right, as victor, to write the story with whatever slant he wished. Also, Caesar could read and write in his language, in my language, the language of the Empire. Even if the conquered could manage to release their pathetic story, they could do so only by word of mouth. The Celtic people do not properly read or write, so they leave no lasting story."

"Yes, my Lady. That explains why we have Caesar's version and not that of, say, Vercingetorix or his followers. But even so, according to the word of mouth that eventually reached

Vebru, many of Caesar's exploits in this campaign were not so daring as in his writings. Caesar paints himself as a much braver warrior than the observer he really was."

"Ah," she said, "so you are saying Gaius Julius Caesar is guilty of embellishment."

"My Lady, I do not know that word."

"When you embellish, Bern, you add and change the fact to make yourself—or your subject—appear better, bolder, more heroic than you or he really was."

"But— "

She held up a palm. "Bern, is Caesar's version not enjoyable to read?"

"Yes, my Lady. It reads like the epic sagas of Homer and Virgil."

"That it does," she said. "So when you write anything—I don't care if it is the list of our supplies for the harvest season—make it interesting for the reader ... But start with the first reader: you, the writer. *You*, Bern, must first be impressed by what you write."

3

After my arrival in the villa, I was separated from my cousins, Frida and Linza, as we were in separate work classes from one another. At the time Vebru purchased them, none of us was aware of the purpose for my cousins' enslavement in Colonia Augusta Rauricorum. Master Caius Cinna had a fine slave stable of strong males from throughout Europe and even as far away as Asia Minor and Africa. Master had become interested in profit from creating the best slaves through selective breeding, yet a problem presented itself, followed by a simple solution. The problem was that he had no females to breed with the males, and Vebru brought the solution back to the villa, namely Frida and Linza.

I managed a visit to my cousins' quarters from time to time, and though we shared a few laughs and old stories, I noticed a pall steadily growing on Linza's countenance. Frida readily accepted her role as breeder and future birth mother. She even appeared to enjoy her work. In two years, she gave Master two strong baby boys, one half-Greek and the other half African. After she weened the first—the Greek-Germanic—at her breasts for a half year, Master had him taken away and then brought in the African slave. That baby followed suit, and none of us knew where either went. Frida didn't care. She ate better and lived in far more comfort than during her childhood, and all she needed to do was allow male slaves to bed her and then raise the resulting babies for a half-year each.

Linza, though, was not as cooperative as her sister. She managed to also birth two slave children, a half-African girl and a half Celtic boy. But throughout the entire process she had to be chained to her bed—as the seeds were planted, as the belly grew, as the babies came through to the world. Two years chained to a bed, and essentially raped at intervals. Unlike her sister Frida, Linza had an uncommon streak of independence and worse, a vivid, undying memory of her life in our Germanic village.

Though it was forbidden without her father's consent, the whole village looked the other direction when she would sneak off in the forest with Broka, son of a farmer with the largest plot of land of anyone among us. I believe now she was in love, a concept far ahead of our understanding of the workings between men and women.

As soon as she realized her plight, the purpose of her life in Master's villa, she pined for Broka—who had mostly likely been killed in the village massacre anyway—and fought as hard as a wolf caught in a snare. In the meantime, she bore the two children to increase Master's inventory.

She would not feed either baby, both of which were handed over to Frida, who was well-endowed and had milk to spare. Only a week after Master sent a local woman to take away the half-Celtic baby boy, my Lady bade me to Linza's quarters. My cousin Frida was in dire need of comforting, she told me.

"And what of Linza?" I said, preparing to back out the parlor.

"You'll understand when you arrive. Go now, Bern, Go to your cousin Frida. In Linza's quarters."

Confusion makes for poor witness, but all the villa had to go by was the baffling witness of a local Celtic nurse. According to her account, she brought a tray of food—apples from the orchards, fresh wine, and bread—to Linza's quarters. She loosened the slave girl's chains so she could eat without hindrance. The next thing the nurse knew, the crazy Germanic slave girl had taken the dull knife, meant for slicing the apples or cutting the bread into smaller pieces, and jammed it repeatedly into her stomach and torso. Blood splattered the sheets and walls from the jagged cuts in her flesh. Though the self-abuse must have caused horrid pain, the girl continued, and screamed out anti-Roman battle cries in her native tongue as the blade sank each time with a sickening *thwack!*

By the time I burst into the room, it was all over. Frida stood beside the bed holding her cousin's red-slickened hand. The blood was draining from Linza's body. She smiled at me, then at Frida. Her face was ghastly pale, as if she had already become her own ghost. "I am free," she wheezed out, "and you both ... are still slaves." Her hand became limp, and through her tears Frida placed it on her chest, covering a couple of her many bloody wounds. Her eyes remained open, and her mocking smile remained frozen. I left her thus.

No nobles wanted Linza's children. I heard they were adopted by local impoverished Celtic families, and whenever I was on my Lady's or my Master's business in the town center, I imagined them running about. Wisps of imagination were all these phantom children had become to me now ... like the notion of freedom.

In the Colonia I learned of the four seasons. Winter gave over to spring leading to the full panoply of summer, then the dying leaves of autumn portended the coming winter. These seasons passed by several times, watching me grow only a little more in physical height but towering anyone else around in linguistics. All the while, Vebru's hair grayed on the sides where it still existed. What grew even stronger was our friendship. Without Vebru I may have fallen into the despair over the loss of my cousin.

An incident involving my best friend created the circumstances that led to my next step in the mini-destinies of my life.

My Lady didn't care for the sport of hunting, though she had no qualms against eating roast pheasant or venison stew. When Master decided the entire villa would begin an annual tradition of moving north for a few summer months to his luxury hunting lodge south of Arielbinnum, she didn't protest, though her hazel eyes flashed at her husband. After he vacated her parlor, she turned to Vebru and me. "You heard the man," she said. "Pack the House of Tavarius for a visit to the wilderness!" She rose from her divan and stormed out, leaving us to shrug at one another and begin the work demanded of us.

Only a week later we were settled in the hunting lodge. I personally found it preferable to the villa. It contained the same number of living spaces for family and slaves, though perhaps a quarter smaller. But the forests were thicker and the many rivers and brooks ran wilder than what I had known since my youth in the distant north.

We all soon settled into our villa routines, Vebru as steward and chief business consultant, myself as the favorite pet and project of Lady Tavarius, my Lady as ... herself, and Master as the rarely-present enigma who ran the entire operation ... in name.

Of course, my Lady continued teaching me the finer points of the language of the Empire, and the more fascinating tongue of Plato, of Socrates, of the poet Homer and the playwrights Sophocles and Euripides. I was by now able to not only speak, but to read and write fluently in both languages. I continued to maintain fluency in Gaulish Celtic by conversing when I could with Vebru.

On a beautiful day, two days past the local midsummer festival, Vebru and I were released from the tight control of the House of Tavarius to gather apples and plums from the orchards north of the hunting lodge. Vebru was not accustomed to such frivolous activity, but the gathering of berries, apples, and plums—all wild—was not that far back in my memory of the northern forests. So I took the lead. We each toted a long gunny sack. Our goal was to return to the lodge with full gunny sacks, enough for a month of cooking and baking, a month of peace in the house.

It happened at the northern edge of the apple orchard. Our sacks were each nearly full, and we were climbing down from the ladders we brought with us from the storage huts on the northern edge. We were planning to move the ladders to another part of each tree we were harvesting, but by the time we reached the bottom rung, Vebru and I felt the sharp points of Celtic spears pressing into our backs.

"Step onto the ground and drop your sacks!" ordered a voice in Gaulish Celtic. We obeyed and instinctively raised our hands in a show of unarmed nonresistance. "Face us!"

We did so, and were surprised that nearly two dozen Celtic warriors had crept from the forest into the orchard without making the slightest sound.

The spokesperson, the obvious leader of this group, stood studying us, his green eyes roving over our bodies. He was tall and lean, but muscular in the way of an Olympian god. His pitch-black hair was tied behind him into a tail resting against the small of his back. "You are the slaves of the House of Tavarius?"

"Yes, we are," Vebru and I said in unison.

The leader snapped his green eyes from my friend to me. "The older slave is one of us, and perhaps before this day is over he shall no longer be a slave. But you," he said stepping forward and boring his gaze down upon me, "what are you? My experience tells me you're a German, but those males are as big as bears."

I smiled up at him and said, "That is who I am."

"What is that supposed to mean?"

"My name is Bern ... named for the bear."

The Celtic leader chuckled. "Well, Bern, and you?" He looked at my friend.

"Vebru."

"So, Bern and Vebru, you will come with us."

"And what is to become of us?" Vebru asked.

"As I said, freedom for you if you cooperate. As for the other," the leader said cocking his head toward me, "we Celts can make use of slaves, too, but we'll have to see what work this small bear can do."

I smiled at Vebru. "Do you know a slave who has been owned by a German, a Roman, and then a Celt?"

"No," he said, "but before your life is over, you must know there are yet other people in other lands to own you."

"A cosmopolitan is a citizen of the world. Is there a word for a slave of the world?"

"You're the language master," Vebru said. "You tell me."

"If not," I said laughing, "I'll create the word."

"If anyone could do it, the bear of many tongues can." Vebru clapped me on the back and joined my laughter as we marched into the forest with the Celtic warriors.

We lived in the Celtic encampment for perhaps a week of sunrises simply eating, sleeping, and occasionally strolling around, though under constant watchful eyes. Finally, the leader entered the hut Vebru and I shared in our captivity. "The council of warriors have met, and they cannot come to an agreement about what to do with you."

"Be short and honest with us, please," said Vebru. "If we are to die, simply say it, so we can prepare ourselves."

"If you are to die, it would be by my orders." The leader nodded at Vebru's perplexed expression. "Yes, the council has placed the entire weight upon my shoulders. Since I decided to bring you here, I must decide your fate." He then turned to me. "Both of your fates."

After a particularly deafening pause of silence, Vebru said, "So tell us, please, what have you decided?"

The leader lowered his gaze to the dirt. "I ... I cannot decide. I acted without plan when I led my men out of the forest and into your fruit trees. And now I pay the price." The formerly intimidating Celtic warrior raised his face to us. I noted his bottom lip trembled. "Can ... can you help me make a decision the council will accept?"

"What he wants," I said, "is to save face." I looked at the leader. "Is that correct?" He nodded. "I wonder something ... Among my people—the Germans—and among the Romans, the leader makes decisions. Can you not do this, simply decide and be obeyed?"

He said, "We all noted that about the Romans when Caesar conquered us. He spoke, and the legions acted. But we always debated and argued before taking a single step. Eventually our form of decision making— "

"Democracy," I said.

"Whatever you wish to call it ... But it defeated us."

"So you need us to help you decide what to do with us," Vebru said.

The leader nodded at the earth beneath his feet.

A thousand thoughts rushed through my mind within a couple breaths. "I know what you can do," I said.

He glared at me like a mother chiding her wayward child. "You? You are still but a boy. How could you possibly know what to do about this problem?"

Vebru rubbed his chin. "Let us hear this brilliant plan," he said to the leader, who darted his eyes from Vebru to me and back. "Aren't you curious?"

The warrior held up his hands in defeat. "All right then," he said, "let's hear it."

I cleared my throat. "The Lady of the house holds me in favor," I said. "If you were to be so kind as to hold me for the ransom of your choice, I am sure my Lady will arrange that payment."

Vebru stepped beside me and bent at the waist. "Bern," he whispered in my ear, "have you lost your mind?"

"That's a distinct possibility," I said from the corner of my mouth. "But if my hunch proves correct, all three of us will profit from this."

"Three? You, me, and who else?"

I shot my glance toward the leader of warriors. "Our nameless Celt."

"In what way?" Vebru said, raising his volume.

"Just let fate lead us."

"In other words, you have no clue!"

I waved Vebru to step aside. "Sir," I said to the warrior, "name your ransom for me, and Vebru here will deliver that message to the House of Tavarius."

"Bern!" Vebru shouted. "I must protest!"

"Then do so, my friend," I said, "but wait until our host has a bag lined full of whatever amount of silver he demands. After that, protest to all the gods you can name."

Grumbling as he packed a sack with food and water, then grumbling with each step he took, Vebru left the Celtic encampment to deliver the warrior chief's demand of 200 silver coins and my Master's promise that he and his people would not be hunted by Roman soldiers. The leader of the warriors and I viewed as my friend and fellow slave stomped south through the forest cursing in his Gaulish Celtic.

The days passed without word from the hunting lodge. The leader sat with me before a fire, though the afternoon was too warm for wolf or bear skins. We each ate from a bowl of stew. As community members strolled past, they stared at us and leaned into one another whispering. The leader swallowed a last slurp, then tossed the wooden bowl and spoon into the fire. "It does not seem the lady you spoke of holds you in much favor at all." He glanced at the passing people from the corners of his eyes. "What they gossip to each other, my strange little captive, is your future."

"My future? And what do they say of it?"

"They hope soon you will be either killed or banished. Preferably the first."

I realized time was running short for both me and my captor. I could not have known how Vebru's message was received, but I had a feeling my Lady wished me back. Yet since my master maintained ultimate control of the purse and since he cared little for my presence in his household, Master most likely walked away from his wife and Vebru with his marble-chiseled, impassive face. I imagined a very cold bed indeed for him, but then I realized as master of a Roman house of nobility and as Chief Consul—and obviously soon to be Governor—of a growing province, Master had the typical Roman nobleman's access to other female comfort. Mistresses, concubines, and other women who were not his wife.

Therefore, unless I acted and did so quickly, all memory of me would fade into the oblivion of the forgotten. I took a deep breath. "Master," I said, "for you are my master of this moment, I have a— "

He pounded a fist into an open palm. "Listen, you— "

"Bern."

"Listen, Bern, as for your status, we are in similar situations. You were a free German, sold into slavery to a Roman family. My people," he said, waving a hand around at the people within sight, "were a free and proud tribe of Celts, defeated and occupied by those same Romans." He spat on the dirt.

"If we are equals, it would be nice for me to be able to address you by name."

"Don't laugh, but my name is Vercingetorix."

"Like the ..."

"Yes, like the warrior defeated by the Roman general we now know as Caesar. My parents believed in the power of names, as all old Celts did. If they gave me the name of a powerful leader, maybe I could live to be his replacement."

"And drive the Romans out of Gaul?"

He snorted in self-mockery. "Needless to say, my parents both died without witnessing such glory. I only hope they are not suffering seeing their son's lack of accomplishments from their place in the afterlife."

I was not sure how to proceed, so I decided to be direct but measured. "Would you believe me if I were to tell you that your best path forward for your encampment here is through and with the Romans?"

"The Romans are our enemy!"

"And I promise you this: if that attitude does not die soon, it will kill you all."

"What would you have us do? Surrender and be marched through the streets of Rome to the auction block?"

"No, not at all ... I would have you cooperate and share what wealth you can gain from your new allies. The Romans."

He shook his head violently, and his hair whipped his face. "We will fight, then retreat to the forest, then strike again and retreat to the forest again!"

"Hear me, please. I have witnessed the result of such bravery in the north. Arminius, the great German fighter, managed to slaughter three Roman legions with only a few hundred men."

"And that is what we must do!"

I held up a hand. "But his people's story does not end there. Yes, his loosely-organized band of fighters who knew their forest were able to defeat three legions that knew only open-terrain fighting ... What occurred next, I witnessed for myself. Germanicus returned with ten legions and more silver and gold than the local tribes had ever seen. He bought the allegiance of the fiercest tribes. Instead of one mighty slaughter like Arminius accomplished, they carried out hundreds, perhaps thousands, of smaller annihilations. For all I know, it could still be carrying on."

"And they would do that here?"

"Of course. And why not? They would do it because they can." I stood and placed my hands on his shoulders. "There is a better way to fight them."

He lifted his dark eyes to me. "And what would that be?"

"Do you speak, read, or write the Roman tongue?"

"Why would I want to do that?"

I winked at him as if I were Vebru and he were me. "I will take that to mean you cannot. Come," I said and stepped toward my guarded hut, "we have much to do and little time." I glanced over my shoulders to make sure he followed me.

Though he was a reluctant student initially, Vercingetorix began speaking simple phrases in the Roman tongue within a week of our tutorial sessions. Recognizing the characters of the writing was a slower matter, but I had patience as his tutor and hoped he would reciprocate as student. I began by teaching him to write his ridiculous name phonetically with Latin letters, as small children learn at first.

Although we attempted to hide away from prying eyes during these sessions, we were discovered by an old woman, and the word got out. I feared we were doomed by those who still scoffed at my presence and would view our lessons as a form of sorcery.

But after a week with my stubborn scholar, a young boy approached me, his father trailing. "You are the German," said the boy, "from the north."

"That I am."

"Your Arminius and his brother were taken to Rome to learn the language and ways. To become Roman citizens and soldiers."

"That's the story I have heard."

"This Arminius used his status as Roman soldier to betray the Roman soldiers."

"I have heard that as well."

"It is possible if I start by learning the Roman tongue, I may follow his path."

"It is possible ... In this ever-growing world, anything is possible. This boy," I said to Vercingetorix, "is smarter than you, my friend. The only way to defeat the Roman Empire is to become part of the Roman Empire. Strike from within."

So my improvised roster of students slowly grew, and I thought it possible I may remain here unharmed. There remained, though, the majority of the eyes, in which I could read only danger.

I realized there would be no ransom for me, and as far as the House of Tavarius was concerned, I was dust shaken off from the sole of a sandal. I knew it when the heat of the summer sun gave over to cooling breezes and rainfall, and the forest's leaves changed from green to yellow and red. The Roman hunting season had passed, and surely the family and its slaves had returned south to the Colonia.

I worked in the fields gathering grain in order to earn my keep. Now and then Vercingetorix would take me aside and teach me to shoot arrows. After our sessions using straw targets, my forearms ached so much my hands hung beside my hips like leaden weights. I noticed my forearm muscles and biceps were growing. For the first time in my life, I looked like the son of a village smith.

One day he took me deeper into the forest, each of us carrying a bow and a quiver full of arrows. "It is time you learned how to hunt," he said. "If you bring meat, even rabbit or squirrel, home to the encampment once in a while, they may forget about torturing and executing you."

"How considerate of them that would be!" I said.

We came across no wild scat or spoor, and the encampment leader explained that if we wished to find game, we would need to trek further north because my Master and his guests had driven everything worth hunting away from the area until the next spring.

"What about trying closer to the hunting lodge?"

He eyed me curiously. "And why would we want to do that?"

"I admit," I said, "that I'm curious to know if the Master or my Lady is still around."

He faced toward the south. I could tell he imagined the Tavarius land, its orchards and buildings. "All right," he exhaled, "I am also curious ... But remember what I taught you about the silent movement."

I nodded. "And don't worry about me trying to escape to them."

"I know you won't. I'll shoot you if you do."

We crossed through the orchards until we crested a hill above the manor house and the livestock barns and slave quarters. We noted nothing but Roman soldiers coming and going between the structures. The House of Tavarius had indeed abandoned me and ridden back to the Colonia, leaving the hunting lodge as a northern military outpost.

"Come, Vercingetorix," I said stepping northward. "I have much work to do until the next summer season when Master and my Lady return. By then all your warriors will be able to dream in the Roman tongue … And you will need to ensure my survival so that my goal can be possible."

I survived through the seasons by tutoring as many as would learn the Roman tongue and by occasionally venturing into the forest and carrying rabbit or squirrel back with me. I was quite appreciated when I ran down a boar until he tired so much he merely stood ten paces away panting while I shot an arrow into his brain through an eye. It took most of the day to drag his carcass back to the encampment, but when I finally did, sweating even through the winter chill, every child, woman, and warrior sang my praise.

Eventually came the thaw of early spring, followed by the growth of thick green leaves from the bushes to the tops of the great oaks. This meant that if the House of Tavarius were to venture to the northern hunting lodge and properties in this year, it would come soon. If not, I may as well become a permanent Germanic Celt if the encampment would have me.

Vercingetorix remained the leader, and as such he held the council at bay from making a final decision about the fate of the little prisoner from the north. When the first buds of apple blossoms appeared, I introduced him to the plan that would restore me to the House of Tavarius, rid the encampment of me, and keep a steady flow of gold and silver flowing into the Celts' pouches ... if it worked.

He, his warriors, and I practiced our actions and rehearsed our words for several weeks until we noticed the signs of game returning past us to the south. The day came in early summer, and we followed the animals. Along the way, I told the leader, "If fate leads us to a meeting with the Roman soldiers, or even the family they protect, I would choose another name for myself if I were you."

"I have thought on that," he said. "From this day forth," he yelled out, "I am Gabrus!" A few warriors looked toward him. "Gabrus! And tell all the others!"

"Gabrus," I said. "A common-enough sounding name."

"It was the name of my father, who gave his son a far more ambitious, far more dangerous name."

"You will be happy to know that writing *Gabrus* in the Roman letters will be much easier," I said.

By the time we reached the hill overlooking the lodge and its supporting buildings, the sun had dropped a quarter way to the horizon from its zenith. Gabrus and I dropped to our bellies and viewed the movement below. Roman soldiers went about from structure to structure, but this time there were also others, slaves from various parts of the Empire. A wagon was parked behind an enclosed coach.

"Do you know those slaves?" Gabrus asked me.

"Only three of them. It appears Master has increased his stock ... And I see the coach. My Lady rides in it when she travels."

"Then the time is right. We'll wait until your Master is outside, but first, let's set the plan with the others." We crawled backwards until we could stand hidden from below.

I had learned the patience of a spider as a hunter in the Celtic world. As the sun sank a bit closer to the distant parts of the western earth—and what would have previously in my life felt an unbearable length of time—my Master finally stepped from the rear of the hunting lodge with his faithful steward, my friend Vebru. They walked along talking, and I imagined Vebru giving advice over some matter of business. They stepped farther from the lodge and closer to the bottom of the hill upon which we crouched. Gabrus raised a sheep's horn and blew into it, blasting a short note.

Arrows arced through the air from three sides landing in a semicircle on the turf around Master and Vebru. Gabrus had trained me to follow my arrow with my eyes so I would know precisely where it landed, and whether it hit or missed an intended target. He trained me well. My arrow landed three paces directly before Master. Roman soldiers raced forward from the rear of the structures, some with swords drawn, some bearing bows and reaching toward quivers for arrows.

Gabrus stood. It was time for him to put my tutelage to practical use. "Caius Cinna Tavarius!" he shouted, drawing the attention of all below. "Your bowmen will drop their weapons to the earth! Behold the ground before you! These arrows came from our third echelon! If a single arrow is notched by one of your bowmen, our second echelon will rid you of protection! You will not want to feel the accuracy of our best, our first echelon!"

Master lifted his left palm to block the sun. He peered up at the encampment leader. "Who are you, and what do you want of us?"

"I am called Gabrus! I am the leader of my encampment, and what I want is to make you an offer!"

"An offer? What would you have to offer us?"

"We protect you, you protect us ... and you become Governor of a real Roman province!"

Master smiled. "Come down and let us talk within!" he said, cocking a thumb toward the lodge.

The newly-named Gabrus spoke from the corner of his mouth to me. "I do not trust this."

"Neither do I," I replied. "Insist you meet where he stands now."

"Please, Governor Tavarius, bring a table and chairs from within, and set them where you stand now! I have some arrows to retrieve anyway!"

"I understand! Trust will be earned! Before we start, though, one question: you are from an encampment north of here, yet you speak excellent Roman Latin! How is that?"

"I had an excellent tutor, my Lord!" Gabrus gestured for me to rise, and I did so. "I believe you know my steward, Bern?" He and I began our descent, bows in hand.

After the negotiations, witnessed according to Gabrus by his *hundred* hidden warriors, he walked away with a bag full of silver coins and the promise that his proud Celtic warriors would resume their former ways as horsemen, with thirty (negotiated down from fifty) steeds of both genders so the livestock could grow. Additionally, in exchange for keeping the Empire's peace among the maverick tribal encampments, the encampment of the leader Gabrus would receive fifty silver coins per season.

"And finally," said my Master, "we thank you for the safe return of our young Germanic fellow."

"He has been valuable to us," Gabrus said.

"I suspect you have him to thank for the new way ... And we have him to thank for the new peace."

"We will sell him back to you for one hundred silver coins."

"Eighty it shall be," Master said, with the gesture of a raised thumb to Vebru, who opened a small chest and began to build stacks of ten upon the table before my captor and student.

My Lady came running out from the back of the lodge. "Is it true?" she screamed. "Someone told me Bern is back!"

I held out my palms. "My Lady," I said with a sweeping, deep bow, "at your service once again."

Her mouth hung open, and she covered it with her slender hands. "It is you? But you have changed so much!"

"Yes," Vebru said, "a year as a Celt has put some serious muscle weight on our little German."

She dropped her hands and clasped them demurely at her waist. She raised an eyebrow in sync with a corner of her lips. "It would appear so ... We shall have some private chat so you can tell me all about it."

"But first," said Master, "you will shave off that beard. I will have no barbarian living under my roof."

I bowed to him. I backed toward the slave quarters, my Lady's eyes following me as she gave her lower lip a little nibble.

5

Just as Gabrus had predicted and promised, the word had reached the far northern borders of this growing province given the name of Gallia Belgica back in the Roman Senate. The Celtic tribes and their encampments in those distant lands were desirous of the gold and silver falling into Gabrus's wooden chests, so Master parted with more of his wealth to gain more protection, more land, and more power.

When we arrived back safely at the Colonia, a surprise awaited Master and my Lady. I had never known the woman Master had been previously married to died giving birth to a son, for no one had ever spoken a word about him. Before the villa, Caius Bruno, an effeminately handsome man in his mid-twenties, supervised slaves unpacking a long cart of goods from the seat of the Empire.

Master grasped his son's forearm and gave it a businesslike pump. "To what do we owe this pleasant surprise, my son?"

"Father," the young man said, "you departed Rome after my eighteenth birthday, and left me with tutors and business benefactors. I have learned all the tutors had to teach me and tripled our assets with the aid of the benefactors. I decided to come and learn the ways of the governance of Rome's expansion directly from the Governor of a Roman province."

"So," Master said, "are they already calling me by that title in Rome?" The young man nodded. "If you are here, then who is in charge of our property outside the city?"

"I named my friend Marcus Janus interim steward in my absence."

My Lady stepped beside her husband. "I am not so certain that's such a good idea."

"Stepmother!" Caius Bruno stepped forward and kissed his stepmother—nearly a decade younger than he—on both cheeks. "It is good to see you! But why do you say that?"

"Do you not think it a conflict of interest to let your lover oversee your business matters?"

Master cleared his throat. He gestured to the slaves unloading the cart. "What do you bring with you, my son?"

"I thought you might wish a taste of civilization out in this wild country." He waved the back of a dainty hand to the gardens. "Artwork ... the best sculpture I could find to remind you of the Empire." The young man looked at Vebru and me, his eyes landing on our wrists. "Father, your slaves have no wrist bands."

"No, son, I've never seen the need here."

"But here the need is even greater. In Rome, the slaves need rebellions like that by Spartacus to attempt escape into freedom. Here?" He pointed to the landscape around him. "Here it's a simple matter of walking away."

"Come inside," Master said. "Let us have some refreshment while we discuss this."

As they approached the front doors, my Lady shook her head. "I am reminded of the true nature of the Empire right here," she said rubbing my forearm, "when I look into your eyes, Bern." My breath caught in my throat, and she giggled. She watched her stepson disappear into the house. "The nurse should have thrown him into the Tiber when he was born."

∾

The next day, all Master's slaves were marched into the center of the colonia where the smith fitted us one-by-one with closed metal bands around our wrists, each band bearing the chiseled letters *C C T*. Out of the end of each protruded a ring just large enough for a chain link.

And as it happened, young Caius Bruno brought more with him from Rome than art and furniture and notions for the proper treatment of chattel.

Out in the growing province, far from the seat of the Empire, the Colonia was relatively free of the problems afflicting the city centers: street thievery, murder in the night, corruption in business and politics, disease. Every few years, according to the news that would reach us, a sickness would break out in the cramped cities of Rome and Neapolis, as well as the conquered metropolises of Athens and Jerusalem. These pests would kill a few thousand. The dead were mourned, and life went on for the living. But then decades would pass, and these cities would be attacked again by veritable plagues resulting in tens of thousands dead. However, in the wild provinces like Gallia Belgica, we were protected—or so we thought—by distance.

A week after Master's son made his way to the villa, one of the slaves he brought with him collapsed in the vineyards and died a few hours later in the slaves' quarters.

Vebru and I were composing a letter to a neighboring provincial governor on Master's behalf when we learned of the poor man's imminent death via a commotion of loud voices mixed with screams. We glanced up at each other with perplexed expressions, then dropped our quills and dashed out of the library. The slaves' quarters where the man lay perishing was the farthest building on the property from the villa, yet the voices of distress rang clearly through the grounds. "Somebody help him!" and "He has it! Get him out of here!" and incoherent cries of panic in various original tongues of the slaves.

Nothing prepared us for what lay on the cot. We had to work our way through the kneeling supplicant bodies, and when we made it to the cot, we both nearly dropped to our knees and joined the others, though not to pray. They had torn off his tunic, now a bloody rag crumpled into a corner, because they feared some sort of wounds from blade or bite. Neither caused these open sores from which blood and pus flowed. The pest had done to this man what I had often heard in oral description, but now I witnessed with my own eyes that he had not been stabbed or bitten from without, but the bad blood and bile was escaping from within, in a violent push through his skin to the air. It was like the eruption of several miniscule volcanoes sprouting from his abdomen and chest. His face had begun to sink in as it would soon enough after his death. Blood seeped from his tear ducts rendering his whole face unrecognizable as such. He broke into a vicious spasm of coughs, shooting out blood, phlegm, and clots of lung tissue, as from a hot spring geyser.

The end came with an intense attack of the dancing sickness, his body jerking furiously until all lay still.

Roman soldiers ordered his body taken someplace away from the colonia where it was disposed of I knew not how, but I hoped by fire.

A week of cautious calm followed, all slaves passing one another warily. Soon we began to forget and lower our guard as the foolish always will. Then, on a lovely day following the first overnight frost, the gods decorated the oak and elm leaves in bright reds and yellows. After splashing cool water over my skin and pulling on my tunic, I trotted to Vebru's quarters to rouse him from bed so together we could revel in the glorious new colors of the forests while ostensibly gathering my Lady's favorite mushrooms for her breakfast.

As soon as I stepped into the little room, I knew something was wrong. When he was awake, Vebru's voice flowed smoothly past his lips like honey poured from a jar, but when he slept the room reverberated so with his snoring, one would swear daemons from the underworld had been loosed upon us. This morning, though, all was still. I stopped in my tracks and gaped at the form on the cot. He lay on his stomach, and the covers rose slightly and dipped with his breaths. I sighed out my relief and stepped up to him. "Vebru, wake up and come! The forest calls!" I leaned forward and touched his shoulder, and when he rolled to his side and faced me, I stepped back with a start.

Blood ran down the sides of his face from his nostrils. My friend's eyes were dead, and I could tell by the way they moved about that he was blind. "Bern?" he croaked. "Bern, is that you?"

"Yes, Vebru, it's me." I grabbed a cloth napkin from his table and stepped forward and wiped the blood from his face as best I could.

"I contracted the pest from Caius Bruno's slave, didn't I?"

I nodded, and then realized he couldn't see my gesture. "Yes, my friend, I'm afraid you did."

His eyes seemed to find mine, and he smiled at me. "Nothing to fear. I have been a slave since I was a young boy. And at last I will soon be a freeman."

Missing him already, I gazed at him. "Vebru, my friend ... you bought me years ago between the two rivers. I pray to the gods I was worth the price you paid."

He chuckled. "You'll receive different answers from different gods. But little Bern, my little bear who is not so little now, yes, you have proven yourself worth a hundred times what coins I handed over that day ... Yet you remain a slave."

"Were I not a slave, I would have long ago died, Vebru."

"Yes. That is the sad reality for our lot. Like working dogs and free wolves. The former tend to live longer because their masters care for them and feed them ... as long as they obey and serve." He was struck by a long attack of coughs from deep within his lungs.

I wiped his lips and chin. "Vebru, rest here while I fetch Master's physician."

He reached out and groped until his hand latched onto my wrist. "You and I both know how this will end for me. It will be slow and miserable. Probably worse for me than that slave of Master's son." He pulled me closer, and I leaned into him, my ear a half a breath from his mouth. "Get an ass and a cart," he whispered. "Put me into the cart, and take me to the northwest corner of the vineyards."

"Up on the hill?"

"Yes. Just a little closer to the gods, and facing the land where I was born. And Bern, my friend ..."

"Yes, Vebru?"

"I will require a knife. A sharp knife for hunting ... or one from the kitchens."

"Vebru!"

"Stop this," he wheezed. "You know if I die on my terms, I will meet my mother and father on the other side ... as a freeman. Please do not let me die a slave."

I walked alongside the sweating beast to the top of the hill past the vines bulging with ripe bunches of green grapes, soon to be picked, pressed, and fermented into rich white wine. We reached the crest, and I helped Vebru from the cart. Our arms around each other's shoulders, we stood facing the villa of the Governor of the province that was being called Gallia Belgica twenty days' ride away from a city known and feared as Rome. I placed my hands on my friend's shoulders and aimed him away from the site of his life of slavery.

We hobbled to a cliff edge, where we sat upon rough-edged boulders and faced the northwest.

Vebru raised his face and smiled, taking in a deep breath of late summer air. "I know we are facing the land of my birth," he said, "and it feels right."

"It is true, Vebru, but how do you know this?"

"Close your eyes." I did so. "Do you feel the sun upon your face?"

I opened my eyes to the sinking sun. "Yes, I do."

"My people say the sun god must die after each day. Then he is reborn after the passing of the danger we know as night to give us another day of light and hope." He reached into his tunic and produced the cook's butcher knife. "Please tell me when he is resting on the earth, so I can join him. But while we wait, remove these damned things from my wrists. I do not wish my family to see me carrying any signs of slavery."

"I put a hammer and chisel in the cart, Vebru. It's all I could steal from the shed. It will be painful for you."

He turned his dead eyes to me. "Bern, you have no idea what pain I'm feeling inside now. Go and get the tools."

I removed the wristbands, and if the pest didn't kill him, he could likely die from loss of blood after the chisel cut into his wrists. I didn't want to do this, yet I understood that I must. I placed my arms around his neck and held his head against my shoulder while he grasped the knife handle in both hands and maneuvered the blade tip between two ribs, behind which his heart—the greatest I had ever known—awaited.

6

For days after sending Vebru's ashes into the sky to join the sun god, I plodded around the villa as though balls of iron were chained to my ankles. I completed whatever chores were demanded of me as the new steward of the House of Tavarius, yet there felt an emptiness, a hole in my soul. Any spare time I had, I spent notching arrows onto my bowstring and sending them on arbitrary flights into the grain fields. I would trudge into the grain, retrieve the arrows, and shoot them again until my arms hung throbbing uselessly to my sides.

One day I entered the villa after this senseless exercise, and my Lady, having heard my shuffling steps, called out from her chamber. "Bern, come in here, please!"

I crossed the threshold and bowed. She was sitting at the table where she kept the colors for her face. "Yes, my Lady?"

"Please sit," she said.

I searched around the room for a chair proper for a slave, but saw only a comfortable divan. "Where, my Lady?"

She pointed nonchalantly to the bed. "There."

"On the bed?" She nodded, and I said, "As you wish, my Lady."

When I sat, she rose from her chair and took a place beside me, her hip against mine. She reached behind my back and placed her soft hand on my shoulder. She rubbed, bringing a shudder forth from me.

"My husband and son are gone north of here surveying the new land of the province," she said. "They will not return until at least tomorrow. Maybe the next day."

"As house steward, I know this, my Lady."

She slid her hand from my shoulder inside my tunic to my chest. "I know you have felt empty since Vebru's passing. He filled a void within your soul ... My Bern, I, too have an empty soul that needs filling." She ran her fingertips over my skin, down to my belly. "Your body has become hard and strong. Is there any part of you that is soft?" she said into my ear.

My breath caught in my throat. "My Lady, what are you doing?"

"What I have long wished to do," she said. She slid her hands between my thighs and grasped, stroking me with her thumb. I gasped and turned to her seductively smiling face, closer than I had ever seen it. She was the most beautiful thing I had ever laid my eyes upon, and I fell in love with her in that moment. "Your hands are free, Bern. Remove my gown, please ... I can't do it at the moment with my hands occupied."

I struggled to calm my racing heartbeat, my rapid breathing. "Yessss, my Lady."

It was everything for which I could possibly dream. I spent nearly all of the next two days in my Lady's chamber enjoying the pleasures of the flesh.

When Governor Caius Cinna Tavarius and his son brought the triumphant news that they had gained the loyalty and protection of further Celtic encampments with the help of Gabrus as translator and negotiator, it was for me business as usual. My Lady and I kept our stoic outward appearances, but as for me, I was racked with desire for her. Those were the most difficult days in my life as a slave in the House of Tavarius. However, in the rare times when we could sneak in an intimate moment in her bed, we made quick, ravenous work of it.

During one of those particularly acrobatic encounters, Master's voice rang from the dining salon. "Bern, are you here?"

With my Lady's help, I quickly dressed and scurried to Master. "Yes, Master?" I said, panting.

He eyed me curiously. "Bern, are you all right? You're drenched with sweat, like you just completed a marathon race."

"Oh ... I, um, I've been practicing with my bow."

He smiled. "That's good. Bring it along. Bruno and I are going to Gabrus's encampment, and we may need your services ... And perhaps along the way, you may find some game. I have a craving for wild meat. And you?"

"Oh, indeed," I said. "Yes ... wild meat."

Before heading toward the stables, he said, "You will not want to go barefoot on a trek this long."

When I returned to my Lady's chamber, she was standing there naked, holding out the sandals I had left behind in my rush.

7

After the House returned to the villa from the hunting lodge, Master and his son could be found for several days scribbling on papers they hunched over in the library. They both would raise their eyes to me as I passed by in the hallway. Occasionally they would call me in and ask for a translation of a Greek word on a document. The words and phrases tended toward business dealings: *profit, annual percentage, interest, loan.*

Finally, one evening as I stood by ready to assist the family at supper, including meat from a wild sow I shot, Master made an announcement. "This House will attempt to make a direct connection in the growing trade of goods coming into Asia Minor from the far lands in the east. We have decided this effort will be under the guidance of Caius Bruno, the successor of my Governorship." He stood and reached out a hand to his son sitting across from him. Caius Bruno stood and grasped his father's forearm. Master faced me. "My wife has suggested that our steward accompanies the future Governor, as he has the capabilities to converse in any language with any parties that may be concerned."

I stiffened. I was to leave my Lady, the only love I've ever known? I said, "But if I may say so, my Lord, I understand in Asia Minor, they speak not only Greek but Hebrew and other Semite languages, which I do not understand."

"But which you will learn, I have no doubt," Master said. He raised a cup of wine. "You will leave with a military escort in a fortnight. So, to a successful journey, adding to the wealth and strength of Gallia Belgica and House Tavarius!" The three family members raised their cups and drank as I sank into a quagmire of disappointment and confusion.

I went about my tasks with none of my previous mirth. Whenever I was required to be in my Lady's presence, I kept my eyes locked on the floor as I performed whatever service was required of me. Then I would quickly exit the room. The day before I was to depart with Caius Bruno, she summoned me into her chamber. As had become my habit of late, I stood, eyes cast downward.

"Bern, lift your chin and look at me." I did so. "Bern, you have dead eyes, and it frightens me to see you so."

"I am sorry, my Lady."

"You've been avoiding me, yet I can tell you have words for me. So out with it ... What is on your mind?"

"My Lady, I— " How could I, a mere slave, deign to question a noblewoman?

"Yes, Bern? I have always allowed you to express your true feelings."

After I took in a deep breath, I said, "My Lady, is it true you suggested I leave the House to go on this journey?"

"Yes, Bern, it is true."

"But why— "

She placed a finger across my lips. "Bern, you must listen and you must understand. I hunger for you. I believe I am in love with you." She placed both soft, slender palms upon my cheeks. "It couldn't last like this forever. It's only a matter of time before my husband catches us."

I mustered courage and defiance, raising my chin and staring her in the eyes. "And what if he does?"

"Then it would be his right under Roman Imperial law to declare it rape and to have you executed. He would probably take that course as it would save his public face."

"And you ... would allow this?"

"Bern, I would have no choice unless I wished to lose my head as well ... So for both of us to stay alive, it is best you leave at least until the child has begun to walk. Then when you return you can be his tutor as well as house steward."

She released her hands and I reached up and rubbed both temples with my fingers. "What child do you speak of, my Lady?"

"I have not lost blood for the passing of the complete moon cycle. I speak of our child, Bern."

My eyes widened, and my breaths rushed in and out in quick spasms. "I ... am to be a father?"

"You dangerously performed the only part you can play in the child's life. There are ways to lose the baby before it grows inside me." She noticed the dread in my eyes and grasped my hands in hers. "But I will not do this. I love you, Bern, and the child—boy or girl—will be my reminder of our love."

"But Master. Will he not suspect— "

"I have been visiting my husband's bed, much as it is distasteful to me. He'll believe the child is his. In fact, it will be a bragging right for him, that at his age he remains potent."

"I don't know what to say, my Lady."

"Before you leave and pack for the journey, you can say *thank you* to me, as I thank you."

I raised her right hand and bowed my face to it. "*Ich danke Dir*," I said in my original tongue and kissed the back of her hand. As per my custom, I backed out of the room keeping my eyes on the stone floor, listening to her sniffle and fight to keep from crying.

Early the following morning I walked behind the cart in which I was to ride, but I thought it apropos to leave the villa and the colonia on foot, just as I arrived many years earlier with Vebru and my cousins. I marched beside the other two slaves, a Celt and a north African. As our caravan—seven carts towed by horses, Master's son, the escort of a dozen Roman soldiers, and we three slaves—passed out of the courtyard, I glanced up at the window of my Lady's chamber. She stood there waving, and I gave her merely a grave nod.

We passed through the gates that shut securely behind us and began our journey toward the rising sun. I had a feeling there was nothing in my destiny behind me, so I aimed my face forward, away from that chapter of my life.

CHAPTER THREE

THE RIVER'S FLOW

1

We had been presented with two options to reach our goal of Asia Minor. We could go by land trekking through what precarious paths the Roman Empire carved through the great mountains, the Alpes, in the centuries following Hannibal and his elephants. It was a path well known, but fraught with peril. No doubt we would lose some men along the way, and if blizzard conditions struck—as could occur during any season—the entire party may be lost. And though Master would save money if we took this route, given such risk along with the possibility of the journey lasting four seasons or more, House Tavarius chose to depart with some of its silver and take the alternate route by water.

Master Caius Cinna chose many of the soldiers based on areas of expertise they brought with them into soldiery from their prior lives. Somewhere after the river widened and the surrounding forests were of tall, thick pines, we would stop and build a few broad barges for our journey to Asia Minor, where the great river emptied into a sea. For this we required lumbermen and woodworkers, engineers and sailors. The officer in charge of our mission had experience in exploration through unknown lands during campaigns in Germania and North Africa. It took a few weeks of recruiting and interviewing before Master was satisfied he had assembled a worthy collection to forge a new aquatic path to the end of the Roman world.

Four soldiers rode ahead a day after we departed the colonia to secure small boats at the source of the great river known by the Romans as the *Ister*, the *Danubius*, or the *Danuvius*, depending upon where along the river one found oneself. This route would last only a season, according to our military escort. And though the way itself would be far safer than overland and through uncertain mountain passes, other dangers would await us.

With four Roman soldiers flanking us on each side, we marched north. Caius Bruno rode in the covered cart lying on his side while eating bits of pork and beef chased by wine from his father's vineyards. Young Master wouldn't allow me to ride in the cart, so at his insistence, I walked directly behind. When we halted to strike camp for the night, he called me to him.

"Slave!" he shouted. To him, I was just a slave with neither position nor name, and until my duties as polyglot steward were required, I was his to serve his pleasure.

I trotted to the cart and climbed the rear ladder until my head rose above the floor. "Yes, Master?"

"I needa shit," he slurred. "Bring me ... cham'er pot."

"Yes, Master."

"An' I'm too drunka clean up."

"Yes, Master, I will take care of it," I hissed through clenched teeth.

I had never held my breath for so long, and after I had finished the labor, I vomited onto the base of a pine tree I braced my hands upon. Then after I cleaned young Master's underclothing, I vomited again. All the while, I could hear young Master snoring away in the covered cart.

Short of a week of marching, cleaning young Master, and vomiting, I took a break as we reached our first goal. Two streams converged to form the mouth of the great river in an area dominated by Celtic worshippers of the goddess Abnoba. The four soldiers sent forth as scouts had promised local Celts a trade of their horses for ten narrow boats to start the aquatic leg of our journey. There would be no room for the two oxen and four large swine, so these creatures were slaughtered and skinned. This labor lasted two days, and when it was over, we dumped the guts and remains into the water, and the strips of meat carved from their carcasses were salted and placed in two of the vessels. I performed nearly half the work, and I was beginning to realize the true plight of a slave in the Roman Empire.

Even though I dipped my entire body into the waters and ridded myself of the blood and entrails, young Master announced to everyone, "I am not riding in the same boat with a filthy Germanic slave!"

One of the Roman soldiers said, "I've seen his work with that bow he keeps around his chest. You would want such protection if we encounter hostiles."

"I lay trust for my protection only in fellow Romans!" he said, and the soldiers spoke low among themselves. "And is he not himself a barbarian? I say we take the bow from him. If we do encounter Germanic hostility, I don't trust him not to join in with them."

"If you try to touch my bow," I said, "I will leave you and join my friends!"

Young Master chortled. "What friends?"

I cupped my hands over my mouth and faced the south. "Show yourselves, my friends!" I shouted in Gaulish Celtic. The thick woods suddenly stirred with shuffling leaves under light steps. Out from behind the cover of trees, vines, and brush, more than twenty Celtic warriors appeared, crouched and prepared to let loose their arrows. The Roman soldiers reached for their swords. "Pull your hands from your weapons," I said to them in Latin. "Before you could draw them from the sheaths, you would all become Celtic pin cushions."

The soldiers raised their empty hands. "This is treason!" said young Master.

"On the contrary, my Master," I said. "As you know, I have good relations with the Celtic encampment north of the colonia, and their leader told me we could rely on another encampment once we reached the source of the great river. These gentlemen, eligible for Roman citizenship, are our local escort until we reach the edge of their territory and the land of the Germanic friendlies." I waved to the Celtic bowmen. "Is it not so?" I asked them in their language, and repeated their generous, though improvised *offer*.

An arrow still drawn in his bow, a chieftain stepped from the cover. "You are the German who was with the Celtic chief now called Gabrus!"

"I am he."

"His encampment speaks well of you ... Do you speak as a freeman, or are you still bonded and chained?"

"I am still a slave in the House of Tavarius."

He aimed the arrow directly at young Master. One eye closed and the other on his target, he gave a half-grin. "Just a few steps out of the water to us, and you are a freeman."

Young Master's wide eyes made me certain he would need another cleaning. "You do not want to harm the son of the House. It would not go well for you. And if I step to you and gain my freedom, I will be forever hunted by their like," I said aiming my chin to the soldiers. "And besides that ... I am setting out on a journey to the edge of the Roman world. Allow me that adventure, and then after I return, perhaps we will meet and you can make the offer yet again."

"I would be proud to be the warrior who helped to free Arth."

Arth. Gaulish Celtic for bear. So now I had a Celtic name to match my Germanic one. I bowed to the chieftain. "Until then, my friend."

He touched his forehead and bowed. "Safe journey, Arth. We will be here in the wood for the next two or three days. Tell the pretty one who cannot handle his wine, the one who soils his clothing, that we are watching him." He and his warriors faded back into the woodland.

2

Gliding along the current, I imagined this must be how it feels when your soul is leaving your body after stumbling through the rocks and tree roots and animal feces along the path of life on earth. And if it were so, as I had hoped, why then would one want to arrive at the next destination? More jostling and grumbling and fighting in some celestial great hall with all the heroes you had heard about around campfires. But simply to glide along a peaceful current. That would be an eternity worth believing in, worth fighting for.

"Needa vommmit!" Young Master had a knack for bringing one back to earth. He leaned over the side of the skiff and released his most recent repast into the water to float past my narrow vessel trailing his. I noted before when I tossed bits of bread into the water, trout and carp immediately broke the surface for a morsel. But young Master's leavings drew no such interest.

"No more wine for this one!" called the officer. I did not know his rank or name until after we reached Asia Minor, and then under the most dire of circumstances.

"What?" young Master called. "You can't do that!"

"You heard the man!" came a voice from the forest in accented Latin. "Puke one more time into our river, and it will be your last puke!" To punctuate that imperative, a Celtic arrow landed with a whack into the side of the boat, directly behind young Master. If not for the boat, there would have been one less nobleman in the Empire.

Following a drunken shriek, the eight boatsful of Roman soldiers and three slaves erupted in raucous laughter.

On the morning of the third day, our escort bade us to dock on their south side bank. We secured the vessels to trees and brush with strands of rope, and stepped ashore to await their word.

The leader appeared from the thicket followed by a dozen warriors from his clan. I knew hidden behind them were dozens more. He raised his right hand as a sign of peace. The Roman officer nodded to me, so I returned the gesture. The leader approached me and held out his arm with his hand formed for a greeting. I clasped his hand, and we pumped together in the Celtic fashion, fingers grasping each other's thumbs. "This is where you leave our lands," he told me in his language. He then addressed the soldiers in their tongue. "German tribes live nearby, over there," he said, pointing to the east.

"How can you know this?" the officer asked him.

"The same way we know you're in the area," the chieftain said. He pointed at his nose and gave the air a sniff, then waved his hand before him as though to drive the odor away.

The soldiers narrowed their eyes at the chieftain. He smiled and winked, then all chuckled except for young Master. Their mirth waned, but then young Master passed gas, and the leader fell backwards to the turf faking a fainting spell. That halted any chance of serious dialogue for several minutes. After the laughter subsided, the leader rose and dusted himself off. "May I retrieve my arrow?" he asked the officer, who waved toward the boats. He brought back the arrow that would have killed young Master had the side of the boat not intervened. He gestured to a warrior, who stepped into the thicket and brought back a large sack. He handed it to me, and I could smell the savory meat emanating from within. "Dried meat from a successful boar hunt. We would offer you some of our strongest ale, but one of you has no further need of strong drink."

All the Celtic warriors vanished into the woody thicket. "Farewell, Arth!" the leader's voice called from the woods in his native Gaulish Celtic. "And come back safely from the end of the world!"

3

The current continued to carry us along, generally toward the rising sun, though occasionally the river decided to send us either north or south. It was said this Danuvius marked the northern boundary of the Empire, at least that part of it in Germanic tribal territory. Rome allegedly conquered the Germanic tribes between the great river and the great mountains, but I preferred the drumming we would hear occasionally beyond the northern banks to the eerie quiet from the south. I wondered how a river could separate wild from tamed, free from subdued. How can a winding band of flowing water divide the spirit? Could the Germanic people on one side be trusted as allies while just across, people with the same Germanic blood were vicious enemies?

One of the young soldiers had experience with rivers, as he assisted with his father's ferry trade across the Tiber a day's march north of the city of Rome. "The current is swift and unknowable nearer the banks," he said. "Our time will go three, four times faster. But it will be that much more dangerous."

"What dangers?" the officer asked.

"The current can change so suddenly it smashes the boat into the shore. Or it can be so fast the boat will snap in two. The boat will be confused. And then there could be the unseen dangers." He pointed downward. "The river bottom is closer there. At such speeds, the hull can run into rocks or tree roots."

"So we go closer to the middle."

"The river is getting wide, which means it is becoming deeper, too. Too deep for this," he said holding up his pole.

"This means we row," the officer said.

"Yes. We row, and we grow tired."

"Just sitting here is putting me to sleep!" cried another soldier. Others grunted their agreement.

"We must take turns," the officer said. He looked at young Master. "All of us."

"If you think I am going to do a slave's labor— "

"I am certain it is possible for a passenger to fall overboard and drown. Am I correct, Bern?"

I gave the officer a slight grin. "Anything is possible," I said.

He rubbed his chin. "And then we would need to go on to Asia Minor without a Roman nobleman to conduct the trade business ... or retreat to the colonia and report the misfortune."

Although young Master did not row all that much, the few minutes with his hands on the paddle brought out blisters on his palms. A soldier rubbed pork fat onto the wounds and bound them in cloth. Young Master grumbled about making us all pay, but no one paid him heed. No one else had young Master's problem since all of us had done labor with our hands. Our muscles, especially our forearms, were another matter.

Around a bend in the ever-widening river, we discovered though we were free of the dangers from closer to the banks as related by the ferryman's son, there were other perils we had not considered awaiting us in the center of the flow.

From beyond the north bank came the blowing of an oxen horn, the like of which I had heard of only among Germanic tribes before an ensuing battle. Instinctively, we all faced to the left, the portside, the direction from which the blast seemed to emanate. The soldiers raised their shields. Then, the same sound blew to us from our right. We reacted, facing to the south, and the soldiers moved their shields to protect from that direction.

We could hear the arrows slicing the air behind us. The assailants beyond the north bank blew their horn at a sheer canyon wall on the south bank, and the echo drew our defense away from the real threat.

The seasoned and trained Roman soldiers reacted to the reality and shifted their defense back to the north side. The paddling had obviously ceased, and our vessels drifted on the slow current in the fat center.

A barrage of arrows from the north sliced the air. The soldiers' shields did their duty, protecting the men behind from a painful meeting. But the slaves bore no such protection. I heard a cry followed by a splash. I looked behind, the direction of the south bank, to see the Celtic slave bobbing face up with an arrow in his chest as we floated past the reddening water.

Spears joined the arrows hurtling toward us, and it was one of the former that attempted to send me to a meeting with the Heroes so young in life. It was difficult to maneuver with a German's spear impaling me to a side just above my waist. In the excitement I felt no pain, but only marveled at the strength and accuracy it had to take for a Germanic warrior to achieve such a hit. I glanced down at the phenomenon, then reached back into my quiver for an arrow and notched it onto my bow string. I pulled with my right hand and waited for my open right eye to find a good target. The target presented itself as a warrior, clad in bearskin loins, stepped beside the cover of a massive oak to receive my arrow into his chest.

A voice called in a Germanic tongue from the north. "We are the Varisci, and you are trespassing on our river!"

Though the wound in my side suddenly became sharply unbearable, I fostered the strength to answer the challenge. "I am from the Tenchteri, and we are passing peacefully! Let us pass!"

A moment of silence slid past. Then came the voice again. "Tenchteri? That tribe is from the north. Far north of here, from what I know ... What does a Tenchteri warrior do so far south from home?"

I looked down at the spear through my side, at the blood spilling from the wound onto the floor of the skiff. I felt my strength ebbing out with the blood. With an effort I took in a deep breath. "I travel with others from the Empire!" I yelled, and nearly fainted from the expenditure. "We go to the end of this great river, and then to the edge of the earth!" I panted for air. "Please let us go in peace!"

Another few moments passed until we received an answer. "Tenchteri warrior, you killed one of ours. We must have one of yours, and then you may pass!"

I stood on wobbly legs and showed their handiwork. "You've already collected! A Celtic slave ... and soon a Germanic slave from the Tenchteri tribe will join him!"

After a brief pause, the Varisci chieftain called out, "I hope to drink with you in the Great Hall! If the spear does not kill you, your plunge off the edge of the world certainly will! Go in peace, Tenchteri!"

I raised a palm and then collapsed onto the floor of the skiff.

4

I awoke to an argument over what to do with me. All boats were still intact, lashed together by rope, drifting along like leaves that gather in bunches and ride the surface of water.

"According to the reports," the Roman officer said, "there's a smaller river a half-day ahead. If we take it, we can paddle south to Augusta Vindelicorum. It's a large settlement where we can find the best Roman physicians."

"We can't make it in time," said the ferryman's son.

"And why not?" the officer asked.

"This is the great river, am I correct? The longest and soon ahead the widest north of the great mountains?" All the Romans nodded. "So it pulls on the smaller river's waters."

"What is he saying?" the officer said.

"He's right," a soldier said. "The other river flows into this one. Its waters flow north, and the settlement is south."

"What would take us a day with the flow," said the ferryman's son, "will take us five against."

"And by the time we reached the Augusta settlement, our German slave friend will be dead," the other soldier noted.

"And we would be near death from exhaustion," the officer said.

"Why are we discussing this?" All turned and scowled at young Master. "He's a slave. A slave who was bought as a boy for a few silver coins by another slave!"

"What will you do for an interpreter?" the officer said.

"I'll buy another ... Take him to the south-side shore, lay him down, and leave him. If the gods will it, they'll save him." He smirked and chuffed at me. "But I doubt they would take interest in a barbarian slave. So why do you?" he said to the soldiers.

The ferryman's son stood in his skiff, causing it to wobble and making his fellow riders grumble, and he glowered down at young Master in his. "Because, if I were born but only three generations earlier in my yet unconquered village, I, too, would have been a slave of the Romans." He swept a hand at all his fellow soldiers. "The same goes for most of us." He plopped back down like some petulant toddler. "But here we are, born when and where we were, conquerors and freemen." He stared at me. "But for an accident of birth, our translating slave who saved our lives suddenly becomes garbage to be discarded on a shore."

"All right," the officer said. "We have had our speeches, and nearly all of us believe Bern is worth saving. But we also know we'll never make it to the settlement Augusta in time. So what can we do except prepare for the end and then argue over what to do with his corpse?"

"Take me to a healer," I croaked. "A German healer ..."

All fell silent. The officer climbed over to the skiff in which I lay. He crouched by my side and grasped my hand. "Are you in much pain?" he said. I opened my mouth to respond but immediately clenched my teeth. "Wine!" he called.

"No," I said. "I think I should drink or eat nothing until a healer allows it."

He took a deep breath and released it through gritted teeth. "We'll paddle to the shore," he commanded. "Two of us will stay with the boats. We'll carry Bern until we find a village."

"I will not walk into a barbarian village!" young Master said. "We will be stepping into a trap!"

"Good," the officer said. "Then you are one of the two who will stay with the boats." After the boats were secured to the trunk of a thick oak tree, he studied his squad. "I need a volunteer to join him." All remained silent. "No one? Very well then ..." He squatted and yanked a handful of dried river grass from the earth. "Draw a straw," he said, passing the grass stems around. When all had a straw, he said, "Short straw loses." The men formed a circle and compared.

"Have I offended the gods?" a soldier yelled and stepped out of the circle. He approached young Master. "Nothing to drink but water until they return! And I am not cleaning after you ... my Lord. And finally, if we are attacked, you better do your part, as either fighter or shield."

The others laughed as they placed me on a canvas and cut saplings for poles.

Four holes had been cut into the canvas, and two poles had been slid through them. Three soldiers and the other slave carried me, each holding the end of a pole. I had to lie on my side as I was still impaled by the spear, which they didn't want to remove as it may be the only thing keeping my blood and guts inside my body. The constant swinging lulled me in and out of slumber, as a baby being rocked.

I came to consciousness at one point wondering how far they had trekked with me into the woods. The answer came from one of my carriers. "The morning has wasted," he said, "and no sign of human life. How much farther before we change directions?"

"Halt and listen!" commanded the officer. All ceased their motion. To the soldiers' right, the distant sound of running water. "Maybe a brook," he said. "Fresh water for us, and perhaps for others who may live in these woods."

Some hundred paces later, the party found the brook. They lay me on the dead leaves and bent to fill jugs with the running water. To save the water they dipped, they all lay prostrate and sucked the water through puckered lips.

Passing over me was a shocking sight the others would soon behold. Two Germanic warriors stepped ever-so-silently past me toward the Roman soldiers. They each gave me a cursory glance, and when I opened my mouth to warn the party, one of the warriors raised a finger to his lips, pointed to me, and ran a finger across his throat. I appreciated the theatre enough to understand good pantomime when I saw it, so I closed my mouth.

"Rise, Roman scum!" a gravelly voice said in a heavy accent. The soldiers got to their feet from the brook and held out their palms to show no aggression. "What are you doing on our land?"

The officer said, "We mean no harm. We were in boats on the great river travelling east when— "

A warrior, likely their leader, cocked his head. "East?"

"Toward the rising sun," the officer said.

"You would let the waters take you until they throw you off the end of the world?" The warrior shook his head. "I understand the Empire's soldiers are brave. I did not know they were also foolish. But that is your business." He stepped forward, eye-to-eye with the officer. "Again, why are you so far from the water? Why on our land?"

"We were attacked on the great river. Our interpreter received a grave wound."

The warrior stepped over and knelt beside me. He rubbed his fingers along the wooden spear and leaned in to examine the sharp head. "Varisci work. A bold tribe on the north side of the water. No one knows how far their territory stretches." He lowered his face to mine and studied me. "Speak, interpreter," he said in a Germanic dialect strange to me. "Speak in my tongue. Let me hear your sounds."

"After your healer cures me, I will teach you how to speak properly," I said.

He regarded me silently with a stoic expression. Then he broke out in a sudden sputter of laughter. "You are far from home, bold one! What tribe?"

"Tenchteri ... if they still exist."

"If they no longer exist in the north," he said, "they do right here in your body ... And we will do what we can to keep the Tenchteri alive." Four other warriors stepped from behind the cover of trees. They raised their weapons as an agreement. "If you are fit," he said to the Roman officer in Latin, "pick him up and follow us to our village healer."

The four bearers hoisted the poles onto their shoulders and followed the apparent leader through the woods, the other warriors flanking and following.

The sun was sinking into the western horizon when the soldiers lowered the canvas to the ground. In that strange dialect, Germanic voices scolded children away from the outsiders: the Roman soldiers, the north African slave, and me. My sight became blurry, but after several moments a face surrounded by long gray hair peered down on me. "Take him to my hut," an old woman's voice said from that face in that strange dialect.

I rose again into the air and floated away rocking back and forth until the world went black around me.

Something sharp flowed through my nose and up into my brain, and I awoke with a gasp. In a dark hut a fire burned in the center, the smoke escaping through a funneled hole in the ceiling and roof. An old woman knelt beside me waving a cloth under my nose. It had been dipped in something that flowed up my nostrils with a sharp, piercing sting. She grinned with her few teeth. "I thought that might bring you back to the awakened. If we are to keep you with the living, you will need to be awake."

My eyes had regained their focus into the old woman's eyes, the color of charcoal. "You are the healer," I said.

"Yes." She put her hand on the spear shaft. "I believe you have met our brothers from across the flowing water," she said.

"One of them sent a message."

"A message you received with full force," she said with a light cackle. She ran a finger along the spear head. "Missing some of the metal. If it broke away and dug itself into you, you may feast soon at the table of the warriors who went before us ... Of course, that depends on where." She leaned close to the pointed metallic head and then over my wound. "If that happened, it went below. Your hip, your manhood ... Who knows?" She rose and stepped to a shelf bearing clay jars. She set one on the floor, then dipped a sheet of animal skin into it and rubbed a liquid along the spear shaft, about three hand-lengths below the head. While she worked, she said, "My grandson—our chieftain—tells me you are Tench-teri, from far in the north."

"Grandson?" I said. "But healers have no children ... because they remain virgins."

A moment passed before she raised her face to the ceiling and screeched out in laughter. She regained her composure and focused again on me. "Tenchteri slave, then I am happy I live here and not in the north. A life without pleasures of the flesh is like a life lived as a handful of smoke." She grabbed a fistful of smoke rising from the fire and opened her hand to reveal the nothing escaping from her palm. "And what pleasure is there in that?" She winked and said, "I outlived two husbands who planted their seeds in me, I'm happy to say."

The old woman faced the hut opening. "Grandson," she shouted, "bring a cloth soaked in fire fuel!" Then she raised a hand and snapped her fingers. "I need a strong pair of hands," she said in Latin. A Roman soldier stepped forth and knelt beside the healer. "Break the head off the spear," she ordered him.

With one hand he grasped the shaft just below the head, and he gripped the metallic head in the other. On an audible count to three, he snapped off the head with a grunt. Though blood seeped from a small cut on his palm, he dropped the spearhead to the floor and stepped back stone-faced to rejoin his comrades.

The chieftain stepped into the hut with a cloth dripping in liquid. "What do you want with this, Grandmother?"

She beckoned him closer. "Soak the spear shaft from here," she said pointing at the line made by the salve, "to here." She pointed to a place a thumbnail-length from where the shaft exited my side. "And be generous ... I want it dripping."

Once he did as she bade, he said, "All right, Grandmother, now what?"

"Now, stand up, Tenchteri slave."

My arm wrapped over the chieftain's neck, I raised myself to my feet. It was difficult to maintain my balance.

The old woman studied me as though I were some new creature. "If you feel like you are about to swoon, you probably will within a few heartbeats." She raised a hand and snapped her fingers again. "Now we require all of you strong Romans," she said in Latin. "Secure his ankles and hold his arms behind him. Hold him with more strength than you think you have."

"Why?" the officer said.

"No questions!" she snapped. The officer motioned to his subordinates, who took places below and behind me. She stepped to the fire, and pulled out a faggot, burning at the end.

"What do you plan to do?" the officer shouted.

"The first liquid near the spearhead end is a salve that will cool and heal the burns."

"What burns?" I said, my words emerging shakily.

"The burns that will be inside you after the healing fire has been pulled through your side."

"You're going to set the shaft afire?" I said. She nodded. "And you'll pull it through me with it still burning?" She smiled with a wink. "Oh, gods, please give me strength!"

"You will need their strength, Tenchteri, but most of what you will need must come from here," she said tapping my chest with her free hand. "Oh, and I lied to you ... I will not pull the burning shaft through you. One of your party must do this. One of your choosing, Tenchteri."

Without hesitation, I said, "The ferryman's son."

"But who will hold your left leg?" he said from below.

"Let me take part of this." The chieftain stepped up and motioned the ferryman's son aside. He dropped to his knees and hugged my left leg tight to his chest.

"What am I to do?" the young Roman soldier said.

"I will set the spear shaft aflame, and when I say so you pull slow, like pulling a heavy bucket full of water from a well."

"Or an anchor from a riverbed," I said.

"I would say like when you pull out of a woman," she said. "But if you are like most men, you have your next cup of ale waiting, so you pop out and run. Do not pull like that!"

He nodded grimly and then wrapped his hands around the shaft behind me.

The healer leaned into me and placed her lips against an ear. "Now show us what you are made of, Tenchteri," she whispered in her strangely-accented Germanic tongue. She pulled a dagger from her hip sheath. "Here," she said, holding the blade so the dagger's handle was before my mouth, "the least I can do is have you clamp down while the demons dance in your brain."

I opened my mouth and held the leathery handle between my teeth. I watched her touch the faggot's fire to the nearer part of the wooden shaft. A tiny flame danced on the wet fuel at first, then a moment later, several hand-lengths were engulfed. The healer faced the ferryman's son. "Now," she said. He took a steeling breath, braced a knee against my hip, and tugged with a twisting motion.

As the fire wormed through me, I bit on the dagger handle, but managed to stifle the scream so wanting escape. Through my tear-blurred vision, I saw the setting sun meant for Vebru's eyes. It drew closer and closer until it consumed me and burned my soul to ashes.

I awoke on a pile of skins and fur in the corner of the healer's hut. A girl of about my cousins' ages when we were taken from our village sat beside me dabbing my hot forehead with a cloth soaked in cool water. I lifted my head and gazed down at my belly and hip wrapped in cloth. The girl spoke over her shoulder. "He's awake, Great-grandmother!"

The healer stepped over the girl and placed a hand on her head. "Thank you, Zieda. Go to your family." The girl rose and bowed to the healer and me before leaving my line of sight. The old woman took her great-granddaughter's place. She reached forward and probed the bandage with a forefinger, bringing a wince and gasp out of me. "It will hurt for a while," she said. "You may limp the rest of your life. I believe some of the iron from the spearhead splintered into your hip. But you will heal fine, otherwise."

"How did you know about the fire?"

She parted her lips and smiled with her few teeth. "I didn't. The answer just came to me out of the smoke. I didn't know if it was a good or evil spirit talking to me, so I gambled."

"You gambled with my life?" I rose sitting and grasped her arm.

"Calm down, Tenchteri. You live, do you not? If I did nothing, you would be feasting with dead warriors far earlier than you would want to ... Besides, if we do not take risks with our life-paths, we live lives not worth living. Each day of life for those of us who live surviving in the forest is a gamble."

I lay back down. "I'm hungry," I said. "I smell something good."

"Some broth is all you should have until we know you can stomach more ... Or if your stomach now has a hole." She held my right hand in both hers. "But before you eat, there is something I wish to know ... Just before you swooned, you had a vision. It showed in your eyes ... Tell it, please."

I relayed the vision of the sun, closing in on me and consuming my soul till nothing but ashes remained. I told her of Vebru and his last moment with the setting western sun on his face.

"You stood face-to-face with your destiny, your fate."

"No," I said, "it was just the pain. For some reason it brought forth a memory, and a hope of what may have been seen through another's sightless eyes."

"You honor your old Celtic friend, but your vision had nothing to do with him. The sun represents your all-consuming destiny. The direction you were facing is where that destiny lies."

"It was the setting sun that warmed Vebru's face as he died. So," I said, incredulous, "my destiny lies in the west?"

She lifted her face and cackled at the thatch ceiling and roof. "My Tenchteri friend," she said, "when you had your vision, you were facing that way," she said, pointing to the side of the hut where she kept her medicines on a shelf. "That is the north."

"The north? In the land of the Germanic freemen?"

"I have met only one tribesman from the north." She patted me on a shoulder. "He is, unfortunately, no freeman."

My stomach had no hole in it, for I ate voraciously and gained strength over the next three quarter-phases of the moon. I had to relearn to walk, compensating continually for the dull pain in my hip that would remain to the end of my days. With the limp, tracking game while trying to remain silent became more of a challenge, but the act of hunting gave me a sense of belonging and purpose.

Every few days, the officer would send a soldier in relief to stay at the boats with young Master. Each time the former guard would bring us the disappointing news that the Roman nobleman, young Master, lived still.

Finally, we could delay our continuing journey no longer. It was mid-summer, and we hoped to reach the heart of Asia Minor before the cold winds of winter set in on the continent of Europe. Though the Roman soldiers offered to carry me, I limped along with them, north to the great river and our awaiting boats.

Our party became one fewer, as a young soldier and the healer's great-granddaughter had become enamored in one another during our short stay, so much so he wished to remain. The officer granted his request under the provision he would officially be declared an outpost guard to protect these people in the name of the Emperor. I believe now the world will someday all claim Roman blood, and the Empire will conquer the world under furs and skins as opposed to under sword and siege.

5

Back in the skiffs, we continued to let the current of the great river take us east. The weeks away from us did nothing to alter young Master's disposition.

"So the slave is cured! So the slave will not perish! How does that serve us?"

The officer, in a separate vessel, glared at the noble-born. "We have already discussed this. Do you speak the Celtic tongue? Do you speak a Germanic tongue? Where we are going, they speak the Greek tongue. I've heard Bern does, but do you?" Young Master offered no reply or rebuttal. "So," the officer said, "speak no more about this matter. We will require Bern's gift, of that I am certain."

"And after we have made our trade connection," young Master said, "his fate lies in my hands."

"What do you mean by that?" the officer demanded.

"He was bought and is owned because he is a slave. And because he is a slave, he can be sold."

"When our mission succeeds," the officer said, "we return to your father with the entire party!"

Young Master smirked, but remained silent and faced forward toward the next bend in the river.

After we awoke the following morning in a clearing in the middle of a weak grove of small birch trees, we set off again. The river banked to the left, so we drifted northeast for the next day.

"If we find no real forest full of pine or other evergreen, what do we do?" a soldier asked.

The officer stared ahead, his face grim. "Reports say where the river banks back south, where this one is fed by another coming from the north, there is a thick forest with what we seek." In his place at the fore, he gripped the sides of his boat and bowed his head. I could tell he prayed to his gods that what he said would be so.

Three days adrift on the strong current, we finally met land on both sides stretching as far as our eyes could see filled with tall, strong pine trees. Our joy was met with apprehension when we noticed smoke rising not far from the south bank. Again we guided the skiffs to the bank and secured them to shrubbery.

"Let's find what manner of people makes this smoke," the officer whispered. He ordered a perimeter detachment to remain with the skiffs and the ever-complaining young Master. The remainder of us crept the direction of the smoke. We knew we had gotten quite close because the campfire smoke stung our noses and throats, and irritated our watering eyes. However, so thick were these woods still we could not perceive the smoke's origin. "Ready for defense," the officer said, and all of the soldiers drew their swords. I notched an arrow in my bowstring. He tapped me on a shoulder. "Call out to them. Tell them they are surrounded and we wish only to talk."

With Germanic tribes, one could never be certain of a reaction. Would they call back and invite a discussion? Would they charge at us shrieking before our slaughter? I took a deep breath, and in my native tongue repeated the officer's words.

Perhaps those who made the campfire had been talking and buffering other sounds, for the crackling of burning wood came clear to us now as well as our own breathing. Then a voice in atrocious German called out. Obviously someone straining with the words. "We ... soldiers ... Imperial Legion ... Roman! You ... under ... Roman eagle!"

"The accent sounds Roman, sir," I said to the officer. "I believe they are also Roman soldiers."

He cupped his palms over his lips. "Hail, Caesar!" he called in the Roman tongue. "In the name of Tiberius, we come in peace!"

"Lower your weapons!" a voice called from the direction of the smoke. Raising a hand in the air, then lowering his palm, our officer made the motion for his soldiers to do as bade. "Men, you may show yourselves now!" the voice said. Suddenly our rear was covered in a semicircle by at least ten Roman soldiers. A Roman soldier—another officer—stepped to us from the cover of a tree before us. "A nice attempt, but in truth we have *you* surrounded." He cocked his head over a shoulder. "Come. We have much to discuss, and perhaps you have need of food and drink." He stepped toward the smoke, and without hesitation, we followed.

As guests, we took the first turn telling our story. After we heard the other officer describe his platoon's adventures, we realized both parties shared a similar storyline, except that our hosts' goal had already been reached. "There are several platoons like ours, sent north from Rome to the Danuvius. Simply put, we are scouts, traveling through Celtic and Germanic territories, to make contact with the locals, establish friendships as best as we can. Then, if we find a suitable area for a future fort on the river, we send word back, and the messenger will hopefully return with reinforcements. One of Tiberius's ambitious plans."

"And have you found such a suitable area?" our officer asked.

The other officer winked. "The most suitable ... Come! Your own eyes will show you better than my words can describe." He rose and stepped into the pine forest, toward the river.

After a trek in the forest, we stood at the south bank of the great river. Our host officer pointed across. "Where the river from the north—the Celts call it the Regana—meets the Danuvius, this is the ideal location for a Roman fort and settlement. Goods from unknown lands out of the Celtic north will land here along with goods from the west. Both can then flow to the end in the east, where you go." The officer's eyes shone with the hope upon which all future is built. A look of hunger. "And we have discovered this is the northernmost place where the great river flows. From here to the east, it is ever wider with warmer climates. Other scouting units like ours are already striking camp along the way until it empties into the sea north of Asia Minor. Merchants like your nobleman will need our protection as they travel through."

"And of course, they will pay a toll to pass your outpost," our officer said.

"Of course! Business is business!" The host officer laughed, but then quieted and shook his head. "Though that is many years from now, and I am not likely to see any of that silver in my lifetime ... But come. You'll need your rest before you fell the trees and start to build your barges." He led us back to the camp.

༄

I had never known work and joy to mean the same as I did among those men who removed their soldier armor to play the roles of the craftsmen they had been in a previous life. A former—and once again—woodsman in our party allowed me to accompany him to the tree line. I observed his technique with the ax and believed I had the basics. However, as soon as I swung and struck the trunk, a jolting pain shot from the healing wound at my side down to my heels and up to the base of my neck. I fell and lay breathing shallowly. Several crewmen gathered and knelt around me staring down with consternation until I sat up and waved them off. "I believe I'm not meant to be a woodsman," I said. "I only want to contribute somehow."

"You're one of the best huntsmen I've ever seen," said the woodsman/soldier. He gestured to the others. "We need to get back to work, which will make us very hungry," he added with a wink to me. "And by the way, why do you always keep your bow around your chest? It's always there, even if you're rowing on the boats."

I thought back to my eventual friend, now called Gabrus. "I lived for a time as a captive of a Celtic encampment. They taught me that a bowman is always prepared." I stepped into the forest accompanied by one of the host camp's soldiers to carry back what meat I may shoot.

For the next week, I marveled at the progress on the barges, and I kept the workers well-fed during breaktime meals with venison, grouse, duck, and the occasional wild pig.

All the logs were cut and hatched at the ends so another log was fixed and nailed across them. Additionally, a hole had been bored through the logs at intervals, and each three were tied together with long strips of deer-hide leather. When wetted then left to dry in the sun, these leather strips tightened to create a secure bond. Finally, where the sides of the logs met, the crew poured a hot pitch, making it all a whole, single, waterproof structure. A guiding rudder was rigged to the rear of each, where a pilot would man the handle.

The three barges would fit the entire crew of nearly a dozen, counting all the soldiers, myself, and of course the spoiled noble child-man. We waited another two days with the barges on the water but tied to trees along the shore so they could get used to the bounce of the water below and the heat of the sun above.

The morning arrived with the sun peaking over our goal— the eastern horizon. A cloudless sky hung over us, and a light breeze pushed behind us. All signs aligned in our favor. I felt it a shame we weren't in a local village or settlement so a shaman, a healer, even a witch, could summon the local gods to send us on with safety and speed.

It was a fairly joyous sendoff. Both parties faced a bright path ahead. We were soon on our way down the great river to Asia Minor, and our hosts would lay the foundations of a settlement to come in time. "I wish you could leave us the translator," the host officer said. "We could use the meat!"

We all laughed as we boarded our new flat vessels. We left the skiffs as gifts to the Roman soldiers of the camp. One-by-one, the ropes securing the barges to shore were untied, and we were off toward the rising sun and our destiny.

6

Young Master complained right away that he should ride in the first barge and not the middle in the convoy, since he was the leader of this expedition.

"Fine," said the officer, "when we find a place to break camp, you can take the lead barge the next morning." Young Master huffed and smirked in a way that said *I knew you would see things my way*. He began to back himself into his tent when the officer continued. "It's a great gesture of your leadership and bravery. Traditionally, if there is a surprise attack on land, it's the front and the rear that receive the arrows and spears. The middle is protected by both ends ... But it may not be so in the water."

After young Master retreated to his pillows inside the tent, we heard no more about his placement in our convoy.

For the next days, the river carried us along without incident. We were making good time, and it felt like the water current had gained speed, but perhaps that was only an illusion created by the swiftly-passing dwarf trees on the bank. Earlier, when we could see distant forest-covered hills, it was as though we drifted at a tortoise's pace, for those hills took forever to pass by. Yet along we travelled, and the men on each vessel suffered no boredom—except for young Master—because they rotated duty, at the rear rudder to steer us away from obstacles like boulders or fallen trees that could smash a barge back into its original individual logs, and at the front to keep a lookout for these obstacles. I learned that true mariners used the terms *bow* and *stern*. We also formed a sort of guard duty to check for dangers on land, mostly on the left side, or *port*, since that was unfriendly territory north of the Empire, but an eye was always cast toward the *starboard* side for the possible rebel attack from so-called friendly territory on the southern bank of the great river.

The mid-day air was becoming tangibly cooler, and noting that the sun's arc across the sky now lay fully on the southern side of the great river and the time of the sun's appearance waned each day, we knew the summer was coming to its end. It was imperative we reach Asia Minor during warmer days, but none of us had an accurate clue as to the length of the river. Our officer estimated at the current rate of the flow we were only eight or nine days away, but his conjecture was based on scouting reports from the early days of Tiberius ... From the days when the Empire and I first met one another.

During nights, we camped at some of the scouting outposts similar to the first one where we built our barges. Each host commander hoped his camp would eventually become a great settlement, a fortress, even a prosperous city for the further betterment of the Empire. One such overnight was spent on high ground above the great flowing river where to the east we could view the water winding widely toward the end of the world. A beautiful sight for even the least romantic ... if it were not for what lay directly across on the north banks.

"They weren't there when we first arrived," said the host officer of the many heads rotting atop the spikes directly on the banks below. "One morning a few appeared. Then each morning since, a few more."

"There must be over a hundred," said a young soldier from our party. He stared across, aghast.

"What people were they?" our officer asked of the heads. "And what manner of people are doing this thing?"

"I can't recognize the victims by race," the host officer said of the dark-skinned faces on the spikes. They were all male, with long pitch-black hair and beards. "Perhaps they're Asian, possibly from the lands east conquered long ago by Alexander. Probably brought to this area by force as slaves ... As to the ones doing this, I hesitate to refer to them as people. We occasionally spot them, but it's difficult to get a clear view this far across. I believe they're Celtic, but I could be mistaken."

"The Empire has fought many wars on this side of the river against the Pannonians," our officer said. "Some of our toughest opponents. Perhaps those are their unconquered cousins?"

"Could be," the other officer said. "But why all the senseless slaughter? It is simply barbaric!"

I looked askance at him. I recalled the Roman *optio* watching indifferently as the Chauci warriors he accompanied ravaged, slaughtered, and enslaved my entire village. Not a single one of the *civilized* Roman soldiers lifted a finger to stop the barbaric brutality. Barbarism as a concept is—and always has been—defined through the conqueror's eyes. "It's a message," I said.

"So, we are to listen to expert advice from a Germanic slave?" the host officer said with a smirk. "All right then, let's hear what a barbarian has to say about barbarians ... What message do those barbarians send to us by placing severed heads upon pikes?"

"Simple: stay on your side of the river."

The host officer chuckled. "In time our numbers will be so great we will overwhelm them. Then our settlement here will no longer be on the Empire's northern border."

"I believe you," I said. "But until then, you should heed their message."

7

For over a dozen days, we let the great river carry us east, and along the way we camped with other military emissaries from the Empire. All were carrying the same mission, and it was obvious to me with the expanse to the southern banks of the great Danuvius, Rome would eventually conquer the entire world, including all the Germanic tribes, heretofore the most uncooperative people they had encountered.

After we drifted out of the Celtic territory the Romans knew as Noricum, and well past Pannonia, we encountered no further Roman camps. Nothing occurred. No attacks. No warnings or gruesome messages from unknown barbarians. We simply floated along and struck our own camp where our officer fancied. We were not bothered. It felt as though there was no one out here to bother us. Did the peace fill us with a sense of security? To the contrary ... The quiet, the dull inactivity kept us all on edge. Surely there waited for us an attack from one side of the river or the other. Yet still, day-by-day, we drifted serenely down the river, to the east.

So focused were we all on imagined danger from the land, we had forgotten to heed the perils of the waters we were in. When a pilot at one of the rudders noticed the speed we uncontrollably gained, it was already too late to make it to shore. He called out the danger. We scrambled to the center of the barge we were on, held on to a log with all the might we had in our feeble fingertips, and prayed to whatever god may favor us at the moment.

Not only did the water quicken its current, but huge boulders also bounded past, surrounding us and churning the brown water into a foamy white. "Rapids!" called the ferryman's son. None of us knew what he knew, but by his tone we understood our situation was not at all good. "We must be coming to the end!"

The pilots frantically pulled on the rudder handles in vain attempts to guide their barges around the obstacles. The men who huddled in the centers clung to each other while screaming with each bump of the logs against rock. And meanwhile our crafts were being sucked along ever faster through the maze of stone. It was as though we had inadvertently been thrust into a race. The lead barge carrying the officer was no longer in the front. Our rear barge, upon which I grasped the tops of log bark with the tentative hold of my fingertips, slid past, and began to spin out of control. I glanced back at the officer shouting through his cupped hands, yet I heard only rushing water and muffled screams of terror and appeals to gods of the moment. Our pilot's forearms strained with the effort. Then we met a massive boulder head-on, and the pilot went tumbling into the angry foam.

When I faced forward, I discovered our barge had become airborne and it had broken into its separate logs. I clung to one, my arms and legs wrapped around as though I were a baby bear shimmying up a pine tree but suddenly frozen in its fear of the height. From my perspective, the clouds sailed past. And then I realized it was me—and the log I held onto with all my strength—that flew into the air over the water. With a jarring slap, the log plummeted into the water atop and below me. The slam forced the air from my lungs, and I briefly lost consciousness. When I revived, I was automatically holding my breath under water, and still clinging to the log that rose too patiently to the surface.

The log finally reached the surface bobbing along while still being shot by the current like an arrow. I opened my eyes and knew I had likely died. What I beheld before me could not possibly be. The river stretched forever forward, and when I turned my face to either side, the northern and southern shores had disappeared. I was either dead or losing my mind. I decided the answer probably lay behind me, so I struggled to maneuver myself around to see from whence I had come. Floating toward me were other logs, likely from the barge on which I road, but no signs of life. It was difficult to imagine only minutes ago I drifted along the current of a great river, for I could barely discern the mouth spewing its contents into this great water, the fabled Pontus Euxina.

This had been our goal all along. Or our initial goal until we safely reached the land of Asia Minor. Pontus Euxina, or the *inhospitable waters*, an apt name at that moment. I sup-posed I had lost the rest of the party forever, and the only hope was the land back either north or south of the mouth of the Danuvius. I hugged my awkward makeshift vessel and kicked toward the shore south of the river mouth, but no matter how hard my efforts, the log drifted further east, further away from land. I attempted again and again until my entire body went numb from exhaustion. I noticed how much cooler the water became farther from shore. Suddenly the wound above my waist throbbed, making me weak. I sighed to myself. *This is it, you fool* , I thought to myself. *You will either slip off the log and drown, or freeze to death—or be taken from this life by a combination of the two*!

I don't know how long I slept, or if indeed it was sleep that overtook me. I had felt a sense of being called to the Under-world by the great dark Voice, but then other voices brought me back to consciousness, back to the log floating on inhos-pitable waters. I opened my eyes and I knew I must have been in a state of limbo between our world and the next, for I saw the barge carrying the officer and a few of his soldiers—fewer than rode upon it on the great river. And secured to it by a rope, the barge holding young Master and some—but not all—of the soldiers who accompanied him. Nowhere among them was the slave from north Africa, who had obviously met his doom in the rapids so far from his home.

Nevertheless, my eyes widened, and I smiled and opened my mouth to shout for joy, but the officer waved his hands as though warding off an approaching evil. Beside him the ferryman's son pointed to me, then to himself, and lowered his head. In this excitement and confusion I heard voices behind me, the voices I had heard calling me back from the Underworld. I had never heard this tongue, spoken in a hurried cadence behind me by three or four males. Again I looked at the ferryman's son. He raised his face, then again pointed to me and lowered his head.

I understood, and lowered my head, resting the side of my face against the log to which I clung so fiercely. I noticed the water felt a bit warmer than before I had lost consciousness. The sun reflected in sparkles off the rippling water, and in this time of the year, its rays warmed the surface enough to save me from a death by freezing. I prayed a silent thanks to Apollo and closed my eyes. But the pain from my wound still throbbed intensely, and I entreated the gods that I could remain still, my body dead, through the agony.

The voices behind me grew nearer, accompanied by the slapping of oar paddles against the water surface. Then I felt a sharp jab between my spine and right shoulder. I gritted my teeth and tightened my already closed eyes to stifle the escaping tears. I learned an important lesson then: the best way to take your concentration away from pain is with another pain even worse. I no longer felt discomfort from my spear wound. To my right, something struck the log and I half opened my right eye. A spearhead jammed into the wood, then the log slid to the left, the spear wielder obviously using his weapon

125

as a tool to push the debris—the log and myself—aside. The water slapping became fiercer, and when the frantic voices passed before my ears, I hazarded to open my eyes. A long, narrow but sturdy boat, commanded by the spear wielder in front and propelled by two oarsmen, speeded toward the barges and my remaining party.

As the boat approached the barges, the oarsmen pulled their oars into the vessel, and each stood holding a bow in one hand and an arrow in the other. All on the barges dropped to their knees and held up their hands in surrender. I knew none of us would reach Asia Minor, at least not as freemen.

A thought flashed into my mind of the last true freeman I knew, Gabrus and his encampment of Celtic warriors and tribespeople. This thought connected my hands to my bow and quiver of arrows. I slipped my bow from around my chest and pulled two arrows from the quiver behind me. As the two oarsmen notched their arrows, I notched one of my own and placed the other between my teeth. Both men pulled back on the strings, but before they could raise their bows and aim their arrows, I loosed my first arrow, which struck the back of the neck of the one to my left. He dropped his bow and raised his hands, clawing at the sky. He fell backwards into the water, and as he sank and floated just below the surface, the arrowhead, having exited his throat, pointed heavenward. As his partner spun, surprised, my second arrow found purchase in his chest. He, too, lost control of his bow and arrow, and grasped at the arrow shaft. He was dead before he hit the now-welcoming waters.

The spear-wielding leader spun and glared at me. He shouted some obvious curse and raised his weapon to hurl at me. I wouldn't have the time to pull out a third arrow, notch it, pull back, aim, and release. My fate was in the hands of the gods, who would either smile upon me and throw off the man's aim or favor this new enemy and put an end to my life of slavery. He cocked back ... and fell face-first into the water as he was pushed from behind. Our officer, water dripping from his face, rose up in the fallen leader's place. The pirate had dog-paddled back to his long boat. He grabbed the side and attempted to pull himself back in.

"My lord!" called a soldier from the barge. "Let me throw you my sword!"

"No," the officer replied, "I'll give him to Neptune!" He struck the man hard twice with his bare fist in his face, then held him by the hair under the surface until it was certain no one could hold his breath for so long. "Are you all right, Bern?" the officer shouted.

I raised a hand, and we both rested a moment, panting and praying our silent gratitude.

After we boarded the pirates' boat, we debated about whether to take it, which was our original plan. It fitted us all—and what provisions and equipment we still held—quite comfortably, and we could sit by twos upon the benches. Yet attached to the sides next to each bench seat were chains and manacles, and on the floor, blood stains where the manacles bit into the unfortunates' ankles.

"I will not ride upon a slave boat!" one soldier said.

"Nor will I!" echoed another.

I looked at each of them and said, "Anyone riding with me earlier rode upon a slave barge."

"It's not the same!" the first soldier shouted. "We're not forcing you to paddle yourself to a slave market!"

"None of that matters," the officer said. "This is a well-made vessel, and the gods have sent it to us. The barges brought us here, but they cannot navigate these waters, not like this boat can." He glanced at the three bodies floating in the water. Each man with long, dark hair, braided beards, leather armor, and scarred faces and arms. "I don't know what manner of people belonged to this boat, but two facts remain. This boat is our only chance to reach Asia Minor in the south, and it is likely there are more boats like this one, carrying their ilk in these waters." He raised the standard, with the Roman Eagle perched at the top. "So let's load our equipment, man the oars as freemen, and travel south, keeping the shore to the west within our sight."

The men grabbed the oars and began the work.

8

For two days we paddled along the western coast, and we believed we would soon make land in Asia Minor, perhaps within a day or two more, but a sudden vicious thunderstorm caught us unaware. The gale-force winds created massive waves sending us off course, north and east. Our oarsmen's efforts could not compete with the will of the gods. Besides, all our attention was needed to bale the rising water from the vessel's floor, so we succumbed to the storm and allowed it to send us where it would. The rain and winds abated in the night, but the clouds remained thick. Since we wouldn't have a sense of direction until morning, we lay upon the floor and fell into an immediate deep slumber.

I awoke first among the eight men who remained. An old habit from years as a household slave, awakening before the dawn to care for Master and my Lady. A sigh escaped from deep within as I thought of her. I leaned over the side of the boat to cup cool water and splash it onto my face, both to wake up and to drive those hot memories away.

I raised my face and nearly fell into the water with fright. An enormous vessel bore down on us, and would overtake us within minutes. On each side at least twenty long oars protruded from holes. I shouted an alarum to our small group, all of whom immediately stirred and sat up. The oars sped their pace to the steady beat of a drum.

The officer stepped to my side. "Prepare to fight or be taken!" he shouted over his shoulder.

This huge vessel was powered by both wind and human energy, and it used both to hone in on us with the speed of my first favorite Roman god Mercury. Yet soon it coasted as the oars raised and the sail dropped. It was now so close we could see the eagle as its front figurehead. "They are us!" one of our soldiers called, and he stood and waved his arms. "The Roman navy! Hail, friends!"

"Remain seated!" the officer called, but the young soldier continued the arm waving and shouting at the Roman ship. "Down now!" our officer shouted.

A long and sturdy harpoon at the end of a rope shot from the front of the ship, and its sharp, pointed head pierced our excited soldier through his torso. Blood splattered his comrades behind him as his body fell into an awkward crumple. A call in Latin from the ship sounded for archers to notch their arrows.

I acted, knowing my action could be my last in this life. I crawled around the floor until I came across the standard bearing my Master's initials and the impressive Roman eagle atop. I picked it up and hoisted it high. "Please do not shoot!" I called. Then I proclaimed a lie concerning myself. A lie that would save us all. "We are Roman citizens! We come to Asia Minor in the name of the House of Tavarius!"

"Lower your weapons!" the voice above us called. A Roman naval officer placed his hands on the ship's railing and leaned forward peering down at us. "You bear no likeness to any Roman citizens I have ever known! You look like barbarians riding in a pirate slave trade boat!"

Our officer stood. "We come from the source of the Danuvius!" he shouted. "Our barges were attacked by the pirates who owned this boat! They are no more! But our crude barges were no vessels for these waters!"

"So you took their boat!"

"Yes!"

"Prepare food for our guests!" the naval officer said over his shoulder. He peered back to us with a wink. "You saved us the trouble of dispatching this barbarian slave boat! You will board this ship and abandon that filthy vessel! We are bound for Sinope, in Bythynia! If you try to reach Asia Minor in that thing, you'll be killed before you reach land!"

Aboard the ship, we understood why they feared us. Compared to them, we did resemble barbarian tribesmen. Our hair had become long and straggly. We each had sprouted a growth of beard. Our Roman clothing had become so sun-faded, it lost its bright coloring. And worst of all, we had become so accustomed to each other's stink, we were unaware of it. The ship's crewmembers pinched their noses upon coming within a few paces of us.

It is perhaps ironic that it was I who asked the ship's captain for a bath, a razor, a clean change of clothes. The only one of our party who expressed his desire to appear and smell civilized was the only one born into a barbarian tribe, and of the worst race—the Germans. The officer was pleased to grant my request, and he ordered his men to fit the rest of us with clothing from their own possessions ... after we had had proper baths and shaves, of course.

During the meal in the galley, we entertained the ranking naval officers aboard with our stories, starting from the settlement in Gallia Belgica. They insisted on viewing my wound, and decided I had been selected by the gods for some special dispensation.

"It is wise of your father to establish a connection for trade in Asia Minor," the captain said to young Master. "All the signs point to this region as the next hub of the Empire."

"Next hub?" young Master chuffed. "I hardly think there shall ever be a city on earth greater than Rome."

"You are undoubtedly correct, my lord," the captain said, "but a great city does not seem to be the goal of Asia Minor."

"What could be more important than being the most powerful city in the world?"

"For each individual, personal greatness ... especially wealth."

Young Master's nostrils flared. "Do you mean individuals become wealthy here, but pay no heed to the power wielded by the Emperor?"

"To answer the first part of your question, yes, individuals become quite wealthy here. In scores. And some become so wealthy they are locally quite powerful. He who holds the bigger purse of gold receives the bigger amount of attention. He gains more customers and suppliers and various business connections, all of which yield more gold."

"And what of the second part of my question?"

"Oh, yes. You will likely meet many wealthy individuals—locals, Arabs, Jews, Africans, and others—in your search for trade connections. But I promise you that you will encounter none who do not pay taxes to the Empire or supply manpower in times of war." The captain leaned forward, rested his chin on his folded hands, and winked. "Oh, and if I were you, I would make sure to find the quarters where the Jewish merchants live."

"And why them?" young Master said.

"They have the true connections. They will trade with anyone. They have a sense for business."

"Jews. I remember hearing about them," our officer said. "Something about being stubborn and refusing to recognize any god but their own."

"But isn't that normal?" I said. All eyes focused on me, the only non-citizen in the room, for the food-serving slaves were awaiting their call outside the door. "We Germans prefer our gods, the Celts prefer theirs, you Romans yours. Yet when we find ourselves mingling, we are able to coexist."

"But there is the difference," the captain said. "They have only one god, and they say he is the only god in the universe."

"They don't recognize the Emperor as a god?" Young Master raised his eyebrows. "They must be dealt with harshly, like any barbarian tribe who refuses to capitulate."

"Like the Cherusci at Teutoburg?" I said, and all others chuckled ... save one.

"Occasionally, an edict comes from Rome, ordering this general or that to deal with the Jews harshly," the ship captain said. "Which often has an effect opposite the desired. So usually tolerance of their odd religion is the preferred policy, as long as taxes are paid and war efforts are supported ... or at least not hindered."

"There are other people in Asia Minor, as you said," young Master said to him. "We will deal with them instead of these Jews."

"If it is trade you seek, you will find you have little choice," the captain replied, "I assure you. Not only will you find that for yourself, but you shall also discover Asia Minor is unlike any Roman region you have ever known ... and for all the best reasons. You may even wish not to leave," he added with a wink.

Our officer stood and raised his cup. "To success in Asia Minor!"

"To success in Asia Minor!" all but one repeated. And the Galatian wine livened the atmosphere.

The party continued to drink and revel. But I left them and climbed up to the ship deck where I stood to watch the shore—and my destiny—come nearer.

Part II

DESTINY'S
DARK HEART

CHAPTER ONE

SAILING INTO DESTINY

1

We made love, the Lady Dalina and I, as though we knew we would never have the chance again. We both sweated like the hunter and his prey, the chaser and the chased, racing through the forest. I could not speak for my Lady, but my entire body ached and throbbed deliciously. Then after more couplings than I could count, we lay in her bed panting with exhaustion, saying nothing because there was nothing to be said. I remember nodding off with her lovely blonde head resting on my shoulder.

"Wake up, Bern," her lilting voice crooned. "Wake up, my darling." She shook my shoulder. "Bern, please ... Wake up now."

I remained in the intoxicating moments between the world of sleep and our world of labor and obligations, of worry and fear. "Come on, German slave, wake up!" This gruff growl preceded the toe of a sandal into my ribs.

I rose with a shriek and sat staring about wildly, my breaths coming and going like a smith's bellows.

"Hey there! Calm down!" said the Roman sailor, his hands on my shoulders. "The Captain sent me. You've slept nearly a full day, and that's enough. I'll take you to the kitchen for food. Then we'll put you to work with someone who's been asking to meet you ... Must've been some dream, eh?" He chuckled as my breathing slowed down. "So let's get some food down you." I followed him to the kitchen praying to my adopted god Mercury that he would carry the lingering memory of my dream swiftly away.

After I ate a meal of some tasteless mush, the Roman sailor led me to the starboard edge on the lower deck, lined with benches where men sat grasping oars, their back muscles straining before they lowered their fists and rocked forward to continue the rhythm of an impossibly round man beating on a kettle drum. "Here," the sailor said motioning to an empty bench seat. "Take that oar and follow the others' motions to the drum beat." I sat and grabbed an oar handle. I observed those on the benches before me until I thought I understood the technique and the rhythm involved.

I was on perhaps the tenth stroke when a deep voice sounded directly behind me. "How long have you been a slave?" At first I was unaware the speaker addressed me. I assumed all down here were slaves, which was why I was put to work among them. I continued rowing until I felt a hard tapping on my left shoulder. "How long have you been a slave?" came the deep voice again. Suddenly I realized the language was mine, or at least an accented version of my native

Germanic tongue. "Just keep rowing, and we can talk. The captain wants to reach Sinope by tomorrow, and with no wind, we must row."

Since he spoke his version of the Germanic tongue, I spoke mine. "Is the captain your master?"

"I have no master after my master died."

"You do this voluntarily?"

"I do this, German slave, because it is my job. It's how I earn what little silver I'm allowed to carry on land."

I glanced around. "But these other men ... Are they also— "

"The only slave down here is the one right in front of me. Which brings me back to my question: how long have you been a slave?"

I paused and stared at the back of the man rowing before me. My rhythmic motion automatic, I thought back through the years to the raid on my village, to my loss of freedom. "Ten, maybe twelve years," I said. "So how long have you been ... How long since your master died?"

"Going on five years."

"And did he free you before he died?"

His silence lasted so long I thought there was some problem in translating from dialect to dialect, and I would need to find some other way to restate my question. "Yes, my master set me free in his will."

"So you found this work because he was also a ship captain?"

"My master knew nothing about boats or the ways of the water. He was a rich man, a Jew."

"And what did he do for his living?"

139

I somehow could feel he shrugged. "As I said, he was a rich Jew. He made money. He would buy things for sale and then find someone who would buy them for more money than he paid."

This confused me dearly. "He had land and crops, right?"

"No land or crops. Only a house in Sinope where his first family lives, and then another where his second family lives ... in Nicaea."

"He had two families?"

"Neither knows of the other, and I was sworn to keep the secret ... So when I found I could have a cot and a few silver coins now and then for rowing on this Roman vessel, I took the chance to live my life and keep clear of both families. None of the family in Sinope ever risk going into the quarter where the sailors drink and find women for the night, so when we're in port, that's where I keep my nose ... We'll be there in two days. Maybe you can pay a visit with me?"

"And maybe Apollo will reverse his course," I said. "But tell me ... what's your name?"

"Raiko."

"I am Bern."

"I know."

"So tell me, Raiko, why don't you just save up some of the silver coins and go where you wish? You have your former master's will, don't you?"

"A lone middle-aged German wandering down the road. Bandits would attack me, destroy the will, and sell me back into slavery. I stand no chance out in the world. I would go back north if I could ... try to find my old people. But I wouldn't make it out of this province. So I might as well live this life." For a moment I heard nothing but the steady slap of oars on water. "Don't you agree, Bern, my German slave?"

"If I were granted my freedom, Raiko, I would take my chances on the road. I would not hesitate to leave."

"And where would a short German bear go?"

I closed my eyes and imagined a forbidden former love. "I have an idea."

"Bern!" boomed a voice from behind accompanied by the sound of steps down from the deck. "The German slave brought from the west! You are needed on deck!"

I stood and saw Raiko, a barrel-chested, one-eyed man with wrinkled skin and briar-bush black hair. He winked at me with his single eye, the other hidden beneath a cloth patch.

2

I followed the sailor to the deck where the ship's captain stood beside my party's commander, both leaning into the railing and looking down into the water. When I reached them, a small vessel containing half a dozen oarsmen sat at their stations, as a tall, lean fellow stood at the center of a craft. All wore turbans, which I would learn was the customary headwear in Asia Minor, and the man standing was obviously in charge. The captain leaned to me and whispered, "Is Greek one of the many tongues you've mastered?"

"My Lady—um, my tutor—taught me what ... um, he knew."

The Captain cocked his head curiously at me. "Good, I suppose, of your lady or tutor, because I speak only Latin and enough German to get me in trouble." He then turned to the standing man and motioned *come on* with his fingers.

The man cupped his hands around his mouth and shouted up at us. I felt a sudden disappointment, for I could understand but a few words. *No. . . land … sickness … doctor …*

I waited until I felt he'd completed his soliloquy. Then I took a deep breath and shouted. "I am sorry, my friend. What is this about land and sickness and doctor?"

He squinted at me while scratching a side of his turbaned head. He mumbled to his comrades. One—a man with the most unruly beard—stood. "What are you," he shouted, "a poet?"

"No, I am but a slave."

" —who speaks like Homer! Do you not understand the modern Koine of the Greeks?"

"No, I suppose I do not."

"Well, it's a good thing for you someone on our boat visited a school when he wasn't being chased by the authorities. I'll try to put it in the old blind poet's words …" He looked off to a horizon and moved his lips, obviously forming the words he must say to me. He finally said, "There has been an outbreak of the pest in Byzantium. Some of those people travel into Rome proper and may have infected people you have supped with … or more. You will not be allowed to step ashore until Sinope's chief physician has inspected you and cleared you to come into the city. Do you understand?"

I nodded and waved. The sailor spoke to his leader, the crew busied themselves at their positions, and the vessel was maneuvered around our ship, away from our line of sight. I relayed the message to the ship captain and my commander. When I finally managed to reach shore later, I decided I would need to learn to navigate this new Greek, this Koine, so I could communicate with all and not only scholars of literature.

"If those sailors were sent to us from the city of Sinope," the captain said, "then Sinope is near. How long since you've laid your eyes on Roman civilization?" he asked my commander and me.

"If the colonia back in Gaul counts as civilization," my commander said, "many months now."

"Then come," the captain said. "Let's go to the bow and take in a distant view of a Roman city in Asia Minor." He stepped away from us, and we followed in single file, my commander in the middle.

3

The water beneath the choppy waves became bluer and greener the closer the ship sailed toward shore. Seagulls and other water birds circled over us in hopes of being tossed scraps of food. There on the distant shoreline, it seemed like Sinope rose from the sand. I noted a single bright hue of white characteristic over all the buildings. The city stretched a great distance east to west, and I imagined it would take the greater part of a morning just to walk from end to end. "How many people live in this place?" I asked.

"I heard it said that ten thousand live within the city walls," the captain said. "But there are villages outside the walls whose people also claim Sinope as their city."

"Ten ... thousand?" I could practically hear my own heartbeat racing within my chest.

"I've never seen a person's eyes so wide before." The captain grinned at me, then returned his face to the approaching city. "Have you never been to a city?"

"Nothing like this ... I can't imagine the number of people in such a place. Where I was born, we didn't believe there were so many people in the entire world."

"Germania, isn't it?"

"Far north ... far beyond the border of the Empire."

"Hmmm ... Far from the civilized world." In his rumination, he rubbed his chin. "But please don't think what the Romans have made of civilization has meant civility. When you step into that city, you'll find greed and immorality along with the progress. The price we pay for Roman modernization, law, and order."

I studied the distant white structures, and in two different locations, I noticed oval green rising above the angular white. "Those green domes," I said. "What are they?"

The captain's expression took on an air of pride. "Great Roman architecture." He winked down at me. "Whatever our faults, we have the best engineers in the world. The larger of the two domes is the temple, dedicated to Mercury—or what the locals call Hermes."

My heartbeat ran the pace of a cornered hare's. Mercury! The god to whom I once owed my life, and who oversaw the course toward my destiny. Could Sinope be my destiny? "And the other dome?"

"That *was* the temple. But as the city grew from its first days as a Greek colony to its present days as a prosperous imperial port, so did the need for other expansion. The messenger god simply outgrew his old clothes … So, the former temple became the city library."

"Library? With books?"

"I know of no other use for libraries."

I gazed up at him, and I knew I could not hide my yearning. "A library is a temple," I said to his cocked-head confusion. "When we are allowed off the ship," I added resolutely, "I must find some time to visit the library."

He put a hand on my shoulder. "You are a slave, Bern. You may enter a city building only if you accompany your master."

"Could you take me inside?"

"Bern, I am not your master." He lifted his hand from my shoulder, then raised his hands as if in surrender. "The only way I could enter the library with you would be with a letter from your master giving me permission."

"Which you shall receive."

"But— "

I held up a palm. "My captain, you shall receive a letter of permission. I am my master's interpreter and scribe. As such, any letter he writes would come from my hand, including his signatory seal."

The captain lowered his hands, clapped my back, and chuckled conspiratorially. The port city of Asia Minor drifted toward us, becoming gradually larger.

4

Two smaller boats, each with armed archers standing beside men at the oars, were about half a league from shore to meet us. A leader in one of them called for the captain to lower his anchor and await a boat carrying a physician representing the city. The captain did as he was bade.

With no work for anyone except for the kitchen crew, every man on board stood on deck, hands against the starboard rails, staring at the city of the white buildings. In their faces I read the sailor's longing for the comforts of the shore. Later while on land I would read in the same faces the anxious yearning for unknown adventure brought on by the lure of the sea. Still, through the day we stared at the northernmost city of Asia Minor, so close we could smell it, yet it may as well have been a million leagues away.

The night came, and still no sign of the promised physician. Sinope now appeared only as several dim lights, likely from oil lamps. There were no maritime chores for the crew on a boat anchored in harbor, so the sailors became restless. The kitchen served a supper of stew in the galley. After all of us had eaten our fill, gambling games broke out, and those involved shouted curses at each other and at minor gods for their bad luck. One sailor fetched a flute from his bunk and played lively tunes while men danced with each other in jovial circles.

The noise and activity extended through the night, but even during it all, I retired to my blanket on the deck floor and slept soundly. For a slave, there is no cause for restlessness in the absence of activity. Time is simply one long stretch, each minute as valuable as the next.

5

The next morning a slender vessel powered by a single oarsman slid slowly on the surface seemingly toward us, though it was difficult to tell.

The sun was at its zenith when the thin craft reached our ship. At the oar was a bare-chested muscular fellow whose head was covered in protection from the sun's heat by a simple cloth. An ancient man, probably in his fifties and constructed mainly of bone, sat on the center bench. He wore a full-length white robe over his scrawny frame and a neatly-wound turban atop his head. His face was deeply wrinkled, and his astonishing gray beard reached his stomach. Beside him sat a young male—perhaps a teenager—dressed similarly to the old man, but the cloth of his robe looked less expensive. Though too young to grow a beard yet, he wore these peculiar curls beside his face as his sideburns.

The old man lifted his face, cupped his hands around his mouth, and shouted up in an oddly-accented Latin. "Hello, I wish to speak with the captain of this ship!"

The captain presented himself leaning over the starboard railing and acknowledged the old man as the promised physician. He said he would lower a smaller craft near the bow and then raise it once the physician was aboard.

Another feat of Roman engineering stolen from the Greeks, the small but wide boat—meant for a small party coming ashore in unknown territory—was lowered via a pulley gear wound with extra-thick rope. The captain halted the movement above the surface, the crest of the waves just lapping the boat's bottom. The oarsman paddled the slender vessel beside the lowered boat and, along with the youth, helped the old man—burdened by a large bag draped over a shoulder—to climb into the boat. After the young man also climbed aboard, the old man said something in this new Greek Koine to the oarsman (obviously that he should wait, for the slender vessel remained where it was throughout the physician's stay aboard). Then, powered by two strong men pulling on either side of the gear, the wide boat carrying the physician and his assistant rose into the air.

6

The captain ordered us to line up shoulder-to-shoulder, starting down at the bow with his men. We from the colonia in Gallia Belgica stood beside each other near the aft. As the only slave in our party of intruders, I stood at the end.

The old man grabbed aimlessly at his side, then searched about his robe looking panicked. His assistant tapped his shoulder and handed him a bag. The physician heaved what looked like a sigh of relief. He stepped before the first man in line.

He probed this and that man with an instrument he pulled from the bag, peered into the eyes and mouths of this and that man, coming our direction with each examination. He would speak over his shoulder to his assistant in some language I had never heard.

By the time he reached our party, the sun hovered just above its disappearance beneath the western horizon. The old physician stood before a young soldier, placed a thumb and forefinger below and above one of the soldier's eyes, and spread them wide. He leaned forward and peered into the blood-shot eye. "Your eye ... more red than white," he said in an accented Latin.

"Sir, I was up most of the night drinking and dancing ... We all were."

"Open your mouth and let me smell your breath."

The young man opened his mouth and exhaled. The physician took a whiff and recoiled, shaking his head. He pulled from the bag something resembling a brass drinking glass, wider at the rim than the base. He placed the rim on the left side of the soldier's chest and leaned the side of his face against the base, pressing his ear into it. He stood shaking his head, his forehead furrowed. He placed the instrument back into the bag and motioned the captain toward him.

The old man pointed to the soldier. "This one cannot come ashore. We shall send a boat to take him to the island for quarantine."

"But there's nothing wrong with me!" the young soldier cried. "I told you ... I was awake through the night!"

Eyebrows raised, the physician scrutinized the young man. "And that accounts for the irregular heartbeat?"

"What's this about my heart?"

"It misses a beat after four or five beats." The old man turned to the captain. "Actually, it would be for the best of everyone if he were isolated now."

"We'll put him in the brig below."

"Because I have tired eyes, because I have a strange heartbeat, I have the pest?"

"You are under suspicion of having the pest."

"And how can I prove I have no pest?"

"We will send a boat with food and necessities to the island once per month. On that boat will be my assistant here who will inspect all the residents. Those free of symptoms will board the boat back for the mainland." Again the old physician looked to the captain. "Please ... take him away."

The captain called out two names, and two brawny sailors broke ranks and came forward. "Take this one down to the brig, but make him as comfortable as you can."

The young soldier whipped his face to our officer. "Sir, is there nothing you can do?"

The officer jutted his stoic face forward, his steely eyes on the white buildings of Sinope. "Not if we are to continue with our mission," he said. He gave the two sailors a curt nod, and they each grabbed hold of one of the young soldier's arms and marched him away.

All the way to the stairwell, the young soldier struggled and screamed. "In a month I'll be alone here! My crew will all be gone! I don't have the pest, but you're putting me on an island with people who do have it!" He continued his protests even as they came to us muffled from below the deck.

As the physician inspected our officer, he said, "It is unfortunate what we must do to protect our own. But you come from Europe, which has the pest. And can you say with certainty you were with no one infected?"

"No, my sire, not with certainty," the officer said.

"Well, you appear fine." The old man raised his point of view over the officer's shoulder by standing on the tip of his toes, and spied young Master sitting on a bench against the railing. Again he spoke to his assistant in this strange language before returning his focus on young Master. "And you back there. Why are you not standing in the ranks with your comrades?"

"They are not my comrades; they are my subjects ... and my slave."

"Subjects? How did the news escape us? We have the Emperor himself on board this ship?" He cocked his head to a side as he studied the figure slouching on the bench. "But I thought Tiberius is far older."

"I am Caius Bruno Tavarius, son of Caius Cinna Tavarius, governor of Gallia Belgica, and you—whoever you are—block the progress of my trade mission!"

"Well, future governor of Gallia Belgica, if you will allow me to inspect you and assure myself that you are free of the pest, we will welcome you to Asia Minor so you may continue with your mission."

"I am a member of a Roman noble family ... We have no diseases!"

"Please be a good Roman leader—leading by example—and allow me my examination."

"You will not touch me, you filthy Jew! I heard you speaking in your foul tongue to that boy, and I've seen your like on the streets in Rome!"

"There are filthy Jewish doctors in Rome?" he chuckled. "My captain," he said over his shoulder, "who is the Roman authority in this situation?"

"The Council of the City of Sinope, sir."

"Yes … And since the Council of the City of Sinope has appointed me to represent it in determining who enters and who does not, what happens to any man—regardless of family status—who opposes my efforts?"

"He goes down to the brig to await a ride to the island of which you spoke."

"Without exception?"

"Without exception, sir."

Both turned their faces to young Master, who finally rose sneering and stepped between our officer and me, whom he bumped aside with his shoulder. "My father will hear of this," he hissed.

"I'm sure he will," said our officer, "and I'm sure he'll commend you for being sensible and allowing our mission to go forth."

After the physician completed his examination of young Master, he stepped before me, the last for him to check. "And what have we here?" he said. "You have the appearance of one from the Germanic tribes, though not as tall as others I have known."

I stepped forward and stood staring, feeling awe, for—except for two of Master's black-skinned African slaves—I had never stood before anyone so exotic as a Jew from Asia Minor.

"And a mute as well?"

"I was born into the Tenchteri tribe, sir," I finally managed.

"Never heard of them," he said. "And in what part of Germania do they loot and rape?"

"My people didn't care much for looting or raping, sir. Only for working to eat and for raising families." I hoped I sounded calm, though I felt myself boiling inside. "They live in the north. Far north."

He chuckled. "I am sorry, my friend. It was only an ill-placed joke ... So the far north, eh? Anywhere near the Teutoburg Forest where Arminius of the Cherusci massacred— "

"Not far from there, sir. But my people had nothing to do with— " He raised a hand and began his probe of my eyes, my mouth. "How do you know of these things? It's a lifetime away from here."

He cocked a thumb behind him, toward the white buildings. "The smaller dome. It used to be a temple for the Romans, but now— "

"It's a library. You read about Arminius and Varus in there?"

He raised his eyebrows. "So a German slave knows about libraries?"

"I speak any language I spend enough time with. I read and write Latin and the old Greek. I'm a translator and scribe."

"And I am duly impressed!" He shrugged. "Well, the bit I read about the trouble up there wasn't really a proper history. Just scraps coming out of Rome at the time ... During

Augustus, I believe it was." He took the bag from his assistant and slung it over a bony shoulder. He looked down at my right leg. "I noticed your limp as you stepped to me. Some kind of cramp or injury?"

"Some flint metal in my right hip, I think." I told him about the attack on the river and the old healer's work. I lifted my tunic and showed him the wound.

"It's too bad you were cared for by that old woman and not me," he said. "You would not have that scar, and you would not have the painful limp. But then, we're not in the habit of hurling spears at one another here in Sinope ... Well, my German friend, you are free of the pest, and I wish you well on your journey."

"Just one favor, please?" I asked. He spread his hands and waited. "Could you please repeat what you just said, but in your own language, the language of the Jews?"

"In Hebrew?" I nodded. "Very well ..." And the most melodic sounds flowed from his lips. He laughed out loud at my reaction of obvious joy. "I shall leave you with a present." He pulled a quill, a small jar of ink, and a piece of parchment from his bag, and wrote what he had said in this Hebrew. His hand was going from right to left. "Here," he said as he thrust it to me. "I'm not sure why I'm giving it to you, though."

I took it and placed it within my tunic. "It's a start," I said. "I shall cherish it." I bowed to him.

"You do not bow to anyone but me!" young Master shouted.

The physician shook his head sadly. "Farewell," he said to the ship captain, then smiled at me. "And may you find your destiny." He stepped to the bow where he and his assistant climbed aboard the landing boat and were lowered to their own.

The captain faced his line of sailors and crewmembers. "I'm sorry, men! But it's too late to dock. By the time we get there, it would be too dark to see what we're doing."

"Does that mean we have to stay anchored here tonight?" a voice called out.

"I'm afraid it does."

"There are two casks of wine left!" the voice returned. "Let's have no wine remaining when we dock tomorrow morning."

The captain raised a thumb up, and the riotous celebration began again for those who live their lives on the water. As for we who traveled from a colonia in Gallia Belgica, we gazed in longing at the city of the white structures.

CHAPTER TWO

THE CITY OF SIN

1

With the small crew—now numbering only seven—from the colonia doing our part, the ship was quickly docked at the pier and prepared for three weeks idle. Though during the previous evening the ship's crew cared more for the fruit of the vine than stepping ashore, they were all now eager to rest—in the form of more drunkenness and the pleasures they would seek in one of the many brothels. So understandably, the work took on a rather frenzied pace.

As I helped a crewmember secure the rear of the boat to the dock with a thick, heavy rope, I noted a strong, sharp smell that rode the breeze coming to the sea from the land to the south. The air was so acrid yet strangely sweet at the same time it stung the back of my throat and watered my eyes. "What is that strong smell?" I asked a sailor.

He nonchalantly said, "The spice market in the square." My expression must have obviously belied my ignorance because he chuckled when he glanced up at me. "Spices, you know, from the distant east ... From what I heard, your master seeks trade?" I nodded. "Well, there it is ... Spices to make his food tastier ... And for other things, like to attract the ladies ... Or for the ladies, spice smells to attract the men."

In a couple of hours, the work was done and the seven of us from the colonia stood on the pier where it met land. The ship captain stepped before us and looked from us to the streets and buildings before us, to which we stared uneasily.

"You've traveled for months through many dangers to reach Asia Minor," he said to us. "Well here it is!" He pointed at the ground beneath his feet. "So get off that dock, and welcome to Asia Minor!" He stepped away, toward the structures. "Come, and follow me to your quarters," he said over his shoulder.

Our eyes searched each other for some signal. Finally, it was the slave among the free citizens, including the nobleman, who took the initiative. "Asia Minor, we have arrived!" I said, and stepped off the dock. I could hear the others following close behind.

We trailed the ship captain down a narrow street leading to a wide market square busy with the cacophony of buyers and sellers shouting their offers and counter-offers for colorful silk cloth and pouches of rich aromatic spices. I heard mostly that new Greek Koine, and a bit of the Hebrew of the old physician among the buzz of hundreds of people. A couple of masculine voices in the familiar Latin came near, and to no surprise, our party was passed by two Roman soldiers on patrol. Mixed into that swirl of tongues was something resembling the old physician's Hebrew, but it was clearly something else.

We took a narrow side street away from the square and soon we were at the guarded gate of the Roman military barracks courtyard. The ship captain vouched for the scraggly lot we were, and the guard stood aside for our entry. "The other ship is out to sea," the captain said, "so there are empty cots for up to two months if you need." He looked at our officer and young Master. "I have private officers' quarters for each of you."

"My slave sleeps in my room," young Master said. "On the floor at the foot of my bed ... as is the custom of a traveling nobleman and his slave."

"Of course," said the captain. "As you wish."

"Fine," agreed our officer, "but one thing: his name is Bern."

We entered our temporary quarters, and I steeled myself for attending to my master's every need, however vile it may be.

2

I will not describe the humiliation I underwent behind closed doors in the following few days as young Master's sole slave and possession. Of course, I expected the earlier degradations foisted upon me, such as cleaning him and the surroundings after a particularly violent bout of vomiting or shitting.

However, I was not prepared for his other demands. Suffice it to say given his preferences, young Master would most certainly never leave the province of Gallia Belgica an heir, not of his blood. What he did most definitely leave behind was my indignation, and my resolved inner strength to someday become a freeman.

In the morning of our third day in the military barracks there came a light rapping upon the chamber door. I rose from the floor and glanced at young Master, draped face-down and naked across his bed. Again the rapping. I shuffled to the door, unlocked it, and opened it to a narrow slit.

The ship captain stood, his arms folded, studying me with his head tilted to a side. "You haven't slept."

"No, I haven't."

He looked over my shoulder at young Master. "But he seems to be sleeping well."

"Wine and exhaustion tend to do that," I said.

"Yes ... Well, get cleaned up and come with me."

"But what if he awakens and calls for me?"

"Like most men who spend the evening pouring wine down their throats, does he take a big drink of water as soon as he awakens?"

"Yes," I said.

He reached into his tunic and pulled out a small pouch. "Here," he said as he thrust it to me, "pour this powder into the water pitcher."

My eyes widened with fear. "This isn't ... you don't intend to pois— "

The captain chuckled. "No ... But what an entertaining idea. It's merely a sleep aid. It works fast and will put him back where he is now long enough for you to satisfy yourself in the former temple ... I'm assuming you've secured a letter from your master ... containing his signature and seal?"

"Yes." I reached out a hand. "Please give me that powder."

He handed it over. "Stir it in well. It evaporates cleanly and has no taste or smell."

The Library dedicated to Augustus was a large but simple round structure topped with a domed roof. As we entered, we were immediately accosted by a Greek librarian. He gave the captain a slight bow, then cocked his head to me. "Who is this one?" he asked.

"Ask him, and he shall be happy to tell you," answered the captain.

I introduced myself by name and status, and handed the man the letter on parchment. He raised it so the light from a window above beamed upon it. He peered over the parchment at me and said with a smirk, "A Germanic slave who reads?"

"And writes and understands and speaks more languages than you will ever be able to, my Greek friend," the ship captain said.

"Hmph," was all the librarian managed. After a moment longer studying the letter he nodded, satisfied. "All right then,

Germanic slave of a Roman nobleman, you have two hours."
He stepped to his desk and poured water from a pitcher into
a funnel device, which the captain later told me was called a
klepsydra, to measure my two hours.

The captain busied himself with the naval records where
he found an old friend, a retired captain, with whom he chatted and laughed. I stood, my eyes roving like a hungry dog
who had wandered into an unmanned butcher shop. But
also, someone with the same lack of plan as that hungry dog.
I was simply thirsty and hungry.

I spent those two hours pulling random books from
shelves and reading several pages before replacing them. I read
about Roman conquests, about military heroes, all of whom
were generals, but nothing about those front-line infantry-
men whose valor actually won the day. I read about strange
customs of those conquered in distant lands. About athletic
events, exotic flora and fauna, genealogy of great families ...
and even of the gods themselves.

I read in Latin, I read in Greek.

I found myself by sheer accident pulling a huge tome that
happened to contain both the *Iliad* and the *Odyssey* by that
god himself Homer "Careful with that one!" shouted the
Greek librarian, who had obviously had an eye on me the
entire time. "It's one of only a few dozen copies in existence!"
I carried the Greek text to a bench and lost myself in a world
of gods and heroes centuries before this one.

Before I was interrupted, I had been reading one of the
many arguments between King Agamemnon and the stubborn Achilles. The legendary warrior mulled over returning

home to a long prosaic life, never to be remembered, instead of a short life ending on the battlefield but living forever in the glory of song. I knew I would have chosen the former, but I also knew Achilles—true to the ideal of the hero—would opt for death and fame.

"Bern," a voice from the present world called to me, "it's time for us to leave."

I felt as if I were being jerked awake from a deep sleep and a pleasant dream. I raised my face to the voice and brought the face of the ship captain into focus. "The two hours have passed," he said. "We must leave."

"Another hour?" I begged.

"No, Bern ... Those two hours were the librarian's terms ... And you know we must hurry before someone wakes up."

I rose and placed the work of the Greek master back on the shelf. I glanced to the left, to a shelf marked in Greek *Plato*, and my heart sank further at the thought of leaving this holy place. I vowed to myself I must someday become a Roman citizen just so I could enjoy as long a stay in libraries as I desired.

Outside the library, on the narrow passageways back to the barracks, I felt as if I were suddenly thrust into deep water. Only a minute earlier, I sat with Homer and his telling of exploits and machinations of heroes and the gods who favored and hindered them, in perfect original Greek. Now I was on a dusty street crowded with people babbling and arguing in all of the petty modern tongues about trivial matters. It was not long before I succumbed to this flood, took a deep breath, and rejoined the present world of the mundane.

The captain and I passed two dark-skinned men in turbans, long robes, and sandals who were apparently arguing over a length of silk they both gripped and tugged, until two Roman soldiers approached them and thwarted impending violence. Again, theirs was the strange language resembling in nuances the Hebrew of the old physician and others later in the marketplace.

We turned a corner into a side street toward the barracks, and I asked, "Those men fighting over the silk ... what manner of people do they belong to?"

My companion shook his head in disgust. "Those, my friend, are Arabs. Their people have mastered the desert from Syria to Egypt. Without their aid, the spices and silk from far east in Asia would never reach the Roman Empire in Europe." He spat to a side. "They are noble people in their native lands ... But the farther they roam away from home, the bigger the scoundrels they show themselves to be." He stopped, causing me to do likewise. "You and your party need a connection to those spices and that silk?"

"That's why we journeyed here. You know that."

He cocked his head back toward the two Arabs. "You won't find it here in Sinope. But since they work cheaply and know the country from here to their homes, and maybe all the way to the Orient, you will undoubtably need to hire their ilk. Guiding outsiders through this territory is something they know how to do, I'll give them that much."

We continued to the barracks, where young Master was just waking up for the second time this morning.

3

The following morning, young Master was slurping down a last swallow of water when another rapping sounded on the door. After a few seconds of studying the door, he gave me a nod. I rose from the floor and opened it.

Our officer stood, dressed in his finest uniform, red and white cloth covered with a shiny brass breastplate. He held his ornate helmet in the crook of his left arm. He bowed his head. "I'm glad uniforms are among the wares in the supply section," he said, smiling at his array. "Master Bruno, I hope all is well with you."

"Under the circumstances," young Master said. "Why the pretty costume?"

"It is time, Master Bruno, for us to investigate our next steps toward a trade connection for your father the Governor."

"I suppose it is," young Master said with indifference. "So what do you expect me to do?"

"I would like to go into the city with Bern and find some-one who can give any information."

Young Master sat up. "Go into the city with my slave?"

"Go into the city," our officer said, "with the mission's scribe and interpreter. With *our* scribe and interpreter. This was the commission given Bern by your father the Governor."

The young man slumped back. He lay on his side and looked languidly to the ceiling. "Very well, then ... You have him until mid-day."

With the door shut behind us, our officer and I walked down the hall. He stopped at the stairwell. "I have a feeling either your master or I will have to go before this mission is over."

With my limp, I struggled to keep up with our officer's pace. He marched with determination to and through the marketplace, and I could tell he knew our destination. "Where are we going, sir?" I asked as I panted for breath.

"The House of the Prefect, to meet with the Consuls of the city, if they are present, which they likely are, as it's a beautiful day and the wine is probably flowing."

We arrived at a guarded iron gate. Our officer pulled a parchment from his tunic and handed it over for the Roman guard's scrutiny. "Please stay here," the guard said. "I will announce your presence inside."

I know not how long we waited, but the sun had moved in its arc across the sky. "If this house is so important as to require the service of a Roman guard," I said, "why does he leave this gate unguarded? We could be bandits for all they know, and storm the house without notice."

"This is an important house," our officer said, "and I have a feeling if we were to storm, as you say, the house, we would most certainly be noted. And most likely with an arrow in each of our chests."

The guard emerged from the great house and handed back the letter of introduction—from the ship captain, I later learned—to my leader. "Follow me," the guard said. He marched toward the house.

"And leave the gate unguarded?" our officer said.

He pointed upwards.

On a second-floor balcony, an archer emerged from the shadows. He stood, his arrow notched, his aim on the gate. I raised my eyebrows at our officer. He gave me a smile and an *I told you so* wink.

In the house we were led to a parlor where four men sat in a semicircle around a table, their backs to us. All sipped wine from ornate brass goblets. The guard halted and gave a deep bow. "My Lord Prefect," he said in the Greek Koine, "I present Legatus Legionus Drusus Garius on mission from Gallia Belgica!"

It occurred to me, until that moment I had never known our officer's name or real rank. So he was of a senator's rank and chose to devote his life to military service. I would from that day regard him with an awe mixed with reinforced respect.

A large man dressed in expensive silken robe, his head covered with a cap of fur and bright feathers, stood apart from the semicircle and faced us. His beard was speckled with gray, and his eyes studied us as if he were attempting to determine what species of animal we were. "So ... visitors from the wilderness," he said in Latin, his voice a deep baritone. He turned to the seated men. "Did they look wild when you first met them, Solomon?"

One of the men placed his wine goblet on the table and stood. His robe was snowy white, and he wore a long shawl around his head and neck. He stepped around the furniture and approached us. "No, Caius Juvus, but neither would I describe them as the most civilized gentlemen I have seen."

The physician who boarded the ship and judged us either fit or unfit to enter the city bowed his head slightly and smiled widely. "So it appears we meet again, officer Drusus Garius and the wounded Germanic slave whose name somehow evaded me on our first encounter."

"Bern, my lord," I said as I dropped to my knees.

"Oh, come! Stop this nonsense! If you are to show such respect, show it to the man in whose house you stand." He motioned to the large man with the booming baritone. Both men laughed.

Prefect Juvus stepped forward and stood beside Solomon, the physician who was also one of the city's Consuls. "So," the Prefect said, "according to the letter of introduction from Captain Tronius, you seek a trade connection for your Governor with the goods of the Orient."

"Yes, my Lord," Garius said.

"From what I hear, they could do with some color and spice in Gaul ... Come, all, and I shall show our guests where they should go." He stepped out of the room, and we all followed, physician Solomon in our lead.

In what appeared a huge banquet room, a large map of the region lay spread across a table surface. All the cities, provinces, and territories were marked and named in Greek. Sinope was a northern port of the province of Bythinia and Pontus. The Prefect picked up a wooden pointer lying across the map and placed the tip on Sinope. "Here we are," he said, "but if you truly want to trade for items from the Orient, you must either go to the source—an option not so practical—or go to a trading hub within the Empire." He lifted the point and placed it on a port far to the south on the great water called *Mare Magnum* by the Romans. Garius and I leaned forward to read the name of the city near the water. Tarsus. "Everything we receive from the east arrives first at the port belonging to Tarsus," the Prefect said.

"And how does it arrive here?" Garius said.

"Sometimes overland, straight north, quicker but also less secure. But usually the goods are brought to us by sea on a Roman naval ship, a journey that lasts up to two months but has the advantage of military protection." The Prefect dragged the point around the southern coast and up through a narrow channel between Europe and Asia Minor. "Perhaps you could arrange to pay for a place on a ship ... Providing there will be one going when you need it."

I peered up at Garius, who pressed his lips tightly together. "I doubt the men will want to go back onto the water anytime soon," he said. "And there's the issue of our nobleman parting with some of his silver to secure berths on a ship."

"Then the only alternative is south overland." The Prefect dragged the point directly from Sinope to Tarsus."

"The distance?"

"Nearly four hundred *mille passuum*."

"And the terrain?"

"Rough. Over dusty desert roads that disappear in the sandy wind. Through narrow canyons not allowing but single-file for travelers ... And you must carry as much water as you can from here."

Garius stood silently staring at the map. Finally he muttered, "Even if the Governor's son would part with enough silver he's hiding under his skirt to buy horses, we couldn't carry enough water on such a journey for the beasts and ourselves. We will need to go on foot."

"And at best that could last three or four weeks," I said.

"There is a solution for you," the Prefect said. We all focused on him and waited for him to continue. "South of town there is an encampment of tents outside the wall. We call it the Arab slums." At the mention of this place, the other members of the council murmured under their breaths. "If you pay this shit hole a visit, you may find a guide and a camel or two for this journey ... What do you know of Arabs or camels?"

A silence ensued, and I decided to break it. "There are neither Arabs nor camels in northern Germania," I said, drawing loud guffaws from the Consuls.

Garius and I decided we would visit this Arab slum soon. We thanked the Council for its generosity and said our farewell.

"Before you go," Solomon said, "I would like to know if you could remain awhile, Bern, so I can give you some tutorial on Hebrew and Arabic ... and the ways of both Jew and Arab."

"I—my master won't— "

"I'll take care of that one," Garius said

"In fact, I will need these tutorial sessions daily, at least two or three hours each afternoon." Solomon smiled at the Prefect and spoke in the new Greek. "Not allowing the German translator and scribe to attend mandatory tutoring would be a basis for his master's banishment, yes, Caius Juvus?"

The Prefect shrugged. "Do you think it should be so, Solomon?"

"Indeed I do."

"Then I shall have my secretary write the decree." The Prefect told Garius in Latin to wait awhile for a copy of a letter of decree he would need to bring back to young Master.

The old physician patted my shoulder and bade me follow him to an anteroom.

4

After nearly a week of sessions with Solomon, I gained confidence with basic polite conversation in both Hebrew and Arabic. I told Garius and young Master we should attempt a visit to the Arab slum, and I was surprised that young Master wished to come along. "Don't act so shocked," he told Garius. "I want to know what my father's silver is buying ... to the exact coin."

In the early afternoon we exited the city's southern or *back* gate where the people dumped their waste and refuse. I thought we could probably cut the stench with a knife, and the flies were thicker than dandelion spores in late spring back in Gallia Belgica. In the distance lay a cluster of tents flapping in the warm breeze. We knew not what we could find, ill or well, within that encampment, but with one look over our shoulders at the filth before the back gate, we hiked on, as the unknown of the tents appeared more hopeful and welcoming.

Once we reached the edge of the few dozen tents, the place looked deserted. No sound, and not a living thing stirred.

"Maybe they're all in the market square," said young Master.

"Maybe," Garius said, "but let's go among the tents a bit."

We stepped within the perimeter a hundred paces, and still not a sign of life. I said, "The physician taught me how to call out what we seek in their tongue … in Arabic." Garius nodded for me to proceed. "We seek a guide to take us south to Tarsus!" I cried out in Arabic. "We will pay a good price!"

"Gods, but that sounds horrid," young Master said.

It may have sounded horrid to him, but it produced results. Suddenly tent openings parted and several men in robes and turbans stepped out and came our way. We stood staring open-mouthed at the sudden throng and listening to the loud babble of their Arabic tongue. They were closing in and reaching for us. I noticed the panic in young Master's eyes. Garius just stood, his steely eyes focused forward on some unknown, unseen point, his jaw jutted out. I didn't know what to do, so I improvised. I grabbed the handle of Garius's sword with both hands and yanked it out of its sheath. Holding it in the air, I shouted, "Quiet!" first in Arabic and again in the new Greek.

The throng of Arabs immediately quieted and froze in place.

"If you will take us someplace where we can sit," I said in Greek, "we will tell you what we need, and anyone who wishes to make an offer may do so!"

A few of them leaned into each other and whispered amongst themselves. Then one of them beckoned to us with his fingers and jerk of his turbaned head. He and the throng stepped away. Garius followed the throng after retrieving his sword, and young Master and I followed him.

At a clearing on the northside of the encampment lay the remnants of a campfire surrounded by several stones. Many of the men—but not all—sat on the flat stones. Three stones remained unoccupied. An Arab man motioned to us, then waved his hand to the unoccupied stones. The three of us sat, and when young Master did so, there came a metallic clanging from beneath his tunic, causing all to crane their heads and direct their eyes toward his belly.

"So," one of the men began in his Arabic, " ... you want a guide to take you south?"

"Yes," I told the man who spoke.

"And what are you willing to pay for this service?"

"That is not how it works, and you know it," I replied. "We are a party of seven. We will carry what necessities we can—food, clothing, shelter, bedding, goods for cooking and eating. We will need a guide with probably two camels." I stood and squared myself to these men. "So, gentlemen, you know what to do now. If you are interested, start making your offers."

The man who first spoke laughed, nearly sending him off balance to tumble off the rock on which he sat. "The short golden-haired one not only speaks our tongue fairly well, but uses it to speak truth!" He narrowed his eyes at me. "What manner of man are you?"

"I am Germanic, from far north of here ... And I am a slave." I held up my wrists to display the metallic bands marking my servitude.

"Which of these men is your master?"

"My master remains at home far from here. He is the father of the one with the red nose, the one who tries but fails at acting like an important man."

"The one who fails hiding his wealth beneath his skirt?"

"The very one," I said, bringing laughter from all the Arab men.

"My little German slave friend," said the apparent spokesman for the slum, "though your Arabic is not bad, you still lack a bit. During this auction, the men will deal in Arabic ... How is your Greek?"

"Far better than my Arabic," I answered in the Greek Koine.

"Good. Then I will translate their offers to you in Greek."

"Then permit a little time to translate to these men," I said with a gesture toward Garius and young Master, "in Latin."

"So be it." He shouted the terms to the gathering. A guide with two camels. "Let the bidding begin!" he yelled out in Arabic.

Thereafter followed the most riotous cacophony of shouting voices. I fought to concentrate on the single voice shouting silver coin amounts in Greek. The first offers were obviously too high, just to test our limits and resolve. One offered a high amount, but only for three camels. I shouted back that we had no need for three. Back in Greek came the answer that the man was in possession of three camels, and what would he do with the third? It would be lonesome remaining here by himself. Another owned only one camel, but would be happy to make two trips. The high bids slowly lowered more acceptably. The lowest was one hundred silver coins, which we got tapered down to eighty.

"On one condition," Garius said. "Show us your camels."

The crowd dispersed back to the tents, and the man led us to the eastern edge of the encampment where we were met with an odor more putrid than that beyond the city's southern gate. The air was thick with flies, and amidst their buzzing came a sort of honking noise, like that of geese, though far less melodious. Lying in a mixture of mud and their own excrement, several dozen huge beasts chewed their cud.

The winner of the auction led us into the middle of these foul creatures to two branded on their rumps with the same odd symbol. He grabbed their reins in each hand and raised them. Both stood to the height of two normal men. They continued chewing and staring forward languidly.

Garius stepped beside each and patted their flanks. "They are strong. Well cared."

"You know camels?" I said.

"Enough to know if they are healthy or sick," he said. "Not enough to drive them ... I saw many in a campaign in north Africa. When I was a very young soldier," he added with a glint of reverie in his eyes. "It's a deal," he said, and the Arab shook his hand. They made an agreement for the man to meet us at the barracks gate right after sunrise in two days.

But as we reached the northern edge of the tent encampment, a lone Arab man stood in our path, blocking our progress. He held up both hands, indicating we should stop, and smiled broadly. "I talk with Roman words," he said in the worst Latin I had ever heard.

"That is good," I said. "Is there something you wish from us?"

"I take you to Tarsus. Two excellent camels."

"But we have already agreed with another," Garius said.

"You pay him eighty. You pay me fifty for same."

"No, thank you." Garius swept a hand to the side, asking the man to allow us passage.

"Wait!" young Master said. He stepped from behind the officer to his side. "You say you will take us for fifty silver coins?"

The man smiled and pointed toward the nobleman's belly. "Yes ... fifty."

"It's a deal!" young Master said.

I pointed back to the camel area. "But what about our deal with the other man?"

"Not worry about him," the Arab man said. "I know this man good. I change his mind."

"Well," I said, "if you and he come to an agreement, very well. You will meet us at the Roman military barracks gate after sunrise in two days."

"No, we must go in the dark. While city sleeps."

"Why?" Garius said.

"Not too hot at night. Travel at night, sleep under sun."

Young Master sealed the deal. "In two days. Before the gates are closed for the night."

The man bowed and stepped aside for our exit from the encampment.

5

I had long known of young Master's tendency to lean toward compulsive and obsessive behavior. His enslavement to the fruit of the vine was a common addiction among the ruling class. In some of the lower societies—from the working class to the classless caste of slaves—it was believed that all the Roman nobility did, especially in the Capital, was to eat and drink to excess, and engage in wild group sex. Such rumors would come naturally to the uninitiated among us. However, those rumors were only mostly true in Rome, but completely true, in young Master's case.

With only two nights remaining until we were to journey north, I discovered another of young Master's vagaries. In an uncharacteristically cheerful mood, especially after I had filled his wine cup for the fifth time, he announced that we—he and I, along with one of our soldiers as a bodyguard—were *going out* for the evening. After I enquired where we were going, I expected a terse none-of-your-business and a reminder that I was an ignorant barbarian, but instead he said, "I'll make our journey to Tarsus completely free of cost. In fact, we'll go with more silver in the coffers than what we have now." When I asked how we were to do that, he said, "Simple: I will find a game and help some of these Greek provincials part with their money!"

The ferryman's son accompanied young Master and me through the streets and alleyways. He didn't appear happy when ordered to come along, but he dared not risk insubordination.

On the corners of buildings at major road intersections, torches burned from bracket holds, but otherwise only weak lamps from within homes provided us enough light to keep us from walking straight into walls. I asked young Master if he knew where he would find the games. "All gambling places contain gamblers, and all gamblers shout in victory or defeat. It will sound like a riot. It is so in Rome, in Neapolis, even in Sicily ... I am certain it will be so in this gods-forsaken Greek provincial town."

True to his words, a distant clamor of shouting voices broke from somewhere ahead of us. We wove our way through the maze of alleyways, and the shouting grew louder. I could feel we were approaching the darkest, most forgotten corner of this city, as our steps disturbed the scurrying and squealing mice and rats all around us on the dirt paths. My eyes having grown accustomed to the dark, I noticed the ferryman's son had a tight grip on his sword's handle. And still the roaring grew.

Ahead, lit aglow by burning torches, a canvas covering stretched across the alley from within second-floor windows, likely from dwellings of those who ran these games producing the shouts. We reached the crowd of perhaps three dozen men screaming in Greek, Latin, and Hebrew, all facing a few men kneeling along the edges of a carpet stretched over the dirt floor. Young Master caught our attention and jerked his head toward the center. We stepped to the carpet nudging through the crowd. The air was thick with oil smoke from the torches and sweat from the packed crowd.

Shouts of protest over our intrusion erupted with each man we passed. The clamor caught the attention of the game manager and the dice throwers as we reached the playing carpet.

"Who are you to come to the center?" the manager hissed at us. "Go to the back and place your bets!"

Young Master reached inside his tunic and pulled out a thick pouch. He held it forward and rattled it, bringing forth a clinking of metal.

"So," the manager sang out with a wide smile, "the newest dice thrower has arrived! Please, sit down!" He beckoned to an edge of the carpet.

Young Master sat awkwardly with the weight of the chest belted to his waist nearly causing him to fall off balance face-first onto the carpet. He was saved such an embarrassing intro-duction to the crowd of gamblers when the ferryman's son and I caught him by both elbows and settled him to the ground.

I never understood these games, nor did I desire to. Yet when young Master placed the die with the spots into the cup, shook them, and tossed them onto the carpet, I per-ceived by the crowd's reaction and young Master's expression of joy, he had done well. In the crowd, silver coins exchanged hands, and before young Master, a small pile of coins grew a bit larger. For the following minutes, young Master rolled and his pile grew.

I glanced across the carpet and noticed the face I had not seen since the ship. Our eyes met each other's—my two and his one. "The German slave Bern!" he bellowed in his native Germanic tongue through the shouting voices.

"Raiko!" I answered in my first language. "It's good to see you again!"

He held out a bulging fistful of coins, then poured them into a pouch. "It's good to be here! I thank the gods you brought this Roman fancy boy to me!" He worked his way around the carpet to stand beside me. "Come!" he said in Latin, for the benefit of young Master. "Come with me and share my blessings with a special blessing!"

"I cannot ... I must stay with my master."

"Go with them," young Master said to the ferryman's son. "Ensure he comes back from wherever this one takes him." He closed an eye and focused the open one on Raiko, mimicking his defect. "Come back before the games end."

"That's more than enough time!" Raiko said.

I had no notion where Raiko planned to go to share his blessings with a special blessing, but I did wish to leave this tent, and I thought it best to take advantage of young Master's mood and uncharacteristic generosity while it presented itself. I bowed to young Master, and the three of us—Raiko, the ferryman's son, and I—wormed our way out of the crowd and into the alleyway where the choking air gave way to foul air. "Follow me," Raiko said in his guttural accented Latin.

Leaving behind the shouts of victory and cries of defeat, we wandered down alleyways guided by our dark-adjusting eyesight and the sound of our guide's sandals shuffling in the dirt. All about, as our sandals kicked bones and fruit pits tossed out of windows, rats and mice squealed in protest as they gave us way. It felt as though we trekked for an hour, and I thought perhaps we should return to young Master, when Raiko stopped before a two-story building with candles burning in all the upper windows.

"What's here?" I asked.

"Pleasure," Raiko said, "the best kind ... Women!"

"Whores, you mean," the ferryman's son said with a sneer. "This is a brothel."

"They have their work, you have yours." Raiko pulled his money pouch from his tunic and poured coins into a hand. "Hold out your hand," he said to me. I did so, and he placed two coins on my palm. "How about you, son?" he said to the Roman soldier. "I fared well at the games, and I'm willing to part with some of my winnings."

"I'll wait here," the ferryman's son said. "If it takes too long, I'll come up and fetch Bern before he catches his master's wrath."

"Suit yourself," Raiko said. "Come, Bern." He grabbed my elbow and we stepped inside.

At the bottom of a rickety set of steps sat an old woman holding a basket in her lap. She squinted up, her eyes like two of the dozens of wrinkles creasing her face. "Ah," she said to Raiko, "you again." She cocked her head at me. "And you bring a friend this time?" She held forth the basket, and Raiko dropped his two coins in. They landed on others with a metallic chink. He winked at me, and I followed his lead, dropping my coins atop his. "Go on up," the old woman said. "All five girls are free right now." She reached up into the murky dullness and grasped a leather cord. She gave it a yank, and from somewhere a bell rang out.

When we reached the upper floor, I perceived the bell was the signal for the girls to step out of their rooms. Five females, from quite young to past mid-life, Europeans mostly—though one at the end favored north African—stood before curtains. Raiko pointed to a young female with long flaxen hair. "Try her," he said in German. "She's not bad ... In fact, she may put a cramp in your good leg and balance you out!" He walked up to the dark-skinned girl, the one I surmised came from north Africa. "You're new," he said in his heavily-accented Greek. She parted the curtain. He stepped inside, and she followed, closing the curtain behind them.

I met the flaxen girl's soft blue eyes, and we stared at one another a moment. She parted her curtain and held it open, waiting. After a moment's hesitation, I stepped through the opening and stood staring at the cot and a carpet resting on a padding of straw. "Could you step inside more, sir?" a delicate voice said behind me. "There's just room for why you came here ... And you will probably want to remove that bow and those arrows from your shoulder."

I had become so accustomed to wearing the bow and quiver of arrows, they had become a part of me, as the Celts who adopted me in a long-ago world promised they would. I shuffled to a side and faced her. She released the edge of the curtain, and it fell to shut out the world with its flimsy protection. As if she were alone and perfunctorily preparing for a bath, she pulled her simple gown over her head and dropped it to the floor. Standing there naked before me, she was young and beautiful, in her impoverished way. I could not help thinking of my Lady Dalina, and how sensually she had removed her gown as she stood before me.

"So, how do you want it?" She cocked her face to the carpet on the floor. "Do you want me on my back? On my hands and knees?" She put her hands on her hips and waited a response, but I only stood looking into her emotionless eyes. "Come, tell me ... What do you want me to do?"

I felt such sorrow in my heart for such a beautiful young body beneath such a soulless face. "What do I want you to do?" I said, sitting on the cot. "I want you to cover yourself and sit beside me. I want us to talk with each other."

"I don't get paid to talk. What if my master finds I didn't serve you?"

"So you're a slave like me?"

"If you're a slave," she said, "you're not one like me. How is a slave allowed to visit a brothel as a customer?"

"It's a complicated story. But suffice it to say this will likely be the last such allowance from my master." I patted a spot beside me on the cot.

She lifted a folded blanket from the room's single chair and pulled it over her shoulders. She stepped over the padded carpet and sat beside me. "You use big words for such a short man. And your accent ... Where is your home?"

I smiled. "I'm a slave. I suppose my *home* is with my master, but I was born far north in Germania." I then gave her an abbreviated version of my life story. "So, as they say, I'm only passing through this city." She was staring blankly at the floor, so I reached over and held her chin between my thumb and forefinger, and aimed her face toward mine. "And you? Where is your home? Where was your home before you became a slave?"

"I am told I'm Thracian, but I was taken by the Romans when I was very little. I don't remember that home." Her eyes drifted off into a shadowy past. "I was told my village rebelled against the outpost soldiers and killed them all. I was told we lived free and happy for many months afterwards ... until the legion came for their revenge. I was sold and brought to this city. I served my master's family for years. But then after my master died, his wife—who never liked me and grew suspicious of her husband's designs for me—sold me to my present master."

"The owner of this brothel," I said. She nodded and sniffled softly. "I am called Bern. What is your name?"

"I am called Zia."

"Zia, you are my sister." I put my arm around her and pulled her into me. She buried her face in my chest and cried, her tears spilling down my torso. She clutched the fabric of my tunic and sobbed with a force that made us bounce on the weak cot. I stroked her hair and let her emotions run their course.

Out in the hallway, a gruff voice bellowed in the Germanic tongue. "Bern! Little Bear! Are you ready?"

"Almost finished!" I called. This answer produced a throaty chuckle.

"I'll be downstairs with your Roman friend!"

"All right! Just give me a few minutes more!"

"A few minutes more? Sure!" The throaty chuckle receded down the hall, and continued down the stairs. I kissed the top of Zia's head. "I must go now, Zia," I whispered.

"I understand." Her sobbing had left her. She sat up, leaned over, and kissed my cheek. "A few Roman nobles have had me on that mattress. And sons of wealthy Greek merchants ... But until you came here, no true gentleman has stepped past that curtain from the hallway ... I shall always remember you, Bern."

I turned and left her.

Down on the alleyway dirt, Raiko asked, "So how was she, Little Bear?"

"She was wonderful," I said.

"What did I say?" he bellowed, clapping my back.

At the tent, young Master had fared so well the crowd had dwindled to nearly half the size it was when we left him there. He was in the best mood ever as we walked home. He had to procure a bigger money bag, and my arms ached with the weight of all the coins by the time we reached the barracks.

6

Just before the closing of the city gates, our party of seven gathered outside the entrance to the military barracks. Young Master had won enough silver the previous evening to pay for the guide and his camels in addition to the mule and saddle he bought from the barracks stable. Soon the Arab guide emerged from the darkness. He had an edginess about him, as he continually took furtive glances all about the surrounding streets.

"Come, come," he said in his horrendous Latin, "we must go to gate now. Camels are tied there."

We nodded at one another and started toward the southern gate.

"No, no," he said. "This gate." He pointed to the west. "This side. Come now."

"The west gate?" Garius said. "Why the west gate? Isn't the southern gate the most direct route?"

But as the Arab guide had already shuffled away to the west, we all shrugged and followed, carrying all we owned with the added burden of food and water for the journey.

Over a hundred paces outside the western gate, the Arab guide untethered the camels from an olive tree, then re-tethered them to each other, one behind the other. With our help—save young Master—he secured all our belongings, food, and water onto the sides of the beasts. "So come," the guide said, "we go now." All the while he glanced here and there, as though spying for imminent danger.

"You," young Master said, "barbarian slave ... Help me mount my horse."

"It's a mule. And this man's name is Bern," said Garius.

I stepped beside the mule, knelt, and interlocked my fingers to form a step. Before young Master placed a sandal on them, he wiped the mud from it onto my back. Now in the saddle, he said, "All right, tell the foul Arab man to lead the way."

The guide cut a small branch from the olive tree and with a curved knife trimmed it to a slender crop. He struck it against the lead camel's flank and grabbed the leather reins. And so, in the dead of night we began our trek to Tarsus.

I noticed we travelled in a wide semi-circle, as though avoiding the Arab encampment, visible to the east by some distant torchlights.

CHAPTER THREE

INTO THE DARK HEART

1

None of us except the Arab guide were accustomed to staying awake all night while marching or riding, so the travelling proved a slow task on the first night. We halted at the break of dawn. And true to our guide's earlier word, we found it was necessary to stop and rest under the shade of stretched canvas during the daylight, for the sun soon scorched the surrounding parched land.

Before we settled onto carpets and blankets for a half a daylight's sleep—with a rotation of a single man on guard (except, of course, young Master)—we amused ourselves in our various ways to pass the time. The Arab guide busied himself brewing strong tea. Always the professional soldier and leader, Garius strode a wide circle around our mini-camp, scouring the landscape for signs of danger. The other soldiers rolled die onto a carpet, playing for small stones that lay all around us in abundance. I pulled sheets of parchment, a quill, and a small clay jar of ink from my pouch and set them on the carpet which would later serve as my bed. In Latin, I wrote scribblings of odd phrases that popped into my head. *My former gods had forsaken me. Therefore, I replaced them with new gods, who are proving nearly as impotent. Must I choose my own destiny? Alas, no, for I am but a mere slave.*

I placed another parchment beneath that one and rewrote the same text, but in the new Greek. I reread it several times until I was satisfied with it. I placed a third sheet of blank parchment beneath the two and rewrote the text yet again, but this time in the Hebrew text of the Jewish people. It felt a bit awkward writing from right to left, but I somehow understood why this had come about, the more I attempted to read and write it.

Though we were all beneath a stretched canvas, I sat in direct sunlight, for my status placed me at the edge of the group, my head barely covered. A shadow suddenly stretched over much of the three strips of parchment. I raised my face and squinted up to the darkened shape of Garius. He knelt beside me and studied my work.

"I understand the top one," he said. "The one below it is Greek, isn't it?"

"The new Greek they call the Koine."

"And the bottom? I've never seen such writing."

"Hebrew of the Jewish people."

He raised an eyebrow. "You learned that much of the language in the short time you spent with the physician?"

"I've learned a bit of it. I'm not sure if I've gotten it right. I can assure you it's far easier to write than to speak."

Garius continued his scrutiny of the script. "But do you really feel the gods are powerless to intercede for us?"

"I can speak only for how I feel, commander. As a very young boy, I watched as my father was beheaded and my mother was raped repeatedly. I'm sure she suffered the same death as her husband after I was taken away to be sold. My Germanic gods did nothing to prevent any of it, though I beseeched them to intervene." I noticed an error in the Hebrew script, so I repaired it. "And since then I've been under the Roman gods who live here as well but bear Greek names—or actually it's the Greek gods who bear Latin names in Rome. Yet I remain a slave. I wasn't born a slave, but I will die one." I thought of my old Celtic friend, the slave Vebru, who died facing the land where he was born a freeman. "I'm still alive, and as long as I help young Master get drunk enough early enough, I'm well-enough fed but not abused."

Garius took a quick glance to the others, then leaned into me. "I've been thinking on this for some time, Bern ... My father is a very rich and powerful man. He's politically smart, and keeps his office as senator while staying alive by always knowing which horse to back. When we return to Gallia Belgica, I will take leave for a few weeks and visit my family in Rome. And during that visit I will procure enough money from him to buy you from your master."

"And then I will be your slave," I said, finding and correcting another mistake in the scripts.

"Yes, and then you will be my slave," he replied. "Mine to dispense with as I wish ... Mine to set free ... Bern, you are too good and clever to be a slave."

I froze for a moment, my eyes wide with doubt. "But if I am freed, where will I go?"

"You could find work with your voice and quill in Rome. The government needs translators with the newly-conquered Roman citizens of Gaul and the north. Or you could live with the Celts, who have high regard for you. Or go back to the people of your birth."

"Would I be able to remain with Master's family?" I admit I thought only of the Lady Dalina.

"That would be your *former* master's decision, if he would be willing to pay for your services as a freeman." He patted my shoulder. "First, let's just make sure we succeed on this mission." He rose and returned to his inspection of our perimeter.

The hot days continued without rain, without even a mere wisp of a cloud to cast a ghost shadow over the baked earth. We lived as nocturnal creatures, though it was nearly impossible for all except the Arab guide to get much sleep in the choking heat. The man snored so loudly he provided serious competition for the noises emanating from deep within the camels' throats.

Garius, from his days in northern Africa, knew about the effects heat could have on a European out of his element. He also understood that without extreme discipline, the temptation for a man to guzzle an entire skin of water in one sitting under the stretched canvas could grow fierce. Therefore, he controlled all water, and the times and amounts for it to be drunk. We would line up, and our commander would hold a skin and squeeze a stream into each open mouth. He would order each man to swish the water around his mouth before swallowing. This included young Master, though the young nobleman would retreat to his carpet and contentedly suck on his flask of strong wine.

The fatigue of the march—steadily uphill—and the sapping of our energy by the sun god Apollo slowed our pace. In the heat I felt nearly no pain in my hip, yet still I limped along perhaps because my muscles were accustomed to such an awkward gait. The dullness of the monotonous heat lowered our alertness, as we discovered just over halfway to our destination.

2

For a few days we could tell the party approached mountains. Each step felt harder. We travelled through hilly country, and with each progress of the stars, the hills grew taller and wider. Then, during a daylight halt we beheld true mountains. Not as imposing as those separating the Germanic people from Italy—or at least according to stories I had heard of them. But still they would be difficult to pass.

We told the guide—whose name we still did not know, nor would we ever learn—of our concerns, and he laughed. "I come here many times, both ways. I know place we pass through. Not worry."

The next evening we reached the mountains. The going appeared simple for the camels and young Master's mule, but for the soldiers and especially myself there was much slipping and falling on the rocky surface, still damp from the previous morning dew. The guide stopped and dug into the dirt with a sharpened stick he retrieved from a bag draped over a camel. After a few minutes he held muddy water in a bowl made by his hands and brought it to the lips of the beasts, who drank greedily. He continued until they were sated, then marched on, holding the lead camel's reins. "Place ahead," he said. "Way through the mountains. We stop there."

As the sun rose in the east, we came to a narrow passageway—just wide enough for our party—that was a rift between two canyons. Our guide led us for another half league and declared the spot as our camp until sunset.

Garius glanced nervously before and behind us. "This doesn't feel safe," he said. "And besides, what if travelers want to pass? There's no room."

The guide laughed. "Travelers? We go now for eight days. Do we see travelers in all this time?" He laughed again and said nearly everyone who wishes to go from the north port of Sinope to the south port of Tarsus—and vice versa—rides on a cargo boat or navy ship. Only Arab guides and their customers go overland.

Our commander nodded but still his eyes darted backward and forward with a nerviness.

☙

The guide had apparently waited until we were all asleep except the shift watchman, walking several hundred paces behind us. We all started awake and stood wide-eyed and alert at the blast of a horn. The guide was galloping away on the mule. He held a goat's horn to his lips and blew, causing the single-note to bounce off the canyon walls.

Perhaps it was instinct, but all of us except the soldier well to our rear began stupidly running after the mule. We suddenly halted with the cry of the sentry behind us. We turned as one to see the man cut down by the swinging curved swords of two figures on horseback, their faces covered except for their eyes. Our man fell with blood spurting from several wounds. One rider raced toward us, and before the other followed him, he made sure the soldier was finished off as his horse crushed the man's head beneath its hooves.

With military precision, the party formed a semicircle, shields out, spears thrust forward, and swords at the ready. The soldier at point broke rank and ran at the men speeding toward him on horseback. The Roman military had learned long ago a foot soldier stands little chance against a man on horseback unless the latter doesn't know how to take advantage of his superior position. But such was not the case this time. The soldier knelt, held out his shield, and jammed his spear into the dirt behind him, holding the point at an angle to meet the steed's chest.

About five lengths away from the soldier, the horse veered wide to its right, well away from the kneeling man's reach. The horseman continued galloping toward us brandishing his curved blade and shrieking shrilly. This maneuver confused the soldier, who stood and turned toward us. The tactic of distraction worked for the horsemen, as the soldier had apparently forgotten the second rider, the one who dispatched the sentry. We watched in helpless horror as the horseman raced forward leaning to his right with his sword arm cocked for a strike. We shouted, we tried to motion to our man to lie flat, but he merely whirled back in time to face the blade swooping toward his neck. His head rolled several paces from the body, which stood for a few seconds before realizing life was over. It toppled to the dirt with blood spurting from the headless neck.

"Shields out! Battle formation!" shouted Garius.

The ferryman's son and the other remaining soldier trotted forward and stood five paces away on either side of their commander. Obviously battle formation was meant to be a semicircle around whatever elements the soldiers were tasked to protect, in this case young Master and his silver. But as we were down to three soldiers, the semicircle was reduced to a weak triangle. And still the horses charged toward us.

The next moments happened as impulse. I must have leaped upon the back of one of the lowing camels, for suddenly I fought for precarious balance as the beast stood. The height gave me an excellent view ... if only I could prevent myself from falling and possibly breaking my neck. As I tottered, my feet planted on either side of the creature's hump, I unslung my bow and pulled two arrows from the quiver. The lead horseman, obviously relying on his previous success, veered his steed to the right. I could sense the panic in my soldier-comrades. What if the horseman broke behind them while his partner charged from their front?

I squatted low behind the camel's neck and head, and notched an arrow. Just as the lead horseman reached even with the triangle's left flank, I had a clear view ... and my only chance. A moving target requires guesswork and precision at the same time. However, this horseman did not guide the steed to move erratically, as hinds or rabbits do. His path was straight and true. I pulled hard on the string and gave my aim a lead of about three horse lengths, then loosed the arrow.

I thought I had missed, and I notched another arrow. Then the rider lost his grip on the reins and slumped forward. Eventually, the bumping motion of the horse tossed him off, and the body fell into the canyon wall. I pulled back again on the string as the second horse began its jump over Garius. I loosed the arrow to time its meeting when the rider reached the zenith of his arc. The three soldiers found a riderless horse standing confused in our perimeter stamping his hooves and snorting. They converged on the rider, clutching at the arrow protruding through his chest. Their swords were raised at the ready, but Garius lowered and sheathed his, and motioned for the other two to do likewise.

I leaped off the back of the camel and ran to join them, nearly tripping over young Master, who lay covering his coin chest, his hands over the back of his head. I thought of informing him that he would likely have been hacked to death lying so instead of standing armed with a sword, but I checked myself and joined the others kneeling around the dying would-be assassin.

The man repeated a word. Garius and the other two soldiers looked at me, but I shook my head. "This is an Arabic word. I don't yet know this tongue very well. But if he lived here, he probably speaks this Greek Koine."

"Then ask him why he attacked us ... what he wanted," said Garius.

I repeated our commander's words in the new Greek. His eyes aimed the direction of young Master. "With that man's silver, ten of us live like kings in the desert for the rest of our lives."

I repeated his answer in Latin. "Ask him how he knows the one guiding us ... the one who owns the camels."

I asked the man the question, and he laughed, bringing globs of blood out his mouth. "The man is my brother. All three of us from the same father and mother. And he owns 10 camels. He stole them after killing owner." He laughed again, and with a great spasm, he stiffened and closed his eyes forever.

We carried his body to the canyon wall and laid him next to the other, supposedly his brother. Garius said, "Should someone say some prayers to their gods?"

"I don't know who their gods are," I said, but I silently asked Mercury to send them swiftly to wherever their people's souls went upon death.

The ground was solid, and resisted any of our spades, so we covered the bodies of our two comrades in stones, of which there were plenty between the canyon walls. We each said words of praise for them and added appeals to our favorite gods and goddesses for their passage to the next life.

We returned to the perimeter where young Master sat before his coin chest. The Arab's horse—a beautiful white stud—stood pawing at the scorched dirt. Garius patted the creature's neck. "Well, Master Bruno," he said, "you've made an excellent trade … That mule for this fine fellow."

"Do we continue to travel by night?" the ferryman's son asked.

Garius rubbed his chin. "Maybe. But one thing I know: I don't want to stay in this canyon. Could be others like these around, for all we know."

We agreed silently and collectively, for we soon began packing up. When we were ready and I helped young Master up to his new horse's back, Garius grabbed the lead camel's reins and tugged. The beast would not budge, merely sat there chewing cud. "Come on," Garius said, and tugged harder. "Come on, you bastard!" His muscles strained with the effort.

"Sir," I said, "may I try?"

"Bern, I don't mean to offend you, but how can you get him up? As short as you are, and weakened by that injury."

I pulled the crop from a pouch near the camel's front shoulder. I gently tapped the top of his head and said some words. Both camels immediately stood.

All the men—including young Master—laughed. "What in Caesar's name did you say to them?" said Garius.

"I have no clue. I merely repeated the phonetic sounds the guide or thief made each time we started out."

"You are too clever," Garius said with a chuckle. And with me—the world's first Germanic camel driver—in the lead, the lead beast's reins in my hands, we began our trek out from between the canyon walls.

3

The following day, or rather night, our progress was slow. There was a tension in the air. We would stop for several minutes and stand in a circle facing outward whenever our surroundings produced the slightest sound. As we had before, we camped under stretched canvas during the day, but none of us—save young Master—got much real sleep even if we were not taking a shift on guard.

On our second day out of the canyon, we found the mule, now a carcass nearly stripped of flesh by carrion birds and jackals. "That bastard rode him to death," Garius said. "Now he's on foot, but how long already?"

"He has no water," said the ferryman's son. "It's all here." He pointed up at the skins and flasks on the camels.

"Don't lose your focus, don't drop your guard," said Garius. "His mother may have produced a dozen murderous sons."

According to the stars it was midnight when we stopped as we heard a faint moaning coming from the dark ahead of us. Garius motioned for us to stay. "I'll check it."

The young soldier whom I knew nothing of because of his taciturn nature stepped forward. "No, sir," he said. "If anything happens to you, we have no commander." He stepped toward the sound. A moment later, his voice called out. "You can come now! It's the camel thief!"

Except for young Master, we gathered around the prone body. He opened his eyes to us and registered recognition in his raised eyebrows and widened eyes. "Need water," he rasped in his broken Latin, "or I die."

"Even if we give you water," Garius said, "you will still die."

"My brothers ... they not come to meet me."

"No," said Garius. "It is you who will go to meet them. You killed the owner of the camels. You stole them. And you intended to kill us." He drew his sword from its sheath. "If any of you wish not to see this," he told us, "go back to the camels."

We all stood and backed up to give him room, but we remained and looked on as our commander knelt and raised his sword. "In the name of the Roman Empire, in the name of the Emperor, Tiberius Caesar Augustus, I sentence you to death." Grasping the handle with both hands, he brought the blade down heavily to decapitate the man, whose scream came to an abrupt end.

We continued south, guided by the stars, for another three nights until we climbed a gradual, gentle slope. Below us were the flickering lights of fires—lamps, torches, and candle flame.

"Tarsus?" asked the quiet soldier.

"Do you smell salt water?" said Garius.

"No, sir."

"Tarsus is near the water. But whatever this place is, from there we can find the right way to Tarsus."

"Commander Garius," I said. "Do we go now?"

He studied the question in silence for a moment. "Good point," he said. "To their eyes, we may appear a band of brigands stealing into their town in the middle of the night." He pointed back at the camels. "And I'm not sure how we could explain those two."

"In the morning," I said, "you can go into the town with whomever you wish. I'll remain behind with the camels and wait for you."

Young Master snorted. "Alone? And then when we're too far to catch up to you, run away?"

Garius stepped to the young nobleman and grabbed the horse's reins. "When are you going to learn that this man is the reason we are here? He saved your life more than once!"

"He's not a man," young Master said. "He's a barbarian, and what's more, he's my property!"

"Maybe for now," Garius said, "but that can change."

"What is that supposed to mean?" young Master said snarling.

"Someone could buy him from your father. Then Bern's fate will be in his new master's hands."

Young Master narrowed his eyes and scrutinized Garius. "I think I see what you're planning. But my father made it clear. I act in his name. I do whatever I wish in the interest of the family business."

Garius cocked his head. "Yes, but what does that have to do with this little disagreement?"

Young Master gave our commander his usual smirk. "It is my right to dispose of my slave as I wish. So he has talent for mimicking various tongues like some parrot, but that has served to little advantage in my father's province. As soon as we make our trade connection, I'll find a slave auction, and be done with this barbarian forever!"

Garius's eyes flashed. He pulled his sword and held it before his chest. "Over my dead body! I swear it!"

"A strong oath," young Master said. "I would be careful if I were you. The gods may be listening."

Garius sheathed his sword and faced the eastern horizon. "Light is breaking soon," he said. "At dawn, Bern and I will go into this town and find the way to Tarsus." He looked to his two soldiers. "You two stay with the Governor's son until we return."

The ferryman's son and the quiet one showed obvious disappointment in their faces, but accepted their orders like the good soldiers they were.

Garius and I were given a long examination under the Roman gate guard's eyes before he let us in, saluting a *Hail Caesar*. "I have an idea," Garius whispered to me after we reached a dozen paces inside. He called to the guard. "Could you tell me where to find your commander?"

"Why? I have done nothing wrong."

"No, no," Garius chuckled. "We seek information. The safest way to Tarsus."

"You don't need my commander. I can tell you that," the guard said. "On the other gate opposite this one, the road leads from Ikonium to Tarsus."

"A Roman road?"

"Yes. The flat stones were laid over the old Greek path only a few years ago. It's in good shape and very safe ... Soldiers of the Empire patrol it."

"How far to Tarsus?"

"A good day by foot."

Our stay in Ikonium lasted that long. Garius thanked the guard and gave him two silver coins. We exited the gate to return to our party.

Just after dusk veiled the landscape into a dark gray, we circled the town of Ikonium until we found the paved road. We decided to trek beside the road until the stars became bright, and then camp for the night. From now on we would be the diurnal creatures we were born to be.

CHAPTER FOUR

MEETING THE TENTMAKER

1

The last leg of our journey to Tarsus passed smoothly. There was a good deal of traffic between Ikonium and Tarsus going both directions, and our party received a share of gawking. We must have been something quite odd to view, three Roman soldiers, a nobleman, and a limping German trekking south with two camels. The Roman road was well-engineered and well-built, as we expected, and before dusk we stood before the northern gate of the great trading city of Tarsus.

With the military authority wielded by Garius, and the signet ring bearing the seal of a Roman provincial governor on young Master's finger, we were granted quick entry without question. We were all still feeling disoriented and fatigued after spending nearly three weeks as nocturnal creatures, so we found lodging as our first priority. We decided to sell the camels during the next day and use the money earned to fund any further room and board we may require in the coming days. Garius and young Master agreed we should focus on finding a trading connection as soon as possible, and shortly thereafter purchase berths on a ship to Italy or, if possible, southern Gaul. We found lodging at an inn with a stable for young Master's horse and even the camels, for which we had to pay an extra fee.

I can speak only for myself, but I believe from the contented faces of the others in our party the following morning, they also slept soundly through the night. Although I slept on the floor at the foot of young Master's bed, I didn't feel the stiffness I had felt every morning in the military barracks at Sinope. We ate a hearty breakfast from our own provisions and set out in two groups to seek a point of contact for trading. All were surprised, by their expressions, when young Master offered to take me with him and venture into the city to search for the man we needed. This was the first time in the entire journey he had exhibited the slightest interest in the mission. I supposed he had grown weary of this life of adventure and uncertainty, and he desired to find success as soon as possible so he could board a ship bound for home. After we finished our breakfast Garius departed with the ferryman's son and the quiet one.

Before young Master and I ventured out together a different direction from the soldiers, I helped him strap the large chest containing the mission's treasury onto a leather belt and around his waist, all of which he covered with his tunic. "Master, why don't you let me ease your burden and carry the chest?"

He sneered at me. "If you could see yourself through my eyes, you would know why!"

I hoped that my indignation remained hidden, but I wished he could see himself through my eyes.

We found a marketplace where the shouting in multiple tongues provided a sound like so many different species of birds singing in the late afternoon in the gardens back in the colonia. I began straight away inquiring buyers and sellers. I received a "I come here to buy fruit!" in Hebrew, and "Do I look like I would know someone so rich?" in the new Greek.

Young Master noticed a group of Arabs under a canvas sharing a skin of wine. He leaned to me and said, "Give me a minute," and motioned me to stay.

He approached them and spoke. One waved at a place beside him on the bench. Young Master sat with his back to me, and after a few moments he rose and rejoined me. I noticed a pouch lay on the table before the place where young Master had sat, and I hadn't noticed it before. One of the Arabs snatched it up and tucked it inside his robe.

"So let's go back to the inn," young Master said. I felt the curiosity boring into me, but I knew it was not my place to ask him about his meeting with the Arabs. All the way to the inn, though, he carried himself with a light, airy mood.

2

As we chewed on the last of our dried meat, young Master suggested we try visiting the taverns where the wealthy were more likely to meet and discuss the business of the day over le and wine during the evening. "Yes," Garius said, "that makes sense. Those who know trading with the east will be of the leisure folk." So we waited until the sun gave the last of its light, then headed into the city center.

We reached the widest, most visited street in the center, and I could smell the ale and wine and hear the lively banter and laughter of soon-to-be drunken revelers just warming up. Men in the dress of Greeks, Romans, and Jews stepped into and out of taverns on both sides of the street. "The slave and I will work on this side," young Master said, pointing to the left, "and you three do the other." Garius leered at him, but cocked his head at his soldiers and stepped away to the right side of the street, and they followed him.

After young Master and I veered down the left side, we passed three Arab men standing together talking. I thought perhaps they may have been the ones young Master spoke with at the market, but I must confess they all appeared the same with their covered heads, long robes, and bearded faces. I noticed after young Master saw them, he gave the slightest glance to his left and what seemed to me a nod. But with the failing sunlight, nothing could be certain.

The third tavern we entered gave us a lead. Young Master and I sat at a table occupied by some old Greeks. While young Master drank wine, I listened to the gentlemen, and heard them speaking of a new trade route bringing in spice and silk. This was my chance, so I took it.

"Excuse me, my good gentlemen," I began in the new Greek, "but my partner and I have travelled from a western province, sent by the Governor of Gallia Belgica. We seek a connection for trade … for goods from the East … Would any of you kind sirs be interested, or know of a possible connection?"

"You speak our Koine quite well," one of them said. "I know someone who is always on the lookout for deals. Go to the road inside the wall on the southside where you'll find other roads leading south to the docks. Find the largest gambling games under a tent connected to a tavern. There you should find a Jew we know as the Tentmaker. He's the one you seek, I promise."

"How will we know him?"

"Simple," the man said. "The man with the biggest pile of coins before him. Saul the Tentmaker always wins." He clapped me on the shoulder and winked.

I waited for young Master to finish his wine, the seventh of the young evening, and told him what I had learned. When we stepped out of the tavern, he said, "We'll wait here and discover which tavern they exit. Then we can surprise them with what we know."

So we stood there, young Master and I, waiting beside the door. After many moments, Garius and the two soldiers stepped out of a tavern. Young Master never touched me in a show of affection, for I was nothing to him but a filthy barbarian, yet to my shock he put an arm around my shoulders and hugged me to him. I was facing the tavern we left, when suddenly I heard cries behind me. I was far stronger than young Master, and broke away from him easily. What awaited me across the street changed the course of my life.

Garius was curled in the fetal position clutching his bloodied belly, and beside him the quiet soldier lay, bleeding out from a slashed throat. Two of the three Arabs I saw earlier had the ferryman's son pinned against a wall. They struck at him with their curved swords, and he fought them off as best he could. The third Arab emerged from the shadows and approached his partners.

I knew the ferryman's son would meet his end without any help. I slipped the bow from my shoulder and pulled two arrows from my quiver. I aimed quickly and released an arrow into the neck of one of the swordsmen. He fell with a shriek. I notched another arrow and pulled on the string. The one who intended to join the two fighting the ferryman's son shouted to his partner. He ran down the street, and his partner ran the opposite direction. My arrow landed into a door.

I darted across and knelt beside Garius. His face had become ashen. I looked at his wound and thought there was more of his blood in the dirt than inside his body. "Lord Garius," I said, "I'll run and find a doctor."

"No, my friend. This is my end ... But I want you to know that before we left the inn ... I sent a letter to my father ... I asked him to buy you from the Governor ... and then release you. Soon you will be ... your own man. By the time the ship you board arrives in Italy ... you'll be free ..." Garius smiled and closed his eyes. I clutched his hands, and through my blurry vision glanced over at the quiet one, who died without a sound, as he had lived.

I looked up. Young Master gazed down at the scene as though he were observing dead insects. "Well," he said, "I suppose we should make some arrangements for them."

The ferryman's son raised his sword, his eyes blazing with vengeance. I stood and put my hands on his shoulders. "Let us take care of the dead we have, and not add to their numbers," I told him. He lowered his sword and slid it into its sheath.

We received permission the next day from the local consulate to burn them both outside a temple dedicated to Jupiter. Although the people of Tarsus knew neither of these men, several gathered to make the sending-off a respectable ceremony.

The morning following the funeral for Garius and the quiet one, young Master made plans to find the games we had heard of. The ferryman's son motioned me to him and whispered, "I know Commander Garius wanted you safe, so I'll take his place and dedicate myself to your protection."

"No, please. My fate is in young Master's hands. He will sell me, and I can only hope the gods will favor me by placing me in good hands. There will be no ship to Italy for me." I put a hand on his shoulder. "You should leave us now. Your part in our mission is over. We would not have gotten this far without your help. But now we should part ways."

He took a deep breath and released it slowly. "Yes, Bern, you're right," he said. "I'll gather my belongings and find the military barracks. Perhaps I can sell my services to the Roman navy." He smiled. "I was born to serve on the water. I am the son of a ferryman."

"That you are," I said, clapping him on the shoulder. "May Neptune protect you!" We clasped forearms in the Roman fashion, then hugged like brothers. When he entered the inn to pack his belongings into a bag, that was the last I saw of him.

Now of the mission's original party, a debauched young Roman nobleman and a Germanic slave were all that remained.

3

When it became dark, young Master and I walked south until we reached the road inside the southern city wall. We strolled east until eventually we heard shouting and laughter, and the farther we wandered, the louder the noise until we found the source. Under a tent for a tavern's overflow was a temporary gambling hall.

We entered the place, thick with oil-lamp smoke, and I was struck by the ferocity of all the voices in all the tongues. I heard some of everything I had learned at least bits of, excepting my native tongue and Gaulish Celtic. Amid the grumblings of the attendees, we worked our way to the center of the huge gathering's focus: three men sitting cross-legged around a carpet. One after the other rolled die from a tumbler. Indeed, there was a nice pile of coins before one of the men, apparently a Jew from his garb. The other two men, a wealthy Roman merchant, it appeared, and a Greek, shook their heads at their losses.

The Jew's gaze landed on young Master. "You appear to be someone of wealth," the Jew said in the new Greek. "Well, if you've brought money and wish to play, there is room for one more."

"Are you the one they call the Tentmaker?" young Master said in Latin.

"You don't speak the Koine?" the Jew said. After he received no reply, he said, "Apparently not ... Well then, my Roman friend," he continued in Latin, "yes, that is what people have taken to calling me."

Young Master unstrapped the coin chest from his tunic belt. He sat at an unoccupied side of the rectangle and set his coin chest before him. I stood behind him.

"You have a rather short shadow," the Tentmaker said in the new Greek, and the crowd exploded in laughter.

"What did he say?" young Master asked.

"I don't know, Master. It was some slang with which I'm not familiar." I knelt and spoke in a low tone into his ear. "Master, please pardon me ... but is it wise to gamble with your father's silver?"

"I'm using my father's silver for the mission. When the Jew has lost most of his pile to me, I'll later be at an advantage to strike a deal favorable to my father, who will be well-pleased. I may not be a soldier trained with sword and shield, but I'm an expert in the war of business and gambling ... Now shut up, and know your place!"

The games continued with young Master in them. When young Master rolled and won, I noticed a slight grin from the Tentmaker. Some of the coins before the Jew moved before young Master. This continued until both the Greek and the Roman merchant raised their palms in defeat and vacated their places, leaving only the Tentmaker and young Master.

The Tentmaker smiled, and I felt he had worked up to this point, that he had planned it all along. For now, the luck quickly favored him. Sweat dripped off young Master's face as roll after roll of the die, more of the mission's silver slid over to the Jew's pile of winnings. I thought when the chest had half emptied, young Master would quit the games, but his addiction to gambling took full control, and the Tentmaker knew this. The games rolled on.

The Tentmaker offered to change the game to the high-risk version, where the die roller calls out two numbers. If the die produce either of the two, he wins double the bid, and he rolls again. If not, the roll goes to the opponent who calls out his two numbers. Sometimes young Master would roll a favorable number matching one of his calls, and he would greedily take coins before him. But most of the time he failed, yielding to the Tentmaker, whose calls were more often correct than not.

The crowd roared with both success and failure, which fueled young Master's desire to go on. The attendees made bets with one another, which added to the volume of the cheers. I felt like I was watching a dog fight back in my childhood village. Young Master emptied the last of the silver coins onto the carpet, and I wanted to intervene, I wanted to plead with the Jew to restore young Master at least a quarter of the silver so we could leave with a semblance of our dignity. But I was rooted mutely to my spot.

Young Master lost the last of his father's gift of silver, and I knew we were doomed to beg on the streets for food. I hoped to beg for enough money to send a letter to the colonia in hopes of finding passage back. What I heard next from young Master's lips sealed our fates. "I am not finished!" he shouted in Latin. Sweat dripped from his chin, and his eyes were widened like those of a frightened horse. "I have more!" He rose, stood behind me, and shoved me forward. "My slave is talented in languages. He speaks, reads, and writes every tongue spoken in this place, and others as well!" He was breathing heavily. He gazed at the Tentmaker and smiled with no mirth in his eyes. "He's worth at least fifty silver coins!"

The Tentmaker merely grinned, meeting young Master's wild gaze. "If he can do all that," he said in Hebrew, "then he would be worth more to me. I would treat him as a secretary, not a slave ... Would you like that?" he asked me.

"As you wish," I replied in Hebrew.

"We roll five times and call the numbers!" he shouted in Latin. "The first to win three times is the victor!"

"And when I win, what do I get?" said young Master.

The Jew waved his hand over the pile of silver coins before him. "You retain your lost fortune ... And you and your slave leave this place."

"So be it!"

"I give you the advantage," the Tentmaker said. "You have first roll."

Young Master snatched up the tumbler and began shaking. It was the first time of the night I could hear the die rattling about inside, for all were quiet as if holding their collective

)reath. "Five and ten!" young Master shouted in Latin and released the die onto the carpet. A *six* and a *four* showed. The crowd roared and coins were exchanged. Young Master cast a cocky smirk over to the Tentmaker, then handed him the die in the tumbler.

The Tentmaker shouted, "Three and nine!" in the Greek Koine. The numbers showing were *five* and *four*. The two stood even at one win apiece.

After the noise from the crowd settled, young Master shouted, "Four and eight!" He tossed the die, to the result of a *three* and a *four*. He heaved a noticeable sigh and slid the tumbler to the Tentmaker.

The Jew waited for the silence he needed and shouted, "Six and eleven!" He tossed the die. The crowd held their silence until the die came to a stop, showing two sets of *three*. The crowd erupted as young Master's opponent held the two-to-one advantage.

Young Master's sweat dripped into his empty coin chest. The Tentmaker handed over the tumbler and die, and young Master shook them violently. "Six and nine!" he called. The tumbler emptied, and the die rolled onto the carpet to the silence of the held breaths. Two *fours* showed.

The Tentmaker gathered the die and stuffed them inside the tumbler, which he had to pry from young Master's fingers. "Two," he said to the crowd's gasp, " ... and eleven." Young Master snorted at the improbability of either number. The Tentmaker jiggled the die within the tumbler and released them. One came to a stop showing a *two*, bringing a shriek of joy from young Master. The other bumped into it, changing its number to *one* and then came to a stop also showing a *one*. The crowd exploded.

Young Master's eyes widened. "That isn't fair!" he shouted. The Jew beckoned to me with his fingers, and I stepped to him from behind young Master.

"Bring me a parchment, quill, and ink!" shouted the Tentmaker. Soon, members of the crowd produced the requested items. "I will have my new translator and scribe write the deed of sale, which you will sign," he said to young Master. "Do you write Greek?" he said to me.

"At present, sir—um, Master—only the old Greek of the poets and playwrights."

The Tentmaker said, "That will give our transaction more of an air of authority."

Working with the Governor—young Master's father—I was familiar with such documents. "I need to know two things," I said to the Jew. "The amount of the transaction, and your name."

Then, with the information, I wrote the bill of sale:

I, Caius Bruno Tavarius, son of Caius Cinna Tavarius, governor of Gallia
    Belgica, hereby sell the slave known as Bern from northern Germania to
    Saul of Tarsus, for the sum of a single silver coin.

After the ink dried, I handed the document to my new master, the apparent Saul of Tarsus, and he dropped wax from a candle below my text. He rose from his place and carried the parchment, along with the ink-filled quill, to young Master.

"I see you wear your signet ring," said the Tentmaker. "Please press it into the wax and sign below."

My former master stared at the document for a minute after I placed it on the carpet in front of him before pressing his ring into the wax and writing his signature with a shaky hand.

The Tentmaker plucked a silver coin from his winnings and tossed it to my former master. "There," my new master said after I handed him the bill of sale. "I am sorry your greed led you to your present status. If you wish, I shall loan you some money to return home and make arrangements to secure repayment from your family."

"No!" said my former master. "We play on!"

Saul the Tentmaker cocked his face and narrowed his eyes. "We play on? But you have nothing with which you can play."

"We play on," said my former master, "and if you win, my life is forfeit to you. I have nothing to lose."

The Tentmaker rubbed his chin whiskers. "But if you win?"

"If I win, I receive half my silver back from you."

"Mm-hmm ... So do you have a game to propose?"

My former master nodded. "Before we toss, we call a number. Whichever of us is closer is the winner."

My new master clapped his hands and smiled. "I like this game! Shall we go two out of three?"

"Yes! Two out of three it shall be!"

"You roll first," my new master said.

My former master shook the tumbler. The silence in the tent was so strong we could hear my former master's nervous breathing. "Six!" he shouted and tossed the die onto the carpet. A *four* and a *two* showed. He shrieked with joy, and the crowd erupted.

He scooped up the die, placed them in the tumbler, and offered it over to my new master, who held out his hands. "I must concede this round to you. Roll on."

Again my new master held his breath as he shook the contents. "Seven!" he shouted. When the die came to a rest, a *five* and a *six* showed.

My new master gathered the die and placed them into the tumbler. "Four!" The die showed two *threes*. The game stood at one win each.

"Eight!" called my former master after a vicious shake . The die showed a *one* and a *three*.

The Tentmaker gathered the die and held them in his hand. He stared hard at the young Roman nobleman. "I propose we halt this game," he said. "I will give you enough money for passage to Rome and expenses."

My former master's eyes showed the whites like those of a rabid dog. His nostrils flared. "I will accept no charity from a filthy, barbaric Jew!" he hissed through clenched teeth.

My new master shrugged. "After this roll, you just may become the property of a filthy, barbaric Jew." He placed the die into the tumbler and shook it a few seconds. In the complete silence, he calmly said, "Two." He released the die, and when they stopped rolling, my former master's fate was sealed. The die showed a *two* and a *three*. The former Roman nobleman lost his freedom by a single dot on a wooden cube.

❧

My former master attempted to escape the tent, but was tacked and held to the floor by several men. In the end manacles were secured around his wrists, and his ankles were shackled with a chain long enough to allow him a regular pace. My new master paid three men to remain with the new slave in a horse stall outside his large dwelling.

My new master and I entered the house. He introduced me to his wife, her bonded servant, and his five children, aged four to twelve. He fed me and showed me to my room on the upper floor and asked if I needed anything before I would sleep. I was amazed at my good fortune and thought to say I required nothing. Then I realized: such a wealthy, educated man must own books. "Master," I said, "do you have any books I can read?"

"Of course," he said. "Any particular topic or author? Any preferred language?"

"Anything. Anything at all."

He led me downstairs to his office where he conducted business. His table, a disorganized mess of parchment and ledger books, stood against a bare wall. Opposite was a wall lined with shelves, on which lay rolled parchment and leather-bound books, all arranged in no order at all. "Well?" he said. "Take a few with you. You live with me now, so there's time enough to read it all, if you so desire."

From the bottom shelf, I scooped up what my arms could hold, and carried my night's treasure back upstairs to my room. *My* room. With *my* bed. And at least for this evening, with *my* books. I set it all on the bed. I sat, opened a book, and began.

❧

I awoke to a knocking on the door. I experienced a weird flashing of images and phrases from the previous night's reading. My new master was a practical businessman, and the books I read were of the geography of lands in the east, which were the points of origin for silk and spice trade with the west, and of the customs and beliefs of the peoples who dwell there.

"Bern?" my new master called. "We leave after breakfast to visit the Magistrate's Office with that Roman slave. I'll need your services."

I was given my own wash basin and a new set of clothes, and after a quick meal we were off to the city center. It was master Saul, my former master Bruno, a hired guard for Bruno, and myself. In only a few minutes we stood before the Magistrate, who studied the bill of sale I wrote and a few scribblings from men who witnessed the transaction at the games. He stamped and signed the bill of sale. Master Saul paid the fee, and we left for the market square. "If we hurry, we shall secure a place for today's offerings," master Saul whispered to me in Hebrew.

It brought back the memory of my time on the platform as potential buyers barked out their bids. I remembered my own machinations to become someone's—anyone's—property back then when I was but a wee child. Master Saul was able to place my former master in the line of slaves for sale. He paid the entrance fee, and we joined the audience to await my former master Bruno's fate.

My former master was number *eighteen* on the list, so the wait was long. Master Saul seemed bored as he shifted balance from one foot to the other. But I? It was exciting, listening to the frenzied shouts in so many tongues. I also realized in a corner of the market square, beside the larger dome of the temple, stood a statue of my patron god Mercury. I wondered if former master Bruno could apply to this deity as did I when I was on the sales platform. Tarsus was much further developed than the fortress between the two rivers in Germania where I was bought by young Master's family. This city had no doubt stood for many generations, perhaps several centuries.

The slaves being sold displayed more variety than those on the day I became property of the House of Tavarius. Every shade of skin I had ever imagined—and a few more—stood before the crowd who shouted its bids. Tantalizing young females and muscular young males from all corners of the Empire were bought for enormous sums of silver.

Finally, my former master Bruno stood alone on the platform. The auctioneer, a rotund Greek with a shiny bald pate, shouted his sales pitch in the new Greek Koine to the silent crowd. "Now we have before you a Roman citizen—I correct myself—a *former* Roman citizen, born and raised in the great city itself. From what I understand, he stands as slave for sale due to acts abominable to the Emperor. So, what say you? Who shall open the bidding?"

In the silence, I could hear men breathing. Finally, a voice shouted out, "Is there any muscle hiding under all that flab?" The silent crowd suddenly erupted with laughter.

"Amusing," the auctioneer said as he stroked his chin whiskers. "But back to the business at hand ... What is the first bid for this slave?"

The laughter had waned to murmurs, which gave way to uncomfortable silence. Since nothing was happening, those who came not to buy but to be entertained began to leave and drift toward the marketplace stalls. The auctioneer begged the crowd. "Come! Surely you won't let this slave go unbid." He looked down at my new master Saul and shrugged. Still the crowd thinned down to only a dozen, Master Saul and I among them. "Any price at all that any of you bid, and you take this slave home!" He shrugged and raised his eyebrows at my new master.

Master Saul leaned down to me, whispering, "There are times when you must cut your losses to rid yourself of damaged goods."

A tall, burly blond man, dressed in an expensive silk robe and some exotic fur pelt around his iron neck and ropy shoulders, stepped from the rear and bumped men out of his path as he made his way to the platform. The auctioneer continued his plea to the crowd, but received no answering bids. Finally the blond man raised a hand.

"Do we have a bid for this item?" the auctioneer said.

"It appears not," said the blond man in an accent faintly familiar to me. "That is, unless you will accept my meager offer of four silver coins."

The auctioneer stepped to the edge of the platform and beckoned Master Saul forward. We stepped up, and with a wince, the auctioneer bent his bulk closer to us. "I believe this may be the best we can do. I suggest you take this slave back home and put him to work in the fields until he resembles the kind of working slave buyers want."

"My fields are doing well, thanks to the slaves I presently own," said my new master. "I have no use for an idiot Roman, whose only talent is the guzzling of wine ... Sell him for the four silver coins you've been offered."

"But with my commission, that means you leave here with only three."

Master Saul smiled. "Then I trade this worthless lump of flesh for a small family banquet ... So be it. Four silver coins it is!"

The auctioneer chewed on his lower lip and heaved a massive sigh from his ample belly. "As you wish, then." He rose and shouted to the diminished crowd, "Sold to the citizen from Germania for four silver coins!"

My former master was led down the steps to stand shackled before the German, who tucked the bill of sale into his robes. He raised a hand and motioned with a snap of fingers. Two slaves, both mixed between Greek and Arab, came forward and grasped Bruno the slave by his elbows. "Where are you taking me?" my former master said in Latin, the only tongue he knew.

"Someday to my villa at Augusta Vindelicorum," the German said.

"You're a German!" Bruno's master nodded. "Put me back on the platform! If I'm to be sold as a slave, let it be to a true Roman!"

"Good luck with that one!" I shouted in my native tongue.

The German whirled and stared a moment at me before speaking. "From the north, according to your accent ... And how do you know this one?" he said with a nod to Bruno.

"He was a brutal master."

"There is a people far east of here who believe in something they call karma, sort of an equalizing. However, I am not a brutal master, nor do I plan to be." He faced his new slave. "But if I cannot train you to behave," he said in Latin for Bruno's benefit, "I will sell you to a brothel where you will know the real meaning of karma." He bowed to us. "Come," he said to his slaves. "We must hasten to meet with a camel caravan in Antioch bringing spices from the east!"

They departed through the marketplace crowd, and I never laid eyes on Caius Bruno Tavarius again. My former master who loathed Germans was now property of a German at the price of four silver coins. One less than his family paid for me.

CHAPTER FIVE

MY NEW MASTER'S BUSINESS

1

I served Master Saul faithfully. Although I was still owned property, I could have lived out the rest of my life contented as his interpreter, his scribe, his conversationalist, his occasional partner in less-than-acceptable exploits.

He proved the penultimate businessman. This man could sell anything to anyone, and he could talk another man into selling him anything he wished for a quarter of what it was actually worth. Thus, he made his family among the wealthiest in Tarsus, and possibly on the entire coast.

"So," he once said to a man passing by whose donkey was weighted down with copper, "where do you go with your load?"

"To the docks where I can sell this copper."

Master Saul looked the direction where the docked ships awaited. "Too bad for you."

"Why do you say that?"

"A rich vein of copper has been discovered in the mountains north of the capital. The empire has all the copper it needs. In fact, there's a glut in the copper trade." He sighed at the pots full of the reddish metal. "I'm afraid you won't be able to sell even a handful of your goods."

The poor man hung his head. "What am I to do?"

"I shall make you an offer. At least you won't have travelled here for nothing, and I can store the copper until I find a market elsewhere."

And so the deal was made. Master Saul sent another slave to fetch a mule and a cart from his home, and together we filled it with the man's copper. The man steered his donkey back the way he came, never to learn he had been duped, and he could have sold his wares at the dock for a handsome sum.

On the way home I brooded in silence. I had never taken part in hoodwinking an innocent man, and though I had no active role in the deceit, I still felt unclean.

Master Saul broke the silence. "So you feel I was wrong, do you?"

"It is not my place to say, Master."

"So you feel I was wrong."

"Yes, Master."

"In your world of honor and scruples, yes, what I did would certainly be considered incorrect."

"What other world is there, Master?"

He patted the money bag beneath his robe. It made the metallic jingle. "The world of profit, young Bern. The world of profit, which leads to the world of leisure and pleasure. Making profit, young Bern, is part of the art of business, and business is a form or war."

"Where did you learn this art, Master? From your father?"

He reached for the mule's reins and pulled back hard. The beast stopped in its tracks. "I learned precious little from my father. At least not what he wished me to learn." Master Saul stared off toward the center of the city as if bringing some memory of it to the present. "My father was one of the most learned rabbis Tarsus had ever known," he said. "And he believed I should follow in his wake."

"Rabbi?" I said. "What is a rabbi?"

He stroked his chin and thought on his answer. "I suppose the best analogy for you would be a priest. A rabbi is the religious leader for the members of his synagogue." He raised a palm, motioning me to remain quiet. "And before you ask what a synagogue is, its best comparison for Romans and Greeks would be a temple."

"Where you pay the priests to say prayers for you to one of the gods." I smiled, feeling proud of myself. Master Saul put an end to that.

"What nonsense! My people pay, but only to help the rabbi keep the synagogue running and for the rabbi's salary, so he can feed his family. Furthermore, my people don't pray to *one of the gods*. They pray to the One God."

"One?" I said. "What about the others?"

"There are no others. Jews believe in only a single God."

225

"No goddesses?"

Master Saul shook his head.

"But ... how— "

"Jews don't believe God has all our physical appetites and bad habits. According to them, God is One, and has always been. That is all."

"So, Master ... why didn't you become a—rabbi, and follow your father?"

Master Saul checked the cinch below the mule's saddle. "My mother died when I was only ten. I was the only child. I was being taught daily by my father the rabbi, and I still know our holy books, the Torah and the Talmud, by heart. But while we would pass through the marketplace on the way to temple, as I stepped along in my father's shadow, I would observe the barterers. I made mental notes about those who succeeded and those who failed. What their differences were." He smiled. "It was all far more exciting than all the blah-blah-blah my father stuffed inside me in that sterile temple ... He died when I had just completed my studies and had the shawl placed around my neck." He rubbed the back of his neck, as though he could still feel the scratchy fabric against his skin. "He left me the house you and I live in, and I've since then built onto it as I've increased my wealth. But I never once led the synagogue in worship or prayer. In fact, I haven't stepped foot into a synagogue since then." He snorted in the direction of the city center, where the synagogue stood. "I don't have patience for such rubbish anymore. As you can see," he said rubbing a cheek, "I even prefer to keep clean-shaven like the Romans. As a Roman citizen and a businessman, I stand

o earn more presenting myself as a Roman than as a Jew ...
Come, Bern, let's go home and put this copper in the storage
rooms."

Instead of mounting the mule and sitting in the saddle, he
grasped the reins and walked beside the creature.

2

After a typical day out in the city making money by any
means available, Master Saul and I would return home where
we continued to work until sunset amid the noise of his three
boys, two girls, and his wife Rebecca, whose favorite pas-
time obviously was to scream at the children to be quiet. She
didn't cook or clean; those tasks were the domain of servant
women. Besides working at cloth with needle and thread, she
screamed at her children.

Master Saul had grown oblivious to the clamor and leaned
over strips of parchment on which he scribbled numbers:
mathematics that meant profit, loss, and future financial
schemes. During these evenings, he would consume cup after
cup of wine, but rarely would it affect him as it did my former young Master. He often offered me a cup, but I always
refused, and he would have me pour him another cup.

There came occasions when he would employ my linguis-
tic skills, and I tackled these tasks with relish. "Let us write
a letter, Bern," he would say, and I would grab the materials
and sit across from him with parchment, quill, and ink at the
ready. "To Marcus Janus of the Council of Elders: You owe

me the sum of five hundred coins silver, which I gave you as a loan for investment in a vineyard. Although no profit to my knowledge has come of this venture as of yet, along with the interest for these three months, the repayment is presently seven hundred and rising. If I do not receive this payment from you, I shall have you arrested and placed in debtors' prison until your family finds the means to repay me, while the interest continues to grow. Saul of Tarsus."

My written version was somewhat different, nearly every time.

> *To the most honorable Marcus Janus, best of the Council of Elders:*
>
> *I have heard excellent news concerning the production of the best wine in the*
>
> *province. I knew you would invest the money I loaned you to your gain. A*
>
> *keen eye for business has always been among your strengths. I look forward*
>
> *to sharing a cup (or two) of this excellent wine soon at a banquet where we can discuss future business.*
>
> Your friend and dearest admirer,
Saul

Master Saul would have me roll the parchment, and he would seal it with wax upon which he would affix his official signet. "Take it to the bastard first thing in the morning," he would order me. And later I would bring him back a pouch bulging with eight hundred silver coins. He would heft the pouch, esting its weight. "This is how you get the result you want n the business world, Bern. Be firm, and never be too shy to wield the sword of justice when necessary."

"Yes, Master," I would say, and as a reward, he would allow me the remainder of the morning free to read his books in my room.

When home, Master Saul slept half the nights in his own room and half with his wife Rebecca. Her room lay directly below mine, and though the noises they made in bed together kept me from a sound night's sleep, I admit they entertained me after an hour or two reading of tedious Roman battle strategy, written each time by the victorious general or by a scribe decades after the general's death. That woman, Rebecca, did love to shriek. At the children during the day and in bed on those nights. And only the gods knew to whom she shouted then.

Most of the household, including Rebecca and the other servants, ignored me as though I were a shadow in the corner of the room. Yet besides Master Saul, only his eldest son Shem valued my skills. He loved studying warfare, but there was nothing written in Hebrew about battles in any detail, and the Greeks wrote only self-serving texts about their military exploits. Those of Alexander or Sparta or even the dubious Trojan War. Shem was most interested in the Romans. 'They're the ones who occupy us now, and have for nearly two centuries, so they are obviously the winners. And I'm not interested in anything but winning." Like his father.

Master Saul spoiled all five of his children, so Shem owned hundreds of expensive carved wooden soldiers, horses, chariots, and battle machines such as catapults. Half were painted with red armor for the Romans and the other half with blue for any Roman opposition. The boy could not yet read Latin, and the best histories containing details of war and battles were written by Roman victors or their surrogates. As I would read the historical account of the Battle of Cynoscephalae, for example, young Shem would set up the Roman army headed by Titus Quinctius Flamininus and Macedonia's forces led by Philip V. Shem moved pieces according to my narration, with the few surviving Macedonians, including their king, fleeing the field. The boy's favorite was Julius Caesar's victory in the Battle of Alesia, leading to the annexation of Gaul as a Roman province, written by Caesar himself, of course.

One time I proposed a battle not yet described by a Roman historian, as it was still relatively recent. "Let's set up the Battle of Teutoburg Forest," I said.

"You mean the Massacre of Teutoburg Forest," young Shem retorted.

I smiled and winked at the boy. "One man's victorious rout is another man's massacre."

"Oh, all right," he said, setting up the figurines. "I suppose even the Romans must lose once in a while ... So they can learn and grow stronger, of course," he added.

Master Saul gave me the role of bodyguard for his wife or children away from the house. One day while performing this duty with my bow slung around my neck and my quiver full of arrows, Shem and I walked along the shoreline, and it dawned on me that it had been over a year since Master Saul won me from my former master, and not once had I witnessed any evidence of his skills as tentmaker. I asked young Shem about this, which nearly brought him to his knees as he bent over laughing. I waited for his fit to subside.

Shem finally ceased his show of mirth and stood upright. "My father never made a tent in his life," he said, still giggling, "and wouldn't know how to begin. He wouldn't even know how to erect one ... It is said that in his early days, shortly after my grandfather died, my father made money buying and then selling canvas to make tents." He began a full, deep-belly guffaw again. "Somehow people in the city started calling him Saul the Tentmaker, and it stuck!" He laughed with his arm around me all the way back home, and after I tried to picture Master Saul making or erecting a tent, I echoed his noise.

To keep the business contacts in his purse, my master spent evenings visiting tavern after tavern, drinking wine with men who knew him well. The more they spoke of possible business coming to Tarsus by boat or camel caravan, the more Master Saul would coax them with free cups of wine and ale. He knew, by man, who preferred wine, who preferred ale, and who favored yet a stronger liquid. And though he would match them drink-for-drink, he maintained level-headed sobriety, thereby plying otherwise strong, shrewd men into giving up more to his gain than they would sober.

231

He enjoyed the company of women on these outings, though it all amounted to mere innocent flirtation. That in itself would drive any other wife to fits of jealous rage if they knew of it. But when we arrived home at night, Rebecca would ask, "And how was Jessa tonight?"

"I didn't see Jessa, but Morah is getting too plump for one man to hug."

Rebecca would nod at this and carry on with her sewing.

Master Saul's pursuit of the carnal delights became more earnest on our trips away from Tarsus. In the nearby towns of Seleucia and Perga to the west, of Derba, Lystra, and Iconium to the northwest, after Master made deals in taverns and homes, I would end up sleeping outside the door of bedrooms while he engaged in midnight encounters with various women. In the morning, the women would prepare breakfast, usually not only for Master Saul and me but for one or several children. My master would occasionally introduce me to the woman and "this is my son Amos ... my beautiful daughter Daria" and other children he claimed as his, in addition to those under his roof in Tarsus. He lavished gifts of expensive clothing on the mothers and exotic toys on the children.

This would not have been beyond imagination in my original Germanic tribal background, but such relationships were kept as clandestine as possible, for Germanic women are fiercely jealous and well-versed in the art of wielding and using sharp objects. However, as I later learned, though Rebecca knew of these women and their children, she never spoke of them, accepting the fact of their existence and her husband's role therein with quiet capitulation. As long as she and her own children were cared and provided for, what her husband did elsewhere mattered not a whit.

One very warm day in late spring, I noticed people regularly passing by on the road before Master Saul's property. It was as though all were headed into the city center for some celebration. I asked my master if it were a holiday and where all the people were going.

"No holiday, but the governor has dedicated the next two days for games in the arena. That's where all the people are heading, and where we'll go, too, after we've eaten."

"Games? Running and throwing? Feats of strength?"

"Oh, we may see some running and throwing. Possibly feats of strength ... But these are gladiatorial games featuring the best fighters in the province."

I had never seen these games, but had heard them described often from those who had seen them in the Coliseum in Rome itself. These games sounded to me like violence on parade for deviant voyeurs.

What I discovered in the Tarsus Arena, dedicated to Mars, shocked me. Eight men fought, two-by-two, in four separate sections of the dirt in the oval. They wore bits of brass armor in an attempt to protect vital parts of their bodies from the swords and spiked maces wielded by their opponents. Each pairing fought until one man fell, struck by a weapon after succumbing to exhaustion. The standing fighter always

stood with a sandaled foot on the back or chest of his opponent while looking to the governor's seat. If the governor
held out a raised thumb, the opponent lived to revive from
his wounds and return later to fight again. However, if the
extended thumb pointed to earth, the fallen opponent died,
in whatever manner the standing fighter chose. The governor
always followed the will of the majority in the stands. If they
shouted, "Live! Live!" with their thumbs raised, then the man
lived. If they roared for his death with their thumbs pointing
downward, it was over for him.

I watched in horror as a standing fighter, having received
the thumb down signal, sliced open the fallen man's face at
the corners of his mouth before cutting open his belly and
gouging out some of his entrails. He held up these pieces,
pierced to the tip of his sword, for the viewing of the audience, who roared in their bloodlust. The fallen opponent lay
screaming until he bled out and his body twitched its death
dance.

I turned my eyes to my master, who wasn't even paying
attention to the spectacle in the arena. He was engaged in a
discussion with another wealthy Jew, for this visit to these
games was nothing to him but another opportunity to conduct business.

Each winner fought another winner, cutting the competition eventually to the championship match, and then that
day's so-called games came to their bloody end.

On the way back home I asked Master Saul who these fighters were. "They are slaves," he said. "Their masters, who stand
to win a portion of the entrance fees and bettors' winnings,

make sure they train so they perform at their best. The longer they last, the more money their masters earn."

Like animals, I thought. Like horses bred to run in races. But unlike the horses who lose, these losers forfeit their lives in the most gruesome ways so fans of the games can enjoy their own lives. *These men are slaves as am I,* I thought, *and only sheer luck of the thinnest margin placed me in this pampered life instead of killing and being killed for the entertainment of freemen.* I was silent for the rest of the walk home, and most of the next few days.

Such was my life for the first two years as Master Saul's property, and as I said earlier in this narrative, I would have been content to live the rest of my days thus. Alas, though, my ever-changing destiny, guided by the caprice of the gods, sent me in far different directions.

CHAPTER SIX

MY LONGEST JOURNEY BEGINS

1

Early in the spring of the fifteenth year of the reign of Emperor Tiberius, Master Saul received a letter from a wealthy merchant in Antioch, a few hundred leagues to the east of Tarsus. A boy of perhaps ten delivered it to the supper table after being admitted by a servant. He handed the scrolled parchment to me. I stood as usual behind Master. I broke the seal and stepped forward to hand it over my master's shoulder. He reached inside his robe, brought out his money pouch, and slipped me a silver coin, which I transferred to the boy, who bowed and departed.

Master Saul read the letter to himself several times, then thrust it over his shoulder. "Bern, read this and tell me what you think."

Written in clear, crisp Greek Koine, the letter described ι "profit of a lifetime" coming from the east via the longest camel caravan the merchant had ever heard of. To avoid Roman and provincial taxes, this caravan carrying not only the traditional silk and spices, but also precious metals, would avoid the larger cities and settlements. Based on strong authority, the letter writer stated, this caravan would pass east of Jerusalem, capital of Judea, and then travel north along the bank of the River Jordan before angling back west and arriving in six months' time (from the date of the letter, which meant four months from my reading) in Antioch. It would be most advantageous to meet the caravan east of Jerusalem, where it would rest a few days before heading north. There, the best deals could be struck, and the deal strikers would become so rich, they could buy the whole of Asia Minor if they so desired. But time was of the essence, for the caravan was estimated to reach that point three months from my reading.

I lowered the parchment and noted that Master Saul watched me over his shoulder. "Well?" he said.

"Well what, Master?"

"Well, what do you think of my friend's proposal?"

"It's not my place to think such thoughts, Master."

He smiled and patted the empty place beside him for me to sit. I did so and shifted my glances from place to place on the table. His youngest child, a daughter whose name I had never heard, giggled at the slave sitting at table as though he were one of the family. "Yet," said Master Saul, "you have such thoughts, and I would like to know what they are."

"I ... try to think from all angles, Master. On one side, you're in Tarsus, doing well in business here and in nearby towns and settlements. You can stay and continue to do well."

"The short Germanic slave sounds wise," said Rebecca, and Master Saul reached over and patted her hand affectionately.

"And from other point of view?" my master said.

"It's as your friend says in the letter. You could become the wealthiest man in Asia Minor if you go and succeed with this caravan of camels and their Arabic drivers."

"Success in this venture could lead to a comfortable retirement," he said. He looked over at Rebecca and added, "Our own island in Greece, away from the filth and dangers of these streets." He closed his eyes and took deep breaths as if practicing the act of breathing, then focused on me. "And you, Bern? How could such a journey affect you?"

I folded my hands in my lap and rubbed my thumbs together as if trying to start a fire with the friction heat. As often when I looked at my hands, my eyes focused on the metal wrist bands prepared at any moment for shackles and chains. I spoke to them as much as to my master. "I was born in the forest and bogs far in the north. Had my village not been attacked as revenge against Arminius, I wouldn't be here. I would never have known of the best and worst of the Romans. I would never have known true nobility, as I learned from the Celtic Gauls. I would never have experienced the adventures with a camaraderie of Roman soldiers as we floated through the beauties and dangers of the great river, the *Danuvius*. I would never have travelled across Asia Minor to live under this roof." I took a huge breath. "And, I would never have gone on this next journey closer to the edge of the world with my Master Saul."

I felt my master's strong hand on my shoulder as my tears landed upon my wrist bands.

We spent the next two weeks preparing for our journey east and then south. We packed light, with only a couple changes of clothing, a bedroll each, and a sheet of canvas for shelter. On the day of our departure, Rebecca was to give us enough food until we reached Antioch and possibly beyond. Master Saul preferred to remain home with his wife and children during our time of preparation. We went out once to a tavern, but his heart wasn't in such merrymaking, so after half a cup of wine he bade his friends—even the women—farewell, and we went back home.

In those nights before our departure, I didn't hear much noise of carnal pleasure below my floorboards, but I could swear there were sounds of a woman sobbing softly and a man trying to comfort her with the songs usually reserved for children at bedtime. In those two weeks with limited sleep, I may have read more in all the languages available in print in that house than in the total of my lifetime.

The morning of our departure finally arrived. Master Saul and I loaded a cart with provisions for the journey and goods we could use for trade along the way. Master kissed his children and Rebecca, then mounted a beautiful black stallion whom he named Narcissus after finding the colt not drinking from the water trough but staring into it at his own reflection. I sat on a bench at the front of the cart pulled by a mule that Master said was mine to name. I decided to observe the beast attached to the reins in my hand and later choose his name.

"Keep your arrows ready, Bern," Rebecca said, sniffling into a silk handkerchief, "and keep the old fool safe from harm."

I bowed to her. "At your service, my Lady," I said.

"Enough of this silliness!" Master Saul grumbled. "*Tempus fugit*, and so must we! Onward! To the journey of a lifetime!" He pulled Narcissus around and leaned into me. "I have a feeling," he whispered, "this journey will change both of our lives forever." He and Narcissus took the lead again. "Come, my noble friend!" he said to the stallion. "We have history ahead of us!"

And with those words, we left Tarsus—and Master Saul's family—behind us.

2

The Roman road from Tarsus to Antioch was well-maintained and regularly patrolled by Roman military. We were confronted only once by a would-be band of outlaws, but a single arrow into the shoulder of one of the brigands squelched their intent, sending them north into the hills from whence they came.

"I will need your language skills, I'm certain," Master Saul said, "but I may need your aim even more."

Master had a wonderful baritone voice, and to pass the time as we travelled along, he sang songs in every language he knew even scraps of. I discovered the Hebrew of the family in which he was raised lent itself well to song, but Latin not so much. Even the bits of Arabic he knew floated through the air like a lovely yet sad memory.

"Come, Bern! Give us a song from your Germanic people! What do they sing?"

"We sing love songs when we're in love, songs of celebration after a victory, riddles for fun. But mostly we sing of the deeds of our heroes."

"Indulge me in one of those!"

"As you wish, but it will last until we strike camp for the night."

He cocked his face and raised an eyebrow. "And why so long?"

"Because our heroes fight and win, then fight and lose. Then they fight and win again, and fight and lose again. Each battle becomes fiercer and each danger more dangerous, until they die and take their place at the banquet table of the gods."

"Well, then, initiate me."

"Please, Master, give me some moments to remember. I have not heard our songs since I was a young child."

As we rode on, in my mind I brought forth memories of the songs of the travelling bards around the village fires. I took a breath and began the song—a saga—of a hero, tracing his life from humble birth, through exploits requiring strength and bravery, to his eventual demise defending his people against the encroaching ice giants from the far north. This took us past dusk, but Master Saul refused to stop and strike camp until the song was finished.

"Though I understood not one word of your song, Bern," he said, "I know now your people are not the barbarians described by the Romans ... Let's take our rest for the evening under the stars that overlook your people as well as mine."

After two weeks of riding along the Roman road, we came upon the wall, towers, and white buildings of the great city of Antioch, sometimes in its history within Asia Minor, sometimes a possession of Syria, and less so within the protection of the Israelites and Judeans. We stood still at the crest of a hill gazing upon the goal of our journey's first leg. "Master," I said, "will you buy donkeys or mules to haul what you purchase from the caravan?"

He chuckled. "Bern, when we meet the caravan east of Jerusalem, I plan to buy as much of the caravan itself as our money will allow us ... We'll become camel drivers!" He rode on, laughing our way to Antioch.

3

"Ah, so the Tentmaker arrives!" bellowed a fat man. His skin, including his bald pate, was bronze from the sun. Silk of many colors draped from his shoulders to the marble floor of this palace-sized manor house. Each of his fingers—his thumbs, too—were adorned with gold or silver rings, and a necklace of pure gold inlaid with jade and other precious jewels hung around his neck of many layers.

"Dan, my old friend!" Master Saul stepped forward and put his hands as far around the merchant's girth as possible. They kissed each other's cheeks and took a step back to regard one another.

"You're getting gray at the temples," the merchant said. "And you're wrinkling like old fruit left in the sun."

"And if you gain any more weight," said Master Saul, "you'll be the only one at your banquet feasts ... because no one else will fit in the hall!"

Both men froze in silence, their visages stern. Then they roared laughing. The merchant threw a chubby arm around Master. "Come, friend Saul," he said, "let us eat while both of us can still fit in the banquet hall!" The man called Dan led my master away, and I followed ten paces behind.

After a sumptuous refreshment for the two wealthy freemen of meats, fruit, and of course good wine, the host had the table cleared and left the room briefly. He came back in with a few scrolled sheets of parchment tucked under an arm. At one end of the long banquet table, he unrolled parchments and looked them over until he said, "Here. This is the best one." Grasping two corners, he pulled it to the center of the table. He spread it out and weighted down the four corners with brass wine cups.

Master Saul stood and leaned over the huge parchment. "Bern," he said, "I think you should want to see this."

I sat at an end of the table eating bread and cheese. I swallowed a mouthful, took a sip of water, and stepped to my master. I gazed down upon a beautifully detailed map of Asia

Minor and much of the lands east. Jerusalem lay well south and a bit east of Antioch.

Dan pointed to a spot about twenty leagues south of Judea's capital and perhaps ten leagues east, closer to the expansive desert. "This is where you will want to meet the caravan. If they reach that place before you, and have already begun north toward Antioch, you should intercept them along this route," he said tracing his stubby index finger along a line to the west of the river marked as Jordan. "Just north of what they call the Salt Sea."

"Is there a Roman road?" Master Saul asked.

"Not there. Nor do you want a well-travelled road." He looked up at my master through the slits obscuring his eyes, making his expression hard to read. "I know you have a stash of silver, and possibly gold as well, in some hiding spot within that cart behind your mule." Master Saul merely locked eyes with his host. "Yes," Dan said, "I thought as much. Before you depart, I will add to that stash, silver for silver and gold for gold. Then whatever you can trade with your excellent skills, you bring back here for a fifty-fifty split."

I raised my face from the map and glimpsed into Master's eyes. In that instant I could read his thoughts in his eyes and he could mine. It was that moment when we began to know each other as friends. I noted in the slightest movement of his head a nod before he returned his focus on the host. "So, my friend," he said to Dan, "I am happy to know you plan to join us on our journey."

"Me? Join you?" When the fat man's guffaws subsided, he said, "I have plenty of business here to which I must attend.

There are three bar-mitzvahs to celebrate in the temple during your journey south ... And besides, there is no beast smaller than an elephant that can transport my bulk."

"So I thought," Master Saul said. "Then if it is to be only Bern here and I doing the actual work of the travelling and trading along unknown and possibly dangerous roads, I offer this: sixty-five percent for me and thirty-five for you."

The merchant's face flattened of his mirth. "That is too much for you, if I finance the mission by half."

"What is your counter-proposal?"

"A sixty-forty split ... Sixty for you, of course."

"So be it!" Master Saul said. "It's a deal!" And both men shook hands, though neither appeared as though he wished to celebrate the deal.

My master's mood grew increasingly more jovial the closer we came to our departure date. He talked of a villa on a Greek island, where he and his family could bask in the sun during a luxurious and lengthy retirement. "And you, my friend," he said to me, "can relax the rest of your days."

I smiled and nodded demurely, but lowered my eyes to the wrist bands only a blacksmith's work away from being bound together by a welded chain.

He rose and slapped me on the back. "Come, Bern!" he said. "Let us go into the city and discover what pleasures lie in store for us!"

"But Master, we cannot leave the cart."

"You don't trust my old friend Dan?"

"I don't know whom to trust."

"I have already planned for this. Come along!" He stepped from the rear garden toward the stables where his stallion and the mule and cart rested.

He instructed me to raise the seat of my bench, and I was surprised to find a dozen traps meant for small animals like badgers or foxes. We opened the traps' jaws and locked the springs open, then placed them all around the cart, just below the clothing, bedding, and provisions. Finally, we laid a tarp over the cart. He winked at me. "Believe me," he said, "before we retire for this evening, we'll know if anyone's curiosity stretched too far."

At a tavern, Master Saul drank more wine and ale than usual, and I had a feeling I would serve as his crutch later that night as he hobbled drunkenly back home to our host. But due to his unsatiable passions, that would prove unnecessary. I knew my master had a taste for women of any hue and shape, but it was not until that night I learned my master had an appetite for variety as well.

I noticed Master staring in a particular direction over the brim of his cup. I glanced over to see what drew his attention. The only people sitting in that area of the tavern were a wealthy Greek and a young man, apparently his slave, by his metal wristbands. Unlike me, this slave also imbibed in the local wine. He smiled our direction. I noticed my master returning the smile.

Finally, Master Saul rose from his seat. "Stay here, Bern," he said. He tottered a bit, but took a deep breath to steady himself, then stepped to the table occupied by the Greek man and his slave. Master sat and began conversing with the Greek, who gestured toward the slave, a handsome, muscular young man with tanned skin and long dark hair. Master spoke with this slave, then leaned in and kissed him on his lips. He reached in his robe and handed the Greek a palmful of silver.

Master Saul stood and came back to our table. "Go on back, Bern. We'll meet in the morning."

"No, Master. I will stay near you to make sure no harm befalls you."

"Bern!"

"This is my duty ... And my promise to Mistress."

He stood regarding me. "I don't deserve you," he sighed. He cocked his head toward the other table. "Come on, then. You can post yourself as my guard outside the door."

It was a long night under the stars outside the slave quarters of the Greek man's house. Noises stranger than had I ever heard emitted from within the room. Men lying with men was rare and even disavowed in my village in northern Germania. I had little knowledge of such things, and could barely imagine what men could do with men for pleasure. The little I could imagine made me shudder.

Master nudged me with his foot. My eyes snapped open, and I broke out of my fetal position and pulled an arrow from my quiver. "Hold, bowman!" he said. "If anyone wished either of us harm, I believe we'd both be dead already ... Rise and come with me, Bern, back to Dan's house."

Although he was the one whose muscles and joints should have been the worse for wear, he walked fine and steady, while I ached from head to toe and hobbled like an old man in need of a cane.

We sat at the table, already full with bread, cheese, sweetmeats, and fruit. I began to carry my plate to the end of the table, but Master Saul grunted and nodded his chin to the place beside him.

With a heavy bandage wound around his right wrist and hand, a servant passed in the hallway. He glanced toward us and then quickly away. "I believe we caught one," Master said with a chuckle.

Dan stepped into the room. "I assume you made other sleeping arrangements last night?" Master Saul shrugged and continued to eat. "It was difficult to get a good night's sleep here, after the physician left. One of my servants screamed out as if he were being murdered and came in clutching a bloody hand. Said a wild dog was sniffing around that cart of yours."

"Wild dog?" Master mused at the hallway as he chewed on a piece of apple. "What kind of teeth marks did this *wild dog* leave?"

"Very straight and deep. Almost as if the beast had jaws of iron." Master Saul lost some of the bread in his mouth as he laughed heartily. After a moment of scrutiny, the fat merchant echoed him. "So," Dan said, "what should I do to our would-be thief? Flog him? Take his hand? Have him tossed into the sea?"

"That's your decision," said Master.

The fat man rubbed a flabby jowl. "Of course ... But what would the Tentmaker do in my position?"

"What did the boy do for you before the, um, attack?"

"He was quite handy—no pun intended. If anything needed mending with wood and nails, Zeb was the one to do it."

"But until his hand heals ..."

"It may take weeks," Dan said. "Until then, what? Feed him and keep a roof over his head? Who's the slave then and who's the master?"

Master gazed at the hallway, where the slave had walked past. "Zeb is a rather remarkable specimen," he said.

"Yes, he is." Then Dan snapped his face to Master Saul in a double-take. "What do you mean by *specimen*?"

"Perhaps you're thinking of punishing him for his indiscretion. But if you rent him out to a brothel, there would be no shortage of customers." Master popped a handful of grapes into his mouth and chewed long before continuing. "The brothel-owner's purse grows, you receive a percentage, and then Zeb comes home with a healed hand and a somewhat altered frame of mind, I would imagine."

The fat merchant clapped his hands. "Bern, your master is the Prophet of Profit!" He stepped out of the room. "Zeb!" he called from the hallway. "Meet me in the rear garden! I have a proposal to discuss with you!"

4

On the morning of our departure, the streets of Antioch lay so thick with fog, it was as though gray vine tendrils wove around the corners of buildings. Dan followed two stout slaves carrying a trunk. When they set it in the cart, the metal clanging and jingling revealed the fat merchant's half in the venture for rarities from the east. "Come back with it empty, but with enough goods to fill a hundred trunks full of solid gold once we sell it all here."

Master Saul nodded, and we headed away from the fat merchant's house and into the fog—horse, mule and cart ... and two fools.

Although the travelling would have been much easier along the coast of the Great Sea on a well-maintained road through several well-known cities such as Tripoli, Sidon, and Tyre, we went east of the mountains following the river Orontes on its eastern bank. Our progress was slow, and we were forced to stop often to rest our two beasts. Thankfully, the river provided them with safe, flowing drinking water.

The settlements along the way were hardly what I would call *civilized*. The inhabitants were wary of the strangers we were, and though these places belonged to the Empire of the Romans, there was no evidence of Rome present. Either these people worshipped no gods, or the gods of the Empire had long ago forsaken them.

We stopped and erected a length of canvas as a makeshift shelter from the sun outside a village, which we learned from the begging denizens was called Apamea. To satisfy my curiosity, I asked one in Latin for the name of the gods he prayed to. He didn't understand, so I attempted Hebrew. In Arabic, he told me he understood some of the language of the Jews, but not very much. I repeated my question in his tongue, which brought about a smile and some tittering from him and a few of his partners to hear their language pouring forth from one so blond and fair as me. He then proceeded to tell me each family had separate names for their home god.

"Do you mean each family has its own god?"

The dark man gave me his ever-present, white-toothed smile.

"But do all these gods help all these families in times of need?"

"Some gods stronger, so clan stronger. Some gods not so strong, so clan sometimes die," he said.

After I gave the man enough grain to share with his comrades, Master Saul asked me the theme of my conversations with these *filthy barbarians*, as he called them. As I began to build a small fire, I let him know I, too, had been referred to by that moniker, and then I explained to him my query. "Why are you always so curious about other people's gods?" he asked.

"I'm shopping, and the world is my marketplace. I should compare the goods first, should I not?"

"That's an interesting way of thinking about it," my master said. "So, Bern, what ... *goods*, as you say, have you found to your taste?"

"What I see here reminds me of what I've known all my life: many gods with focused powers and responsibilities. In Germania, in Celtic Gaul, and here among these—what do you call them? filthy barbarians?—too many gods to keep track of. How does one know which one to pray to?"

He gave me a condescending grin. "So what is the solution?"

I studied his face a moment. "I believe your people may have it right," I said, "with one god to handle all issues ... So how does one become a Jew, Master?"

Shaking his head, he narrowed his eyes at me. "Jewry is best achieved by birth," he said. When a question formed on my lips, he raised his palm face-out for me to keep my silence. "I'm not saying it's impossible, for I've known a few members of my father's synagogue who were not born into Jewish families and the Jewish faith." He poured water from a gourd into a small kettle and added a handful of tea leaves. He set it at the edge of the new fire. "But being a Jew, a true Jew, is not just belief in the One True God—whom we know as Yahweh—and the memorization of ancient scribblings. It's an entire lifestyle. It affects what we do, with whom we associate, even what we eat."

"Master," I said, "you don't eat anything other than what those around you eat."

"Yes. Because I'm not what my father would have called a true Jew. In fact, he would have been so ashamed of what I've become, he would probably disavow me as his son. Disinheriting would not have mattered; I've made my own fortune, such as it is." He picked up the kettle by its wooden handle and moved it circularly in the air to stir the tea leaves into the heated water, then placed it back. "Do you like pork, Bern?"

"Yes, Master ... And so do you."

He smiled. "A Jew is not allowed to eat pork, my Germanic friend."

"Really? Why not?"

"It is written in those ancient scribblings of which I spoke. In short, there is a list of things we are forbidden to eat. Things I love to eat: pork, shrimp, all of those nasty but tasty fruits of the sea ... Yahweh has decided those are unclean."

"Yahweh," I said, and the name came off my lips like the gentlest of whispers.

"Bern, there is one last thing I haven't told you. Of course Yahweh would accept you as one of His own. But He would require you to sacrifice a bit of your flesh."

"My ... flesh?"

"Specifically, flesh from your penis." Master rose and retrieved two cups from the cart. He handed me one and poured it full from the kettle. "Here," he said, "allow me to try to explain it to you over a cup of tea ..."

After he finished his description of the act of circumcision, I swallowed the last of my tea with a shuddering gulp. "Maybe the One True God is not quite right for me after all," I said.

"Best to be a student of all faiths, but an adherent to none," Master Saul said. "Enjoy all that life offers. But most of all, keep your integrity—and your penis—intact." He tossed the last of his tea into the embers producing a hiss that ended his elucidation. He rose and pulled a blanket from the cart. "I'm getting some sleep," he said, "and since you fed those Arab beggars, stay awake to fight them off if they come around for more."

I pulled off my tunic, wrapped a blanket around me, and sat before the flames. "So that's what causes your limp?" Master said.

"What, Master?"

"Quite a remarkable scar you have."

"Oh that ... Yes, Master, the old healer who saved my life told me I would probably limp the rest of my life. There's a piece of a spearhead in my right hip."

"Now this sounds like quite a story! I've known you for a couple years, and I haven't heard it. Tell it to me," Master said. "Make it worth the wait."

He lay beneath the canvas and pulled the blanket over him while I told him a bedtime story of pain and suffering.

5

Two weeks after leaving Antioch and what felt like the last of Roman civilization, we passed through, or actually passed *past*, several villages and settlements east of the Orontes River. I had created a smaller version of Dan's map we viewed back in Antioch, and after we passed the town of Heliopolis, I knew we were less than a day from Abila. A tiny village of five dwellings—likely the settlement of a clan—lay about a hundred paces from the river's east bank.

Master Saul nodded to the mud and stone structures. "I can't make sense of their words, Bern, so go and see if you can barter for some firewood."

I climbed down from the cart and stepped toward the nearest of the houses. I thought it odd no smoke rose from behind, where most of these people placed their fire pits for cooking and boiling river water clean for drinking and cooking. These fires burned more or less nonstop under normal circumstances. I detected no sound of barking dogs or bleating goats, though there came a distant, constant buzzing. There should have been other noises like the squealing of children at play and the squawking of their scolding mothers, under normal circumstances ... But I discovered no normal circumstances on this day.

I approached the front opening of the small building, and about fifteen paces away hailed my presence aloud, but no one showed in the arched opening. Only five paces away, my nostrils were hit by the foulest stench. I lifted the hem of my tunic at the neck and held it over my nose. I stepped inside and waited for my eyes to adjust to the darkness of the hovel. When they did, I wished they hadn't.

Two adult human bodies lay on the floor, most of their skin ripped away, and likewise with much of the muscle tissue and internal organs. There were no faces to speak of, but an eyeball hung loosely from one dark, blank socket off one of them. A faint lapping came to my ears from a corner, and I turned. Three dogs feasted themselves on the bodies of two small children. One of the canines gorged itself on the tender throat of what had been a little girl, I believed. The creature raised its face to me with nonchalant disinterest, licking blood and tissue from its lips before continuing its repast.

I backed out of the place into the blinding sunlight. I fell to my knees and jerked my tunic away from my mouth and nose so I could vomit into the dirt. I had had nothing to eat yet that day, nor did I think I would be able to for a while. My stomach produced only a thick yellow bile. "Bern?" Master Saul called from behind me. "Bern, are you all right?" His footsteps crunched nearer and louder on the dirt and pebbles until they came to a halt directly behind me. He placed his hand on my shoulder. "Bern, what is the matter?" I tried to tell him, but only retched more bile from within me. I pointed lamely behind me to the dwelling. His footsteps crunched away in that direction.

A moment later, the master joined his slave emptying his stomach. I wiped my mouth with the back of a hand. "What happened in there?" I asked, my voice tremulous.

"I've seen it before. Travelling Arabs dead in their tents, blood and bits of lung hanging from their lips and chins. None of our physicians could determine what it is." He paused and took in a breath. "Some kind of a pest we don't know in the west. Obviously contagious." He stood and helped raise me up, his hand under my arm. "Come. I need a drink of water before we leave."

"Leave? Shouldn't we bury them?"

"Bern, we should get no closer to those corpses than what we've already done. They should be burned, but not by you or me. So let's leave this place while we are still alive to do so."

He stepped toward the cart and his horse. I looked from his back to the cart a few times before deciding to join him. Master Saul clicked his tongue and gave the reins a jerk, signaling Narcissus to move on. I did the same with the mule I decided to call Vanitas because he was undervalued and seemed to know it. We didn't get far when we heard an infant crying in one of the hovels. I pulled Vanitas to a halt. "Master?" I called.

"Yes, Bern, I hear it, and if we keep going, soon we'll no longer be able to hear it!"

"But it's only a baby!"

He halted the stallion and twisted around in his saddle. "Yes, a baby who's infected with whatever in God's name it is that killed these people."

"We don't know that, Master!"

"Even if the baby doesn't have this pest, what do we do with it? We can't sell it in the slave market. We can't visit home after home hoping to find someone to adopt it. We have business to attend to, and time will not allow us to alter our course."

"But— "

He held up his palm and brought the horse next to me. "There is nothing we can do for this baby." He glanced up at the sky. "Pray to whatever god you wish that it will be saved. I would pray to Yahweh, but I've never had much luck with that. And besides, He is God of our people, not these Arabs ... So come. Our destiny awaits. I'll become so rich I shall move my family to my own island, and you may become a free man. But not if we meddle in matters that belonging to the realm of the immortal." He guided Narcissus around and continued to follow the river south.

I knew of no god whose domain was abandoned Arab babies, so I breathed a silent prayer to Mercury to at least speed the soon-to-be-dead child's soul to a better world as I guided the mule forward in Master Saul's path.

CHAPTER SEVEN

OUR DESTINY CHOOSES US

1

We strode through the central marketplace in the Syrian provincial capital of Damascus. Master Saul and I walked along holding the reins of the stallion Narcissus and the mule Vanitas. All manner of mankind mingled around us, yet no one paid us any attention. At the city gates, my master had told me he wished for a proper bed and water for washing. I asked a Jewish man buying fruit from an Arab where we could find accommodations, and he directed us to a side street on the other side of the market square.

Just before we reached the narrow lane, we happened upon a small crowd gathered around a man at the intersection. The short, frail man was a Jew who shouted with much enthusiasm in the Greek Koine about some fellow he called the Christ who had lived and died in Judea. The apparent preacher spoke of this Christ person as though he were somebody truly special. I asked Master if we could listen for a while, for a bit of diversion before we found our room. He nodded, and leaned against a building, folding his arms and observing, a slight grin playing on his lips.

The man ranted about this dead man, who had a brief career as a wandering healer and teacher. He spoke of a movement he called *The Way*. Though this preacher spoke the familiar new Greek of the region, his speech was laced with the accent of an unfamiliar tongue, which I later learned to be Aramaic, widely spoken in Israel, Judea, and Samaria. This Christ—a word I found later to have multiple meanings—performed many miracles, proving him to be the Anointed One sent by Yahweh Himself to save and even raise the Jews to their proper place as His chosen people.

There was a break in the preacher's ramblings allowing Master to challenge the man. "Did you say your Christ gave sight to a blind man?"

"That is correct!" the man said.

"And speaking of sight, did you yourself see this miracle?"

"No. I was told of it."

"Told of it. By one who witnessed it."

"No. By one who was told by a witness."

"So you don't know."

"I believe! I have faith!"

"Because you were told of this so-called miracle by some-one who was also told of it ... And what if I tell you my friend here," he said motioning to me, "walks on water?"

The preacher laughed. "That is absurd! No man can walk on water!"

"And you should be careful spreading your own tales." Master Saul waved his hand over the crowd. "Incite these people into believing God's Anointed One has been walking among us, and you're playing with Roman fire." He headed into the lane where our quarters awaited, and cocked his head for me to follow.

As I followed Master and his horse into the lane, I listened to the receding words of the preacher who continued his praises of this Christ.

Both Master and I were exhausted, so after securing the horse, mule, and cart—and setting the traps—we opted for sleep instead of going out for something to eat and plenty to drink for my master. While Master Saul prepared to lie upon the bed in this inn room, I asked him about this preacher and the Christ fellow of whom he spoke.

"Nowadays, there are many like him preaching of what we Jews know as the Messiah."

"Messiah?"

"*Christ* is Greek for the Jewish Messiah, as best translated. This Messiah is supposed to come from a specific family line,

nd will be the King of the Jews who will restore our people
o their former glory forever."

"But didn't the preacher say this Christ was killed?"

"Which is why he couldn't very well have been any Mes-
iah," my master said.

"You said there are many preaching this."

"These are hard times for those who cannot or will not
iccept the reality of things. We are occupied by the Romans,
ind have been since well before my birth. Roman rule is all
iome of us have known, and we tend to look at what it gives
is—the peace and security, the health and abundance—
nstead of what we fantasize life would be like without the
Empire. Some preach of a military victory, yet others follow
lifferent dictates. This cult called *The Way* has no chance to
iurvive for very long. Mark my word."

"So they dream of a Christ or a Messiah to drive the
Romans out so they can starve and have their freedom," I
nused.

"Yes. And they see signs of his coming in every cloud and
inder each rock ... But in the end, life goes on, and our real
eader is a gentile who lives in Rome but is not appreciated
'or what he gives us." Master Saul lay and stretched out on
:he bed. "In the end," he said to the ceiling, "that man's gods
ind mine are the same ... gold and silver, and the peace and
:omfort they can buy. And speaking of which, I think I paid
:oo much for this rock-hard mattress." With that, he closed
iis eyes and commenced his usual raucous snoring.

After probably an hour, Master Saul awoke suddenly and
iat up. "Let's find a tavern," he said. "Wine calls."

The fruit of the vine wasn't the only siren calling that evening. From a tavern just one street away, Master Saul returned to the inn with a young Arabic male *on loan* from his master.

Instead of lying in the comfortable bed next to Master, I rolled a blanket from the cart for a pillow and lay on the floor at the foot. I never heard the usual sounds from Master's encounters in bed. I was so tired I fell into an immediate deep slumber. As I drifted off, I hoped for an encounter or two with my Lady Dalina, but the following morning I couldn't remember any dreams I may have had.

2

We were making good time, for we had reached the settlement Canatha, only about fifteen leagues north of Jericho, east of which we were to find the caravan, with two days to spare. It would have been out of Master Saul's character to simply have a good meal and rest for the last leg of our journey before heading back home wealthy beyond our dreams. In the airy mood of one certain of an impending victory, Master decided to go out for a night of pre-celebration. He paid the old lady, the owner of our inn, to watch over our cart and beasts in the barn, then asked if there was a road to Jericho. She replied there was only a rough path to Jericho, then a true Roman-built road from Jericho to Jerusalem.

So, true to his usual form, he drank more than his fill of wine at a tavern, and before long he had coaxed a young, plump blonde to sit on his lap while they drank and sang.

She was obviously a *gentile*, as he called non-Jews, but where she came from, I could not tell. Her manner, her laughter, her coarse Latin, all marked her as an obvious whore. And no doubt she would earn some of Master's silver for parting with her special talents this night.

"Shall we go an' spen' the res' ofa night findin' whish posi-ion we like bes'?" he slurred while he held a wine cup to her lips spilling most of it onto her chest.

"First, clean up what you spilt!" she said, and cackled as he licked wine from her ample bosom. Then she hopped off his lap and led him out of the tavern.

I rolled my eyes and followed them through winding alleyways until we reached the edge of the settlement where white tents were erected outside a gate. "This one is mine," the woman said. She opened a flap and led him by the hand inside. Soon after she closed the flap I heard the expected sounds of pleasure, in this case his grunting and her cackling.

I had never known of a prostitute who travelled in such luxury as that complex of fancy tents exuded. I decided she must be quite successful in her profession.

I awoke beside the tent flap. The sun had just risen, giving more clarity to my surroundings than I had had the previous night. A few Roman soldiers stood talking around a fire. One, after warming his hands, ducked into one of the white tents. He exited with another. It finally dawned on me. This was some kind of mobile Roman military unit. I supposed the prostitute travelled with them for her existence, and for extra money found customers such as my master.

The tent flap opened behind me, and Master Saul's head poked out. Wide with panic, his eyes darted from side to side. He focused on me and exited. "Come, Bern, we must leave."

"Of course, Master, but is something wrong?"

"She's dead!"

"The girl from last night? She's dead? But how?"

"I don't know ... But she's not breathing. There's no heartbeat ... And her skin is growing cold!" He lifted me to my feet. "Come on. Let's get our things and go."

"But shouldn't we ..." I glanced to the Roman soldiers.

"What are they doing here?" he said. "No, let's get out of here!"

We had just stepped inside the gate which was not manned, likely because of the soldiers just outside, when we heard shouting behind us. "She's dead!" a woman's voice screamed. "The Vice Governor's daughter! She's dead!"

Master Saul's already-widened eyes seemed as though they would pop out of their sockets. "Vice Governor's daughter?" he muttered.

"She was with a man and his slave last night in the tavern!" came the feminine voice from the tents. "They left together!"

Another voice shouted, "Do you know who he was?"

"No, but I remember him!"

"Come on! Let's find him!" a male shouted.

"Do we take him to a judge?" another said.

"The nearest judge is in Jericho! No, we'll get the truth out of him ourselves, then hang the bastard and his slave!"

Master Saul grabbed my tunic. "Come!" We rushed together through the narrow alleyways until we came to the inn. I started to step inside, but Master put a firm hand on my shoulder. "Forget whatever we have in the room," he said. "Let's take what we have in the barn and leave this place."

We made it to the gate we entered the previous evening, and Master Saul halted Narcissus. I pulled the cart up beside him. "Where to now, Master?" I asked.

He chewed on his bottom lip and gave an emphatic nod. "We can't go south. The soldiers will discover the inn. They'll either bribe or torture the owner into telling what she knows. I asked her about a road to Jericho, so they'll go south to find us." He shook his head. "So we have to go back north."

"But what of our destinies?"

"I venture to say, my friend, we each have new destinies now ... We have enough silver and gold in the cart to live out our lives as fugitives, if we are so lucky. This means we'll have enemies in uniform to the south, and perhaps those more dangerous to the north."

I knew by the latter he meant the fat merchant Dan in Antioch. The man would want something to show for his investment. The expedition was his plan, and he would be furious if we brought back only his gold and no wonders from the east. He would undoubtably give us over to the Roman authorities, especially if there was a price on our heads. And if we failed to return? A man that wealthy could hire assassins to come after us, take our heads, and bring them along with the gold and silver to the fat man.

"Back to Damascus," Master said. "We'll buy a place to hide along with our keeper's silence."

So north we rode, away from Master Saul's dream of a luxurious retirement on an island ... and my fleeting dream of freedom.

PART III

DESTINY'S SLAVE AND THE ACCIDENTAL APOSTLE

CHAPTER ONE

NEW PERSONAE

1

M aster Saul and I traveled north from Canatha, the scene of the crime. We didn't stop for nearly a full day, and it was only my tearful pleading that prevented his horse Narcissus and my cart mule Vanitas from dropping exhausted along the path.

"Our pursuit believes we're heading to Jericho and thence to Jerusalem," I said, hopping down from the cart. "They're at least two days south. It will be another day or two, and maybe more, before they realize their mistake."

"And they might go west to the sea, thinking we would hide on a ship bound for Greece or Italy," Master Saul said.

I agreed with him. "Which means we're safe enough find a suitable place to strike camp, Master."

He dismounted the stallion and looked at me long, smiling. "So the Master follows the slave's plan." We began walking north, leading our beasts by the reins. "Pretend I'm a cruel master, one you must escape for fear of being brutally killed. Think like the prey doing what he must to stay alive and hopefully gain his freedom. Whatever you decide to do, Bern, I will be your accomplice."

So my master followed me. When the sun hung over the western horizon, shining down in mid-day on a people far to the west, perhaps a people over which the Empire held the slightest, most tenuous hold, I spied a gathering of boulders around a thousand paces off the path to the east. I left the path toward the boulders, and my master followed me.

I made a fire with wood stored in the cart. I prayed the embers would burn through the night, for there stood not even a shrub within line of sight. We still had some of the salted, dried meat packed for our journey by Master's wife back in Tarsus. Tarsus ... it seemed years behind us, though it had been but a mere couple months since we set out on this expedition.

I still thought of this as a business expedition, an excursion to barter with drivers in a camel caravan somewhere east of Jerusalem. Were it not for Master Saul's wanton debauchery, we may be camping with those Arabs now, listening to their desert songs around a glowing fire under the myriad stars.

Master Saul pulled a piece of goat meat from the end of a pointed stick. He chewed and sipped alternately hot tea from one cup and cool wine from another. "At what point," he asked, "do we give ourselves over to the authorities?"

"I suppose," I said, "at the point of desperation."

"I've never despaired ... How does one know when that moment arrives? When things have become desperate?"

I thought of being taken as a slave to the colonia in Gallia Belgica along with my cousins Frida and Linza. For the latter, the point of despair had arrived. She could not remain a slave, so she took her life, and the last of her blood left her body as Frida and I stood by helplessly. I remembered her smiling at me, then at Frida. Her face was ghastly pale, as if she had already become her own phantom. "I am free," she wheezed out, "and you both ... are still slaves."

Though I had never felt as low as I did when facing the abuse, the humiliation at the hands of young Master Bruno, I had obviously not reached the point of despair. For I lived on to belong to Master Saul, who treated me more like an employee than an object owned by him to enjoy as he so desired. And I had a feeling Bruno was likely to meet his desolation well before I would.

"I suppose when one ceases to truly live, that is the time to give up the struggle." I stirred the coals below the flames with a stick. "You have no idea, Master, what it is to live in bondage. However, I have been through moments of freedom. In my first few years with my tribe in the north. Living with another race and tribe, the Gaulish Celts, for a time." I thought of those moments in bed with the wife of my master, the Provincial Governor. Though I felt free there in that bed, I knew once my master came home, I would know my place. I ripped myself free of those memories. "Life as a bondsman is no real life, where I'm concerned. But, Master Saul, I have never felt the remotest desire to leave the living and become free in that respect. My life is not yet at an end, and until it is so, there is still hope. And that dark beast lurking in the shadows, the one called Despair, will have to wait its turn."

"I asked when we know to despair," Master Saul said. "You took the longest, most poetic route to say, 'I don't know.'" We locked eyes in silence for a moment until we could no longer hold back our laughter.

2

After nibbling on dried dates, we set out the next morning north hoping to reach Damascus before sunset. Along the way we chatted about comical incidents we had witnessed together in the marketplace square and in the taverns back home in Tarsus. In the mere two years that I lived there with Master Saul and his family, Tarsus had already become a home to me, nearly as much as the colonia in Gallia Belgica, and certainly more so than the forests and swamps of my birth, that distant, shrinking memory of northern Germania.

The sun was perhaps an hour away from its mid-day zenith when shadows swept over us with a slow regularity. I raised my eyes to the sky and spied a pair of vultures circling overhead, directly in our path line. "Something dead before us," I said.

"Hopefully if it's edible, it hasn't already gone bad," Master Saul mused.

Perhaps the dead thing may have been edible, but it was the one delicacy even Master Saul wouldn't serve or eat. The dead thing on the path was a man. His turban lay on the dirt behind him, revealing his skull cracked in several places. The blood dripping from these wounds was nearly dry in the warm air. We both knelt for a closer inspection, then turned simultaneously to each other with wide eyes.

"The preacher," I said. "The one who shouted praises of the slain Christ and the cult of the Way."

"Yes," Master Saul muttered. "In Damascus."

All around this man's body lay stones, most of them of palm-size. A few of them held faint spots and streaks of a copper color.

"He was killed. Stoned to death." I felt a strange empathy for this man I never knew. "But why?"

My master stood and shrugged. "A man preaching his dangerous words cannot last long. The Jews would despise him for praising a false Messiah. The Romans couldn't abide a man stirring up people with a message that there is or was someone—a non-Roman—greater than the Emperor, which would mean preaching the fall of the Empire ... But it was the Jews who killed this one."

"How do you know?"

"How much did it cost to execute this man?" he chuckled. "Besides, the Romans always make sure to put on a show to keep the lower castes entertained and to leave an example for anyone who harbors interest in following the criminal's footsteps." He glanced up at the circling vultures. "Come, Bern, we're in the way of someone's supper plans." He stepped toward his horse.

"Wait!" I said.

He stopped in his tracks. "What?"

"The men pursuing you. Maybe they'll eventually come this way."

"Yes, maybe. So let's go!"

"And by the time they get here, the body will be stripped to the bone."

"Yes," he said, "very likely. So what's this about?"

"And if they find this body and believe it's you, you may be saved."

"Bern, you have always made good sense. Now, though, I think your addled brain is in need of some rest. So let's go and find some shelter so we can make plans."

"I already have a plan."

"All right, then out with it!"

"You remove your clothes, Master, while I remove his." He merely remained standing there, mouth agape. "Then you dress in his clothes while I dress him in yours. The unrecognizable corpse will be wearing the clothes you were wearing. For all anyone could know, this man may be you." I began undressing the dead preacher.

"This is a good beginning of a plan, Bern." While he removed his robe, he said, "But what about you?"

"What about me?"

"You were with me." I handed him the poor man's threadbare robe, and he exchanged it for his. "Those who wish me dead may believe I am already so when they come upon this unfortunate creature." He pulled the fabric over his head and fitted his arms through the sleeves. "A near-even fit," he said. "But Bern, after I died, what happened to you?"

I hadn't tried to dress dead-weight—literal this time—since young Master Bruno, and it was a struggle now as much

ιs it was back then. I sat the body up to pull the expensive
robe over his shoulders, then laid it back down to slip the hem
ιo the ankles. I took a break and thought awhile. "It could be
ι'm the one who killed you. I stole the money, and I'm seeking
ι corrupt magistrate to bribe for my declaration of freedom."

"So you killed me. I stood still while you threw stone after
ιtone at me?"

"Oh," I said. "You have a point there ... We'll need to move
ιhese stones away from this spot." I stood and pointed at a
ιmall boulder about fifty paces away. "Behind that boulder,"
ι said pointing.

Master Saul sighed. "I remember Dan saying something
ιbout the master becoming his slave's slave ... Well, let's get
ιo it."

After we'd hidden the last of the stones behind the boul-
ιer, I convinced my master to help pick up the body and lay it
ιn the cart. After what I estimated an hour north on the path,
ιve removed the corpse and laid it back beside the path. "He
ιtill appears like he was stoned to death," Master Saul said.

"He won't within a few days after the vultures and dogs have
ιeasted," I said. "Besides, you didn't suffer death by stoning."

"No? Then how did I meet my demise?"

I pulled my bow off my shoulder and an arrow from my
ιuiver. "I put an arrow through your neck." I notched the
ιrrow on the string and pulled. Stepping over and planting
ιny feet on either side of the corpse's chest, I aimed downward.

"Bern! What are you doing?"

"I'm putting an end to your miserable life, Master."

"But— "

I opened my thumb and forefinger, releasing the arrow into the middle of the corpse's neck, nailing it to the earth. Corpses held no sacred status for my people, the Tenchteri, as they seemed to hold for Romans. They were merely the material husks for immortal souls, and as such worth the dirt they would soon join. "Too late," I said. "The deed is done."

"I hope this pays off," he said. He started toward the horse.

"Your turban."

"What?"

"The turban on your head is the expensive one you wore. It belongs on or near him," I said cocking my head to the body. "The one you're to wear is in the cart."

"His robe scratches my body. Do you think he carried lice?" He removed his silken turban and tossed it next to the corpse's head.

"There's only one way to find out," I said.

3

The road to Damascus finally brought us to Damascus, whose wall loomed on a hill in the distance. We halted our horse and mule, and surveyed our surroundings. Except for a few shepherds and their flock ahead just outside the wall, there was no traffic arriving or departing the capital of the Syrian Province. "Well, what are we waiting for?" Master Saul said. "Let's go."

"I don't think it's a good idea just to go in."

"And why not? I'm a Roman citizen and have the right to enter a Roman city."

"This is true," I said. "Saul of Tarsus is a Roman citizen, but though these people don't know Saul of Tarsus is wanted for murder in Judea, they eventually will. You are not that man, but whoever we decide you are."

"And who may that be?"

"I don't know yet. We'll have to decide later ... But some of these people inside those walls were the ones who took that preacher a half-day out to kill him. And I don't think it would be wise to enter the city dressed as him. If they killed him once, surely they can kill him again."

"I never thought of that," Master Saul said. "And I can't put on the change of clothes I have in the cart, for they would mark me as what I truly am."

"What you truly are needs to change," I said.

I noticed he was eyeing my wrist bands. "Also, what you truly are. Let's find what we can in the cart to remove those things from your wrists."

"But I remain your slave until I have an official deed of freedom. Otherwise I'm an open target for anyone wanting to earn silver by capturing me and placing me on an auction platform."

"Agreed," he said.

We spent the next hour or so hammering and chiseling at the metal bands until they were loose enough to fall off. My wrists were bloody, but the air felt good on the open wounds.

"We should bury these." He hefted the bands.

"No," I said. "Put them in the cart. Someday they'll be mementos of this life."

"The scars on your wrists will serve as much."

But I kept those metal bands, and carried them in a bag for many years. The scars eventually faded.

"One last thing before we enter the city," I said. "You need to climb into the cart and cover yourself with the tarp. I'll somehow get us inside so we can find a place to hide."

"But what about Narcissus? What about my horse?"

"We should have released him back at your body. There's no way I could explain such a fine animal in the hands of a simple German merchant on his way back north."

"A what?"

"If you're dead, Master, I can live whatever fantasy I wish." I looked ahead at the sheep and received an idea. "Just get in the cart, please, Master, and prepare for company."

"Company?"

"Just do it, please."

With Narcissus tethered to the rear, I drew the cart to the edge of the flock and observed the three shepherds to select the one who could fit my plan. The youngest, wearing the most tattered cloth, won me over. I was prepared to climb down from the cart, but his curiosity brought him closer to me. I hailed a hello to him in the Greek Koine, and he bowed, his hand on his chest.

He stepped to the mule and patted his neck, then peered around at the black stallion. "That's a fine horse," he said.

"Yes," I said. "I found him wandering along the path."

"But surely he belongs to a nobleman or even someone of royal blood."

I imagined Master's chest swelling with pride, and he was struggling to keep his silence under the tarp. "I doubt it," I said. "He has no brand."

"But the saddle, it's so expensive!"

"Yes, it appears so. But likewise, it carries no markings indicating the owner."

"All right, so what do you plan to do with him?"

"I plan to give him to you, if you do me a favor."

Soon I lay beside Master under the tarp. We jostled against one another with each stone and rut the wheel rolled over. Finally, we felt the cart come to a halt.

"It's the shepherd boy!" a voice cried out from above. After a pause, the voice called, "What do you have in the cart?"

"Sheep dung!" the boy shouted.

"Why in the gods' names are you bringing sheep shit into the city?"

"My father sells it for fertilizer."

The following pause was long, and both Master and I feared the guards would climb down and inspect the cart. But then the voice from the wall shouted, "Come on in ... you and your shit!" The cart rolled forward.

It felt like perhaps an hour had passed when we halted and the boy tapped on the tarp. I crawled out and inspected the narrow, deserted alleyway. "He's a fine horse," I said. "Treat him well. Call him Narcissus."

"Why?"

"Go to the library and read about it."

"The library wouldn't do me a lot of good. I can't read."

"Oh ... well. So call him whatever you want and note how he reacts. Then call him Narcissus. You'll understand," I said. The shepherd boy walked away to get acquainted with his new horse. "All right, Master, it's clear. You can come out for now."

He lifted the tarp and climbed out the back of the cart. "This scratchy robe will kill me before anyone else gets the chance." He frowned down upon me. "You gave Narcissus, that work of art, to an illiterate idiot!"

"Yes, an illiterate idiot who probably kept us both alive by sneaking us into the city. I'd say that was worth the cost."

"I shall miss that horse," Master Saul said.

"I'm sure you shall," I said, and patted his shoulder. "Now get back under the tarp while I find us a place to hide."

With a pouch of silver under my tunic, I wandered through less-traveled alleyways like the one in which Master Saul lay under the tarp. Surely there would be someone fitting the description I sought. Someone with a dwelling large enough to accommodate two men, and a shelter for the cart and mule until we could figure a more permanent plan. Also, someone destitute enough to need a steady flow of silver. Finally, some-one who—with a bribe enough—could keep a secret.

I passed several candidates sitting outside their doorways or hanging out window openings just staring at nothing. I had to get this right the first time, for approaching the wrong person with my illicit proposal could mean a quick trip to the jail for the both of us ... and an eventual death sentence.

The one I sought seemed to be seeking me. I strode down a narrow alleyway, and an old man stepped out his doorway. He watched me intently as I neared. When I was directly before him, he said, "You. You're the slave traveling with the Tentmaker from Tarsus, are you not?" I stopped in my tracks and faced him. I held up my wrists, free of their bands. "And what's that supposed to prove?" he said. "A slave's bands and shackles can be removed, even as badly as you have done, according to those marks. And please don't try to shoot me. I just say the word and Cerebus will be at your throat." He whistled, and a huge mastiff trotted from within and stood growling beside him. From every part of the beast, especially his teeth, exuded the desire to pounce and maul.

I must have reached for the bowstring without realizing it, for I found it in my fingers. I relaxed my grip and lowered my hand. "How do you know me? And what do you want?" I said, my eyes steady on the dog.

"Two questions. All right, then, the first one first." He placed a palm on the mastiff's head and patted it reassuringly. The dog kept his beady eyes on me. "I was in the tavern when your Master went home with another slave boy. By the way, did that make you jealous?" he added. I didn't answer. "And I know he's Saul the Tentmaker from Tarsus because he said so, many times ... Oh, your master's a talker when he drinks."

He paused so long I thought he'd forgotten my second question, so I reminded him. "And what do you want from us?"

"Ah, yes, the second question. That depends on your answer to *my* next question." I clenched my teeth. "You were heading south, but now suddenly only a few days later you're back. Are you in trouble?" Again I remained stoic. "If you don't answer, you will hand me your quiver of arrows and take a walk with me to the magistrate. But only after Cerebus has had a taste of you."

I fought to steady my breathing. I realized I was trapped, and thus so was Master Saul. "There was an incident in Canatha," I said, "involving my master and a woman. My Master is innocent of any wrongdoing, but there is no way to prove it."

"And so this, um, incident might seek you out, even here?" I nodded at the dirt. The old man rubbed his chin with one hand while he continued to pat the dog's head with the other. "Well, I think I may have at least a temporary solution to your troubles."

"And what would that be?"

"Me, my friend. I have plenty of room since my wife died and the children grew up and left for greener land." I narrowed my eyes at the doorway. "Oh, don't let appearances deceive you. I have many rooms and a courtyard big enough for your cart, mule, and that beautiful horse." He laughed at my expression of surprise. "I saw you leave the south gate while I was walking with Cerebus."

"We no longer have that beautiful horse," I said. "Just the cart and mule." I had forgotten till then I carried some silver under my tunic. "And what will we pay for this?"

"For now, two silver coins per day."

"For now?"

"They raise the price of fruit in the marketplace or ale in the tavern, I must raise the price of your rent. Business is business."

"Business is business," I echoed. I pulled the pouch from within my tunic and handed him the first day's rent. "I'll be back soon with the cart, the mule, and the master."

"I shall be here to lead you around to the courtyard."
I stepped away from the old man, whom I hated already.

4

Within the dwelling of the old man whose name we never learned, Master Saul wore his one remaining robe of fine silk. Neither of us left the place for the first several days. Our room facing the inner courtyard afforded us an excellent view of our cart and mule—and a skeletal fig tree in name only. Ours would become a life of veritable house arrest, yet protection from capture and execution.

We had run out of our own food, and I told the old man of our dilemma. "For an additional silver coin per day, I'll feed you," he said.

I said, "I'll go to the marketplace myself!"

The old man merely smiled and winked while Cerebus sat panting and filling the dwelling with his hot breath. I rummaged through the cart until I found a long strip of cloth we had packed for emergency cover from the sun. I cut the cloth with a knife until I had a small enough piece to do the job. I wound it around my head and face until only my eyes showed. "How do I look?" I asked Master.

"As long as you cover your blond mane, at least you won't be so obviously misplaced."

So we lived, so we survived through several weeks. I left the abode every few days to venture, dressed like a leper, into the marketplace for food. I would carry an empty basket and return with a basket full of fruit, bread, and cuts of meat and fish we would roast over a fire in the courtyard—and of course, skins of wine.

There was nothing to do, no direction or purpose for us. I spent time cutting wood and whittling shafts to make arrows. I had found a smith who crafted arrowheads for a decent price, and I thought that larger chicken feathers from the fowls in the courtyard might do the trick to balance the ends.

Master Saul had no such work to occupy his time and keep his mind sharp. He had begun to lose his normally robust personality, becoming taciturn. Sitting in the courtyard, he would stare up at the sky, framed within four walls, while drinking cup after cup of wine. One time I stepped into the courtyard to find him standing next to Vanitas the mule engaged in a single-way conversation in hushed Hebrew. The man was losing more than his former personality.

I had no idea what month it was, for each day that passed melded into the next, and unlike in my memories of Europe, there were no distinct seasons in the Province of Syria, only very warm and less warm. But the air felt cool and the leaves of the fig tree that bore no figs rattled a bit in what could be considered a breeze when I entered the courtyard to ask Master Saul if he wished me to bring anything in particular from the marketplace.

He had become quite drunk. He raised his glassy eyes to me and said, "I'm tired of living like this, Bern. Can you bring something to put an end to my weariness?" He then poured more wine down his throat.

At that moment I knew I was losing my master, my friend.

࿐

As usual I had filled the basket with the customary food and drink meant to keep Master and me alive another few days. I wandered away from the marketplace square knowing in the side streets just off the main market, one could find wares deviating from the conventional. I intended to seek out an apothecary that may carry powerful powders whose sole purpose was conveying someone from this life to the next one. Just as I headed toward a narrow lane, I noticed a small gathering around a man shouting and gesturing.

I reached the edge of the people and found yet another vagabond preacher of the Way of the Christ. I skirted the small crowd and stepped into the lane. A woman was pulling a little boy along and scolding him in a shrill voice. "What in the name of Zeus is wrong with you, Paul? Why can't you behave yourself like your brother Barnabus?"

Three steps later I froze. The whole plan, the entirety of the next years lay suddenly before me. I dashed back to the old man's dwelling and prayed to Mercury I would not find my master already dead. But I later realized there were few opportunities. He couldn't very well hang himself from the fig-less tree, which would snap in two even from his decreasing weight.

I found the rooms empty, but a candle burned in the old man's chamber, on a table by his bed. This was an annoying habit of his, to leave a flame burning when he was out. He could afford such waste after he raised our rent by a coin. I thought of snuffing out the flame but was distracted by the thought of the plan I wanted to discuss with Master, so I took my basket outside.

I entered the courtyard to find him debating with the mule. "Master, sit down and hear me out!" I called.

"What?" he croaked. "It took all the energy I have to stand and walk over here. This idiot mule won't come when called."

"Please sit down."

"You seem to have your heart set on my sitting, so as you wish." He shuffled to the stool beside the would-be tree and eased himself upon it. "Did you procure a poison for me?" He eyed the full basket I laid at my feet. "So let's prepare a feast to see me off."

"I have no poison," I said. "I have something much better."

"Something quicker? Something less painful?"

Something less ... deadly. Master Saul, you're going to stay alive."

"But I don't wish to, not like this."

"I know. You can't stay cooped in this space forever. And you won't."

"You found another place for us to hide?"

"Master, we're going to leave this place and go wandering."

"And get ourselves arrested and executed." He glanced over the courtyard wall, someplace where the air carried the sounds of children playing and dogs barking into our little space of confinement. "One look at me, even after all this time, and I'm theirs. Justice has a long memory."

"You haven't seen your reflection in a long while," I said. "You don't look like Saul of Tarsus anymore. For one thing, you've grown a long beard."

He touched his face and stroked the beard which hung below his neck. "By Jove, I have, haven't I?" The stroking ceased, and he narrowed his eyes at his hand as if wondering why it was there. "You were saying something about leaving this place. You know that's not possible."

"It is, Master. You wear old robes and keep your beard."

"And that's it?"

"That's just a start. We go by different names."

"What names?

"It won't be such a change for you because you'll be Paul."

"And you?"

"Well, I shall be ..." I feigned a search in the air for a name. "Something like ... Oh, I know: Barnabus."

"All right, so we're Paul and, uh, Barnabus. And what do we do?"

"As for me, Master—and I can't be heard calling you that anymore except as my guide and teacher, I'll be your assistant."

"My assistant ... of what?"

"This is why I wanted you to sit." I took a breath and let my plan flow out. "You will be a wandering preacher of this Christ of the Way."

He stared at me stone still for the longest, then his shoulders began quaking, and a wheezing sound escaped his mouth. This grew until it became uncontrollable laughter making tears flow down his cheeks. He coughed into a clenched fist, and his laughter became light chuckles. Finally, he calmed and smiled at me. "Thank you," he said. "That was good. Now, where's the poison?"

"I told you. No poison." I knelt at his knees. "You must leave this place and continue to do what you know how to do. But you can't sell goods, because to do that you have to be Saul of Tarsus, the Tentmaker ... You are the best businessman in the world, so use that skill to sell something else."

"What?"

"Sell people the Christ."

"But I don't believe in the Christ."

"Master, you often didn't believe in the quality of the lumber, the copper, the grain you bought and then sold for a handsome profit. Yet you did it with resounding success." I stood, and his face followed me. "I remember you once selling a flock of sheep. I wondered at the time why you even bought such obviously underfed, starving animals. But when you approached men wanting to restock, you kept trying until you found the buyer. By the time you reached success with him, you had him—and even me—convinced this was the finest flock in the province." I leaned forward and placed my hands on his shoulders. "You didn't believe in the sheep ... You believed in yourself, Master. So believe in yourself again, and sell this Christ even though you don't believe in him." I grasped one of his now thin hands in both of mine. "Let's leave this place ... Master Paul."

He stroked his beard. "Sounds like a challenge, and you know I'm always up for a challenge. I suppose we'll have to go out and do some research, should we not, um ... Barnabus, is it?"

CHAPTER TWO

FINDING THE WAY

1

We didn't trust the old man, so we led the mule Vanitas and the cart out of the courtyard behind the dwelling. We walked down the deserted alleyways and busier streets, the mule's reins in my hands. I kept the cloth wound over my head and around my face, but Master merely appeared as he had for the past year-and-a-half in his ratty robe, dull-white turban, and long, unkempt beard.

At a corner of the market square, we found our mark, as Master called him. A small group of men gathered around a lone speaker. In those days, if one accepted life as it was, there was nothing to speak about. One simply lived life, paid the Romans the appropriate taxes, and that was that. However, if one believed there was a better way, he may be so bold as to speak publicly and hopefully draw others toward his belief. The same went for religion. But as I would later come to conclude, religion and government were in the end one and the same entity. We guided Vanitas so he faced away from the speaker, and we sat in the back of the cart to observe and listen. I pulled a scrap of parchment from my tunic and took notes as the follower of the Way spoke.

"The only salvation is through the Christ, the one who gave his life so we can all be truly free. He will soon reappear, and when he does, the cruel oppressors will come to their reckoning, and our land will once and for all belong to God's chosen people." The man, who resembled the one stoned to death nearly perfectly, went on about miracles this Christ performed. He healed sick people with the touch of his hand, in the name of Yahweh. By his command, he calmed a stormy sea.

This preacher was ineffectual, and his tiny audience diminished one-by-one as men left shaking their heads. Finally, the man stood alone leaving Master and me in the back of the cart with no words to hear because even he had wandered away. Master and I looked at each other for a moment before he said, "Well, I can't say I got anything out of that. I could do far better."

"That's what I've been telling you," I said. "But if this Christ really could do all those things, he must have been powerful. He must have known something the rest of us don't."

"I wonder about that," Master said. "The other fellow, the one who met his end on the path, described a slightly different Christ. His was the Jewish Messiah, meant to unite his people against the Romans, even though he died leaving us ll still provinces of Rome. This one spoke of similar notions, but added something about salvation, like something spiritual and magical. It's almost as if they were talking about two different men."

"But what was his name?"

"I don't know. He's probably wandering around the marketplace somewhere. You can find him and ask him."

"No, not the preacher. This Christ fellow of whom these preachers speak."

"Ah, him. I'm not sure it matters. He sounds to me more of an idea than a man." In his grin, I saw the old Tentmaker. "Also, I'm not sure it's the same man. Or any man at all."

"But surely, Master, both preachers aren't inventing stories."

"No, I think they believe. They're sincere about someone they've never met or something they've never personally observed. I imagine if you knew these preachers, you'd discover they come from poverty themselves." He climbed down from the cart and motioned me to join him. He grabbed the mule's reins. "Desperate times create desperate stories. And you know, Bern—pardon me, I mean Barnabus, that if you tell someone you knocked over a burning candle and you killed the tiny flame with a slap of your palm, by the time the story gets to the tenth person, the whole house burned down, and the hundredth person will say the entire city went up in flames." He walked along, back toward the dwelling, and I walked beside him. "And if the story spreads enough, under the right circumstances to the right people, people with creative imaginations, you may very well have called upon Prometheus himself to bring fire from the heavens to destroy the whole province." He shook his head. "If I am to join this cult of the Christ, I will likely need to invent my own version."

"And I shall help you do so, Master, um ... Master Paul."

We arrived at the lane leading to the back courtyard, and the air became thick with smoke stinging and watering our eyes. The closer we came to the courtyard gate, the thicker the smoke. At the gate we found something that altered our life-course much quicker than we had planned. Not only was the dwelling burning to the ground as men splashed buckets of water onto the flames in vain, but the old man's charred body had been pulled out of the inferno and laid on the dirt below the fig tree's flapping leaves. In that setting, the tree seemed more alive than ever. The old man's mastiff stood by the body staring down as though awaiting a command to sit.

"Well," said my master, "I believe this is a sign for us to move on."

2

For the next few months, we wandered south of Damascus as far as Jericho, and north to the outskirts of Antioch (though we were smart enough not to enter those city gates). We followed no plan except to learn what we could of this Way of he Christ. When we could, we stayed in inns and rooms of people who were willing to let us invade their privacy for a silver coin or two, which we still had in abundance. When we were outside populated settlements, we camped out for the night.

I learned much of a new tongue, the Aramaic spoken widely in Judea, yet Master had no time to learn the *primitive gibberish*, as he called this language.

After the first few scares, coming near and even face-to-face with Roman soldiers, we became more relaxed, as it appeared our presence sparked no interest. On occasion I would even ask these men for directions to an inn or the next town. The soldiers were pleased to help the travelers along, especially for silver to spend in the taverns.

We stumbled only a few times upon men who appeared more destitute than beggars while spreading the word of the Christ. On each of these occasions I took notes, and later that evening Master and I would discuss what we heard and what we could use.

"This one today was heavy on miracles, but vague when asked for specifics," I said.

"Yes, I noticed," Master said. "And we have yet to meet any-one who personally met the one he preaches about."

"But what was this Christ's name? Where was he born? And how exactly did he die?"

"I don't think any of that matters." Master stroked his beard. "In fact, I have a suspicion it's not a *he*, but rather a *hey*, which is why we're getting so many conflicting stories."

"Do you think so?"

He nodded. "One says the Christ traveled alone. Another says he wandered with a group ... One says he was unmarried. Another says people came to the house where he lived with his wife to hear his words." He perused my notes and then raised his eyes to me. "In the end, my friend, we must create our own Christ."

"That should be easy enough," I said. "Let's start with where he was from."

"If we knew that, it would make him human."

"But he was human, wasn't he?"

He shook his head. "The Christ I envision may be based on a real human, or perhaps an amalgam of several real humans. But the one I plan to sell is a spiritual idea. The less I talk about an actual person, the more veritable my version."

"I'm not really sure what you mean. The only real person with a story would then be you."

"Precisely!"

"All right then ... So how did you come to know about this Christ of the Way?"

"That's just it. It's got to be something dramatic. It's got to be about *me*, not about *him*, whoever he was."

For some reason, I thought of my former master, that horrid Bruno. If something occurred to make him suddenly kind and caring, it would have made quite an impression. "Master," I said, "I have an idea." I told him about the transformation of good coming from evil.

"Yes!" he said. "I like it!" He rose from the cot and paced about the confines of the room, his eyes wide. "Yes ... I was one of those who oppressed the followers of the Way. I directed

he stoning to death of that preacher a few years ago. We'll
have to give him a name."

I thought of names I had heard. Children called out by
their mothers in alleyways. "Stephen," I said.

"Stephen. That's a good one." He stopped pacing. "And
then what?"

I could think of nothing religious but of the Greek and
Roman gods. Lightning bolts and flashes of volcanic erup-
tions. "Blinded!" I screamed. He narrowed his eyes at me. "On
your way back to Damascus, you were blinded by a white-hot
light in the sky!"

He sat back on the cot. A smile spread across his face. "And
out of the light came the voice of— "

"The Christ!" we said together, and we laughed like little
boys creating naughty images. "And what did he say to you?"
I asked.

Master stood and lowered his face to the floor. He cupped
his hands over his lips and his voice became a deep baritone.
"Why do you persecute me?"

He looked up at the ceiling shielding his eyes and acting
fearful. "Who are you?"

"The one you persecute," he said, cupping his hands over
his lips.

"You don't sound like my wife!" And we both lay on our
cots laughing wildly until there was a knock on the door and
a call for us to be quieter.

As we talked through that evening until we were both too
exhausted to stay awake, we decided there would be no mention of this Christ's name, or his birth, life, or death. The

focus would be on Master Paul and his ability to sell the Way. The less said, the less likely to offend and be stoned to death or arrested by the authorities. We both decided to test our abilities tomorrow.

3

We decided at Jericho to wander northwest to Arimathea, an obscure town at the northern edge of Judea, to initiate the mission of Paul and his assistant Barnabus. It lay in the dry valley of hills bald of vegetation, the nearest natural water source a stream over five leagues to the west. The people procured their water from many wells dug into the hard-packed earth. It was at one of these wells where we began our new careers.

My master stood at the well and began speaking when one middle-aged woman stepped up to lower her bucket by a rope. As she struggled to raise the full bucket, I came up to her and motioned that I would help, and she accepted with a shy smile and bowed head.

"Good people of Arimathea," my master said in the Greek Koine, "I have news for you. News of a new and abundant life for those who hear with their ears but listen with their hearts."

The woman thanked me for my aid and whispered in Aramaic, "If your friend wants us to understand him, he will have better luck in our local tongue."

"I am Paul, and I come to you from Antioch." I held out my palm to him and repeated his words in Aramaic. We continued hus with a pause after sentences or phrases. "I was against fol-owers of the Christ of the Way, even supervising the execu-ion of Stephen ... But the Christ was stronger than my efforts. While I traveled on the path to Damascus to ferret out other nembers of this cult, he came to me from the sky in a flash of blinding light. He showed me how I erred and told me to con-inue to the city and seek out followers of the Christ, one of whom would restore my sight with the touch of his hand ..."

As I repeated his text in the language of the people, I viewed him from the corners of my eyes. I had never heard his story. It felt as though he were improvising this fantas-ic, compelling narrative. He continued to speak, to sell the cult of the Way, and I noticed the woman had been joined by a small crowd. Many of their faces were struck with awe; he held these people spellbound. The difference in Master and the wandering vagabond preachers was the cadence of his words and timbre of his baritone voice, the flash of his eyes and fluidity of his gestures.

He spoke for perhaps half an hour, and during this time a small pile of silver disks bearing the image of Emperor Tiberius—recently late and replaced by his nephew Caligula—grew at the base of the well.

At that night's campfire, I counted the coins before dumping them into a pouch. "I never thought there would be profit in this Christ stuff," I said, "But we could earn a living doing this."

"Yes," Master said, "and it's so easy. Far easier than selling sheep or metal."

"And where did you get that story of being blinded, then cured at the hands of those whom you wished dead?"

"That was a good one, wasn't it? Some of the best stories passed down from the old Greeks contain irony in justice. I thought of my favorite blind man, the old prophet Tiresias, and how he lost his sight after gazing on Athena. Then I thought of a story in which he played a major role. How Oedipus's search for justice led back to himself." Master chuckled, staring into the dancing campfire flames. "I really don't know how one led to the other, how I got from being blinded by the light of the Christ to being cured of blindness by his followers, but I rather enjoyed telling it."

A few days later we happened upon another traveling preacher speaking to three listeners outside the town of Sychar. He seemed uninspired, and his small audience even less so. "This cult needs to become a movement if it is to survive," Master said to me. "The men who want others to believe and follow are killing it with stories of a Christ who was merely a man. He needs to be the stuff of the very heavens!" The preacher lost his tiny crowd, and we moved on.

We spent a few weeks circling the Sea of Galilee from the southern shore and around going eastward and then north. At Capernaum, Master preached the same sermon as he had in Arimathea, but his tone was ever more vibrant. He added something that initially bothered me, and I translated it hesitantly into Aramaic for those who didn't know the Koine.

"And the Christ told me he would return during the lifetimes of most who are hearing my words!"

"And he will defeat the Romans who occupy us so brutally?" shouted a man in the crowd gathered before the synagogue.

Master raised an index finger to the sky. "Know this," he said. "The Romans shall be defeated, but not with the sword. They will be overwhelmed by the perfect love known as *agape*, and they will also come to embrace the Christ."

"The Romans—the worst of the Gentiles—following the Jewish Messiah?" shouted another man. "I say this Paul before us speaks blasphemy!"

I urged my master to sit in the cart and grab the mule's reins while I pulled the bow from my shoulders and notched an arrow. Walking backwards behind the cart, I aimed toward the crowd, and no one within it dared to challenge me.

That evening while sitting at the campfire, I breathed a silent prayer to Mercury that we were far enough away from the dangers of Capernaum. "Master," I said, "what is this *agape* you spoke of?"

"Obviously not a concept these Jews are yet prepared for. It's an old Greek term. A perfect, brotherly love. Loving all humans equally, with the knowledge that our enemies are people, too." He grabbed a stick and stirred the tip into the glowing embers at the bottom of our fire. "You see, the Jews have a long history, written into the books, of believing we are Yahweh's chosen people. Through us and only through us does God work his plan for the world. So when people after people—Egyptians, Assyrians, Greeks, and now Romans—barge in with their military superiority and run our affairs, it tends to rankle us because it runs contrary to the plan."

"But if Yahweh prefers that the Jews win," I said, "then why doesn't He simply intervene and make it so?"

"That would be logical, would it not?" he said. "Something I asked my father, who merely said I was too young to understand how to ask the right questions."

"So am I too young to know the right questions?"

"No, and neither was I. It's the absolute, right question. The Jews are not the chosen people. Those who have been elsewhere know this little strip of dusty land we sit on now cannot possibly matter that much to a creator of the universe." Master stood and looked off into the darkness surrounding us. "You, my friend, are one of the wisest people I've ever known, and you come from a far different people than these. Do your people believe they are chosen by the divine?"

"I never heard anyone say so."

"That's because your people, and the Celts you've spoken of, are truly free. Only those enslaved in their hearts and minds believe they are God's people." I could see in his eyes he had come to a decision. "It's time for us to spend some of the silver and gold we have in the cart."

"What will we buy, Master?"

"A ship ... or at least passage on one." He raised his face to the stars as though speaking to them. "If the people in the land of the Christ are not willing to accept his Way, maybe it is meant for the lands of the Gentiles."

4

From Damascus a well-built Roman road led to Tyre, a major port city of the Province of Syria. Two days later, we arrived at the marketplace, a short walk to the shipyard. For nearly a week, we unloaded the goods in the cart and sold my beloved hooved friend Vanitas and the now-empty cart to a widow who needed a way to transport her grain from field to market. When she gave him a hug and pat, I knew he was in good hands. The old mule had served us well, and I prayed again to Mercury he would live out his life useful and respected.

Our gold and silver secured in locked chests, we boarded the ship as the only passengers bound for Thessalonica in the Province of Macedonia. Master and I took shifts staying close to the chests in the hull. Master cared little for the sight of distant shorelines, surrounding waves, and passing vessels, so he took the daytime watch over our goods. I enjoyed the time holding onto the rail on deck, my face stinging in the cool saltwater breeze. Looking out at the endless rolling water, I felt a momentary freedom.

I stood on the top step of the hull as Master tried his luck selling the Christ of the Way in the Greek Koine to the sailors, who enjoyed the odd digression. "Add a li'l strong ale to your fancy talk, an' ya just may win me o'er!" a sailor said, to the delight of his comrades. They then drowned him out with an argument over which was better—strong ale versus a special wine home-made by a specific member of the crew. They reminded me of the one-eyed former German slave Raiko. I thought he would fit right in with this lot.

As we sailed along the southern coast of Asia Minor, the captain called out, "Passing Tarsus!" as he did with all landmarks. The ship sailed close enough for a distant view of Master's home town, walled in and perched atop a hill. Although it was a dark night, we could perceive the firelight of the torches on the battlements. I watched from the top step. Master's back was to me. He leaned against the railing, and I sensed in him a longing for a fleeting memory of some past life. He remained so until the city drifted out of view to the east.

After passing the eastern point of the great island of Crete, the ship maneuvered through a series of islands, some of which belonged to Asia and some the Province of Achaia in Greece. With fair weather, we were but a couple days from our goal of Thessalonica.

We met at dawn at the entrance to the hull below for Master's shift guarding our chests. I asked him, "Why Thessalonica? Why not great Athens?"

"From my childhood I learned that the Athenians are proud people. They believe all great things in the world originated with them, and most of them probably did. They couldn't produce conquerors like Alexander of Macedonia, but they made up for it in the thinkers like Aristotle, Plato, Socrates, and writers like Homer and Sophocles." He braced against a sudden splash of water from the sea. "The great city also gave these seamen their Poseidon and all the Greeks their Olympian gods. The Athenians know the Romans adopted the Greek gods and gave them Latin names. Their form of religion has withstood the test of time. In short, they believe theirs is the true way, and we would come to a painful end in that city if we come marching in with our talk of the Christ and his Way."

"But don't the Thessalonians hold belief in the Athenians' gods?"

"Yes ... in name. But distance creates a laxness in all things. Even devotion ... So if we are to succeed among the Gentiles, Thessalonica is a safe start."

We found an inn with our own lock on our room door for the duration of our stay. For the first time, we didn't worry about our chests full of silver and gold. After a night's sleep in beds in a space that didn't rock with the motion of waves, we set out for the temple dedicated to Aphrodite where members of the cult of Dionysus worshiped.

Master had begun to dress as before in fine silken robes ... yet he retained the flowing, wavy beard and longer hair, now his costume as much as a disguise. Before the steps leading to the temple entrance, Master looked impressive. He began his introduction in the Greek Koine, and since this temple was situated on the busiest thoroughfare in the city, a crowd soon gathered. Unlike in the Jewish provinces of Judea and Samaria, these people interrupted him often to make comments or ask questions. He was asked if he were a Jew, and he stated that he was born into these people, yes, but most importantly he was a citizen of the Roman Empire.

He was asked if this Christ was a Jew and a Roman citizen. He leveled his eyes at the growing audience. "Labels such as Jew or Greek or Roman or German do not apply to the Christ. He belongs to the Kingdom of God, which serves the spiritual needs of all human beings. Perhaps he was a Jew in earthly life, but he is now the Christ for all people, Jew and Gentile alike. He is your Christ, if you will but accept him, believe and follow. He will set you spiritually free in a way your many gods were never able to do."

Though he didn't impress everyone, three friends remained to speak with us after his talk finished. We were invited to the home of one of them, a man named Timothy, and together we feasted and spoke of the Christ and the freedom the Way offered. "I must admit," said Timothy, "I feared your talk would lead to subversion against Caesar, and we in Thessalonica accept Caesar as our ruler."

"Your earthly ruler," said Master. "But the Christ rules your heart."

"And for those who go so far as to worship Caesar as their god?"

"That is their choice. But if it is to be the preference of the city government, then we must tread carefully in public about the Christ. Dead, his followers cannot spread his word."

The next day around noon, we hired men to move our chests to the house of Timothy, who—to our incredible luck—operated a secure bank where we could deposit our money, which would be loaned on interest to grow into more money. Master was fascinated by this passive method of creating profit, and when he wasn't meeting strangers with his word of the Christ, he spent time learning the ways of the bank. He relayed to me privately that if someday he could cease running with an eye over his shoulder and settle somewhere, he would open his own bank.

᳐

"I met a man who would be happy to host meetings of the Christ and the Way in his home," Timothy told us at supper after we had been in this city for a little over a month.

And thence was founded my master's—Paul's—first church dedicated to the Way of the Christ. Master had known only the Jewish synagogue of his first two decades as his place of worship, so out of habit he met with the followers once per week on the Jewish Sabbath. However, this changed to Sunday since that was the local day free of work. We gathered in the courtyard, and Master's voice competed with bleating, mooing, and neighing from the various pens and stalls. The host built a makeshift wooden platform upon which my master stood and spoke. At first there were only half a dozen polite, intent listeners, but the followers multiplied with each passing Sunday until the courtyard was packed with only room to stand shoulder to shoulder. Master would place a basket on the dirt before him, and when we went home, it was half full of coins to add to the bank account.

From one of these gatherings, Master brought two young women home to his room in Timothy's house. I pored over my notes under a lit taper in my small chamber next to his larger one with those familiar sounds of pleasure seeping muffled through the plaster wall. The next morning we all enjoyed a hearty breakfast, and after the two women—one brunette and the other auburn-haired—departed, Master took a long sip of water and wiped his lips with the back of a hand. He said, "Being an emissary of this Christ has more benefits than

I imagined! The young ladies love a man of God! You really ought to enjoy these fruits while we're both alive," he added with a wink.

We had been living this way for nearly three months when two members met with us after one of Master's courtyard sessions. They each offered to host followers at their homes, and they wished to spread the news themselves. "I have heard you so many times," one told Master, "I feel confident I can do it, too." My master told him if he believed in himself, then he could convince others to believe in the Way of the Christ. So the church in Thessalonica was firmly established, and Master told Timothy it was time to spread the word elsewhere.

Timothy left the business of the bank in his brother's hands, and sailed with us to Corinth. With his good name—and with our good silver and gold—another church dedicated to the Way of the Christ was successfully established. We remained in this city for over a year, and our fortunes grew.

At one of the Sunday meetings in a Corinthian host's courtyard, a man stepped forward trailed by a younger fellow who wore a slave's wrist bands. "Master Paul," said the well-dressed rich man, "your Christ sounds filled with purity and goodness."

"That he is," replied Master.

"And he sounds like he has a heart for the lowest among us."

Master nodded. "He has indicated so to me."

"What does he feel about slaves and slavery? What should I do with my slaves? How should I treat them? Does the Christ compel me to free my slaves?"

Master gave me a slight look. We locked eyes and then turned them quickly away from one another. He knew these were dangerous questions that could get us arrested and executed for treason to the Crown in Rome if he answered incorrectly. He took a deep breath. "Slavery has always been with us. Eve was subordinate to Adam in the Garden of Eden. Even in Heaven, the angels belong to God. Slaves must accept their status and serve their masters well in hopes of securing their freedom. They should not rebel in attempt to gain their freedom, for such acts run contrary to God's plan." The rich man nodded in approval, but Master held up a finger. "However, as master you have an obligation to treat your slave with kindness and respect, for we are all slaves."

"How am I a slave?" the rich man protested.

"If you follow the Way of the Christ, you belong to the Christ. He is your master, and you are his slave. And don't forget it is also your duty to indoctrinate your slaves to the Way of the Christ."

I knew Master would never set me free as long as he lived, and though I had many questions over his words to the rich man, I never posed them.

When Master's reputation as lover of lovely Greek girls began to rival the popularity of belief in the Christ, especially when it resulted in one young lady beating another nearly to death in a fit of rage and jealousy, we decided it was time to move on, choosing Philippi, east of Thessalonica.

There the power of gold proved superior to the power of the Christ. We had been in Philippi for nearly half a year when a Greek council member visited us at the house of Tychicus, a wealthy merchant originally from the lands east of Judea. We were in the garden planning the talk for the following Sunday while Master enjoyed a rather good wine, according to him.

A man barged into the garden dragging a young girl along with a strong grip on her wrist. He halted before us. We glanced up from the parchments we had been reading to his glare and sneer. "What do you have to say about this?" he shouted at my master.

"About what?" Master asked casually. "About the lovely girl you hold?" There was a slightly perceptible wink from him to her.

"This *lovely girl* is my daughter! And she's pregnant!"

Master gave away nothing. He smiled at the man. "I suppose congratulations are in order. If we remain in Philippi long enough, will you invite me to the naming ceremony in the temple? Or even better, may this child be the first baby brought before the Christ as a future follower?"

"Stop these games, you pervert! You were not careful and didn't know or care who you lay with. As City Council member, I give you two choices. Either you are arrested and brought before the court, or you marry my daughter Miriam and legitimize her child. *Your* child," he said, pointing his accusing finger at Master.

I could tell in his expression Master had never known this girl's name. "My dear, um, Miriam, would you be so kind as to wander in the garden so your father and I can talk? There are the loveliest flowers in the back."

Timothy and I rose from our stools, but Master motioned us back down and told the angry father whatever the two of them had to say needed to be said to us as well. He bade the man sit in an empty chair, and now the two of them looked each other in the eyes. "Your threats seem sincere enough," Master said. "But to whom am I speaking now?"

"My name is Nikodemus, and I am a member of— "

" —the City Council, yes ... All right, Master Nikodemus, what price do you demand to settle this problem?"

"Price?" The man leaned forward, his clenched fists trembling. "What do you mean? Are you trying to bribe me?"

"Yes," Master replied calmly, "and I will likely succeed." He looked at Timothy, then me. "So will you forget it all for, say, fifty silver coins?"

The anger in the man's face softened, and he folded his hands together on his lap. "You would part with so much? All right then, one hundred ... and you leave the city immediately, and you are never again to step foot inside the city gates."

The old businessman who was Saul of Tarsus returned in that garden, and Master was able to negotiate the bribe down to seventy-five silver coins and a month for us to prepare our departure from the city gates. The city councilman and his daughter left the three of us. Timothy spoke through his gritted teeth. "This is how you spend the money we raise to build the church? On bribery to cover your selfish appetites?"

"This, Timothy, is money well-spent. Barnabus here and I will leave soon to Asia Minor. You have the three churches— Thessalonica, Corinth, and Philippi—to tend to. May they grow and spread, making you and your bank the richest enterprise in Greece." He rose and spread his hands as though encompassing the garden in his embrace. "This Way of the Christ is becoming the biggest business in Greece, and with any luck, the Roman Empire."

CHAPTER THREE

RETURN TO THE FAMILIAR

1

Six weeks later, we rode a man-powered ferry across from Byzantium in Europe to Asia Minor. We brought with us five hundred silver coins as a parting gift from Timothy to continue our so-called mission for the spreading of the Christ and the Way. On a hunch, Master decided to go south along the coastal cities and stop in Ephesus, where he said the worship in both Jewish synagogues and Greek temples was nearly non-existent. We bought two old mares for the journey. Master forbade us to name either of these horses, to make it easier to sell them and part with them once we reached our destination. The journey was tedious, and relatively safe. I had to shoot only one would-be bandit attacking us on the open road with a partner. Both were on foot, and the last we saw of them, they had run away on three good feet since one had an arrow in a thigh.

We arrived in Ephesus after enduring a days-long thunderstorm on the road. I had beseeched Master to let me find some shelter such as a cave until the rains abated, but he was insistent on reaching the city in the southwest of the provinces. A weak sun attempted to peak through holes in the clouds when we entered the city's northern gates. Master barely moved on the back of his mare, and he had begun a cough that sounded fluid and deep.

I tethered our steeds outside an inn and from the silver in the chest, paid a few nights in advance for a warm room. Past several passers-by, I practically carried Master into the building. I sat him on the bed and pushed his chest to ease him down. I left him and retrieved hot broth and a pail of boiling water from the kitchen. He lay with a rag soaked in the boiling water draped over his forehead and slurped the soup from a wooden ladle I guided to his lips. Thus we spent the first week in Ephesus, by the end of which Master's cough had abated and he was able to pace about the room.

Little did I know, hot soup down the throat and a steamy hot cloth on the forehead, which is what my people in the far north employed to cure the coughs and chills, would lead to the conversion of so many to the cult of the Christ in our first stop in Asia Minor. For when we stepped out of the inn and onto the dirt street intending to find some busy thoroughfare, we were immediately surrounded by several locals. "This one was close to death," a young man said, pointing at Master. "When they entered the inn, the short one carried him inside. The bearded one appeared like he was struck by the pest. What happened?"

I said, "I merely gave him— "

"Barnabus here gave me the touch of his hand as he prayed over me, filling me with, uh, the Holy Spirit of the Christ."

"A miracle!" one of the men shouted. "Please tell us about this Christ and the Holy Spirit!"

The small crowd walked along with Master in the lead until we all reached the Temple of Artemis. By the end of his talk—and he began to refer to these talks as sermons—the largest gathering ever surrounded him. Word had spread about his miraculous healing through the Holy Spirit with his servant Barnabus as its conductor. Many in the audience asked specifically about this phenomenon, and Master described it as "God permeating the very air so all can be touched by the power of the Christ." If we truly believe in the Christ, Master told them, each of us, though we are of a lowly status among our peers, can perform great deeds through his Holy Spirit with which the Christ has filled the believer.

Back in our room later that day, I asked Master what this Holy Spirit thing was all about. "I only kept you warm and fed you hot broth. That's what I filled you with."

He chuckled. "Like all of my best ideas, my friend, this just came to me out of nowhere. The idea of Yahweh's spirit alive and working in the world is as old as the oldest scriptures, which means the average working Jew wouldn't know of it, and absolutely none of the Greeks who believe in the Olympian gods, though I've heard the Romans have something like a traveling spirit."

"So I suppose this Holy Spirit will become a part of the Way now."

"Yes," he said, "I believe we have no choice. The people seem to fancy this concept."

"But what if they try to cure a friend who's suffering the chills and a cough? What if they lay their hands on him and try to fill him with this Holy Spirit thing?"

"Then they will cure him with the Holy Spirit ... and hopefully they'll have some hot broth and a steaming cloth close by."

2

During one of Master's sermons, a man in the front of the congregation suddenly fell to the ground and began making unintelligible noises from his throat and mouth. Master stopped speaking of the now multiple visions he had had in which the Christ spoke to him, and stood over the babbling man. He asked if this were some form of language. I replied that I had never heard it before, and during Master's inquiry and my reply, the man continued the sounds.

Finally, a friend of the afflicted man stepped forward. "Master, he has been known to do this from time to time. He stops after a while and has no idea what happened ... I'm glad he's doing it now," he said, raising his voice to be heard, "for now you have proof of his possession by demons, and now you can use the Holy Spirit to drive them out!"

Master looked at me, and I could only shrug. In another moment of improvisation, Master said, "This man is not possessed by demons! The angels themselves are speaking their

anguage through his lips! I will tell all of you what they wish
ou to know!" He knelt and placed a palm on the man's fore-
1ead. Master's body jerked and stiffened as though he were
truck by lightning. "The heavenly host guided by the Christ
greets you!" he said. "If you do not support this new church
vith your tithings of ten percent of your earnings, the moun-
ains will erupt, and you will be lost in the flowing fire!" Mas-
er then fell backwards to the ground, and when I knelt by his
ide, he opened his eyes and winked at me.

Miraculously, the babbling man ceased his clatter and
tared about himself stupidly. "Oh, no!" he said. "Did it hap-
en again?" His friend helped him to his feet, placed an arm
around his shoulders, and led him away. The empty basket
hat always sat before Master as he spoke to the people sud-
1enly filled to the brim as those present tossed in coin after
coin.

The phenomenon of speaking in unknown tongues soon
ecame a common practice, often with Master soliciting men
o play the roles of those suddenly struck by the Holy Spirit
hrough their tongues so he could lay his hands on their fore-
1eads and *interpret*. He'd invite these men to our quarters,
and the rehearsals were among the most absurd things I'd ever
1eard. "No," Master would say, "it's not *flabalaladum*. That
ounds too much like baby talk. Try *fealadalaciricum*."

The church in Ephesus grew so much in the next months,
everal congregants spoke of using the funds gathered during
he Sunday meetings to construct a new building since there
vere no empty places to renovate. This would have been good
1ews, but such activity would direct more attention to Master

and me than we would like. We were, after all, still fugitives on the run as far as we knew. The solution to the problem of our popularity, as often occurred, came to us from without.

A man who had visited our meetings while he conducted business in the city from his home town lingered after the followers left us and we were counting the collection. "I am Simon of Colossae," he said with a bow. "In my town we already have many followers of the Christ and the Way, but we have no one to lead us correctly. We also already have a large hall where we can meet."

"So," said Master, "you need some leadership?"

"Yes, Master Paul ... Is there anyone you can send to us?"

I had learned to read the subtle glint in Master's eyes. "I believe it may be time for us to move on," he said. Leaning in closer to me, he whispered, "Colossae is that much closer to Tarsus."

"And soon we come full-circle?" I said, and he winked and nodded.

In the heat of the summer, we arrived in the small city in southern Galatia. As Simon had said, loose followers of the Way had been gathering in a former temple dedicated to a Greek god now forgotten. The locals were quite devout, but to what, exactly, was the ultimate question. There was a thriving *cult of the angel*, in which the archangel Michael sat in center focus. Also, people from the town and neighboring villages flocked often to a spring dividing the city east to west. Its waters held supposed healing properties, though no one could point to any concrete examples of cures.

The people were friendly, especially the young ladies toward Master and his seductive personality. A group of carpenters built a dwelling for Master and me, situated directly over a hot spring. For the time of our stay we lived in comfort. The new church thrived in this dwindling town of relative obscurity. This could have easily been our home for the rest of our days. But my master's success in his business of the cult of the Christ rendered that end impossible.

It was in Colossae where Master received the first of letters from another church petitioning for help. It came from a messenger passing through, and had originated from the church of the Christ in Rome. "Am I reading this correctly? There's a church of mine in Rome?"

"I believe it was founded by a follower of Timothy," I said, bending over the parchment.

"A follower of a follower. Well, this can't last long in the Capital. Emperor Claudius won't stand for it." Master sat with his feet in the warm water and lay back, his folded hands on his belly. "Well, what do these people have to say?"

I held the parchment, faded in the long journey, closer to my eyes. "It appears they have a problem with homosexuality, Master."

"Doesn't surprise me in that city," he chortled under his breath. "So what do they want?"

"They wonder where the Christ stands on this issue."

He reached blindly above his head, missing the pillow each time. I laid the parchment upon the table and placed the pillow under his head. He stretched back on the stone floor and pulled his shawl down covering his eyes.

"So what should I tell them?"

"I'm too busy for such silly matters," he said. "Just fix it." And his slow, heavy breathing told me he was soon sound asleep.

Just fix it? I had no idea what advice to give them over this matter. I knew Master had demonstrated an occasional leaning toward young, fair men. For him, they were the exotic side-dish in a normally routine diet. I thought of my people in northern Germania. A man who preferred to lie with another man was considered a deviant, and was most often put to death when his deviance was discovered. For my people, it was simply a matter of running contrary to the dictates of nature. Sex, though pleasurable, was meant to create babies, hopefully Germanic male babies. And homosexual pleasure was of no benefit to the race; therefore, it was unlawful.

I had had the opportunity to read the old Hebrew scriptures, the *Torah* and the *Talmud* of Master's people, both clearly against the activity which concerned the Roman church. So I wrote back as Paul, forbidding homosexuality in the strongest language possible. I affixed his signature underneath my script, rolled and sealed the parchment, then found and paid a courier to send the reply on to the addressee.

I have no idea why, except to give the first letter an air of validity and to have some fun of my own, I wrote to the Corinthian church stating Paul's edict to the Romans, yet with even

stronger language. I sent this letter, by way of Simon to Ephesus on his next business trip, forbidding not only homosexuals
but all fornicators from entering the Kingdom of God. Hopefully from thence it would find its way to Corinth.

Only a few months later a courier brought a reply from
Corinth stating they agreed with the ban on men who lie with
other men. But as to the sanction against all fornicators, they
hoped there were some error in the script, for in their judgment,
without fornication the church would be empty within a generation. I decided not to share this communique with Master.

During the next spring, the city held its annual festival in
honor of the old angel cult and in the name of the archangel.
A play was staged in which a beautiful teenage boy, playing
the role of Michael, was lowered from a crane to found the
city and bless the spring which nourished it. This year, it was
cult meeting cult, with Master and his church of the Christ
at the center. Master sat in the front row admiring the youth
as he touched ground and blessed the spring in his character's
name and the names of the host of angels. Master leaned into
me and whispered, "After the performance, go meet that boy
and bring him to our house."

"For what purpose, Master?"

"What do you mean, 'For what purpose'? For the usual
purpose. He's a beautiful boy. I want him."

"But you can't have him, Master."

"Do I need to remind you that you are still my— "

"—slave. No, you don't need to remind me of that. But the
problem lies with what you wrote to the churches in Rome
and Corinth."

319

"What do you mean? I never wrote to anyone."

"The leaders of the church in Rome wrote to you, remember?"

He stared off, trying to bring forth the memory. "Vaguely. But I never wrote back."

"But you did. You told me to fix it, so I did."

"Oh, Bern ... What did you write, in my name?"

"The Christ is completely against men lying with men, to begin with."

His eyes widened. "What compelled you to tell them that?"

"The ancient scriptures of the Jews, who stoned such men to death. And my own people, who chopped effeminate men to pieces and fed those pieces to the pigs and dogs."

He clamped his lips together. His eyes landed on a dancing girl, one of the water nymphs. "Oh well, I still have the young ladies," he said.

"Perhaps I should tell you what else you wrote to the Corinthians," I said.

3

It had been over a decade since the unfortunate death of the daughter of the Syrian Provincial Vice Governor. Master longed to visit his hometown in hopes the lust for justice against him would be just as dead. He packed enough silver and gold to appease his wife, and with a chest full, we bade a fond farewell to the now-thriving church of Colossae, and rode two stud horses, which we decided to eventually name, eastward.

Tarsus had little changed in all the years since I first walked through the northern gate. The market square was still abustle with the noise of bartering in so many tongues. The air was still thick with the smell of spices, citrus fruits, and sweat. We led our horses, his named Lucrum and mine Dubium, past the synagogue and into an alleyway, the end of which would give us a view of the front court of Master's house.

Master froze a few seconds. Roman soldiers stood at the gate, as they had probably done for several years. So Master was still a wanted man, and the hunt was still on. Our long-ago attempt to fool authorities into believing my master dead failed. We turned our horses around and wandered through the streets and alleyways until we reached the southern gate with the view of the Great Sea below.

We both listened to the waves attacking the shore. "What now, Master?" I said.

He sighed, dejected. "We move on. Let's go into the land where this Christ supposedly lived. Maybe we will discover *what now* there."

"Back to the lands where the incident occurred? Is that wise?"

"It would be the last area where I would be expected. The Vice Governor is probably dead by now, or in his final days in retirement in his Roman villa. They obviously expect me to return here." He looked to the east. "So I plan to disappoint them and remain a step ahead. To Judea," he said, "where we can fade into obscurity."

He guided his horse Lucrum east along the coastal road, and I followed.

321

For weeks we traveled without speaking a word to anyone about the cult of the Christ or the movement of the Way. Although we could have found a night's rest in a comfortable inn in the Syrian city of Antioch, that was the last place we should light. So we skirted its walls and rested instead in Seleucia on the coast of the Great Sea.

Riding south on the coast, Master stopped and stared west into the waters at each shipping yard we passed: Tripolis, Sidon, Tyre. At the southernmost of these, Tyre, it seemed almost as though he planned to book a berth on a ship. He took his horse directly to the docks and ambled along, looking at each ship we passed. Finally he motioned for me to come up beside him. "Do you wish to board a ship?" he said.

"If you desire to go somewhere, of course."

"I have no desire to venture into the sea, ever again ... But do *you*, Bern, wish to go?"

At last, his meaning came clear to me. "Master," I said, "if ever I am to part from you, it will be as a freeman. Legally, with the signature and seal of Saul of Tarsus. Since you cannot sign as that name without fear of capture and execution or imprisonment, I go where you go."

"Very well, then," he said. "We go south." He clicked his tongue and gave the reins a slight jerk, and off we went south along the coastal road.

At Caesarea a preacher of the Way was speaking before the synagogue. "It is said," he proclaimed to the small crowd of nen, "there have been churches set up in Gentile lands in the name of Christ. But do they truly follow the Word of God? Do they know of the Blessed Trinity? Three divine beings in one? God the Father, God the Christ, and God the Holy Spirit!"

"I wish I had thought of that," Master said to me. "Remind me to install this trinity if ever we return to Asia Minor."

"Christ has come and gone, but he is still with us in his spirit," the preacher continued. "Within your lifetime, he will reappear in Jerusalem, and then the world will know the meaning of Messiah!"

"Let's go," Master told me, turning his horse Lucrum away from the crowd.

"Where to, Master?"

"It is time for me to finally visit the holiest of cities for my people. To Jerusalem!" He sent Lucrum into a canter.

"Well, Dubium," I said to my horse, "what are we waiting for?" And toward the rising sun we went, following the dust wake of Master and his steed.

4

The gates of Jerusalem were well-defended by teams of Jewish and Roman guards. There had been many attempts by outside groups and forces in the past decades to infiltrate this city, key to the control of the region, and set a rebellion in motion. Therefore, entry by unknowns had proven next to impossible.

Master decided to make the town of Bethany, within walking distance to the southeast of Jerusalem, our post until we could find a way into the old city. We could have afforded to simply remain quietly in a rented room for as long as we needed until an opportunity to enter presented itself. That's what we could have done. But Master was never one to sit quietly for long.

I awoke one morning to find myself alone in the room. I dressed and searched the house and barn, but no sign of Master, and both horses stood feeding from sacks hung over their heads. I went back to the room, grabbed the small chest of coins, and left the house.

At a well, Master stood surrounded by a large crowd. He spoke to them of his conversion, of the holy trinity, especially the power of the Holy Spirit. He told them if only they believed, they would receive the gifts of healing and speaking in the tongues of the angels. He had rarely been so enthralling, so inspired. And I realized the meaning of that word *inspired*. The spirit having come within. To the Greeks it meant a muse giving the artist ideas for a song or painting. But in Master's fictional world of the Way of the Christ, it meant being filled with the so-called Holy Spirit. The businessman made these people believe he believed. It was then that I realized: the whole crux in selling religion is to make people believe in belief.

Early that evening we were startled by an unexpected knock upon our door. I had been reading a history of Alexander which Master had stolen for me from the library in Ephesus. I marked my place and rose to answer the door.

An old Jew dressed in a simple robe, his head covered by a shawl, stood looking at me through tired, glazed gray eyes. He leaned on a walking stick. "Does Paul, the so-called apostle of the Christ, stay in this room?" he said in the Hebrew tongue.

"And who calls upon me? And what was that other thing you called me?" Master stepped beside me.

"My name is Jorma … And some have taken to calling you an apostle of the Christ."

Master took a backward step. "Please come inside." He motioned to a chair. The visitor sat in the chair I had occupied. I leaned against the wall.

"Do you intend to shoot me with that thing?" the old man said, pointing at the bow.

"I don't believe you will give me reason to do so," I answered.

"You wear it for protection?" I nodded. "It appears quite foreign. Celtic, perhaps?" He smiled at my surprise. "Come now … The Romans are not the first foreigners in our lands."

"My good sir," Master said, "you didn't come here to query my companion Barnabus. So what did bring you here?"

"No, Paul, I did not come here to ask questions of your … companion. I represent the Council of Jerusalem."

"A man dressed like you are, you are a member of the City Council?"

"Not that council, but the Council of the Jerusalem Synagogue who follows the Christ."

"Synagogue. A Jewish gathering for the cult of the Christ?"

"First," the visitor said, "we are no cult. We began with men who were with him."

325

"And where are these men now?"

The old man gestured the direction of the great city. "The Roman authorities infiltrate any new group with Jewish spies. They crush these groups in the usual ways: imprisonment, death. None of these men survived. What's left is a loyal group forced to worship underground."

"Back to my original question. What brings you here to me?"

The old man leaned forward, both hands atop of his walking stick. "You have brought the word of the Christ and his Way to Gentiles."

"Yes. They thirst for the same thing as Jews do."

"You do not demand these Greek men undergo circumcision."

"No, of course not. Circumcision is a physical act that does nothing to boost a man's spirit. If anything, it accomplishes the opposite."

"We Jews—*true* Jews—say since the time of Abraham, circumcision is what has set us apart as the chosen people. The Christ, as the Greeks call him, was the Jewish messiah. And as a Jew, he was circumcised."

"Of course," said Master. "But what has his circumcision to do with my mission to the Gentiles?"

"Everything!" the old man said, pounding his stick on the floor. "It has everything to do with your activities among those people. We Jews are the chosen people of Yahweh. The messiah is our leader. He was circumcised, so all who follow him must be likewise circumcised."

"So it comes down to a man's penis?"

"Hmmph!" The old man looked at me. "And you. Are you circumcised?"

"No, sir," I said.

"You carry a Celtic bow, yet you appear Germanic." He refocused on Master. "The Way is not meant for heathens such as this one who accompanies you. Only true Jews are to be accepted, not uncircumcised swine eaters."

"The Christ told me otherwise," said Master.

"Ah, yes, I forget he appeared to you."

"He did."

"And tell me about him. Describe his appearance."

"He has come to me in the sky as a blinding flash of light. He is not of flesh."

"And what language does he speak? Hebrew? Aramaic? Surely not Latin or Greek."

"As he is spirit, not flesh, he speaks not with the mouth but with his heart. His words come to me in the language of the angels."

The old man raised his eyebrows. "And you speak this language, the language of the angels, as you told the people this morning at the well."

"I do when the Christ gives me his meaning."

"How convenient." The old man stood, his knuckles white as his hands grasped the walking stick. "Back in Jerusalem my advice and judgment over you are expected. I believe you are a charlatan. The Way belongs to the Jews. We are to spread the word in this land as we travel by foot. These so-called churches in Gentile lands have nothing to do with our Way."

"Before you leave," Master said, "I want to know if you believe the Messiah will restore God's chosen to their greatness."

"Of course I believe that, as any true Jew does."

"Including defeat of the Roman occupiers by war and violence?"

"By any means necessary. Whatever God wills."

Master stood and stepped forward, face-to-face with this old man Jorma. "The Christ I'm selling to the Gentiles is gaining in popularity. If its growth continues, the Roman government will someday become our puppet. When Caesar is no longer a god, when Caesar has been replaced by the Christ in the lands of the Gentiles, Caesar will have no real power over the Jews here. The Way will cover the Empire like a vine. The Empire will remain, but only in name."

The emissary from Jerusalem started for the door, then stopped. "By your accent, you come from Asia Minor. Return from whence you came. Your people are the Gentiles, not us. Go and enjoy your swine-flesh. If you are still here tomorrow, we will have you arrested."

"On what charge?"

"Plotting to overthrow Caesar's government." He smiled back at us. "We, too, can gather enough silver to bribe men into witnessing what we tell them they witnessed."

I opened the door for him, and he exited. I closed the door and stood facing Master in the silence. "Well," he finally said, "you heard the man. Let's pack our things and go back north."

DESTINY FINDS ME

1

We traveled at a leisure pace to the coast and northward. To earn money for our expenses until we could reach the church in Colossae, Master preached at every village and city. Sometimes we left a settlement with enough to buy bread, and other times we hauled in enough for a small banquet in a tavern and a room for the night.

Away from the prying eyes of congregants in the growing churches in Asia Minor and Greece, Master felt free to enjoy the other bounties of his ministry. Young girls, as always, were drawn to this man, even though now past middle age. He promised this Kingdom of God after this life, but delivered his own form of paradise at night in darkened rooms or under the stars. After turning east, we again skirted the Sea of Galilee, and Master's earnings increased so much, we had to buy and fill another small chest, the weight of which caused old Dubium to slacken his pace.

In Abila we found shelter in the home of an old couple. Master ordered me to carry the chests along, and we left to find a tavern so I could eat and Master could drink. The room was like so many others, dark and dank with the smell of roasting meat, old wine and ale, and sweat. Two Roman soldiers sat on either side of a buxom young brunette. All three laughed as they drank from wooden cups. After each drink, both soldiers kissed the woman's neck and fondled a breast. She looked our way and said something to them. One of the soldiers put his lips to her ear and rose. He drained his cup, gave her breast a squeeze, and departed with his comrade. Something felt off to me, but since Master seemed at peace, I concentrated on the bread and chicken leg.

Master was now free to concentrate on the woman, a dark and curvy Syrian. She sat running a finger around the brim of her cup. When her eyes met Master's she dipped her finger deep into the cup, then stuck it into her mouth and pulled it out slowly. She gave him an encore, causing him to suck in a breath, which caught in his throat. His eyes turned sidelong to me. "As you wish, Master," I said, "but you know I'm not leaving you alone."

"Yes, yes ... But surely we can find you a girl to keep you warm tonight." I shook my head. "Bern," he whispered, "whoever she was, she can't still remember you."

I froze. "What do you mean, Master?"

"Whenever I want some fun, you get this faraway look. You're not a eunuch, and you don't prefer men. There was some woman in your past, and you won't let her go."

The dark woman affixed her attention on my master. "Go on, Master, while you're both still in the mood."

"I plan to make her happy she met me." He rose and stepped to her table.

After another two cups of stale wine, a few laughs, and some groping, Master left the tavern with the woman. I took a chicken leg with me and followed them.

I thought it odd she led him not to a house but a tent complex. "This is where you live?" he asked her as they approached a tent.

"While my father herds the sheep, this is where I live," she said.

"And when he's not herding sheep?"

"Then I live in our palace," she said, laughing. They entered the tent, and I sat outside the entrance listening to their special sounds. After a pause, she said, "So am I as good as the Vice Governor's daughter? You remember her, don't you?"

"Oh, I remember, all right," he said. "You are far better than she— " He stopped there in mid-sentence.

Suddenly she screamed, "It's him, it's him! I knew it was him!"

The two soldiers who earlier sat beside her ran to the tent from behind another. "Stay with him," one said to the other pointing at me before rushing in. "Get dressed, old Jew!" his voice came muffled from within. After a few moments, he shouted, "Come in ... and bring that fair one with you!"

Master appeared to have shrunk sitting at the foot of the bed. The dark woman sat against pillows at the head holding a blanket against her bosom. I stood there helplessly as the soldier who brought me into the tent stood behind me with a dagger to my throat. The soldier who rushed in first bore his eyes into the woman's. "Well? Are you certain about this?"

"I was her handmaiden," she said. "I was in the tavern that night in Canatha. He left with her, and that one walked behind," she said, pointing at me. "I followed. They entered her tent, but that one stayed outside." She glared at Master. "I stepped out of my tent the next morning and saw them run away. Then I entered her tent and found her dead."

"Are you sure it's him?"

"I don't know what he's calling himself these days, but take away that beard and the years, and sitting there before you is Saul of Tarsus. Saul the Tentmaker ... Saul the murderer! But that one," she said pointing at me, "is the exact same now as then."

The soldier sneered down at Master. "There has been a reward for you for something like fifteen years now. In that time the Vice Governor of the Province of Syria has become Governor. How unfortunate for you." He turned to his comrade. "Let's bring them both to our tent and bind them ... We have some cargo to deliver to the palace in Damascus, and we ride at dawn!" He reached in his tunic and pulled out a small pouch of coins. He tossed it to the dark woman, then marched us out.

2

After three days without food and only two cups of water from a bucket after the horses had drunk from it, Master and I felt close to death. We sat back in the cart unable to move, with our ankles bound before us and wrists behind. Master called for a morsel of bread at least, but the soldier riding in the back with us said if he didn't shut up, he'd shove something in his *old Jew mouth*, and it wouldn't be bread. I kept my eyes on my bow and quiver of arrows by the soldier's side and prayed to Mercury to release my bonds so I could put those weapons to use. He answered me with silence, like the Christ, like the Holy Spirit, like Yahweh.

At Damascus our bonds were cut and we were tossed into a prison cell in a dungeon to await a trial before the Governor. Master had lost his tongue, for he merely sat staring at the sand floor no matter how I prompted him with small talk. A guard would bring a bucket of water and another half-filled with some kind of slop, which we had to lick from our hands. There was nothing rigged for relieving ourselves, so we had to use those same hands to wipe ourselves after urinating or defecating in a corner on the floor. After nearly a week by my best reckoning, a guard entered our cell and made us disrobe. He splashed us with buckets of water, gave us each a scratchy cloth with a hole for our heads, and marched us out.

We were made to stand barefoot on a stone floor before an empty throne-like chair for probably a couple hours. A herald announced the arrival of the governor, and a soldier stepped behind us, and with a heavy hand on our shoulders, forced us to our knees. Accompanied on each side by centurions, an old man of perhaps Master's age of fifty stepped before the great chair and sat. He was well-fed, though not fat. His white hair was trimmed short, allowing the ivy garland to stand out prominently.

A younger man, dressed in fine silken robes, came from some-where to our left and stood between us and the governor. He held a thin scroll and unrolled it. In a booming voice, he read aloud in Latin. "Brought before the Governor of the Province of Syria, the Jewish merchant from Tarsus named Saul and his Germanic slave, whose name we know not." I opened my mouth to give him the missing information, but the soldier behind me slapped the side of my face. "This Saul is guilty of the murder of Dressa, daughter of the Governor, and awaits the Governor's judgment." He re-scrolled the parchment and held it to his chest.

The governor took a deep breath. "We have awaited this moment for many years, praying to Iustitia for her gift of justice, and today she delivers." He studied us before continuing. "Have you anything to say on your behalf, Saul of Tarsus?" Master merely bowed his head. "Very well then ... You shall die tomor-row. I shall ask the goddess for her counsel as to the method."

"My lord!" called Master.

A hushed silence fell over the great hall. The governor pursed his lips and narrowed his eyes. "You have something to say, condemned man?"

"What is to happen to Bern?"

"What is this Bern?"

"My companion, my ... slave."

"I plan for his death alongside you, as he, too, stands accused beside you."

"But he had nothing to do with your daughter's tragic fate. He sat outside the tent during her death."

The governor stroked his freshly-shaven chin. "As a con-demned man, if you were a Roman citizen, you have forfeited your citizenship. As I am sure you are aware, non-citizens cannot own slaves within Roman territory. Therefore, you have also forfeited ownership of said slave." Master nodded. "So your former slave may speak, if he is able to."

I leveled my eyes on this man who held my fate in his hands. My memory drifted back to the little boy I was on the auction platform back in the fortress between the rivers in Germania. His gift of the many tongues saved his life by delivering him into slavery. I opened my mouth and braced for another slap that didn't come. "In which language would my lord the Governor wish me to speak?" I said in Latin. I then repeated the question in the Greek Koine, in the old Greek of the poets, in Gallic Celtic, in Arabic, in Hebrew, in Aramaic, and finally in my own Germanic tongue.

The governor's eyes widened with a shine. "Come forth, court interpreter!" he shouted. "Come forth, Tinius!"

A thin man slightly older than me stepped forth from our right. His hair was of some undetectable color, so thin it was, hanging in wisps from various random spots on his head. "Yes, my Lord?"

"How many of this Germanic slave's many tongues do you speak?"

This Tinius held out a hand and counted on his fingers as he named them. "Latin, my Lord, and the current Greek. A little of the Hebrew of the Jews."

"We live in a land settled mostly by the Jewish people. And you can speak but a little of their tongue?"

"My Lord, you have never had such a need."

"And when I do have such a need? Then you would be worthless to me at such a time."

"But my Lord, I— "

"You are dismissed," the governor said with a backward wave of a hand.

"But where am I to go?"

The governor looked to a group of men gathered on our left. "Counselor Boramas, where does one go when one is dismissed?"

"Elsewhere, my Lord," a voice replied.

The governor returned his disinterested focus on the interpreter. "Well then ... there you have it. Begone!" The interpreter spun and left the hall. The governor's eyes landed on me. "If you do not wish to join your former master on his last journey, you will be my new court interpreter. I bind you to two years of service to the court of the Governor of the Roman Province of Syria. Consider yourself a *servus publicus*, and when two years' service have passed, you shall receive your *manumission* to stay if your service is deemed satisfactory or to leave as a freeman if you so desire." He stood and took three steps toward us. "If you are to work for the court, we will be compelled to call you by some name, I assume. What is your name, German?"

"I am Barnabus ... I mean Bern."

"Is it Barnabus or Bern?"

I turned to Master. He nodded. "Bern, my Lord. My name is Bern."

With the back of his hand, the governor motioned to the soldier behind us. "Were you the one who brought them from ... Abila, was it?"

"I was one of them, my Lord."

"First, you shall receive the award of one hundred silver coins. Divide them among your party in such a way that does not lead to bloodshed ... Second, restore Bern here his possessions, if he had any."

"A bow and a quiver of arrows ... and two small chests tied together with a rope he had slung around his shoulders."

"Restore him these things." His steely-brown eyes aimed into mine. "Rise, Bern. Counselor Boramas, see our new court interpreter to his quarters, and find new garments for him ... and ensure he bathes before donning any of them." He clapped his hands twice, signaling the hall to empty. A ring was fitted around Master's neck and locked. As I was led out through the door the governor exited, Master was pulled out by a chain the way we had entered. We both craned our heads around and met each other's eyes for the last time.

The next morning I was awakened by a servant who urged me to dress and follow him to breakfast. Nibbling daintily at his piece of bread and that piece of fruit, Boramas sat across from me as I stuffed bite after bite of everything available into my mouth. I felt not only could I sleep another day or two, but I could likewise keep eating until I fell asleep exhausted from eating. "If you could be so kind as to take a pause," the counselor said, "the governor has given you the choice as to how your former master will meet his death."

I chewed and stared at him. "Something fast," I said.

"Archers with arrows as he stands tied to a stake, perhaps?"

"Archers often miss," I said. "It may then be painfully slow."

"So what do you suggest?"

"One swift blow by an expert axman," I said. "One swift blow to remove his head."

"So be it," the counselor said, rising from his seat. He left the dining room, saying over his shoulder, "You may come and watch if you wish."

I didn't wish. And I suddenly lost my voracious appetite.

3

For the next few months, I spoke the tongues of the governor's true subjects, Jews and Arabs, who petitioned for settlements of land disputes. In the past, these disputes were never settled because they were never negotiated in the court. They were simply ignored as one ignores the background chattering and chirping of birds while sitting in a garden with friends. And this, of course, would lead to the locals deciding matters for themselves with the edges of swords. By simply introducing a competent interpreter into the situations, disputes were settled without bloodshed. Of course, I embellished the government's official word now and then. I learned much from Master Saul through our years together. There was no unnecessary spilling of blood among disputers in Syria, and my personal treasury grew with each settlement.

I had developed a friendship with one of the governor's servant families, Samaritans who were taken during one of many failed local rebellions against the Empire. The father was put to work rowing on a ship, and the remaining family members never spoke of him. The mother kept the chambers of the governor and his wife clean, and performed a little of the cooking duties. The only children were two daughters, Jezaria, a fair young lady who said she was sixteen, and a very young girl, who was dressed like a doll and doted over by the governor's wife. Her only duty was to exist and remain cute. Her name changed by the week, according to her mood. Jezaria was the handmaiden of the old lady of the court, so I met her often when I had duties there.

I was called to court for a meeting one autumn day, and as usual I showed early. I met Jezaria passing through. "I am pleased to see you again, Lady Jezaria!" I told her in Aramaic.

"I am no lady. I am a handmaiden to a lady."

"You are a lady or not here and here," I said, pointing to her head and heart.

"Bern!" a tiny voice squealed, and I found the little one running to me. She leaped into my arms and popped the bow-string against my chest, something she always enjoyed doing.

"And who are you today, little princess?" I said in Greek Koine, the tongue she preferred.

"Today I am Cleopatra!"

"So you are. But you must understand her name didn't serve her too well in the end."

"I'm Cleopatra before she met Marc Antony!"

"Oh ... Very well then."

Giggling, she kissed my cheek and gave the bowstring another pull and pop, then wiggled from my grasp and skittered away.

Jezaria smiled at her little sister's exit. "You would make a good father, Bern."

"Perhaps I would." My mind drifted to an opportunity missed, thanks to fate determining otherwise. "If you wouldn't mind, Lady Jezaria, I need to prepare for a meeting to settle a dispute between two shepherds."

"And which one will walk away with more sheep?" she said.

"The one who tells the more entertaining story," I said. She smiled and walked away. As I watched her go, a shadow appeared on the floor, stretching from an outer corridor to my feet. I followed the shadow with my eyes until I found the governor's wife leaning against a caryatid. She had been silently listening and observing the conversation I had had with Jezaria.

Following the successful meeting with the shepherds and Boramas, a light rapping on my door took my attention from my reading. After all these years, I finally had my own copies of both *The Iliad* and *The Odyssey* by the old blind poet. "Come in!" I said.

The door cracked open a moment, then wider to allow the governor's wife inside. "Are you alone?" she said.

I glanced at the books and thought a lover of books is never truly alone, but I didn't believe she would care for such philosophical minutiae. "Yes, my Lady."

She closed the door behind her and stepped to my desk. "May I?" She nodded at the other empty desk chair.

"Oh, please, my Lady." After I stood, she sat in perhaps the most uncomfortable chair in her cozy life. She appeared uneasy, glancing about the room. I sat back down. "Is there something I can do for you, my Lady?"

"Um ... you have been doing good work for my husband."

"Well, thank you, my Lady."

"Are you happy here, Borg?"

"It's Bern, my Lady, and yes, I suppose I'm as happy as I can be."

She had been staring at the tiled floor. She raised her eyes to mine. "But would you be happier with a young lady in your life?"

I admit I wasn't prepared for that. I rubbed my temple. "Uh ... Why do you ask this, my Lady?"

"I've seen you with my handmaiden— "

"Her name is Jezaria."

"Yes, well ... and you two are getting along well."

"We are friends, my Lady, as I am with all of her family."

"She's a sweet girl, don't you think? And very pretty, too."

"I agree on both counts, my Lady."

"So then ... why not marry her?"

My breath caught in my throat. "My Lady, I— "

"If you two were to have a baby girl, why she would be simply a doll. Don't you agree? With you as a fair blond and the young handmaiden with her dark beauty ..."

So she's finally reached the crux of it, I thought. She knows the time will come when the little girl with the ever-changing

341

name will grow out of her cuteness. She will need a replacement to dress up. She will need a new doll.

"Perhaps you are right, my Lady. However, I have only ten months left on my servitude, at which point I am free to leave. And if I were to marry Jezaria, I would take her with me, for if we were to stay, any children we would have would be born into slavery. And I cannot condemn children to that."

"Why in the gods' names would you want to leave? You have everything here your heart could desire. And your wife and children would live in this comfort."

I leaned forward and stared hard into her eyes, making her obviously uneasy. "You and I, my Lady, have something in common. At present, we are both slaves. But in ten months' time, only one of us will remain enslaved here."

I was afraid she would pull some wicked machinations against me, but after she left my room, we never so much as glanced at each other again.

4

I had assumed my final day as a *servus publicus* in the position of court interpreter would pass unceremoniously, and I would simply leave and be on my fragile way. However, since the governor held a fondness for pomp, I left feeling a status greater than even my previous two masters held. The governor summoned me to an audience before him and all the court, and all eyes were fixed upon me as I stood alone on the stone floor before the throne-chair.

"You have served the court well, Bern," the governor said, 'and I would prefer you remain in our service. However, I am a man of my word. Your period of two years has expired, and as you have expressed the desire to leave us, you are to leave this court a freeman." He held out a hand, and Boramas stepped behind him and placed a small scroll in his palm. He unrolled the scroll and held it to a side for his chief counselor to read aloud.

"To any and all persons who read this: The bearer of this document, Bern of northern Germania, has been granted his freedom by Janus Caius Maximus, Governor of the Province of Syria as of this date." The counselor produced a quill, and the governor signed and dated the parchment. Then, a spill from a red candle and a pressing from the governor's signet ring, and the deed was official. The governor re-scrolled the document, but did not yet hand it forth.

"Another matter must be resolved. We cannot have you wandering alone out there, armed with merely a bow and a document from me. Not much protection in the latter, is there?" Again, he held out a hand. This time, the document gave me my status as a full Citizen of the Roman Empire.

I felt a surge of blood flow throughout my body, filling my brain and making me suddenly light-headed. I dropped to my knees, bowed my head, and cried.

"Rise, new citizen!" the governor said. "I understand you wish to leave us, and we wish you well. Outside the palace, you will find a parting gift to help you on your way. As long as you remain within the boundaries of the Empire, you have your traveling expenses taken care of." Again he held out a hand, and again a scroll rested in his grasp. "Go to your quarters and pack your belongings." He stepped forth and clasped my forearm, as the Romans do with equals.

I did not know how I could possibly carry anything with me as I wandered away on foot, but that was not how it was to be. For when I stepped out of the palace and into the gated courtyard, one of the soldiers who arrested me two years earlier stood holding the reins of a beautiful black horse, very similar to Master Saul's Narcissus, and a pack mule. I immediately decided the mule would be called Vanitas II, after my old friend. And though the stallion resembled Narcissus in every way, I chose to call him *Libertas*, for like me, he was a free spirit. Vanitas II was loaded with empty pack bags, which I filled with all my possessions. I attached his long reins to Libertas's saddle so he could follow along.

I mounted the steed and guided him toward the gate. I twisted in my saddle and found the Samaritan family standing on the front porch waving at me. "Stay strong," I mouthed to Jezaria, and she wiped tears with the back of a slender hand. "And who are you on this last day?" I called to her little sister.

"I am my birthname today … For you, Master Bern. I am Dariana."

"Farewell, young Lady Dariana. May Yahweh keep you in the palms of his hands."

I rode through the palace gates a free man in the fourth year of the reign of Emperor Claudius. Free for the first time since the second year of the reign of Emperor Tiberius.

CHAPTER FIVE

RETURN TO UNCIVILIZATION

1

I guided Libertas and Vanitas II to the western gate, and put Damascus behind me forever. I knew as soon as I left the palace grounds I would travel to Tyre where I would secure berths for a man, a horse, and a mule, but to which port in Europe, I had yet to decide. The path from the great Syrian city to the port harbor town was infamous for lawless activity of bandits, so my bow rested on the saddle horn before me, as did the strap of my arrow quiver.

This path was void of settlements. Why would a people settle in a waterless stretch of sand and stone? Twice I stopped and camped, once before and once after we forded the river Jordan. On the second night, not only did I find the protective boulders I hoped for, but a cave as well. And not only did

I find a cave, but trouble into the bargain. Not in the form of highwaymen or bandits, but in a revenge-seeking party from a past belonging to other men and other times.

I learned from my time with the Celts that horses are particularly sensitive to foreign sounds, and that night I learned mules are even more so. I had just sparked a fire with my flintstones when Vanitas II began snorting and stamping the ground with his forehooves. Libertas soon joined him. If some carnivore were out there, I could not lose these valuable, loyal friends. I guided them as far as I could inside the cave, a mere dozen paces and stood by the small fire facing outward.

In the quiet I heard the whinnying of at least two horses. I picked up my bow, slung the quiver around my neck, and notched an arrow. I listened, and the horse-sounds of snorting and hooves pounding dry ground grew closer.

Now a human voice joined the noises made by the horses. "We know you're there, slave!" came a Greek Koine accented as I remembered hearing from early in my journey with Master Saul. "Tell us where you hid the gold and silver, and you live!"

"There is no slave here!" I replied. "And I know nothing of gold or silver!"

"We come from Antioch!" I felt pinpricks race throughout my body. "We know your master is dead. It was a fine beheading ... You should have seen it!" With that pause, the hooves on the ground came closer. "We watched you leave the city, and you cannot have such an amount of money on you! So tell us where you hid it!"

Another voice broke out. "Come, Bern! Be sensible!"

Dan himself. "Where did you find the elephant to carry you, my Lord?" I shouted.

"I've lost a little of my bulk worrying about my money," the merchant said. "And besides, I ride in a wagon! I have spies in the court of the Governor who let me know of your arrest and your master's end. Pity I couldn't be there to watch it ... So when my spies told me you were being released, I just had to come and meet you personally." Then his voice commanded, "Get the slave, men! But do not kill him ... I need information first."

I stomped out the fire and climbed to the top of the cave overhang. I crouched behind rock cover, and as I learned from the Celts, I let the men's sounds guide my night vision. Although pain shot through my spine from my hip, my breathing slowed, allowing me to listen. Men on a mission of killing—soldiers, assassins—can rarely keep quiet. Their emotions control everything about them, including their voices. As I listened, I counted four voices distinct from Dan's. The merchant likely remained in the wagon awaiting the sight of his men dragging me, defeated, to him.

I stood from behind the rock cover. The trotting and sudden halt of horse hooves followed by the slapping of sandals on the earth, carried clear and true by the thick and still air, directed my aim. My fingers relaxed, releasing the arrow. There was no cry, only the thud of a fallen body. Another set of sandals accompanied by heavy panting to my left. The assassin was climbing the slope and nearly upon me. This would be dagger's work if all went as planned. I pulled the blade from my belt sheath and leaned back into the rock. The man's path would lead him directly in front of me. The running steps grew closer. And closer. One pace away, and I stuck the blade before me, landing smoothly into the center of his throat. He clutched and gurgled himself to his death.

Another set of running steps scrambled up the rock in the same path as the man I had just dispatched. I bent, hoisted up the dead man, and held him before me, positioning my bow horizontally in front of his body. An arrow notched, the string pulled, I held the corpse up with the wrist of my firing hand under his armpit. The footsteps slid to a halt. The man gaped at the sight before him. "Joppa, is that you? Are you all right?" He leaned his face forward and squinted. "What are you doing with that bow? Put it down, you fool, it's me!"

I released the arrow into the left side of his chest, and he fell off the cave roof with a final shriek. My wrist ached with the strain of holding up the body. I released the dead man back to the earth. From below came the nervous grunting of Libertas. "Gold!" shouted a voice. "And silver!"

"Leave that alone!" shouted Dan from beyond the cave. "Catch the slave and you have more gold and silver than you can carry!"

I leaped and landed on the warm ashes of the extinguished fire. Reaching down I felt the hot end of a stick and jerked my hand away, then grasped the other end and slipped silently into the cave. A jangling of metal against metal told me where I could find the last of these assassins. Instinct guided my aim. I jammed the stick forward, and the cave filled with a cry of anguish. I pulled another arrow from my quiver and thrust it forward in my fist with all my might. A sickening hiss came from my opponent's mouth where the arrowhead entered and lodged itself into the spine.

I stepped toward the sound of a fat man's panting. Deliberately stomping and sliding my feet, I tried to mimic the sound of struggling. "Bring the barbarian bastard here!" called Dan. His eyes went shock-wide at the sight of me alone with an arrow pulled and aimed at him. "Clever boy," he said. "So show me you are really clever and take me to where you hid the gold and silver ... *my* gold and silver."

"It's a long ride to Thessalonica," I said.

"What?"

"That's where Master Saul deposited all the gold and silver. In a bank in Thessalonica."

Even in the dark, I could tell his mouth hung open. "That's impossible."

"Maybe so, but the impossible happened ... So consider it a miracle."

At a loss for words, he scowled at me. "You'll pay for this, slave boy!"

"I have spent the past two days as a free man and a citizen of the Empire. And it feels so good, I plan to remain so."

"Impossible!"

"Another miracle, then ... But to make me pay, as you threaten, you will need to pay men far better than these," I said cocking my head behind me. "And that will be rather difficult without gold or silver ... or clothes."

"What are you talking about?"

"Get down from the wagon, Ben, and remove your clothing. You may keep your sandals on. Do it, or join your hired men."

349

A few moments later, the most grotesque sight of naked blubber stood before me. I unhitched the two horses free of the wagon and removed all their leather restraints. With a shout, I slapped the flank of one, and it galloped away joined a second later by its mate. A quick prayer to Mercury had them and the others ridden by the assassins in good hands soon, I hoped. "Now it's your turn," I said to Dan. "Antioch should be due north from here. That direction, about three hundred leagues," I said, pointing. "Go, or I'll put an arrow in your ass. Go, and may you be chosen by Yahweh."

Whimpering, the fat, wealthy merchant—who could have continued to live his fat, wealthy life save for his vengeance lust—began the trek towards his death.

2

At the seaport of Tyre, I tested the governor's line of credit, and found myself, my animals, and my possessions welcome aboard on a ship bound for Neapolis. I spent as much time in the hull of the ship with the horse and mule as on deck. The animals were obviously agitated by the steady rocking of the vessel in the cramped space amidst the Asian goods on their way to Italy, and they appreciated the reassurance of my rubs and pats and my gentle voice.

For three weeks the ship sailed over the Great Sea, and in the warm waters south of the island of Crete, dolphins accompanied us, dancing as only the free and joyous can. At night I would lie on the deck staring at the stars and scudding

:louds before the movement of the vessel rocked me to sleep.
[kept dreaming I was bound in chains, and I would awaken
n a fright. The stars above reminded me of my freedom. I
vould go down to the hull for another visit with Libertas and
Vanitas II, and it would be these two fine friends who reas-
ured me I was truly free and all would be well.

The ship arrived in the port of Neapolis on a beautiful spring
nidmorning. I stood on the docks with Libertas and Vanitas
.I for perhaps an hour to let them get re-accustomed to stable
Mother Earth. I had no immediate plans but to travel north
along the coastal Roman road, so I secured a room and stable
stalls for a couple days, as much for the horse and mule as
or me.

   In the early afternoon with the scrolls displaying proof of
ny status as both freeman and citizen stuffed into my tunic,
[took a walk along the impressive coast toward Mount Vesu-
vius in the background. I ate a bowl of broth and bread outside a tavern on the outskirts of Herculaneum. I asked the
avern owner about the name of this town. Was it not named
after the Greek demigod Hercules? I asked. Indeed it was,
[was told. There was a glint of pride in the man's eyes, as
though he had something to do with the exploits of the hero.
[finished my meal and walked further into the town and
ound a temple dedicated to Hercules. So they worshiped a
nan who walked upon the earth, a man who was blessed by

the gods with extraordinary gifts. The priests told me Hercules ruled over the distant mountain that occasionally rumbled as the mighty demigod strolled past. And permeating it all was a *genius*, a spirit which fills all things and follows each man from birth to death. How fortunate these people were, I thought, to live under the protection and bounty of this most blessed, benevolent mountain.

I started to walk back to the city and my room in the inn, but suddenly I stopped and realized: not only am I a freeman, but also a Roman citizen. And as such, I would be admitted on my own into a library! I quickened my pace to find the library in Neapolis.

With perhaps two hours before sundown, which meant closing time, I found the library. The head librarian stopped me immediately upon my entrance. "Who ... what are you? And what do you wish here?" he said.

"I am a citizen of the Empire, as are you," I answered, producing the scrolls which he unrolled and read. "And I wish to use this library." He handed back the scrolls and stepped backward a pace.

This domed building was likely a temple in its past, probably customary for libraries. Again, I thought how fitting that a place meant for reading began as a place intended for worship. I realized there was nothing I immediately wanted to read, for I had already read most of the fascinating adventures available in the Roman and Greek world. I asked a librarian for any works over the history of this area, and he led me to what he called the eastern arc. He took some books off a shelf and laid them on a table. I sat and read of the Greeks who originally settled the city and surrounding towns. They were the ones who established Hercules as the local god in flesh, and the *genius*, the spirit inside everything. Master Saul, or rather *Paul*, must have heard these tales from somewhere, and they hid within his mind until they forced themselves out as a Holy Spirit. I realized then the followers of the Christ and the Way were following nothing new at all. They had merely adapted existing stories to fit their Jewish faith.

Two days later, I decided Libertas and Vanitas II were rested enough to travel, so we left the city and headed north on the best-maintained road I had yet discovered. We were also well-protected by patrols of Roman soldiers every five to ten leagues. It would have been an unbearable nuisance to most travelers, but I rather enjoyed being stopped and asked to produce my papers proving freedom and citizenship, just because I could. One older soldier, a Praefectus castrorum, said he had spent a year in Syria when the present Governor was Vice-Governor. It was a shame, he said, what happened to the man's daughter, and I agreed. When he saw the Governor's signature and signet seal, he had his platoon reverse course and escort us as far as Rome. "And where is your destination?" he asked me.

"After Rome, sir, my destination and destiny may become one and the same," I said.

3

Three days later, we entered Rome. This was the city of so many myths I had heard in my lifetime, from those who had experienced it firsthand, though from the limited perspective of the noble class. All around us, I found no evidence of the perfection others had painted in my mind. Instead, I saw only crowding and squalor.

"So where is it, exactly, are you wanting to go?" the old soldier said. "It's not a festival, so finding a room and hay for your animals is easy enough."

"I'm seeking the father of a man I knew. A nobleman-soldier called Legatus Legionus Drusus Garius."

The soldier stopped and bore his bright eyes into mine. "You know him? You know Garius?"

"Yes," I said, "I knew him."

"He was my officer in my first assignment overseas. North Africa. How is he?"

I bowed my head. "Perhaps I should see his father first."

"Oh … A shame. He was a fine man. Really cared for his soldiers."

"That sounds like him."

"Were you there when he went? Did he die fighting, like a soldier?"

"That he did," I said, my head bowed. I remembered him sprawled on a dirty street after an ambush outside a tavern.

"I know where he lived. I know his father's house … Come. I'll take you there."

꙰

After being admitted into the house of Senator Pomulus Garius, I sat waiting in an anteroom while within, two male voices discussed something of importance to both, if the liveliness of their muffled voices rang true. It was an opulent house, framed and sculpted in marble, the white of which dazzled my eyes. The door opened, and two old, regal men dressed in togas stepped out. The host bade his visitor farewell, then his quizzical eyes met mine. "And what have we here, Quebus?"

The servant who had let me in stepped forward and bowed. "Master Garius, this man says he has news of your son, Drusus."

The old senator stepped back into the inner office. "Please come inside, Bern."

I half-rose and froze in place. His servant had not used my name. I followed Senator Garius into his office. He sat at a huge oaken desk and pointed to a chair opposite him. "After your emancipation," he said, "I gather young Bruno Tavarius was none too pleased?"

I didn't know what to say. It was as though I was deep under water and he spoke to me from above the surface. "My lord, I don't understand. My ... emancipation?"

"My son wrote to me asking me to buy you from Governor Tavarius in Gaul. I did that and one better, having you declared a freeman in the Senate." Elbows on the desk surface, he clasped his hands together and leaned forward, smiling. "I can't say it sat too well with the governor. But after all, it's the loss of only one slave ... So tell me, how goes it with my son? I expected to meet you eventually, but as his escort."

"My lord, how long have I been ... emancipated?"

"Has it been so long you've forgotten?" He looked to a side and pursed his lips, and I visualized him calculating the passage of time. "It's been about fifteen years, I would imagine."

"My lord, your son ... He died in battle nearly eighteen years ago. I doubted you knew, so I thought I must deliver the news to you personally."

I remembered Garius for how he cared for those in his charge and for his stoicism. He had obviously inherited the latter from his father. The old man showed nothing. He stood and said, "Thank you, Bern ... Is there anything you need? I could argue for your citizenship before the Senate. Perhaps even a direct declaration from Emperor Claudius himself, if the old man will give us an audience."

"No, my lord ... Thank you, but I have all I need already."

I left him standing there. I unhitched Libertas and Vanitas II from the post at the gate and led them toward the city center. I was a freeman even before I left with Master Saul to Antioch, and the last decade-and-a-half had been a charade. Or had my entire life, from the time I was captured by the band of Chauci warriors, been nothing but a charade?

I spent a week on the streets in the center of the universe, the great city of Rome. I had expected to hear Latin wherever I went, but this was a polyglot city, with oddly a slight propensity for Greek Koine. Every language I knew was spoken somewhere here, though not so much of Germanic tongues except where one could find slaves or soldiers ... or both.

The city served as refuge for those who feared attacks in the countryside, and more poor people moved in with each passing day because of the lawlessness outside the walls. The newcomers took what work they could find, and those who could find no work begged on the streets, often including whole families. Though they came inside to escape potential violence from without, a network of crime had still spread through the streets. Rival gangs supporting ethnic backgrounds fought for control of swaths of city sections. If one was not careful, one would easily lose all his possessions, often at knifepoint.

The various libraries were mostly deserted because nobody but the nobility could read or write, and they had their own personal libraries in their gated homes. After I was only a few days in the city, games began declared by Emperor Claudius a month previous to celebrate victory in Britain, and during the various competitions the streets were bare, leaving them safe for me to wander from library to library.

I never entered the Coliseum. The thought of watching slaves kill each other for the hopes of limited freedom, but mostly for the chance to live another day, repulsed me. As I passed the great rotunda and listened to the blood-lust roar of the entertained, I knew the true meaning of barbarism.

Often I would ask a passerby if he or she knew where I could find a church where congregants followed the Christ of the Way. "I know nothing of them" and "Never heard of it" was all I received. All around me, I noted if any people needed a direction in their lives, it was here. And if the cult of the Christ was unknown on the streets, the church here—if it ever truly existed—had already failed and faded.

For reasons known only in the halls of the dead heroes or in the caverns of Pluto, I hesitated to leave this city, though chaos ruled every street corner. I doubted the existence of destiny. Or maybe this was my destiny, to live out my pointless life as a freeman in a pointless city. I thought of ending my life on my terms as a Roman citizen, a dagger driven into my heart by my own hand. But then as I slept exhausted in my room provided courtesy of the Governor of Syria, a haunting dream forced my hand.

I wander down from the hills over the villa. The Celtic tribes are celebrating the coming of spring with their rites in the forests, and I join at their invitation. But the villa draws me back to Roman civilization. I step through the orchards and reach the garden. There playing with a baby goat is a young boy, blond and blue-eyed. The goat bleats and the boy giggles as they play a chasing game. A woman, also blonde and fair-skinned, exits the rear palace doors and watches the spectacle with a love that permeates the garden. I step past the flowers and stand before the most beautiful lady in the world, the most beautiful lady in my life. "Hello, My Lady," I say. "I have long waited to see you again." She faces my direction as if she heard something. She looks right through me, then focuses her attention on the boy at play.

I am but a spirit. I am dead, a forgotten memory. A blinding light from the sky blots out all my surroundings.

I sat up on the cot, breathing like a panting dog on a hot summer day. Sweat drenched my clothing. I cupped water from a bowl and splashed it over the top of my head. A roar from the bloodthirsty Romans—citizens and slaves—in the Coliseum filtered through the thin walls of the inn. I splashed more water onto my face and felt the beginnings of a thick beard. If allowed to grow, it would mark me as a barbarian physically, as those in the Coliseum had become in spirit. With a hunting dagger, I scraped the stubborn beard off my cheeks and chin until the water in the bowl had reddened with my blood.

I had to leave the city. I had to go north, to know once and for all if I was truly free. The owner of the inn would be among those enjoying the spilled blood of the unfree, so I wrote a note letting him know my stay in this room had come to an end. I packed my belongings and left the note and ten silver coins on the cot.

CHAPTER SIX

AND SO A LIFE ENDS, AND SO A LIFE BEGINS

1

The way up the western coast of Italy was smooth but tedious. For days we traveled through fishing villages where the people were too busy with their boats and nets to note the passing of a short, blond German riding a black horse, a pack mule trailing. We stopped at a Roman naval base, the municipium of Portus Pisanus, established originally as a launching site for protection against Ligurians, Carthaginians, and Gaulish Celts attacking from the sea.

None of these former enemies threatened northern Italy by sea in the present time, due to the superiority of the Roman navy. In fact, a few of the soldiers manning the gates and walls were descendants of former enemies, Celts from deep in Gaul. They marveled at the short, stocky blond man who appeared Germanic but spoke a fair Gaulish Celtic, and who also bore what very closely resembled a Celtic bow. They insisted on hearing any tales I could deliver, so starved were they for diversion. I told them my entire life story with little embellishment. Enthralled, they sat encircling me as I strode around the fire. They kept silent but for the occasional gasps or cheers or even laughs at points in my narrative until I came to my arrival here. Roman officers had gathered outside the circle and bade me repeat my words in Latin or the modern Greek. I chose the latter, but spiced it with the language and style of the old language, the Greek from my introduction to the art of letters.

Though it was a chilly evening in mid-autumn, I dropped to my knees perspiring when I finished my story for the second time. One of the officers approached and knelt before me so he could face me eye-to-eye. "You can read, that I can tell by how you handle the words. But you should also write so your story lives on. You must dedicate your life to this." He placed a hand on my shoulder. "All men should have a destiny to guide them. This should be yours."

That night as I lay covered with blankets and drifted to sleep under the ancient Etruscan stars, those words from the officer echoed through the caverns of my mind.

Out of love and respect for my hooved companions, we remained at the naval base for three days so they could rest after the long journey from the seat of the Empire. I put in as much work as I knew how to do in order to earn my keep. In earlier times, I went into the forests and brought back meat for my companions' provisions. But ever since the great river known as the Danuvius dumped my comrades and me into the Pontus Euxina, I had had no such need, nor had there been such forests where game could thrive. So I toted what needed toting. I helped to dock incoming vessels. I fed and groomed my hosts' horses. There was a stark difference, I realized, in work done for pay or trade and work done by force of slavery. After each task on the naval base, I felt I accomplished something of need instead of something required. I felt like a man, through each aching muscle.

We road north along the coast to the cheers and songs of the men on the walls and watchtowers.

Following the coastline, we were soon heading west on the Roman road called Via Julia Augusta, with the great mountains, the Alpes, looming in the distance to the north and stretching to the western horizon. A steady cold breeze pressed against my right side, and I came to realize I had not felt any type of real cold since before the journey down the great river, what felt like a hundred years ago. The cooler temperature affected Libertas as well, slowing his pace. The soldiers and sailors back in Portus Pisanus had given me abundant rations

)f dried and salted meat and fish, and as long as I could scrounge dry weeds and wood for a fire, I could remain warm and fed. I often needed to ride off course to find grass for Libertas and Vanitas II.

We found shelter from the wind in an abandoned hut nestled into the edge of the woods at the base of foothills. At the time, I knew not why the place was empty and what could have happened to those who built it. The creatures barely fit through the door. There was just enough room inside for us all, and their body heat soon had the place warm with steam rising off their backs. We remained only until the following morning.

The next day we found other such huts and finally discovered their purpose. A huge flock of sheep ate what grass was available around a hut exactly like the one in which we slept. A shepherd stepped outside from within as we passed. These structures provided shelter for such men as their flocks grazed this valley between the sea and the mountains. I had heard bards in Greece and Asia Minor sing in taverns about the lovely, carefree lives of shepherds as they tended their flocks. In truth, there never was anything romantic and carefree about the lives of men and women who eke out their livings from the earth. But I knew I could live such a hard life, as long as I lived it as a freeman.

We reached the edge of the mountain range according to my view northward. The settlement of Monoecus in the province of Gallia Transalpina provided us a last rather spartan accommodation before we headed north toward Gallia Belgica. A woman whose hard life made it impossible to gauge her years sold me a room and a lean-to structure for the horse and mule, all for a single silver coin. We found nothing to eat, but I had the last of the provisions from Pontus Pisana, and the hooved ones had eaten grass alongside the sheep until their bellies bloated.

In the bare light of early dawn, we passed the temple known as the House of Hercules on our way out of the settlement. Legend said the demigod came into the area and evicted the local gods. I needed a real god, like Mercury, instead of a wandering demigod, to guide me to my goal. Perhaps he guided me through the genius spirit. Honestly, though, I was slowly losing grip on belief in any gods. I had never seen or heard one of them, but I had had many encounters, both ill and well, with humans in whom I had no choice but to believe.

2

Every step northward grew colder, but we trekked on, the western edge of the mountains beside us to our right. The air felt thinner as well, and we had to stop for rest so often, we made little progress per day. One advantage I discovered was the plentitude of game, especially deer and pigs, in the surrounding forests. We found a last shepherd's hut, and this one contained troughs full of grain in the back. Libertas and Vanitas II munched away without a care, as if this was how it was supposed to be, eating rich barley and oats in the middle of an abandoned nowhere, on the way to wherever it was their master was leading them. I started a fire and cut up the sow I had shot.

A week later, the edge of a body of water whose other shore was too far to see lay in a valley below us. We traveled around the lake, Lacus Lausonius as I later learned, on its western shore, and happened upon a fortress manned by Roman soldiers. They called this place Colonia Julia Equestris, since it was settled by career cavalrymen. It had served, along with other Roman colonies in the area, to control the Helvetii who were settled in the area against their will after their defeat at Julius Caesar's Battle of Bibracte. Though they were taken aback at first by my appearance, the soldiers accepted the veracity of my scrolls. As seasoned horsemen, they gave Vantas II and especially beautiful Libertas the best of care and grain in the stables.

I spoke no Gaulish Celtic while there, nor spoke of my friendship in the past with renegade tribesmen from the very Helvetii they watched over with wary eyes. During a meal in the banquet hall, I asked the commander in Latin if he knew the best way to reach Augusta Rauricorum, being extra careful to call it by the Roman name. He stopped chewing venison I provided from a hunt a few hours earlier. "And why do you wish to go to such a place?" he asked.

"When I reach the colonia, I will come full circle in my life's story ... literally."

"The latest wave of the pest swept through the area about ten years ago," he said. "Augusta Rauricorum was hit with the brunt of it. Even the governor himself was not spared."

"Governor Caius Cinna Tavarius? He's ..." I could not finish with the finality of the word.

"The man you named lives no longer ... There is a governor, order remains, but the old man you named, the one who built up that colonia, is dead and gone."

"And ... his family?"

"He had a wife who lived there. She was far younger than he. I don't know what became of her. I understand his son went on some mission to make his family richer than it already was. Somewhere to the east."

"And ... this son of his," I said. "Where is he now?"

"He left with a small party, and was never seen again. None of them were ever seen again."

And never will, I thought, *save one*. "So do you know how to reach this place? I used to live there."

"I understand. You wish to visit a place you knew before, and perhaps you still harbor fond memories of it. But please know this: things change. Nothing is later as we remembered it." I nodded. "You have not so far to go. There is a path north from here to the settlement of Aventicum, and from there a proper road to your Augusta Rauricorum. The colonia you knew lost its former splendor. The seat of the Province of Gallia Belgica has moved far north and east to Augusta Treverorum. The present governor thought to rule from a distant southern corner was dangerous." He drew an imaginary map on the table with his finger. "Here we are now, and you will need to go here, to Aventicum. Then from there to Augusta Rauricorum. In good weather, maybe two or three days. In fouler climes, a week or more."

As a parting gift, I went out and shot another deer buck and brought back the carcass for the garrison's nourishment.

From the backside hide, I fashioned proper winter bootlets, turned inside-out, the fur against my skin. I kicked off the sandals and never wore such footwear again. The commander insisted I take some meat from my kill.

As fate preferred it, these were fouler climes. It was not but six or seven weeks into autumn, but a snowstorm blew in on us from the mountains to the east. It took nearly a week for us to reach Aventicum, only fifty leagues northeast of Julia Equestris. The soldiers in Aventicum surrounded us outside the fortress, their swords drawn and their bowstrings pulled. I raised my hands and asked for their commander after giving him the name of the commander in Julia Equestris. A soldier cautiously took the parchment written by the commander I had left earlier and ordered me to remain seated on my horse.

While the snow, now become sleet, pelted us from the northwestern edge of the mountains, we all waited until a runner came from within the fortress. He led us inside and brought me to a cabin where a grizzled old centurion sat scowling behind a desk. He addressed me in Latin. "It is not wise, German, to be traveling in our region this time of the year."

"Perhaps not, sir, but this is the time of the year fate has chosen for me to be traveling in your region."

He nodded. The scowl remained. For the next few days in the fortress, that scowl remained.

On the fourth day waiting for the storm to abate, I walked Libertas and Vanitas II in the soldiers' training area at the center of the fortress. The commander walked beside me. "You have a way with these animals," he said.

"Thank you, sir. It's about mutual respect."

"Mutual respect? But these are animals."

"As am I, and with due respect, sir, as are you."

"We won't enter into a discussion about some religion you learned in the east. I came out to offer you a position with us. We could use someone with your obvious talents. You're German, and we will be receiving Germanic replacements as our men are taking their leave of this place and going home to Italy. Someone should talk with these Germanic soldiers, tell them in their own tongue when they can eat and shit." He grabbed the reins, stopping both the mule and horse. "There is nothing for you elsewhere, anyway ... And besides, I hate it here. Always have. But I think I could tolerate it with someone I can talk to once in a while."

I took the reins from his hands, forcing him to walk along with us in the wide circle. "Maybe I'll return if I find nothing in Augusta Rauricorum."

"I can tell you that now," he said. "There is nothing up there since the governor moved north. Nothing but the savage Celtic tribes. You wouldn't want anything from them except maybe to hump their women." He scrutinized my body from head to toe. "But then, you wouldn't make it past supper ... because you *would be* supper."

"They are not cannibals," I said.

"And how would you know that?"

I understood then the ignorance of the occupying, domi-nating forces from foreign lands. Although this man com-manded a garrison outpost in Celtic territory, he never recognized I wore a Celtic bow over my shoulders. "I just can't believe people in Europe are that wild."

"Well, you obviously know nothing about these savages you call people."

4

The three of us left Aventicum when the snowstorm let up. The Roman road was slippery, so we trod with care. In the summer we could likely make this last leg in a day, possibly two at most, but making such good time would prove impos-sible now. The Roman soldiers we left were not as generous as were the Celtic soldiers at the naval base Pontus Pisana. They gave us nothing, and though I personally needed noth-ing as long as I had my bow and arrows and my flintstones, the horse and mule would never find vegetation in the snow cover. I had to buy an overpriced large bag of barley for my hooved companions, and Vanitas II was content to carry it.

The further north we came, the less snow on the ground. Four days after we left the garrison behind us, we were free of the slippery white surface, and it appeared as though we would arrive at the old colonia by the next mid-day. Around a bend in the woods, a great fir tree lay across the road. I halted Libertas and surveyed the fallen tree. I could tell it had been deliberately cut so it would block a traveler's progress.

It would be a simple matter of leaving the road briefly and maneuvering around the obstacle, and I started to do so. But a chorus of high-pitched shrieks surrounded us.

I pulled the bow from around my back and reached for an arrow out of the quiver when two arrows landed into the trunk of the fallen tree. "Freeze, you fool!" shouted a male voice in Gaulish-accented Latin. I complied, holding the bow high in one hand and no arrow in the other. Several Celtic warriors wearing face paint ran out of the cover of trees and ferns. They either had their swords lifted and ready to hack or arrows notched in bowstrings and pointed at me.

A man with long black hair and steely eyes rode on a spotted horse out of the forest on my right. "You ride from the soldiers' fort," he said in that voice I heard a moment ago. "Where do you go now?"

"Perhaps it would be easier for us to speak in this tongue," I said in Gaulish Celtic.

"And from where do you know our tongue?" He led his horse beside Libertas, and thrusting his short blade forward, used it to lift my hair from my right shoulder. "You look more a German than a Roman." He touched my bow with the tip of his blade. "And which of our warriors did you kill to take this bow? For that is the only way another man—an outsider—can have possession of a Celtic bow. Right, men?" The men in the party roared their assent.

"I was born a German but lived among your people. They taught me to shoot, to hunt, how to move in the forest."

"Our people? I don't know you."

"In the hills and woods north of Augusta Raurica." I made sure to use the Celtic term for the colonia. "The chief of this encampment, who goes by the name Gabrus, became my teacher, my friend, and my chief. A neighboring encampment later named me Arth."

"Dismount," the chief ordered, "and show me your bow." We both climbed down from our mounts. I handed him the bow, and he ran his fingers across the interlaced markings. "Definitely from our people," he said, "with the markings showing our end is at the start, and our start at the end." He flipped the bow and inspected the inside. "These symbols. Do you know them?"

"I've always thought they were decorative drawings. Something added by the chief's son."

The man chuckled. "Decorative drawings that speak words! This one means *leader*, or your Gabrus. Then a wavy line showing a giving. Finally, this one means *bear*. So put together, this bow is a gift from the encampment leader to you." He handed me back the bow. "Tell me, Arth, where has this bow taken you?"

"On a circle around the world, starting at Augusta Raurica."

"So now you've come full circle. Your end is at the start. Come, men, let us move this tree off the road. It's blocking our way."

"*Our* way?" I said.

"These woods are dangerous. From what I've heard, they're full of savage Celtic warriors hungry for man-flesh! We can't let you risk your life alone!" All the warriors laughed with their leader. "Besides, I'm a good Celt, which means I like a good story. So as we ride together, tell me yours, and we shall know how it ends." He winked and mounted his horse.

"But I don't ride with strangers," I said. "What's your name?"

"Segomaros, at your service," he said with a touch of his forehead and a bow.

Once the men pulled the tree off the road with ropes, we all marched northward, Segomaros and I riding beside one another.

5

The colonia had lost its former glory. Many of the buildings had fallen into disrepair, but life carried on, just not with the iron-fist order and thriving commerce as under the rule of the House of Tavarius. It was difficult to believe this place once housed the governor of a Roman province. Dreams had been born here, dreams of riches and power that sent me on a wild journey for naught.

I dismounted Libertas and spoke with those whose eyes would meet mine. I sometimes used the Latin of the house in which I served and sometimes the Gaulish Celtic of those with whom I served. I asked each what had happened to this once great settlement, and they spoke of the slow death brought by a pest. This disease feared none, neither the poor nor the mighty, and took nearly half of those who had lived here in the colonia's prime. I asked about Caius Cinna Tavarius, and hose who remembered my first master said one day he grew ired and lay in bed, and for days he grew ever weaker until ie faded unto death. One resident took me to the old man's mausoleum behind the charred ruins of the palace.

My eyes were attracted more to the pile of rubble that was nce a great house of a great family than to the small mon- iment under which the moldering body of an old Roman ay. "What happened to the palace?" I asked the man who rought me here.

"It burned down as you can see."

"But how? What started the fire?"

He leaned in close and whispered his answer. "After the iew governor and his people left, they came from the north. They took whatever remained and burned it down."

"Celtic warriors?" In the man's silence I gleaned the answer. walked through the debris and imagined the rooms when I cnew them. The office where I worked as scribe for Master Caius Cinna. The slave quarters occupied by my old friend Vebru and me, and many others. The room where my cousin Linza bled to death after stabbing herself multiple times with a dull knife. "The other slaves who lived here in the time of he former governor," I said, thinking of my cousin Frida, 'what became of them?"

"The pest killed most in this villa. Others were sold off .. The new governor had his own, and took them with him iorth."

I knew I would never learn Frida's fate. I closed my eyes ind breathed a silent prayer to Mercury for her safety, or for he transport of her soul to comfort in the afterlife.

I stepped through what was once an immaculate house filled with sculptures from the Empire's Capital. All of them were absent now, either taken away or smashed to pieces. I didn't want to go where my feet were taking me, yet an unknown force drove me to go there. Gazing at the place where my Lady's bed was positioned for her to face the rising sun when she awakened, I felt weak. Tears welled in the corners of my eyes, blurring my vision. Fire had burned this room and its bed, but it could not have matched the heat of the forbidden love that occurred here.

Again I turned toward my escort. "The former governor's wife, did she also perish?"

"No one knows what became of her and her child, sir. Rumor has it she left to her family's lands near Rome."

At first I focused on the words *and her child*. Then it came clear to me what the man had said. "She went to Rome?"

"According to rumor, sir."

Could it be while I was in the city wallowing in my own self-pity, my Lady was nearby, in some villa just outside? My heart felt like it was dying, and I wanted to lie down in the charred place where the bed had stood. I wanted to sleep and not awaken. A voice called me from my perverse misery.

"Arth? Are you here?" Segomaros stepped through the charred memories toward me. "What is this place to you? Is this the great house you spoke of? The one where you served as a slave?" I nodded. "Then it's a good thing it burned ... You need no reminders of your bondage." I had not told him of the Lady Dalina and our forbidden pleasures. "There's nothing in this place worth living for anymore. So what now?"

I pointed north. "I seek old friends in the hills and forests."

"And I go with you," he said. " ... For your protection against those barbarian Celts!" He shouted for his men to return home without him, and laughing deep in his belly, he strode away. With one last look at the room, I turned and followed.

6

Before we were within an hour of the Celtic encampment, Segomaros and I were halted by three archers, their arrows aimed for the kill. My companion talked us ahead. They knew of him, but knew nothing of a Germanic who had lived among them seventeen years ago. None of them were old enough to remember me, and for all I knew, I may have played with them during pauses as I tutored their older siblings or parents the Latin tongue. Two remained on perimeter duty while the other led us toward our goal after retrieving a horse from the woods.

The encampment moved a few times while I lived among them. Celts in Gaul have always been basically a nomadic people, following game in the forest or allowing fields they had harvested to strengthen the soil for future growth. A tribe's movement also kept them one step ahead of the occupying forces of the Empire. Once per generation, an ambitious Roman officer would choose the offensive strategy of seeking out the rebel tribes for extinction instead of the defensive of protecting the forts they built from marauding Celtic warriors.

Without the warrior as a guide, it would have been difficult to locate the new encampment. But soon we heard the singing of women at work and the joyous shouts of children at play in the distance. Moments closer, the escorting warrior halted us with the signal of his raised hand. "The pigs ate all the grain!" he shouted.

A moment later a voice answered the apparent code of the day with "Come in!"

The escort lowered his hand, and our party of three men, three horses, and a mule continued into the encampment. We reached the center, and the escort said, "Dismount and remain here. I'll bring our leader." He leaped off his mount and strode away.

The sight of a blond-haired man in Roman garb with a Celtic bow strapped around his shoulders was too much for a group of children nearby. They danced a circle around me singing and miming shooting arrows at me. I couldn't help it; I mocked a painful flinch with each shot, much to their giggling delight.

"Enough!" bellowed a male voice. The children stopped their game and froze in place, staring wide-eyed as children are wont to do when they're caught doing something they ought not. The muscular man with hair showing hints of gray hanging to his shoulder blades smiled at the children and winked, showing them they weren't in trouble. They each touched their foreheads, gave a slight bow, and trotted off. The man turned his attention to me, and his smile dropped.

My old friend Gabrus and I stood gaping at one another. "Bern?" he finally managed. "Is it really you?"

I touched my forehead and gave a bow. "My chief, you still ive, and that gladdens my heart."

We both lunged forward and fell into each other's arms. We clutched each other like the long-separated brothers we vere. We cried and we laughed.

We pulled apart and regarded each other. "What has it)een, Bern? Sixteen winters? Seventeen?"

"There are no winters where I have been," I said. "But sev- :nteen winters have passed here while I wandered in the sun."

He looked at my wrists. "No bands," he said. "So you're a "reeman now?"

"No bands on my wrists." I patted the pouch at my waist, ind the metal pieces within clanged against each other. I "eached in my tunic and pulled out a scroll. "And I have some Roman scribblings declaring me a freeman."

He unrolled the scroll and read the Syrian Provincial Gov- :rnor's declaration. "Writing words on parchment can make you free?" He placed his palm first on my head, then on my :hest. "You have always been a freeman, Bern. It has always)een so in your head and in your heart ... It will be forever so."

I tried to control my emotions. I fought to keep my voice "rom cracking. "Could ... could I live here ... among your peo-)le ... as a freeman?"

"Bern, we are your people. Being a Celt, like being a freeman, s as much in your soul—in what you believe in your heart— is it is in your blood." He put his arm around my shoulders. 'Besides," he whispered in my ear, "I believe you will want to :tay with us. There are some people I think you should meet. Come along." He led me to a hut at the edge of the encampment.

Several children sat on the ground in a semicircle around a beautiful blonde woman dressed in Celtic leather. She sat on a stool reading aloud to them in Latin from a book on her lap. Lifting her eyes momentarily, she stopped in mid-sentence. She lowered her eyes and finished a section. Marking her place in the book with an oak leaf, she told her audience the lesson was over for today. The little ones rose and ran away shrieking and giggling. She lifted her face and stared at me. Her eyes became glassy with tears, and her lips trembled.

"I think I'll leave you here," Gabrus said as he squeezed my shoulder, and he stepped away.

I trod forward until I stood directly before her. Still we said nothing, simply stared into each other's tear-glazed eyes. I fell to my knees and buried my face in her lap. She ran her fingers through my hair. "My Lady," I said, my voice muffled. "Oh my Lady, I feared we would never— "

"Stop, Bern. There was always hope, and that's what kept us both alive. That's what brought us to this moment." We remained so a long while, until I finally raised my face so I could look at hers. "I've become old," she said.

In my eyes, she was still the most beautiful woman in the world, even more so than the woman I had left behind so many years ago. I told her so, and stood, raising her from her stool. We embraced and kissed, and I had never felt so blessed, so free. I hugged her close, my cheek against hers.

"You must meet him, Bern. I named him after you." She called out his name ... my name.

"I'm coming, Mother!" From behind the hut carrying an ax, a young blond man of my age when I left the colonia stepped toward us. He wore a bow and quiver of arrows around his chest and shoulders. "I've cut enough wood for everyone's fires this ev— " He stopped and cocked his face in a pose of puzzlement.

"Bern," the Lady Dalina said to the young man, "please come and greet your father, also named Bern."

"My fa— " He looked at his mother. "So what you told me, Mother, was the truth."

"And what truth did your mother tell you?" I said.

"After the Governor died, she told me that my real father is a German gentleman. That he shall return from a long journey and live with us as a family." He took a couple steps toward me. "Is it true? You shall live with us?"

I took a breath and felt my heart racing in my chest. "If only the both of you would have me, Bern."

He dropped the ax and bounded into my arms. He said words that suddenly sounded so normal. "Welcome home, Father." I stood holding my son in an embrace for all those embraces I had missed over the years.

The three of us fell into the routine of life as a family. I took young Bern out regularly to hunt, and together we supplied many families with meat. He was good with a bow, but that was to be expected from one raised by the Celts. He knew his mother and I wished to make up for lost time, so he erected a deer skin lean-to behind the hut for himself so the Lady

Dalina and I could enjoy the pleasures we once knew but were forced to hide. She loved running her fingers over the scar left by a spear wound in another world, in another man's life. "If I had been the old woman," she said, "your cure would have lasted much, much longer. I would have made sure of it," she whispered as she kissed first the entrance wound, then rolled me on my stomach to kiss the exit side. All over again, I felt the ecstasy of the young man I was once with her. Any after-life could not possibly match the bliss I felt...

... I thought nothing could threaten my new life of peace, freedom, and serenity. But a warrior on the eastern perimeter came rushing in while I shared boar meat from a kill with Gabrus and his advisors. "My leaders," the man shouted as he gasped for breath, "Roman soldiers, a scouting party, coming this way! Twenty leagues from the northeast!"

"I'll order a move now," Gabrus said.

"Wait," I said. "Have you tried speaking with them?"

"Speaking to them about what?"

"A truce ... A declaration of a permanent peace."

One of the advisors stood and threw a bone on the ground. "Permanent peace? With the Romans who want us annihilated?"

"They don't want to annihilate us," I said. "I have traveled around the Roman Empire. The people in those lands are not Romans, yet many of them are Roman citizens. The Romans cannot live in those lands they conquer without the help of the conquered people." I stood and paced within our circle. "The only thing the Roman Empire has of its own is military might. They took their building and engineering, even their gods, from the Greeks they conquered. They took their courts and banks from the Jews they conquered. And in exchange they give citizenship and protection to the lucky."

"And what can they take from us except for our lives?" said another advisor.

"Ask Julius," I said. "Vercingetorix had a system of rank and file that worked. He would have defeated the Romans if not for their superior numbers. But Julius brought that system back to Rome with him. It's in place today in the military and in government." I lifted my bow free of my shoulders and held it high. "But the Roman military, for all its might with superior numbers, loses too many good men in battle with hand-to-hand combat. I say we give them archers with Celtic bows. I say we become their companies of archers in this province and in all provinces throughout Gaul."

"And then we lose Gaul!" an advisor protested. "We become Romans!"

"There was a man I met in my travels. A Saul who as Paul told a Jew in Bethany that Rome would be defeated by being swallowed with the concepts of those they conquered. He was speaking of a new religion, a cult. But it works for us in the same way. We as Celts, and perhaps the Germanic tribes as well, become the Roman military here in Gaulish territory and Germania. And soon enough, we swallow up everything that once was Roman, even their language."

"You mean they'll start speaking Gaulish?" laughed the protestor.

"No," I said with a smile, "but something more Gaulish than Latin, at least in this part of their world."

We set out on foot to find the Roman scouting party. It was Gabrus, an advisor named Damos, and the two Berns—the younger and myself. I insisted on a handful, all of whom spoke fluent Latin, and I insisted no matter what we may hear of Gaulish from the Roman soldiers, we speak nothing but Latin. Campfire smoke wafted through the air. We crept as we knew how, stealthily toward the sound of crackling firewood. Then we found them, a dozen soldiers setting up a temporary camp.

At Gabrus's signal, we pulled our bows free and notched arrows. Our chief gave a hand signal telling us to put an arrow into the fire, and then for me to speak. He nodded, and we loosed our arrows. Before they reached their zeniths, we had another four arrows notched. "We come in peace!" I shouted. "Allow us in, or the next arrows take four of you!"

We heard the low grumbling of voices, then "Enter!" We crept inside the perimeter, all of us panning our aims. A Roman officer stepped forward. He offered the Roman salute, fist at the chest, then palm out. "What do you want?" he said.

"Peace," Gabrus said. "And a future of your people and my people working together for that peace ... "

A few hours later our party of four left with some tenuous agreements. At a point when it felt grim for us, I reached into ny tunic and pulled out the two small scrolls granting my freedom and citizenship. I advised the Roman soldiers if they attacked us, they would be attacking peaceful Roman citizens. The officer asked me how many of us in the encampment were citizens, and for the sake of our people, I lied. I had found in my travels one man sees a ceiling while above him another sees a floor. One man hears truth in another's lie. I told him there were a dozen, some with children. To this, the soldiers huddled on their side of the fire and whispered a discussion.

The discussion ended, and the officer assured us of our safety, that we four could leave their camp unharmed, but with no guarantees what we discussed would become reality. That would ultimately be up to the Governor of Gallia Belgica in Augusta Treverorum. But if he agreed with our terms, our encampment would send a dozen archers to the provincial capital in one moon—which the Romans called a month—as guards stationed on the battlements. They would swear loyalty to the Empire and defend the walled city against any attacks, even from fellow Celts. Every three months these twelve would be replaced by a fresh twelve. In exchange, we would be left alone to live in our encampment in peace, as long as we fought against future common enemies, come what may.

We didn't know whether we could trust this accord, but we thought it may be our only chance for survival.

7

Six Celtic moons after the meeting in the forest with the Roman scouts, the encampment had sent two dozen archers to Augusta

Treverorum in rotations of a dozen each for three moons each. The peace was holding, and the Roman military in the area began to send soldiers to the encampment to rove the wider perimeter as our protection. With an eye on the future, the governor sent us military engineers to aid our building projects.

In the ensuing peace, the encampment dwellings developed touches of permanence, with cellars dug for storage before the living spaces. And the living spaces became houses instead of huts. They were larger, with two or three spaces for living and sleeping and cooking and eating. A large granary kept us fed during winter months. The life of the nomad had come to an end for us. We were home but as yet had no name. To give an encampment a name meant those within would stay. And those within belonged to the place and not merely to the tribe. A name would come if that was to be our destiny. If not, we belonged to time itself.

I sat with my Lady Dalina before our hut. With the aid of a Roman engineer, I had since added a proper room to the side, the first young Bern had ever had of his own. My wife reached over and grabbed my hand. I squeezed and raised her hand to my lips. I knew if I turned my face to hers, I would not be able to look away, but I did so. I had become a man who lived his life staring into the sun.

"Are you happy here?" I asked her.

She smiled, a sight that always melted my heart. "Without you here, I was happy seeing you in our son," she said. "But with you here now, happy is not a strong enough word."

"Would you ever want to leave? Go back to Rome? But of course, I would hope you would take me with you."

She tittered, grabbed my hand and gave it a light squeeze. She stroked my thumb with hers, and that always made me shudder with pleasure. "In the colonia, that was all I wanted when I was young ... when you were only a boy. I prayed to different gods for the old man who was my husband to die so I could be released and go back home. I didn't care how. But none of my prayers delivered any results. None of the gods listened." She hung her head, and tears dropped to her lap. "Until finally they all descended on us with the pest, killing him and half the innocents of the colonia."

"The gods didn't bring the pest. I've come to the conclusion there may not be any gods. Or if there are, they are merely observing and hoping we take control of our own destinies. We disappoint them time after time with our vain prayers."

Her eyes narrowed curiously. "Is it proper to think such thoughts?"

"Here as a freeman, I can think how I wish, and can even speak those thoughts aloud." I leaned into her and kissed her lips. "Why believe in wisps of air when I have you? I believe in you."

"And I believe in us, all three of us." She smiled out toward the center of what had become the village. Bern was talking to a lovely young lady, daughter of our smith. "He will marry her."

"Do you think so?"

"If you see them with a woman's eyes, a mother's eyes, you would think so, too. You would know it."

"My father was a smith," I said. "Maybe Bern will learn the trade and bring life to its full circle, beginning at its end."

"We were both slaves, you in your forced service and I in the charade of my life," she said. "But we are both finally free … I love you, Bern."

"And I love you, Dalina."

We collapsed into each other's embrace and kissed with the passion of young lovers.

LIFE BEGINS AT ITS END

I finish that final sentence knowing it is the proper end to my story, that kiss.

Young Bern and the smith's daughter did marry, and the smith taught the young man his skills. My son had learned well, and had become respected in the village and surrounding villages for his skills. People come to him for metal repair and for the creation of knives, swords, and arrowheads, and his father-in-law has settled into a contented life of semi-retirement. Within two years, his beautiful young wife of the raven hair and eyes bore him a son and a daughter, both of whom their grandparents, the Lady Dalina and I, spoiled as much as we could. That is, after all, the right and the destiny of grandparents.

My dear friend Gabrus lived out his life in peace. I could see in his eyes whenever Roman emissaries visited the village, this was not how he wanted to achieve that peace. Like his first namesake Vercingetorix, he would prefer to have won independence from the Empire with a fight. Yet he gave over to the inevitable.

Epilogue

The various tribes and encampments throughout the vast land of Gaul could never unite as one people, which is all they needed in order to defeat the occupiers. This ignoble peace was good for the village, but it is probably the beginning of the defeat of Celtic culture in Gaul, and maybe elsewhere. I am both proud and ashamed of my role in this. Would it be best for the Celtic culture to die fighting for their freedom, or to live free but Roman under Roman terms and law? My friend faded into old age and died in his sleep. Perhaps as his heart ceased beating, he dreamed of wielding his sword and bow against the last of the occupying forces. If so, that is where he is forever in the afterlife.

The Lady Dalina and I lived most happily together as the outsiders, two of the three non-Celts in a Celtic village. We had talked of journeying south together, perhaps to Rome or even in the shadow of that beautiful mountain near Neapolis, to settle in warmer climes as we grew older. Both of us knew it was just talk to keep our minds occupied. In truth there was no way the doting grandmother would pry herself away from those grandchildren.

In the late spring, the fruit trees were in full bloom, and the bees danced from blossom to blossom. Our grandchildren occupied much of their time chasing butterflies in the field full of flowers, and they were doing so when their grandmother, the most beautiful woman in the world, my Lady Dalina, closed her eyes for the last time and expired her final breath.

I know if my scribblings find any readers in future days, some—especially the soft-hearted—will find the loss of my love a sad turn. But she lived a long and beautiful life. She was ten or eleven years my senior, and few women are so blessed to live her fifty years. Yes, I was indeed distraught for a time, ʝut I came to accept her end as a Celt, knowing she left life ıs another entered. I knew her love would live on when I sat ʝefore the hut with my granddaughter on my lap telling the ʂtory of my adventures floating east on the great river, the Ɖanuvius. At one point she lifted her face and watched me in ʋonder. I believe it was the part of my story when I was cured ɔf the spear wound by the ancient Germanic healer woman. Ɓut when I looked down into the little girl's eyes, I froze for a ɱoment, and my story stopped in mid-sentence, for my eyes ɱet the Lady Dalina's captivating hazel eyes. So my love lives ɔn, and I can no longer feel sorrow for her parting.

One could think it is for lack of creativity, but my grandchildren are named Dalina and Bern. Yet I feel again it is the ɕompletion of a circle.

ɱy life has been a strange one. Taken captive in a revenge raid ɔr an act against a Roman general and his three legions, yet to ıs in that remote village the Roman named Varus or the Gerɱanic rebel named Arminius were only rumors and therefore ɪgnored. Sold as a slave because of my gift for foreign tongues ɵo the House of Tavarius where I met a Celtic slave named Ʋebru and where I met the Lady Dalina whom I grew to love. Ƭhe wild journey on the Danuvius and the trek across Asia Ɱinor where I lost a cruel master but gained a kinder one.

I learned people are not happy with the lives they have, so ɵhey create gods and then replace them with other beliefs, other gods. The cult of the Christ must surely have withered away by now. Everything has its beginning, its birth, and everything has its ending, its death. So it is for all people, and so it must be for the gods they create because they haven't faith enough in themselves to do the greatness they were born to do as individual humans.

My old hooved friends Libertas and Vanitas II still live, but I wonder how much longer they have. Do they have enough life and strength to make one last journey?

Tomorrow I pack for the final voyage of my life. I will travel north until I find the people who speak my first tongue, people who live a hard and unforgiving life, eking an existence from deep woods, swamps, and frozen earth. People whose religion changes depending on the teller of the tales. People who are truly free.

Along the way, I will pass through *Castellum apud Confluentes*, where I began my life as a slave. I've heard it's becoming a thriving Roman city. There, somewhere in the woods or fields outside the walls, I will bury the bag containing the wristbands marking me as a slave.

And when I reach some village in the north that will accept me, with any luck I can teach some to read so I may live on after this life in my scribblings the old mule will carry on his back.

Perhaps that is my destiny.

Thank you for reading this work. Please go to amazon.com or amazon.uk.co and leave an honest review and let me know how I did. And go to my website, www.tklaverents.com, and sign up as a subscriber. I'll let you know when my next work is coming, as well as other updates. Again, my heart-felt thanks!

Made in the USA
Middletown, DE
21 February 2022

61619115R00236